ALSO, BY R.W. MARCUS

The Fate *of* Tomorrow: Tales of the Annigan Cycle
Book One

Shadow *of the* Twilight Lands: Tales of the Annigan Cycle
Book Two

Whispers *from* Nocturn: Tales of the Annigan Cycle
Book Three

Agents *of the* Void: Tales of the Annigan Cycle
Book Four

The Bane *of* Empires: Tales of the Annigan Cycle
Book Five

The Pride *and the* Fury: Tales of the Annigan Cycle
Book Six

R.W. Marcus

The TRUE BELIEVER

A Tale of the Annigan Cycle
in Three Acts

BOOK SEVEN

R.W. MARCUS

LAUGHING BIRD
PUBLISHING
GALAX, VA USA

R.W. Marcus

Published by Laughing Bird Publishing
Galax, Virginia USA

Visit us on the web!
https://AnniganCycle.com

Cover art and design by Kilson Spany
Cover layout by Laughing Bird Publishing

Laughing Bird Publishing® is a registered trademark of Mark W Phillips

Manufactured in the United States of America
10 9 8 7 6 5 4 3 2 1

First Printing, 2023
ISBN 979-8-9877180-3-2

The True Believer

Dedicated to the memory of
Edgar Rice Burroughs...
with a wink and a nod to
Philip José Farmer &
Quentin Tarantino

CONTENTS

ACKNOWLEDGEMENTS

A legion of talented, dedicated people that make up Team Marcus and all deserve recognition for their behind-the-scenes efforts.

As always, my first and foremost thanks goes out to my partner in crime, Cheryl Pepper, who shares my writer's life with all its idiosyncrasies and crazy ideas.

Of course, no project would be the same without my oldest friend and creative muse, Mark Phillips, whose fingerprints are on just about every imaginative endeavor with my name on it.

My awesome beta readers keep my twisted tales on the straight and narrow; Max Yrik Valentonis, Lynn Marie Firehammer, Dave (Chainsaw) Hollman and Ivy Maxine Elissa. This would be all but impossible without them spotting plot holes and inconsistencies.

Thanks are also in order for my growing group of technical support: Jessica Pepper RN, physicist Keenan Pepper, analytical chemist Dave Holman and artist extraordinaire Kilson Spany.

Not to be ignored, Laughing Bird Publishing for taking on and seeing this project through.

To all goes my most profound and heartfelt thanks.

WELCOME TO THE ANNIGAN

This mostly aquatic planet travels in a geosynchronous orbit around a small yellow sun. It's set far enough back in the solar system's Goldilocks Zone so that it maintains an atmosphere conducive to a wide variety of life.

Sentient creatures, terrestrial, marine or amphibious, share a hyper-fertility devoid of genetic boundaries. Any sentient creature may mate with any other and produce offspring.

Lumina basks in perpetual sunlight on one side of the Annigan. Humans dwell alongside many other sentient races thriving across its various continents and island chains. The fertility enriching rays of the sun, and the warmth of the Shallow Sea, support a vibrant and rich ecosystem.

Although life is abundant there, Lumina is hardly a serene place as you will see. Millennia of feuds, ruthless ambition and individual hatreds forged a fragile peace, barely sustained under the rule of the Great Houses.

Because of the incredible diversity of sentient creatures, all races, genders and hybrids in Lumina enjoy social equality, judging each as an individual based upon their own merits. Beneath the veneer of peace, however, dwells a hotbed of totalitarian torture, raider uprisings and a constant escalating cold war between the Great Houses.

Nocturn languishes in constant darkness on the other side of the Annigan. Only moonlight, starlight and bioluminescence illuminate the land of endless night. Without the warming rays of the sun, Nocturn's oceans froze over, but constant geothermal activity heats the land masses, creating a temperate and misty terrain teeming with exotic and predatory sentient races.

Imperialistic cat people rule aboveground and hive nations of humanoid mantises swarm beneath the surface. In the Ocean Deep, a race of sentient octopoids dwell in vast underwater cities worshiping the ancient ones of the abyss. You are predator or prey in Nocturn's despotic societies.

The Twilight Lands reside at the fringes of the Annigan and remain in constant gloaming. Here, warm and cold air currents clash, generating a perpetually stormy climate.

Ruled by the amphibian Bailian race, the Twilight Lands serve as a neutral zone for cultures from every corner of the Annigan. Many encounter the other races for the first time, and like the weather, their clashes can prove tempestuous.

Only the sun of Lumina keeps back the nocturnal predators of the dark side. Legends tell of a prophesied great eclipse stripping away all boundaries and igniting an apocalyptic war. Until then...

...these are the tales from the Annigan Cycle.

My name is Taleeka Konrad
My friends call me Tally
I fix dangerous situations
For total strangers
...and I do it for free
If I believe them

ACT ONE

Fledgling's Quest

Captain Vanir de Tuath watched the late autumn storm clouds roll in off Narian Bay and considered the coincidence of how the weather mirrored his mood. At thirty-one, the head of the Investigative Division of the Zorian Guards had only been in that position for six grands. Notwithstanding, the man walking to his left had been a thorn in his side the entire time.

"Dammit Karta, we finally had him!" Vanir said, as a gust of chilly wind blew about his shoulder-length red hair.

"Apparently not," said the handsome, clean-shaven barrister. "The judge obviously didn't think so."

"Now, he's going to go back to the Commodities Exchange and keep skimming money!"

Karta Lushi stopped in the middle of Judgement Square and glared at the passionate city guard. All around them stood an assortment of sinister looking devices, designed to exact punishment on the miscreants of the High Holy City of Zor.

"Look Vanir, "you know the rules as well as I do. He could afford me, so I spoke on his behalf."

A frustrated Vanir stared at the well-dressed lawyer in the expensive high collared jacket with ruffled shirt and knew he was right.

"We all know who really paid you," the red head replied, running his hand through his matching red beard.

1

"Be that as it may…" Karta said, glancing upwards at the gathering storm clouds.

"Now, I gotta start from scratch building a case against this guy."

Karta gave an exasperated sigh. "Vanir, that's not my problem. I did my job. You just need to do yours better!"

At this point in time, all Vanir wanted to do was punch the smug little bastard in that honey filled mouth of his. He realized that would prove counterproductive, with Karta Lushi being the best, and most expensive barrister in the High Holy City, and by default the entire Goyan Islands. Nothing good would come from assaulting him. What Vanir really wanted was a drink.

The two resumed their trek by the gallows where a man hanged last cycle still dangled. The noisy host of crows feeding on him scattered in a flurry of wings and squawks of protest when they passed.

"I can appreciate your situation, Vanir," Karta said, when he felt the first drop of rain. "However, my client is not your run of the mill street thug. Si. Dalaal has powerful and wealthy friends. The bar is set considerably higher as far as capturing his particular brand of criminal."

"So, you *admit* that he's a criminal!"

"Oh, there was never any doubt!" Karta exclaimed, looking shocked. "He and his kind have practically taken over the Commodities Exchange since the new head of the Zorian Monetary Council rose to power. The place is a nest of financial vipers."

"You mean *Lord Banavor*?" Vanir practically spat the name out.

"If you really wanted to clean things up in the finance industry, he's the one you should go after."

Vanir remained silent. Karta was right once again but the Zorian Guard's hands were tied. Just before his command, the Zorian contingency of the Society of Whispers struck a deal with the provocative, young, financial genius. The city's predicament turned dire and Banavor was in the position to save it. So, everyone reluctantly agreed to look the other way from his shady dealings as long as he caused no calamity to befall the capital city.

The deal held up because not only Zor, but the entire Goyan Islands saw nothing but unprecedented growth and prosperity since they forged the pact. Of course, it also meant Banavor de Moras, the unscrupulous trader and priest of the greed god Pa-Waga, grew more powerful with each cycle.

"You think pinning something on Dalaal is tough, try making a case against his boss," Vanir said, attempting to cover his inaction.

"I can believe it," Karta said, just before the Grand Turine rang twenty-three bells. "I gotta get going. You gonna be at the card game tonight?"

"Nope, too much to do," Vanir said, moving towards the street. "Right now, I'm due at the forum."

"You know, you were a whole lot more fun before your promotion," Karta said, wincing slightly as the rain slowly picked up.

"I was a lot less stressed, too," Vanir said, raising his hand to hail a passing hackney.

The slow moving four seat Ukko wood craft came to a stop and hovered just in front of the investigator. Vanir reached for the door handle, when he felt the crackle of electricity fill the air and a loud clap of thunder erupted directly overhead. He managed to hop inside just as the sky opened up and it began to pour.

Vanir watched Karta run for cover from the dry interior of the cab. He smirked at the thought of the rain soaking his expensive suit when the sense of electricity strengthened. Another deafening roar of thunder reverberated over them and a bolt of lightning streaked downward, striking Karta and causing everyone in the vicinity's hair to stand up. Vanir stared wide-eyed in shock out the coach's window.

"Wait here," he instructed the driver.

Vanir exited the cabin and bolted towards an unconscious Karta lying on his stomach. He knelt over him in the driving rain to check his pulse and found it strong. To his utter amazement, it did not kill Karta. It blew his clothes completely off him and left a large, intricate burn on his back, but otherwise he seemed unharmed.

Vanir picked up the body and carried him back to the waiting hackney. The driver looked anxious when the rain-soaked Vanir placed an equally saturated unconscious body in the seat beside him.

"Clerria House," he ordered, "fast as this thing will go!"

Taleeka Konrad banked her converted four-seater scout craft over the roofs of the Kampo Plat of Zor, just as the Grand Turine in the harbor rang twenty-four bells. It was the first day of the fall semester and she silently chastised herself for running late.

Down below, the buildings and plazas of the University of Marassa shimmered from the storm which just passed, and the Autumn sun felt good on her face. The celestial orb on permanent station directly overhead gave welcome respite from the chilly winds starting to blow in from the north.

She spotted the university's recently constructed landing pad on the roof of the library. After gently putting her ship down, she grabbed her backpack and quickly set off towards the flight of stairs up the side of the two-story building.

The campus bustled with activity as the mostly younger human student body struggled to navigate around their new world. In stark contrast, Marassas in their red robes, as well as older returning students, casually sauntered about the sprawling grounds encompassing almost the entirety of Kampo Platt. Luckily for Taleeka, the building containing the new Department of Policing and Investigative Science sat just next door to the library.

She threw open the double doors at the entrance and kept a brisk determined pace through the crowded hall, nodding to people she recognized along the way. The wiry sixteen-grand-old, with chocolate brown skin and short black hair, eased open the door to the lecture hall and slipped unobtrusively into the room.

The large space was set up theatre style, with rows of seats gently sloping down to a stage, and a lectern in front of massive chalk board mounted on the wall. Marassa Zekoff de Corab, the former commander of the Zorian city guards, stood at the thin reading stand in the process of welcoming his newest students. At first glance, Taleeka thought his kindly face and grey beard contrasted with the bright red Marassa's robes.

"Mz. Konrad," he called out upon seeing her, causing all heads to turn her way. "I was hoping your name wasn't placed in error when I saw it on the roster."

"Sorry I'm late, Colonel, I mean Marassa Zekoff," Taleeka said sheepishly, finding a seat halfway towards the front on an aisle.

"As I was saying," Zekoff said, returning to his introductory lecture. "The days of the city guards using brute squad practices is over. With the new laws and regulations recently passed by the High Council, as well as the proliferation of barristers and judges willing to listen to them, doling out justice now requires a new methodology.

"Of course, being caught in the act still generates swift and most times brutal punishment, but for almost all other crimes, the gathering of evidence, as well as a bevy of modern techniques, have proven exemplary in their success. That is what I am here to teach you.

"So, I would like to begin by posing a philosophical question for your consideration. Is there any instance you can think of where there should be no punishment for a crime? If you have anything to offer, please rise, state your name and give me your thoughts."

Immediately a hand shot up a dozen seats away from Taleeka, on the same row. A young Amarenian teen confidently stood. She appeared thin with a stern expression and her short black hair contrasted against her pale white skin. In keeping with Amarenian tradition, she wore the traditional Amarenian brown cropped pants with her chest bare. Taleeka studied the Amarenian's profile while she faced the teacher, entranced by her petite, upwardly turned alabaster breasts, proudly thrusted forward.

"I am Noorim Sheed," she proclaimed assertively. "I say no! If a crime is committed, there must be a price paid by the offender. To not punish sends the wrong message to others who would attempt lawlessness."

This statement prompted a hand to go up from the second row in front of Zekoff. A young Bailian female, just over five feet tall with pale blue skin and a beautifully symmetrical face, stood to address the professor. She had captivating large eyes, as do most of her race, and she wore a simple grey tunic covering a blouse and pants. Unlike the Amarenian, unyielding in her traditional garb, the Bailian clearly attempted to fit in.

"I am Barr-Ani," she said softly and lyrically to Zekoff, and then turned to face Noorim Sheed. "What if their family is starving and they steal food or perhaps medicine? Surely there must be exceptions made for compassion?"

"There is always begging," Noorim said coldly.

The statement drew a loud sardonic laugh from Taleeka.

"Not in *this* city," she countered.

"You have something to add to the conversation Mz. Konrad?" Zekoff asked, leaning on his lectern.

A sly grin crossed Taleeka's face and she slowly stood.

"Taleeka Konrad, and begging is illegal in Zor," she said defiantly. "That will get you a serious beating from the Piety Watch."

A hand went up from off to Taleeka's right and a heavy-set human female teen stood. Her shoulder length brown hair framed pleasant light brown features and her ample frame filled the plain green dress she wore.

"Nibira de Awa," she introduced herself to Zekoff, and then confronted Taleeka. "Technically, it's not illegal. I mean there is no law prohibiting begging. There is a social edict from the clerics of Pa-Waga discouraging it."

"Yeah," Taleeka scoffed. "I saw a beggar discouraged almost to death the other cycle."

Noorim furrowed her brow in shocked indignation. "If these are not laws, how does this Piety Watch get away with openly beating poor people?"

Nibira shook her head woefully. "Rules concerning the governing of the Pa-Waga religion are incredibly lenient in their favor. Several laws enacted several grands ago, allow the Piety Watch to operate with practical impunity. This is a by-product of the Pa-Waga leader sitting at the head of the Zorian Monetary Council."

Taleeka nodded. "Yep, as my mom would say, 'as long as the greedy little fuck is making people money, they're going to keep kissing his ass.'"

The sudden use of profanity in an academic setting caused an amused titter to pass through the students. Zekoff smiled but said nothing, allowing the discussion to continue. He noted how the rest of the pupils remained silent, content to let the very diverse women debate.

These four, he thought, *will be my prize students.*

Karta Lushi woke up groggy, laying on his stomach, and directly smelled the fragrance of freshly laundered sheets. However, a splitting headache and a brash metallic taste in his mouth offset any pleasant sensation around him. Two sets of hands tended to the cool compresses on his exposed back and he could hear female voices speaking softly.

When one of his attendants moved through his field of vision, he saw her purple robes and yellow palm frond symbol on her back. The barrister had no idea what had befallen him, but thank the gods, he somehow made it to Clerria House. He knew the Clerria Sisterhood ran the infirmary serving as the working arm of the University of Marassa's Isarod School of Medicine. The care given there, long known as the best in the Annigan, remained unequaled.

Groaning, Karta attempted to roll over, but a gently positioned hand kept him in place on the bed.

"Just lay still and rest," he heard a woman's voice say melodically. "It's not everyday someone gets struck by lightning and lives."

Lightning! Well, at least now he knew what happened.

"How are you feeling?" the same disembodied voice asked.

His badly parched mouth opened and he uttered one barely discernable word, "Water."

"Of course," came the kindly reply and a glass full of cool water slowly made its way up to his lips. After several swallows he finally felt able to communicate.

"Besides a headache and the inside of my mouth tasting like a foundry, I feel fine. What's wrong with my back?"

"The lightning left a large, unusual looking burn across your entire back," the sister reported. "Otherwise, you appear unharmed. You must have found favor by the gods."

"Not enough favor to keep me from getting struck in the first place."

"The gods' ways are mysterious," she said wistfully. "We were just getting ready to change your bandages. Are you in any pain?"

"No, no pain."

"Good, let's see what we've got here."

Karta could feel the large swath of cool padded cloth being removed, followed by a lengthy, uncomfortable pause.

"Go get Sister Sararwaan," the same woman said and the other rushed from the room.

Karta felt a sudden rush of anxiety charge over him.

"What? What is it? What's wrong?!"

"Nothing to be concerned about," the Clerria answered soothingly. "The burn mark has somehow… changed."

"Changed how? I didn't feel anything."

"That makes it all the more mysterious. Normally we would have to give you something for the pain, but you say there is none?"

"No. Like I said, I feel fine. How long have I been here?"

"Captain Vanir brought you in this morning. You've been here most of the cycle. The Kan will be starting in a few decis. He's been outside this whole time waiting for a word."

"Huh," Karta said with a perplexed grin. "I didn't think he liked me that much."

The sound of curtains parting and two women entering, interrupted the conversation. They quickly stepped over to the bed.

"How long has he been like this?" an older woman asked sympathetically.

"We just removed the bandage and found this," the sister staying with him said calmly.

"Pain?"

"He says no."

"Si. Lushi, I'm Sister Superior Sararwaan," the older woman said soothingly. "You initially had us all concerned, but you seem to have come through unharmed except for your back."

"Is someone going to tell me what's wrong with my back?!"

Sararwaan sighed. "It appears quite different than when they brought you in. I'm reluctant to say what it looks like. I'm going to touch it very gently. Please tell me if there is any pain."

"Oh, you can count on that."

Karta could feel the Clerria's touch, but otherwise nothing else.

"Anything?" she asked.

When Karta shook his head, she moved to another spot on his back with the same results.

"Is Captain Vanir still outside?" Sararwaan asked the other Clerria.

"Yes, Sister Superior."

"Bring him back here please, perhaps he can shed some light on this."

"Yes, Sister Superior."

Vanir stood by the front doors to the busy infirmary watching the Clerria bring in the sick and wounded. The investigator couldn't stay too much longer, he had surveillance teams to coordinate this Kan and it promised

10

to be a long one. When the sister came to fetch him, and informed him of Karta's stable condition, he felt relieved.

Taking the last swig off his flask, he slipped the empty vessel into a tunic pocket and followed through a sea of curtained-off bed spaces. He winced at the smell of the cleaning fluid constantly used and tried to ignore the groans of the afflicted coming from behind the partitions.

When she parted the curtain to Karta's area, Vanir saw the naked barrister, bottom half covered by a sheet, laying on his stomach in a single bed. Two purple robed Clerrias, with head coverings so only their faces showed, stood beside the bed tending to the barrister. The older Clerria supervised his care. The red trim of a senior Marassa lined her robe. They watched the city guard captain enter and nodded.

"I wanted you to see this, Captain," Sararwaan said, indicating the markings on the lawyer. "You're an investigator. Have you ever seen anything of the like?"

"Vanir, I never thought I would ever catch myself saying this but am I ever glad you're here!" Karta interrupted, struggling to look over his shoulder. "I can't get a straight answer from these people. Will you please tell me what in the name of the gods is going on with my back?!"

Vanir leaned over Karta's prone body and examined the burn marks covering the entirety of his back. Although asymmetrical, they appeared to be clean, deliberate lines, markings of distances and elevations, and even topographical illustrations of water and landmass.

"We may just be dealing with the gods here, my friend," Vanir said, with a touch of wonder. "This appears, to me, as some sort of map."

The quartet of young women exited the lecture hall still carrying on their debate long after Zekoff shooed the main body of students on their way. The enthusiastic young women paid no attention to the throng of students passing in either direction in the hallway. The foursome remained so absorbed in their conversation, they barely took notice of the direction they walked.

"Hey Nibira," a youthful male called out, interrupting the girl's spirited banter. "Headed to the cafeteria?"

"Make sure you leave us some!" another called out.

The group stopped and Nibira embarrassingly lowered her head as they passed the source of the harassment, a group of five human teens leaning against the wall. Four of them appeared to be first grand students, like themselves, and about the same age. One stood a full head taller and Taleeka judged him to be a second or third grand student, and considerably older. All sported short haircuts and expensive looking clothing.

"Looks like you've got some ugly friends," one of the younger ones taunted. "You gonna fatten them up too?"

Nibira's honey brown skin flushed with embarrassment and, keeping her head lowered, she started off again.

"Come on," she said in a humiliated whisper. "Don't pay any attention to them."

Taleeka eyed them warily but set off with her companions until the boy who initially called out to them started making oinking noises. She stopped when she heard the offensive sound and a scowl crossed her face.

"Tally don't," Nibira said in a panicked whisper, tugging at her arm. "That's Boraton Jeffries and his crew."

Taleeka scoffed, not taking her eyes off the abusive group. "As my mom would say, 'I don't give a fuck who they are.'"

Pulling her arm free from Nibira's fearful grasp, she clandestinely slipped a small Ukko wood truncheon from her backpack slung over one shoulder. Concealing the club up her sleeve, she marched over to the gang and stood directly in front of the oldest boy.

He stood slightly taller than Taleeka and carried an air of wealth and privilege. Slender, with high cheekbones and a pouty mouth, he sported a head full of unkempt whiteish blonde hair.

"I'm guessing you're the brains of this outfit," Taleeka challenged fearlessly.

Boraton chuckled contemptuously and glared at her.

"Hey Borr, she's calling you out!" one of them chided.

Taleeka ignored the others and continued intensely staring at the leader. "I think your rude little buddies owe my friend an apology,"

The tension in the air reached a palpable level. Other students in the hall gawked while slowly backing away from potential conflict. Barr-Ani and Nibira timidly held each other when Noorim stepped up beside Taleeka, her pale face taut.

"Oooh, looks like someone else is upset now," one of the boys called out, pulling a dagger. "What *did* you cut your hair with? A meat cleaver? Maybe I can trim it up for you."

All four bullies aggressively stepped forward while their leader stood leering at the girls with a mocking smile. With a flick of her right arm, Taleeka sent the truncheon into the stomach of the nearest boy. The Ukko wood club struck with a dull thud and the sound of the wind driven from his lungs. The magical wood's natural repellant properties launched the boy back against the wall where he began vomiting up his breakfast. The weapon swiftly snapped back on its two-foot lanyard and flew back into her hand.

The teenager with the dagger lunged at Noorim. The Amarenian girl batted aside the attack and lodged the dagger in Taleeka's backpack. Noorim grabbed his wrist before he could dislodge the blade, barred his elbow and thrust upward. The teen screamed in agony, trying unsuccessfully to escape the joint lock. She maintained her calm, with a determined expression, while guiding him down to his knees. Desperate to escape the pain, the young man willingly went wherever she led.

The remaining bullies halted their advance once the violence started and stood back, frozen in shock. Taleeka maintained her silent staring contest with Boraton while she removed the knife lodged in her backpack and tossed it on the ground next to the boy in Noorim's armlock.

"You and I both have bespoke names," Taleeka said disdainfully to Boraton. "My family earned ours by risking our necks, so pampered little rich boys, like yourself could get yours handed down to you. Now… about that apology."

Boraton's confident demeanor cracked seeing half his crew quickly neutralized. When he finally turned away from Taleeka's intense stare, he saw one of his boys leaning against the wall, dry heaving, and the other kneeling at Noorim's feet, whimpering in pain.

He looked over at the two unharmed companions and nodded towards the girls. The two teens looked at each other uncertain what to do and this prompted Boraton to grimace and nod his head again insistently.

"We're sorry,' one said meekly.

"Yeah, we're sorry," the other chimed in.

Taleeka glanced back at Nibira. "Apology accepted?"

Nibira timidly nodded.

"Great!" Taleeka said cheerfully. "No hard feelings."

Her sunny disposition instantly turned serious again. "Now beat it."

Noorim released her armlock and the boy rose to his feet nursing his sore joint. The other two assisted the one against the wall clutching his stomach. Boraton menacingly glared at Taleeka one last time before leading his comrades off through the dispersing crowd.

"He won't forget that," Nibira warned, she and Barr-Ani stepping up to the combatants.

"I sure hope not," Taleeka said firmly, hefting her club. "I hate repeating myself."

"I sensed so much anger in the tall one," the Bailian assessed. "Rage flowed from him like crashing waves."

Taleeka fixed her gaze on Nibira. "So, how do you know what's his name?"

"I'm a second grand student, majoring in Library Science," she explained. "His name is Boraton. I got the full treatment from his crew last grand. He almost always has his toadies do the bullying. He just incites it."

"Just like a coward," Taleeka said disgusted.

"You are most proficient with that," Noorim said, curiously examining the foot-long club. "May I?"

"Sure," Taleeka said handing the baton to the Amarenian.

"It is light as a feather," Noorim marveled, hefting the short cudgel.

"Ukko wood," Taleeka said, "given to me on my eleventh birthday by the man who just delivered that lecture."

A look of surprise crossed the group's faces.

"I knew he called you by name when you came into class," Nibira said, clearly impressed by the news, "but I had no idea you knew him that well."

"Yeah, Zekoff and my family go way back," Taleeka said, returning her attention to Noorim. "Speaking of proficient, you've got some pretty serious moves, yourself."

"Thank you for your kind words," Noorim replied with a touch of pride. "It is called Kovos, the national martial art of the Amarenian people."

"Nice!" Taleeka said enthusiastically. "You'll have to show me a few moves someday."

"I cannot," Noorim replied flatly. "It is forbidden to teach Kovos to anyone not Amarenian."

"Oh," Taleeka replied disappointedly.

Noorim handed the club back to Taleeka, who placed it back in the special side pocket of her pack.

"Okay," Taleeka said, lightening the moment. "One of those goons mentioned a cafeteria. Anyone know how good the food is?"

"Actually, it's pretty good," Nibira answered. "They serve a roast duck rivaling any I've had."

"Sounds delicious," Taleeka said beaming. "So, what do you say? Lunch is on me. I'm hungry. Fighting always gives me an appetite."

Many consider mornings in the High Holy City of Zor its most vibrant time. With the Kan fog finally receded, marked by the Grand Turine in the harbor ringing sixteen bells, the city always awoke to the possibilities the new cycle offered. The buzz usually began on the docks.

Dockworkers loaded merchandise and other various commodities for transport to destinations across Lumina. They unloaded and prepared fresh seafood of all kinds for sale. Along the adjoining streets and in the squares, shops and food vendors greeted their earliest customers with the hopes of a prosperous day.

Captain Vanir de Tuath, however, slept through all of it. The lead investigator for the Zorian Guards stayed out late on a case and toppled into bed the moment he returned to his modest apartment in the Bogat Plat. He slumbered through all the Turine bells and the clatter from the streets two stories below, but the brilliant detective, with flaming red hair and beard, could not snooze through the sound of the human greeting him from inside the same room.

"Time to get up there, sunshine!" Rafel cheerfully pierced the serene curtain of slumber.

Vanir rolled over onto his back and opened one eye, confirming what he'd heard wasn't a dream. Captain Rafel, the Zorian Guard's spymaster stood beside his bed staring down and grinning.

"What?" Vanir asked. "How did you get in here?"

Rafel chuckled at the question. "Have you forgotten who you're talking to?"

"I don't want to be talking with anyone right now," Vanir grumbled, opening both eyes and looking around. "Speaking of which, why are *you* so chipper this morning?"

"Whilst you were out traipsing around in the cold Kan fog, I was having sex," Rafel replied proudly.

"That will do it." Vanir slowly sat up. "How is Muuky by the way?"

"Gone," Rafel said, scratching the neatly groomed shadow of facial hair on his cheek. "He pulled some classified mission for House Calden on the east coast."

"Ovora?" Vanir asked, swinging his legs over the side of the bed and feeling the cold floor on the bottoms of his feet.

"Probably," Rafel confirmed. "Ovora's always had problems with smuggled agriculture, but it seems to be getting out of hand."

"Okay," Vanir said wearily. "You don't have to babysit me. I'll be down there in a little bit."

"Nope, we got a live one," Rafel insisted. "You're with me this morning."

The detective stared blankly ahead. "What now?"

"Patrol found a body."

Vanir sighed. "What's so special about that? Every morning the Verr Corpse Cart picks up at least a half dozen killed during the Kan."

"True, but this wasn't a nobody."

Vanir groggily began looking side to side, searching for something. Rafel reached over to the nightstand, picked up

Vanir's silver engraved flask and handed it to him. It took a moment for Vanir's vision to focus in on the vessel being held out to him, but he accepted the gift Colonel Zekoff gave him, so many grands ago, with an appreciative nod.

"Thanks," he said popping it open.

"It's the least I can do to get you moving." Rafel said glibly.

"So, who exactly was this somebody?" Vanir asked, before taking a large swig.

"An Imperial Judge by the name of Quadi, his wife found him hung in his home this morning."

"Suicide?"

"Unknown, that's for us to determine."

"Is there a female guard with the wife?"

Rafel nodded. "Gasata has one in route."

Vanir took another hit from the flask and, finally becoming animated, he stood.

"All right!" he said. "Let's go see what we can find out."

Rafel didn't move and gave him an amused look.

Vanir squinted at the spymaster, confused at his colleague's expression.

"What?"

"Pants."

City guards filled the narrow front lawn of the upscale private home in the northern Tuath Plat. They stood calmly talking with one another while the small crowd of curious neighbors huddled in the street, nervously speculating as to what transpired during the Kan. The crowd moved aside when the hackney came to a stop in front of the residence and Vanir and Rafel climbed out of the carriage doors.

"Wait here," Rafel ordered the driver, knowing they would obey his command. All hackney drivers in the city of Zor maintained a contract with the Zorian Guards and, in order to get a charter to drive the public transportation vehicle, city guards on official business received priority status. Accounts, settled at the end of the Quinte, ensured law enforcement's swift passage through the city without them having to fumble around for coinage.

"Captain Vanir," an elderly woman still in her bathrobe called out when they passed. "What's going on?"

"That's what we're here to find out," the investigator said, not breaking stride.

"What have we got?" Rafel asked the uniformed guards standing around the open door.

"The body was found hanging in his private study upstairs," the patrol sergeant answered dispassionately. "No sign of forced entry. A guard arrived on scene a short time ago. She's taking the wife's statement right now."

"And the body?" Vanir asked.

"The crime scene is intact, sir."

Vanir nodded his thanks, and then led Rafel into the spacious foyer. As they passed the living room, they heard them interviewing the wife between her distraught sobs. Both sleuths moved cautiously up the wide staircase and carefully took in their surroundings, alert for any possible clues.

"Smell that?" Vanir asked, when they reached halfway up the flight.

Rafel stopped and sniffed. "Yeah. Kinda smells like the wharf."

Vanir nodded and then sniffed at one of the many ostentatious tapestries decorating the wooden paneled walls leading up to the second floor.

"It's coming from this one," Vanir stated, his face inches from the tapestry.

Rafel watched the redheaded detective take in the strange odor. "What do you think it means?"

Vanir stepped back and surveyed the intricately woven pastoral scene. "I don't know, but we're quite a distance from the water."

"The cord from the right side of the tapestry is missing," Rafel noted.

"Curious," Vanir said, continuing their climb.

The guard stationed by the door made finding the study easy. Upon entering the room, they winced at the smell of released bladder and bowels. Floor-to-ceiling bookshelves, richly appointed in dark wood and marble, ran the length of the wall and behind a large ornate desk facing them.

Imperial Judge Quadi dangled motionlessly in front of the desk, suspended from a beam in the ceiling with the missing tapestry cord. His normally tired-looking eyes bulged in terror and his bloated tongue protruded from his grimacing mouth. An open robe revealed his soiled blue silk pajamas stinking of feces and urine. His mangled office chair, now badly broken from the dying man's flailing legs, lay directly in front of the hanged man.

Vanir stood in front of the dangling man carefully examining him while Rafel walked the perimeter of the room.

"Looks like there's a suicide note," Rafel said peering down at a disheveled piece of paper laying on the foot of the bed next to his neatly folded clothing of the day.

Vanir stepped over to the spymaster, picked up the note and read it.

"This handwriting looks forced," Vanir noted, while glancing over at the corpse, "like the hand was trembling when written. That face conveys terror, not just discomfort or a last-minute change of heart. And then there's the scuff marks under the chair, they tell me he struggled standing in the chair while someone held him in place."

Vanir placed the note back beside the clothing.

"Smell that?" Vanir said sniffing the air.

"All I smell is shit and piss," Rafel admitted.

"Colone," Vanir said, running his hands over the meticulously folded clothing. "Expensive cologne at that. He was cleaned, well-groomed and ready for the day. So, no sign of depression. I also don't think a man this vain would want to be found in his bathrobe."

cThe investigators paused on either side of the suspended body examining every detail.

"What's that on his wrists?" Rafel asked.

"Rope burns," Vanir said. "It appears someone restrained him and the ropes came off after death."

"Rope burns on the ankles, too," Rafel said, examining his feet.

Vanir studied the judge's hands. He held one up to examine it thoroughly in the light.

"There's something under the fingernails."

Suddenly Vanir let go of the hand when an idea came to him. "Let's get this robe off."

Each of the Zorian Guards grabbed the shoulder of the garment and gently removed it.

"Just as I thought," Vanir said, pointing to massive bruises on each of the victim's upper arms. "He was held up by someone very strong."

The duo shared a unified look of acceptance.

"I'm ready to call this a murder," Vanir said, before calling out to the door guard. "Sergeant!"

"Yes, sir!"

"Get this body over to Clerria House. Have the Marassas examine it thoroughly. I want to know *everything*, what he had for dinner last Kan, *everything*, and especially what's under those fingernails. Then, have an evidence team take this office apart. Examine *everything*, down to the books and papers. Someone killed this man for a reason and I've got a feeling the answer is in this room."

Taleeka enjoyed nippy fall mornings and the warm sun on her face. She decided to walk to school from their family's townhouse on the hillside in Tuath Plat. The nice weather and the squawking gulls above the busy streets comforted her.

On this particular morning, she didn't take the direct route to the Kampo Plat and University of Marassa but diverted through the northern docks. Ramoc, one of her contacts, had hastily called for a meeting before class. Taleeka wasn't sure what he might have for her, but the low-level Bailian scrounger sometimes came up with amusing trinkets to sell.

She turned the corner into a less congested side street, headed for the docks and a small warehouse backroom where the meeting would take place. Taleeka rolled her eyes and smiled at the thought, *clandestine meetings in mysterious back rooms*. Ramoc had a flair for the dramatic.

He also wanted to get into her pants. Ever since he found out her preference for Bailian men, she constantly had to fend off his less than subtle advances. She doubted this meeting would be any different.

Passing a group of five human merchants standing at a storefront in a heated conversation, she heard the distinctive sound of a physical altercation. A small crowd of human onlookers surrounded the conflict just ahead. When a two-man patrol of Zorian Guards walked by without intervening, she realized the nature of the struggle.

The Piety Watch had found another victim.

She drew closer and heard the telltale crack of their canes striking flesh and the cries of pain. She saw three of them, wearing their distinctive red shirts and black half capes, with high collars resembling cat ears when viewed from the front.

Their victim, this time, happened to be a naked beggar, cowering against a wall. They overturned his shallow bowl in front of him and the few copper coins he had managed to collect lay scattered amongst the cobblestones.

Taleeka fought the urge to stop the beating. She had acquired her father's revulsion of those armed with weapons preying on the unarmed. She knew getting involved now would be unwise.

Her adopted home city had changed in the last six grands since the end of the Etheria War. A new religion took hold, one of greed and ruthlessness. Taleeka thought all religion stupid. She considered devoting your life to some being from another plane, who didn't care whether you lived or died, pure insanity.

However, under *this* new religion, at least most everyone's finances were doing well, with commerce thriving. She imagined that as long as the money kept flowing, the populace would put up with the draconian measures imposed by the acolytes of Pa-Waga.

Taleeka kept her head down and briskly walked past the spectators and overheard their softly uttered commentary.

"He had it coming."

"He should know begging is despised by the lord."

"Why doesn't he just get a job."

And Taleeka's personal favorite, the mantra of the unscrupulous faith.

"Productivity is the only path to prosperity."

She left the holy beating behind, turned into an alley, stepped up to the third door on the right and knocked. After a brief moment, the door cracked open and a young man's pale blue face appeared. The initially suspicious look rapidly changed once he saw to whom it belonged, erupting into a broad, toothy grin.

"Hey, Tally, glad you could make it!" he said, opening the door. "You look good this morning."

Taleeka ignored the compliment and stepped inside. Tall and thin, Ramoc wore a cheap gaudy suit with ruffled cuff and collar. He kept his head full of bronze colored hair piled up into a pompadour.

"So, what have you got?" Tally asked, getting straight down to business.

"You mean besides some sweet, sweet loving for you?"

Taleeka brushed off the salacious comment. "Yes, Ramoc, besides that."

"Honestly, Tally, why don't you forget about that guy back in Immor-Onn. I'm right here and right now."

Taleeka drew a heavy sigh. "Come on Ramoc, quit messing around. I gotta get to class. Now, what have you got?"

The Bailian's face fell in defeat and he walked over to the solitary desk in the room.

"One day," he said, hopefully.

He rested his hand on a long wooden box on the desktop.

"I picked this up last cycle," he said, "and was saving it for you. See? That's another perk of being with me. You'll always get first dibs on anything I get."

"I thought I got first dibs, anyways."

Ramoc paused. "Okay, not the best example."

"Ramoc!" she urged.

"Alright," the Bailian acquiesced, opening the container.

Inside, lay a small sleek pistol crossbow nestled in its own individual section. The miniature, vertical bow, near the end of the barrel, contained a half-inch, clear-sighting devise. Beside it, rested two empty magazines and twelve bolts lined in three rows of four. Each row appeared to hold a different type of round.

Taleeka whistled softly in appreciation and picked up the pistol.

"I've never seen anything like this before and figured you might be interested," Ramoc said hopefully. "I'll let it go for a hundred secors."

"I know exactly what this is," Taleeka said, examining the weapon. "This is a Landagar Mark Seven pistol. My mom's got one. Where did you get this?"

"You know, I got it from a guy, who got it from a guy who saw it fall off the back of a wagon."

Taleeka huffed in amusement. "More like the back of an airship. This is the latest in Valdurian hardware."

"The latest huh? Maybe I should be asking two hundred."

"If I were you, I'd take the hundred, and then forget you ever saw it," Taleeka said ominously. "The Valdurians take a dim view of anyone caught with their newest toys. Once they realize this is missing, you can bet every one of those hundred secors they're gonna send a fixer after it. It won't be pretty. They'll want to make an example out of you."

Ramoc laughed contemptuously and said, "They gotta find me first."

Taleeka rolled her eyes. "Not a problem. All their newest stuff contains Etheria tracking chips. This little item will lead them straight back to you."

"So, how are you going to get around it?"

Taleeka grinned knowingly. "Let me worry about that."

His eyes shifted back and forth weighing his options.

"So, you still want to buy it?" he asked hesitantly.

"Sure," Taleeka said with a victorious smile. "I gotta keep up with my mom."

A frigid haze hung in the air. It clung to the city's dull white buildings, making them glisten. This was Mal's first time here and she marveled at the architecture comprised entirely of elaborately carved whale bones. All throughout the small whaling city, they had constructed entire walls solely from slats of massive whale ribs. The murals adorning their surfaces showed elaborate scenes of great hunts and battles. Door jambs and handles displayed delicate scrimshaw patterns. The gables of roofs gently sloped upward, each topped with various nautical themes.

The maps marked the Ice Land's City of Mokalla, also known as the City of Bones, as the northern-most place of habitation in Lumina and it tested one's endurance and resolve. Just beyond, to the north, rose the Dra' Tar Mountains and glaciers forming the dividing line between Lumina and Nocturn.

To the south, the dim distant orb of the sun floated directly over Zor, the city she called home. Just offshore, the Mokalla Turine rang six times. Mal mused that back home, the Kan would be just starting, and she would be a whole lot warmer. However, the Kan fog didn't exist in this frozen recess of northern Lumina.

Mal slipped her Mark Seven pistol from the holster under her parka and cocked it. She absolutely loved her newest piece of hardware. The Landagar Group had done it again. Mal had owned every version of the pistol crossbow since its invention and she considered this lighter, more concealable piece of hardware twice as deadly.

She looked at Alto and shook her head in amazement. Dressed only in his traditional black robes, the man showed no signs of discomfort from the bitter cold. In stark contrast, a half dozen heavily armed city guards stood ready in their bulky winter gear behind the swordmaster.

"You're absolutely sure they're in there?" the command sergeant asked hesitantly.

The Spice Rat continued peering through the dimming illumination at the warehouse doors.

"Yep," she said, smiling confidently, "followed the fuckers here, personally. My people in the air say their ship is about a deci out and the moon is setting, so we gotta work fast. Are your people ready?"

The sergeant nodded but Mal could only see his ice-covered, long, black beard and the glint of eyes peeking out from under his head covering. "Yes. We have the place surrounded and my breaching team is here."

"Good," she said. "Let's get this done. I've got a teenager back at home getting into who knows what, and I fucking hate the cold."

"Squad, prepare to breach!" the sergeant addressed his men, causing them to heft and ready their weapons.

Mal raised her pistol and aimed it at the latch holding closed the double doors. With a final glance around to see if all were ready, she pulled the trigger. A small shower of orange sparkles erupted from the barrel when the Trinilic powder ignited and sent the two-inch projectile racing toward its target at just under the speed of sound. The new semi-automatic feature returned the cocking lever to ready position and dropped another round in the chamber.

The Na-Kab Carbon bolt struck the latch with a thunderous crash, blowing a two-foot hole in the sturdy bone barrier, obliterating the lock and sending what remained of the doors swinging wildly on their hinges.

"BREACH, BREACH, BREACH!" the sergeant cried, sending his men streaming through the broken opening.

"Impressive," Alto said with an appreciative nod.

"Yeah," Mal agreed, "you gotta hand it to the Valdurians, they know their shit when it comes to making things."

Hearing no sounds conflict from inside caused the Spice Rat to pause cautiously.

"It's pretty quiet in there," Mal said, eyes narrowed. "Let's go see what the fuck's going on."

The two stepped into the darkened interior. Mal tapped the orange disk in the wall to the right of the door and pulled back the head covering of her parka. Up above, long crystal rods began glowing, filling the interior with a warm light.

The fifty-foot square room contained an office to the rear on the left. They had broken open the single door on the far wall leading outside and several guards stood blocking the exit. The space itself contained long rows of small barrels neatly stacked four high. City guards moved around the casks, searching for anything to aid their investigation.

"Well, the stolen whale oil's all here," the sergeant said, approaching, "but the thieves are nowhere to be found."

"What! How the fuck did that happen?" Mal asked, holstering her pistol. "I saw them come in here and you had the place surrounded!"

"Your guess is as good as mine," the sergeant replied, clearly perplexed.

"Sir?" a young guard called out, standing by the open door to the small office.

"I'm pretty sure I'm gonna fucking hate this." Mal sighed and took off with Alto and the sergeant in tow.

The office only contained a solitary desk and chair. An old woman, small in stature with long gray hair and dressed in a simple shapeless frock, knelt over a square, purple rug in the center of the office. Her pale face and hands revealed her to be one of the inhabitants of the Ice Lands.

A faint blue glow ran along the rug's edges. Ignoring the intrusion, she tossed a handful of ornately carved whale bones on the carpet. A small shower of blue sparkles erupted when the intricately adorned objects landed on the fabric.

"Right on time," she said, examining the seemingly random patterns the tokens formed upon landing. "The bones do not lie."

When she looked up, her gaze bore into Mal and a devious smile crossed her face.

"Captain Maluria," she croaked happily. "It's good we finally meet."

"Metoke?!" Mal said astonished.

This caused the old woman to laugh. "One of my many names."

"You know her?" Alto asked, not taking his hand off Defari's hilt.

"By reputation only," Mal replied, keeping her eyes locked on the rival smuggler. "What I don't understand is, why the fuck are you stealing from your own people? You're held in high regard on the Rhune Coast."

"Stealing not *from* my people," she corrected, "*for* my people. We got a better offer than those fat merchants in Zor are willing to pay. And that's why they hired you."

"Double dipping," Mal said appreciatively. "Nice! But did you really think you could get a shipment of this size past the Quartermasters and Ironmark?"

"My generous client is not in the Goyan Islands, so those brutes are of no concern to me."

"I'm the only one you should be concerned about," Mal said smugly.

"Oh, you're no concern to me either and I bear no grudge for this interruption in my plans. It's the cost of doing business."

Mal chuckled wryly. "Yeah, and it doesn't hurt that you've already been paid by my client. So, where are your friends? I saw them come in."

"My men? They're gone," she said flippantly, waving her hands.

"This establishment is completely surrounded," Alto declared. "How is that possible?"

This caused Metoke to laugh. "There are many other ways to leave a room than just doors and windows."

"I see," Alto replied stiffly.

"Actually, Maluria," Metoke said, picking up the bones and tossing them once again, "I stayed behind to give you a message. Think of it as professional courtesy."

She pointed to the arrangement before her. "The bones have spoken, and they tell of your daughter, Taleeka."

Mal and Alto both immediately perked up in astonishment and concern.

"What about my daughter?!" Mal growled.

Metoke's eyes widened. "Not just your daughter, but the very gods themselves! There is a great imbalance and your daughter is at the very center of it."

"What the fuck are you talking about?!" Mal stepped forward menacingly. "If you've done anything to…"

"I've done nothing. I am merely a messenger, Goodbye Maluria. I feel our paths will cross again."

Before anyone could move, she pulled the ends of the rug up and over her. The fabric gave off a flurry of azure sparks and a swirling blue vortex opened beneath her. The rug completely engulfed the old woman and she vanished into the portal which swiftly closed, leaving only the original stone floor.

Mal sighed in frustration. "Well, at least we know how her men got past the guards."

"What of Taleeka?" Alto asked, apprehensively.

"We need to get back to Zor," Mal said, her timber matching Alto's, "and I mean fast."

Taleeka couldn't help feeling particularly proud of herself for the deal she had just struck. She decided she would keep the pistol in the box for now, safely stowed away in her backpack. She already concluded that for everyday protection her Ukko wood truncheon and knife would do fine. However, she took solace knowing heavy firepower could be called upon if needed.

When she made it to the university campus, the Grand Turine rang out over the city, telling her she still had well over a deci before class. This should give her plenty of time to visit the library. Her friend Nibira, who worked there, informed her of a special meeting of several key Marassas that she would find very interesting. Never one to turn down a curiosity, Taleeka added it to her hectic morning schedule.

Students of almost every age filled the wide staircase leading up to the busy library, filing in and out of the entrance. Taleeka marveled how the three-story structure remained in a perpetual state of growth, as more and more books from across the Annigan found their way onto the shelves. Even Mal and Alto had donated a sizeable sum, mostly to ensure their daughter's acceptance to the university and unfettered access to the knowledge within.

Passing through the front doors, Taleeka saw Nibira chatting with a Picean clerk by the massive front desk. They spoke in hushed tones and the humanoid fish's gills fluttered over her ears, translating Nibira's Common Tongue into the Picean's high pitch language.

When the library science student saw her friend, she hurriedly broke off the conversation and went to meet her.

"Good, I'm glad you were able to make it," Nibira said, leading Taleeka into the main library. "They just started."

"What's going on?" Taleeka asked, sensing urgency in her friend's demeanor.

"That passing storm, yesterday morning?"

"Yeah?"

"Well," Nibira added, lowering her voice, "one of the barristers got struck by lightning in Judgement Square."

"Wow, talk about starting the day off on the wrong foot."

Every time Taleeka entered the main atrium its size impressed her. Bookshelves lined the walls of the first and main floor. People quietly read and took notes at six long tables surrounding a large cabinet in the center containing the card catalogue of the library's contents.

Looking up, both the second and third levels appeared as stocked with books and as busy as the first floor. The large glass paneled roof allowed ample sunlight to stream through. An intricate system of mirrors ensured the natural light flowed into every recess and corner, eliminating the need for artificial illumination.

"Here's the weird part," Nibira continued. *"He lived."*

"No kidding?!"

"Nope," Nibira added, "and not only did he live but he made it through practically unscathed."

Taleeka raised an eyebrow. "Practically?"

"Yeah, the lightning made some kind of weird pattern on his back. The Marassas are trying to make sense of it."

"How do I fit into this?"

Nibira shrugged and guided her down a wide side corridor. "I don't know. You're always looking for an angle on things. I thought this just might be the kind of odd occurrence that could turn a profit for you."

"Thanks," Taleeka said.

"Okay, we're here." Nibira came to a halt in front of a single nondescript door in a long row. "We can quietly slip in the back."

Taleeka nodded and the duo crept softly through the door into the small, thirty-foot square lecture hall, containing ten rows of tiered, theatre-style seating in front of a circular, raised center stage.

Karta Lushi stood shirtless, facing away from the doors, with three red robed, senior Marassas examining the extensive burn on his back.

"And you say it doesn't hurt?" a slight man with a scruffy haircut and beard asked.

"Not at all," Karta replied. "I don't even know it's there."

"That's Marassa Sajarah," Nibira whispered. "He's head of the History and Lore Department."

Taleeka nodded. "And the other two?"

"The Bailian is Marassa Karru, he's head of the School of Air Magic. The other bald one, with the blue, circular tattoo on the top of his skull, is Marassa Osius. He's head of the Osaya Runeists' School."

Sajarah turned from the barristers back to his colleagues.

"Karru, you deal in the magic of the air, storms and the like. What do you make of this?"

The Marassa's ice blue eyes narrowed and he shook his head. "I've never seen anything like it. By everything I know about lightning, and the power it possesses, this man should be dead right now."

"And the pattern is like no rune, glyph or ward I've ever seen," Marassa Osius added, her voice drifting off.

While the two senior Marassas conferred, Sajarah took a few steps back and intently studied the pattern, while scratching at his disheveled beard.

"Can we hurry this up?" Karta asked irritably. "I've got work to do."

Suddenly, Sajarah broke from his contemplative trance with a startled cry. "I know what this is!"

He pointed at the burn pattern on the shirtless lawyer. "It's a crude map. Here are mountains. That's definitely a river, and there, in the center, looks like a village."

He traced a line with his finger. "See? This trail leads into the mountains, through the village and proceeds even further up a specific mountain, where it abruptly ends."

The other two Marassas looked on in amazement.

"Why present a map in such a form?" Karru asked quizzically, running his hands through his short white hair.

"If your theory is true," Osius added cautiously. "What is it a map of? Where is the location?"

"I don't know," Sajarah admitted. "We need to study it further. Barrister Lushi, I know you need to go, might you come back tomorrow so that we can copy it?"

Karta gave a frustrated huff. "Yes, yes, anything to get me out of here."

Nibira leaned over to Taleeka, her eyes sparkling with exhilaration.

"Tally, I know what that's a map of!" she frantically whispered. "It's a map of my home island of Awa. I should tell them."

Taleeka loosely gripped her arm and shook her head. "No, but we should definitely have a private talk with the good barrister over there."

Nibira gave her friend a puzzled look before turning her attention to Karta, who turned around facing them while putting his shirt back on.

"Sure," Nibira said, with an admiring gasp at the man's clean-cut, good looks. "I'll talk to *him* anytime. He's a muffin!"

Taleeka chuckled at the reference and motioned to leave.

"Hey Tally?" Nibira asked, once out in the hall. "Why don't you want the university to know about the location? Don't they need all the help they can get?"

"You said it yourself, Nibira." Taleeka said, smiling slyly and reassuringly patting her friend's shoulder. "I'm working an angle."

Anak Bramoul, also known as the Antiquary, strolled leisurely through the gardens of his sprawling estate on the outskirts of Zor, his hands clasped behind his back. The wealthy shipping magnate loved the fall colors and the crackling of the dried leaves under his Kell skin boots.

He paused briefly, stroked his thin black moustache and silently nodded to the gardener, seasonally pruning a rare Tashen Bush. The older indenture nodded back.

Anak loved the delicate purple flowers on the bush one of his finders acquired from the only place it grew naturally in the world, a small speck of land off the coast of Soril Island in the Otoman Group.

The Antiquary prided himself on his vast array of rare, exotic plants from across the Annigan, but he always coveted more. Walking past the Nocturn greenhouse, he resisted the urge to stroll through the flora of the dark side of the world.

His current destination was his private zoo, on the other side of the estate. He didn't want to miss feeding time. The zoo complex, almost as vast as the manor house, contained over three dozen of the rarest creatures collected from the most remote lands.

His beast master, a burly hulking slave with a natural affinity for animals, greeted him with a bow when he entered.

"How are my babies today, Milos?" he said, leading the way back to a large picture window and adjacent door. The thick glass pane looked into a hundred-foot square tropical rainforest. On the other side of the room, the only other door was closed and locked.

"Hungry, sir, always hungry."

"Well, I've got a special treat for them today, and a little sport for me."

"Very good, sir."

"In fact, here comes the treat now."

From down the hall two tall muscular men in green tunics jostled a pudgy naked man who whimpered, looking about fearfully. They stopped in front of Anak and he looked him over. At five foot six he stood as tall as Anak, but unlike Anak's cruel good looks and neatly slicked back short black hair, this slave was homely with flapping jowls.

"So, you decided that being my indenture wasn't good enough," Anak said mockingly. "A soft job with my accountants didn't challenge you enough, so you decided to add a little excitement by stealing."

The terrified accountant started to stammer out a pleading explanation, but Anak shushed him.

"Now, normally, I would just have you killed in front of your colleagues to discourage this kind of behavior in the future. Today I'm in a sporting mood and with your need of a challenge, I think I can provide."

Reaching into his pocket Anak produced a solitary key and handed it to the naked slave.

With the thugs still holding his upper arms he accepted the key, stared down at it and then up at Anak with a bewildered expression.

"That key unlocks that door," Anak said pointing to the door just beyond the forest. "All you have to do is make it there and you are a free man, released from your contract."

The slave began pleading when the men forced him to the door. He struggled futilely when the beast master opened the levered handle. Giving out his last utterance of protest, the henchmen quickly threw him into the room. The door slammed shut behind him and the naked man anxiously scanned the forest standing between him and freedom.

The two henchmen exited down the hall, the same way they arrived, leaving Anak and Milos standing before the window, watching intently.

The slave looked around apprehensively at the lack of sounds or motion. Without the noise of birds or insects, every step he took crunched dried leaves underfoot which sounded unnaturally loud.

He paused when he heard a lone squeaking sound up above, which reminded him of a child's toy but he still saw nothing. When the trees began to rustle, the sound of the monkey's chattering spread, he took off running through the forest, his rolls of fat flopping with each step.

Halfway across the enclosure, the primate's chattering soon rose to a cacophony of screeches and howls. The trees above the running man now violently shook, showering the ground with leaves. Peering up in terror, he tripped on an exposed root and toppled to the jungle floor.

Rolling over onto his back, he screamed when two small gray monkeys dropped onto him from the branches. The creatures stood no more than a foot tall and had long gangly arms. Their hands, perfectly proportioned, contained hooked claws for nails.

One landed on his stomach and shrieked, revealing a mouth full of sharp teeth. The slave screamed when the monkey's front and rear claws dug into the soft skin of his stomach. It then bit down on his right nipple, tearing away a large chunk of flesh. Ripping the creature from him, he attempted to stand, only to have three more drop down from the trees and attack. He tried punching them, but they grabbed onto his arm and bit down.

The slave now crawled with all his might towards the door. At twenty feet from the egress, dozens of small monkeys poured out of the trees, swarming over his body, biting off chunks of his now badly bleeding body.

Anak stood smiling, holding his hands behind his back and watching his pets eat the man alive. Yes, the exotic carnivorous monkeys from Scoth Island did not disappoint and always entertained. When their voracious sounds of feeding replaced the agonizing screams, the Antiquary looked over at Milos.

"I would say his contract has been officially terminated."

"Yes, sir, definitely sir," came a nervous reply.

"Sir," a soft voice beckoned from his left.

His aide, Redati, stood beside him holding a note.

"It's from our contact at the university." At six feet tall, the thin young man, with light brown skin, angular face and snow-white hair, towered over his boss.

"Thank you, Redati," he said accepting the paper. "That will be all, Milos."

Anak waited until his beast master left before reading the message. All the while studying the lengthy note, he kept repeating the word "interesting" with increasing zeal.

When finished, he stared quizzically into the pen where the monkeys still gorged themselves and an exuberant smile slowly worked its way across his face.

"Redati, I do believe we're about to embark on a grand adventure."

"An adventure, sir?"

Anak then filled in his aide on the story of the barrister, the lightning and the map. Redati patiently listened with an unsure look.

"I'm not following you, sir," Redati asked with the greatest care so as not to squelch his employer's enthusiasm. "What does that have to do with an adventure?"

"The map, Redati, the map! A map doesn't appear in that fashion if it doesn't lead to something extraordinary! I must have that map!"

"But, sir, it's physically attached to someone."

"Details," Anak said dismissively. "It can be removed."

"But, sir, the map's owner is a barrister of the high council."

Anak sighed loudly. "Redati, I don't want him *dead*. I just want the skin off his back. Now, this note says he'll be at the university library tomorrow. Take a couple of men and get me that map!!"

Vanir heaved a dreaded sigh before ascending the steps to the Imperial Bank of Zor. He had come to despise this place, even though in the last six grands he had almost no reason to visit.

The explanation for his revulsion had more to do with what the institution had evolved into of late. While true, the economy for the entire Goyan Islands was surging like a team of runaway horses, a relative few experienced the full benefit of this boom. The rich were getting richer, the poor had been getting poorer and all the people in the middle found themselves getting squeezed. All because of the financial policies put in place by the young economic prodigy he would now be questioning. The lead investigator for the Zorian Guards had had virtually no interaction with Lord Banavor since he assumed leadership because of the deal they had struck at the end of the Etheria War. However, things had recently changed. His investigative team had uncovered certain papers in the office of the deceased judge. It was time for he and the eccentric economics prodigy to have a little chat.

The lobby of the bank bustled with activity, much like he remembered it. Though now it was much busier, just as the offices of the Zorian Monetary Council, which occupied the same building.

Banavor's assistant, a mousy brunette he had delt with before, knew better than to stall and led him immediately back to her boss's office.

The young man, now twenty-three, looked virtually unchanged. His beautiful face with golden brown skin and full pouty lips, oozed sensuality. His provocative style of dress also remained the same. With the colder weather upon them, he had covered more of his body, but the skintight Kell body suit revealed his every attribute.

Even though he carried an Etheria ward against Banavor's salacious effects, the detective kept his distance, cautious about getting too close or allowing the beguiling young man to touch him. His two EEtah bodyguards standing dutifully behind him at his desk also followed suit.

"Why, Captain Vanir, so good to see you!" he said, coming to his feet. "It's been ages. And as I recall we still have to christen my office at the university."

The suggestive comment sent a jolt of sexual energy surging through his loins and he thanked the gods for the Etheria protection he carried, or he would have been pulled under the comely young man's licentious spell.

"As enticing as that sounds, I'm afraid I'm here on business today." Vanir said formally.

"Oh, nothing bad I hope," Banavor replied with a pout. "Please, have a seat."

"Did you know or have any dealings with Imperial Judge Quadi?"

"No, I've heard of him, but we've never had the pleasure to meet. Why do you ask?"

"He was found murdered in his home yesterday morning."

"Why that's terrible, of course, but how does that involve me?"

"Were you aware he had paperwork ready to file which would order an investigation launched against you and the entire Zorian Monetary Council?"

The young man seemed genuinely surprised by the news. "Me! Whatever for?!"

Vanir shrugged. "You tell me."

"I can't imagine why!" Banavor said innocently. "Through my guidance, the lord has bestowed an abundance of bounty and prosperity on the entire Goyan Islands and beyond. As for the poor judge, I'm a lover, not a fighter."

With the last statement, Banavor began playing with his nipple through the bodysuit. Vanir caught his breath when another wave of targeted lust crashed over him and then quickly waned.

"You are aware of the agreement we made at the end of the Etheria War. I'm to be left to my own devices so long as I cause no calamity. Prosperity, my dear Captain, is hardly a calamity."

"I'm aware of our agreement, Lord Banavor. I'm just doing my job, following up on any possible leads."

"Well, I'm sorry I can't help you, but it certainly was good to see you."

"I trust you'll make yourself available if I have any further questions," Vanir said standing and heading for the door.

"Why, Captain," Banavor said seductively, now actively pinching his nipples so that they pushed against the tight fabric covering them. "I thought I made myself clear. I'm available for you anytime. You really do need to drop by my office at the university."

Vanir stepped halfway out the door when Banavor called out again, causing the investigator to pause.

"Oh, and Captain, I still don't wear anything under those stuffy Marassa robes."

"Is it my imagination, or is Professor Zekoff getting stricter?" Nibira said adjusting the books in her arms and transferring them to the bookbag on her shoulder.

The quartet of friends exited the building and made their way down the steps and onto one of the many of the university's busy plazas.

"It is just he expects more of us because of the aptitude we have shown," Noorim replied.

"He is a good man," Barr-Ani noted. "Deep down, I sense a feeling of profound loss within him."

"You know he lost his wife awhile back," Taleeka said watching her breath materialize in front of her on the crisp fall air.

"Oh, I'm so sorry," the Bailian sensitive replied, bringing her hand up before her open mouth. "What happened?"

"Cul-Ta killed her in retaliation for something. I don't know the full story," Taleeka replied. "It's why he hates them and you don't see any in Zor. He pretty well had them eradicated here."

All three friends stood open mouthed, in muted surprise.

"Nice old Professor Zekoff?!" Barr-Ani finally stammered in astonishment.

Taleeka chuckled. "From the stories I've heard, Zekoff was a force to be reckoned with in his younger days. Later, when he commanded the City Guards, he was so well respected on the streets, he never even carried a weapon."

"I had no idea!" Barr-Ani said, clearly impressed by the news.

"Yeah, the good old days," Taleeka said wistfully. "Okay, Nibira and I have got something to do over at the library. Dinner, seven bells at my place. Peshk is fixing something special."

"What is she fixing?" Barr-Ani asked eagerly.

"It's a surprise. You'll love it."

"I didn't think Piceans cooked," the Bailian pressed.

42

"She pretty much runs the house. Before the university she was my tutor as well."

"You are sure this will be acceptable with your parents?" Noorim asked in concern.

"Sure," Taleeka said with a wave of her hand. "Besides, they're on a job up in the Ice Lands. We'll have the place to ourselves. We really have to go. I don't want to miss this."

Redati tugged at the ill-fitting red Marassa robe and tried to blend into the river of students and instructors, flowing through the halls of the university's library. He hoped no one noticed that the sleeves only came up to his mid-forearms and the normal floor-length hem crept up almost to his knees.

Up ahead, moving towards him on the opposite side of the hall, his target seemed oblivious to his surroundings. He easily stood out from the students, just as described. Handsome, short hair and clean shaven, wearing expensive clothes. There was no doubt, their target had been spotted.

Si. Lushi," Redati kept his demeanor friendly. "The examination has been moved to another location. If you'll follow me."

The barrister paused and looked the fake Marassa over. "You're not one of the ones from yesterday?"

Redati kept his affable smile. "Yes, sir, I'm just the one to get you there. The rest is for the experts."

Karta gave a frustrated sigh at the change in plans. "Very well."

Redati led him towards the back of the library down a less traveled hall.

"Where are you taking me?" Karta asked suspiciously when he saw the thinning crowds.

"Given the nature of the examination, a more secure sight needed to be chosen." Redati replied, before stopping in front of a nondescript door. "And we're here."

"Alright," Karta said watching Redati open the door. "Let's get this over with. I've got work to do."

Stepping into the room Karta froze and gasped in shock. An old man lay motionless on the floor in the center of the room. The last thing the barrister saw was a large sinister looking man with a bald head lunging for him before being struck from behind and his world went black.

Redati quickly closed the door behind him and locked it.

"Get him on his stomach," he ordered the two henchmen while he stripped of the academic's robe and tossed it onto the body of its prior owner.

"Get that jacket and shirt off him," he ordered, and then pulled out a thin bladed flaying knife.

The thugs gruffly ripped the shirt and jacket off Karta and tossed them aside.

The Antiquary's assistant nodded appreciatively at the map burnt into the barristers back, and then knelt down to begin his grisly task.

When Redati lowered the knife to begin the first cut, he recoiled in surprise. The lines on the map began losing their shape, rapidly transforming into a formless blob of dark marking. The moment he moved the blade away the amorphous shape began transforming back into the map.

Redati gave his two nefarious companions a questioning glance only to be met with similar perplexed looks.

Several more tries yielded the same results. Any attempt to remove the map would cause its destruction.

"Quick, get him up," Redati ordered. "We're right by the back door. Let's see if we can get out of here with as few people spotting us as possible. Looks like the boss is gonna get the whole package."

Taleeka knew something seemed wrong when she saw the same three Marassas from yesterday standing outside the lecture hall expectantly scanning the crowds passing them in the corridor.

"I don't like the looks of this," she said to a confused Nibira.

Changing direction, she pushed her way through the throng of moving students until she reached an intersection which afforded an unrestricted view of all four exits.

Near the rear of the building, in a less used hallway, two men carrying a bare-chested Karta by each arm could be seen. A tall thin man rapidly led them towards the rear exit. Several stunned students stood frozen, watching the abduction.

"Shit!" Tally spat, and then turned to Nibira. "Get help, Hurry!"

Taleeka bolted down the hall to her right, heading for one of the side exits.

When Redati threw open the library's back door he halted abruptly and sputtered in surprise. There, standing in their way, a lanky teenager with attractive brown features and short black hair stood smiling. She appeared totally at ease, with her hands placed casually on her hips.

"Hey boys," she said pleasantly. "Where ya going?"

"What the..." Redati blurted out. "Who the fuck are you?!"

"Just a concerned student," Taleeka politely replied pointing at the unconscious Karta. "He doesn't look too good. You're taking him over to Clerria House, right?"

Redati sneered and stepped forward. "It's none of your fucking business where we're going. Now move aside."

Keeping her pleasant demeanor, Taleeka shook her head. "I don't think I want to do that."

Redati kept up his antagonistic advance. "You either move, or I'll move you."

In a rapid, fluid motion, Taleeka reached up and back, with both hands, to pockets on either side of her upper backpack. When she returned them in front of her, a foot-long knife occupied her left hand and a Billy-club loomed in her right. Her face, now serious, accentuated the fighting-ready stance she stepped into.

"Look, I don't want to hurt you," she said resolutely.

All three of the Antiquary's men gave a condescending smirk at the brash sixteen-grand-old and Redati lunged for her with open arms.

Instead of backing away or cowering under the onslaught, Taleeka pounced forward towards her assailant, driving the head of the Ukko wood club into his stomach. The magical wood's natural repellant properties catapulted the startled mobster five feet away. He landed flat on his back, gasping for air.

"Next time, I follow up with the blade," she said sternly.

The shrill sound of an alarm whistle suddenly cut through the air, interrupting the conflict. The two men holding Karta looked at each other, and then down at their fallen leader with a panicked expression.

"Looks like the city guards are about to join our little party," Taleeka said confidently. "I completely understand if you don't want to talk with them. No sense of humor, I'm told. I'm not going to prevent you from leaving, just not with him."

The approaching guard's whistles grew ever louder, causing visible anxiety in the kidnappers.

The two men standing finally gave in to the fear, dropped Karta, quickly helped Redati to his feet and raced off around a nearby building. Deftly slipping her weapons back into their holsters, Taleeka made her way over to the still unconscious lawyer.

"Well, this just got real interesting, she muttered aloud.

○   ○   ○

"Alright Redati, you want to tell me what in the name of the gods happened?" Anak impatiently asked, turning away from watching his carnivorous Scothian monkeys devouring the pig his beast master released into their habitat only a short while ago. The pig's anguished squeals had only just faded away, when the Antiquary's assistant returned from his failed mission at the university.

"I'm sorry, sir, but things really went sideways on us."

"I gathered that. I'm looking for the details."

"Well, first, we couldn't cut it off him. The minute my knife blade got close to the map it turned into this formless blob."

"What?!"

"I'm not kidding, sir. All the lines lost their shape right there on his back."

Anak nervously sucked on a tooth while considering Redati's explanation. If anything, this recent development convinced the Antiquary even more as to the map's importance.

"So," Redati continued. "I figured we'd snatch the guy and bring him someplace where we could copy the map. That's when the girl showed up."

"Girl?! What girl?!"

"She didn't give her name, but she had a cudgel and a really big fighting knife."

Anak paused and a grin of recognition crept across his face. "About five foot nine, skinny, pretty with short black hair?"

Redati's face furrowed in confusion. "Yeah, how did you…"

"Taleeka Konrad," Anak announced with an assured nod of his head.

"Sir?"

"Maybe you've heard of her parents, Mal and Alto Konrad."

"Who hasn't? I can tell you one thing. That cudgel packed quite a wallop."

"Yeah, I've never met her, but I've heard stories. Her mom did some work for me a while back. We've gotta change strategies. Have our people at the library keep an eye on the map and anything that has to do with it."

The Antiquary paused, stroking his chin. "So, the Konrad's are now players in this little quest. Let's just see if Taleeka is as formidable as her mother."

Peshk set the platter of steaming food in the center of the table and stepped back. All watched the Picean's opaque blue-green gill flaps flutter excitedly and could see the look of pride on her face.

"Roasted Wouvian duck, assorted tubers over rice," she cheerfully announced.

"Wow, Wouvian Duck," Taleeka said excitedly, leaning forward and taking in the pungent aroma. "How did you get ahold of that?"

The humanoid fish smiled coyly. "Your mother's rubbed off on me. I've been cultivating quite the list of contacts."

"This smells wonderful Peshk, thank you," Nibira, who was sitting across from Taleeka, said gratefully.

"Yes, thank you," Barr-Ani and Noorim Sheed chimed in.

"It was my pleasure. Now, you young ladies have a wonderful evening. It's been a long cycle. I'm going to climb into my tank and get some rest."

All said their farewells and the Picean seneschal descended the stairs to the lower level containing her room and the small garage.

"So, I would like to hear more about this altercation," Noorim Sheed said, grabbing a drumstick.

"Don't ask me," Nibira said, pouring Taleeka and herself a glass of wine. "By the time I got back with the city guards it was over."

All eyes turned to their hostess carving herself a piece of duck.

"Well, it looks like there's a new player who wants that map. So much so that they're willing to snatch an Imperial Barrister. Two of them were your run of the mill street goons. Their leader, the tall skinny one with the white hair, something about him is familiar."

"What about the barrister?" Barr-Ani asked, concern clinging to her question. "Is he alright?"

"He's over at Clerria House right now," Taleeka replied waving a forkful of duck. "They think he'll be okay. But the person you really should be asking is Mz. Nibira over there. She was the one giving him quite a bit of loving care all the way to Clerria House."

All eyes shifted to Nibira who lowered her head and blushed.

"He is very handsome," she said meekly.

"As I recall," Taleeka said with a grin. "When you first saw him last cycle you called him a muffin."

The table erupted in laughter, which allowed Taleeka to take a bite of her food.

"And what of this *muffin*," Noorim quizzed Taleeka. "Do you find him handsome?"

Taleeka shrugged. "Sure, he's just not my type."

"If you don't mind me asking," Noorim pressed. "What exactly is *your* type? I've not seen you in the company of a man *or* woman. And you do not seem to possess the obsessive behavior towards sexual activity I have witnessed in many other students."

Now Taleeka took her turn in an awkward moment.

"Well," she began after a lengthy pause. "Well, I kinda have a thing for Bailian men."

"Really?!" Nibira said almost spitting out a mouthful of wine.

"You favor the males of my race?!" Barr-Ani asked, putting her fork down and staring in surprise.

"Yeah, they've got the curly-cue thing, you know, down there," she said circling her finger in the air.

"This caused a squeal of delight to erupt from around the table.

"You mean you've done it before?" Nibira shyly asked.

"Sure," Taleeka confirmed. "I've been exposed to sex my entire life. My first nine grands were on the streets in the slums of Toriss. The sex I witnessed there, most often defined itself as brutal and degrading. I had to learn quickly who and where to avoid. I almost got raped several times, but I was fast. When I finally became old enough and living with mom and dad, all mom wanted was for me to be careful. That's when I found out most human guys are just out for themselves."

"And the Bailian men?" Barr-Ani asked.

"Gentle, and they were always concerned that I had a good time. Then there's their eyes."

"Not to mention their curly thing," Nibira teased, which set off another round of laughter.

"Is there anyone special?" the Bailian continued.

A sad smile played at the corners of Taleeka's mouth, and she nodded.

"I met him last grand in Immor-Onn. He's a low-level aide in the royal court. We had a great three cycles together. But, you know, he had his job. I'm traveling around with my family and getting into trouble. It's kind of a long-distance thing now. It's probably not going to work out."

"Don't say that!" Nibira optimistically rebuked.

"I am glad to be free of such distractions." Noorim said definitively.

"You mean you don't think about sex at all?" Nibira said in disbelief.

"Certainly not with *men*," the Amarenian replied. "My race has had a long-standing hatred of human males."

"Well, then, um, how do you have babies?"

"The Derek Witches, our shamans and midwives, perform a breeding ritual called the Kaefom. Male slaves, chosen by the Derek as breeding worthy, are given Nord Root which causes them to become erect. Their seed is then milked into a special sleeve without the necessity of a sister's hand touching the male organ. It is then transferred into the vaginas of the most prominent daughters of the Banjas. The males are then sacrificed to Tamoil, the many teated crone of the mountains, to ensure a female is born. A daughter ensures great honor on the Banja and a potential rise in status."

"And if it's a boy?"

"It is a great disgrace. His manhood is removed and he becomes a house slave in the service of the Banja. If the Crone of the Banja thinks that too many males have already been born, he may be killed outright."

"Will you ever have children?"

Noorim shook her head. "The Derek decreed me unfit for bearing children to the Sheed Banja. My hips are too narrow and my breasts are too small. I have been chosen to be a warrior."

"That sounds sad," Barr-Ani said sympathetically.

The Amarenian shrugged. "It has been this way for thousands of grands. Now, with diplomatic relations and trade with the Goyan houses, things are beginning to change. But many still cling to the old ways."

"You've been awfully quiet down there," Taleeka said to Barr-Ani. "Any potential romance with you?"

The Bailian hesitated and gave a thoughtful smile.

"No, I belong to an order of sensitives called The Mingan-De. Extreme sensations like those caused by arousal interferes with our abilities."

"Talk about sad," Taleeka said, taking another bite.

Suddenly, the sound of the latch turning and the front door opening interrupted the conversation. They all turned to see Mal and Alto enter the living room at a determined pace.

"Mom, Dad, you're back!" she cried out, bounding from the table and hugging Mal. "That job certainly didn't take long."

"Are you alright?!" Mal asked, watching her kiss Alto on the cheek.

"Sure, I'm all right, why wouldn't I be?"

"I was concerned, so we hauled ass back here."

"Why would you be concerned? Come on I've got some friends I want you to meet."

Mal remained adamant. "Mz. Tally, you got shamans invoking *your* name way the fuck up in the Ice Lands. Now, has anything strange happened around here since we've been gone?!"

Taleeka wavered, finally taking her mom's sense of urgency seriously. "Well, now that you mention it…"

Karta Lushi awoke abruptly with a splitting headache. Glancing around at the curtains surrounding him and hearing anguished moans from beyond, he knew he had been brought to Clerria House, again.

This is getting old, he silently grumbled, sitting up.

When the bed creaked from his moving, a purple robed Clerria sister stepped into his cubicle, accompanied by Taleeka and Nibira.

"Good, you're awake," the Clerria said cheerfully. "How do you feel?"

Karta rubbed the back of his head. "Like a blacksmith's anvil. You know, it hurt less being struck by lightning."

"We'd like to hold you for observation," the Clerria said compassionately. "That's a pretty nasty bump you've got there."

"No way!" Karta said, swinging his legs over the side of the bed. "I've already lost enough work."

"Good," Taleeka said. "That means you're up for some visitors."

The barrister studied the pushy young lady for a moment and then scowled.

"Who in the name of the gods are you?"

"I'm the person that saved your ass," Taleeka said with a confident grin. "My name's Taleeka, Taleeka Konrad."

Karta's annoyed disposition faded slightly. "Thanks. Konrad, any relation to Maluria Konrad?"

"That would be my mom, and this is my friend Nibira," she said, indicating the heavy-set teen beside her. "She works at the library. She remembers things, *everything*, she can accurately recall everything she has ever seen or heard."

Nibira, who had been adoringly staring at the wounded lawyer, glanced down and blushed. Karta nodded at the introduction but remained silent.

"I think you should hang out here until we can get those Marassas back and make copies of that map." Taleeka cut Karta off when he started to protest. "Look, some pretty ruthless people are after you for that map. As long as you have the only copy of the map, it may as well be a target. Let us take some of the heat off of you."

The barrister sighed in defeat. "How old are you?"

"Sixteen."

"The apple sure didn't fall far from the tree," he said exhaustedly.

"You have no idea," Taleeka replied, and then glanced over at Nibira. "Okay, go get them."

Nibira nodded, and then disappeared behind the curtains. She returned a short time later, with the three Marassas as well as the university's lead scribe and a stack of paper.

"Okay kids," Taleeka said taking command of the situation and motioning towards the design on Karta's bare back. "It's arts and crafts time. Everyone gets a sheet of paper. Let's make some copies."

The art session itself didn't take long. The crude map seemed easy to duplicate. They thought the process had gone without a hitch until the renderings made their way to the head scribe for examination. The old Marassa with short white hair and a sour expression shuffled through the six drawings with a furrowed brow. He then glanced over a Taleeka with a baffled look.

"All of these are different," he said confusedly, holding up the stack of papers.

"What do you mean?" Taleeka asked, stepping over to him.

"I mean every one of these drawings is different!" he proclaimed, spreading out the sheets on the bed next to Karta. "I mean, radically different."

Everyone looked on in bewilderment at the scribe pointing at the original, covering Karta's back and the completely different images resting beside him.

"It's like everyone copied a different drawing," Taleeka said, closely examining each illustration and comparing it with the original.

"How?" the scribe asked, his voice cracking.

"Sometimes the mind can play tricks on us," Nibira offered. "It's like Professor Zekoff said in class the other day. Sometimes eyewitness accounts are the most inaccurate."

"Well, this has been a colossal waste of time!" Karta said in frustration. "We may as well burn them and be done with it."

Taleeka had been watching the exchange, playing with a curl of her hair, deep in thought.

"No," she finally said. "Don't get rid of them. I've got an idea."

Six middle aged members comprising the elite Zorian Monetary Council sat nervously around the polished wooden table in their austere private meeting room.

The four men and two women, dressed in professional suits, anxiously followed a pacing Banavor who strolled around behind the seated council.

The young man's two EEtah bodyguards, Luft and Nagrada, stood watch guarding the door both inside and out.

The council members, surprised to see their leader dressed so conservatively, in a shirt, leggings, and tunic, watched his every move. They had to admit, the autumn air did contain a bit of a chill, making their boss' conservative dress completely appropriate.

"I think we can all agree that this organization works best from behind the scenes," Banavor said calmly. "Let's face it, decisions made here affect scores of peoples and whole governments."

Everyone around the table mumbled in agreement.

"So, you can imagine my shock and dismay when I was visited a few cycles back by an investigator from the Zorian Guards. You see, he's investigating the death of an Imperial Judge."

Banavor paused his circumambulation and diatribe for effect. His monologue continued when he began his trek around the table.

"Now, the death of a judge certainly would have no effect on our little group. So, I asked what this had to do with me."

Banavor paused again and chuckled. "It turns out the judge's papers contained an order to begin an investigation into the practices of myself and this illustrious organization."

Banavor halted at the head of the table and waved his hands dramatically. "I was understandably alarmed. What could they possibly be suspicious of? I mean, the economy is booming thanks to us. Why would anyone be troubled enough to launch an investigation? Then, I considered some of our more, oh, how shall I put it, time saving measures we had to employ to fast track such prosperity and I could see their point."

The young man, still calm and cordial began circling the table once more. "This caused me to ask myself, who would or better yet *could*, betray our actions to the Imperial Court?"

Banavor now leaned with both hands on the opposite end of the table surveying six anxiety riddled faces.

"The answer is quite simple. The betrayal had to come from someone in this room."

The accusation set off a round of nervous whispers and panicked looks back and forth at one another.

With a devious smile Banavor set off again, "Who amongst us could conceive of such duplicity? We are doing the Lord's work and our success is evident in the favor we have found in his eyes. Naturally, my curiosity was piqued. So, I launched my own little investigation. My findings were as fascinating as much as they were disturbing."

Banavor came to an abrupt halt behind an older clean-cut man with short salt and pepper hair.

"Wouldn't you agree, Si. Bosch?"

The acolyte of Pa-Waga abruptly reached under his tunic and retrieved a pistol crossbow. He rapidly but calmly pointed it at the back of Bosch's head and pulled the trigger. The unsuspecting victim's skull exploded, showering all at the table with blood, bone and brain matter.

The woman seated next to her now headless colleague screamed when the body, pumping blood like a fountain, toppled over onto her. Still maintaining his pleasant demeanor, Banavor holstered the pistol and returned to the head of the table.

The ruthless young man surveyed the grisly scene with a wide, friendly grin. Blood covered the tabletop, soaking the stacks of papers, dripping over the edges and running onto the floor. The council's gore-stained faces stared back at him with terrorized expressions. Several of the members visibly trembled and the woman with the corpse in her lap became paralyzed with fear, mumbling incoherently.

"Alright," Banavor said exuberantly. "I believe we understand each other. Meeting adjourned. Good talk!"

He then turned to the EEtah standing by the door.

"Nagrada, Get a clean-up crew in here. I'm sure you're hungry. You and Luft can have the body. Speaking of an appetite, who's up for lunch?"

The Kan fog had already begun to settle over the campus of the University of Marassa when Nibira and Noorim exited the Social Sciences building. The political philosophy workshop had run well over its scheduled parameters due to a number of spirited debates and Nibira's stomach now growled.

"Hey, what do you say we get a bite to eat," Nibira said, pulling her coat tight against the damp chill.

The Amarenian teen peered around at the milky whiteness slowly enveloping everything and shuttered.

"If we are able to find our way," she said skeptically.

"I know this little place just off campus that serves the best Lamprey Pie. Perfect for a chilly Kan."

"Anything will do," Noorim replied, following. "I am not an admirer of gourmet foods such as Taleeka and yourself."

"Don't worry, this place isn't fancy at all. You'll love it, come on."

"Very well, I must admit you do know many good eating establishments."

"Oh yeah," Nibira replied. "I mean come on; does it look like I miss any meals?"

Noorim scowled at her friend's self-deprecating question.

"You are too hard on yourself."

"Nah, just realistic," Nibira's statement was laced with melancholy and accompanied by a sad smile. "I know it's why guys don't look at me. A good meal is so *satisfying* and you know, it doesn't care what I look like."

"When the time is right, a proper partner will present themselves to you." Noorim said optimistically.

"From your mouth to the ears of the Goddess."

They walked the next block in reflective silence until they found themselves passing the library. Noorim unexpectedly stopped and studied the building suspiciously.

"Did you see that?"

Nibira, who had been dolefully staring downward while walking, glanced up in surprise.

"No, what?"

"Inside the library, first floor, I saw lights. There's someone in there."

Both students stood and carefully watched the darkened windows of the empty edifice until a brief moment later they saw a small orange point of illumination moving about.

"There it is again," Noorim announced. "Something's not right. I must investigate."

"Wait, shouldn't we get the city guards or something?"

"There is no time," Noorim said starting off towards the front doors. "You may remain here if you wish."

Nibira watched the Amarenian skulk up the walkway. When she reached the wide stairs, Nibira gave a resigned sigh and went off after her friend.

They found the front door unlocked and shared a concerned glance before quietly opening one of them and slipping inside. The warm and quiet interior seemed to echo and amplify their footsteps. Beyond the large front desk, they could see multiple lights moving about the main room and heard hushed voices.

Crouching low, Noorim rushed over and ducked behind the checkout counter. Nibira, unaccustomed to sneaking around, clumsily mimicked her companions' actions.

Squatting down next to Noorim she attempted to calm her ragged breathing and heaving chest.

The Amarenian pointed to the moving lights in the next room and then held up four fingers. A trembling, wide eyed Nibira nodded, and then nervously stared in the intruders' general direction.

Quickly peering around the desk to check on the burglars, Noorim indicated for Nibira to stay put. Then, still in a crouch she snuck over to the doorway and flattened herself against a wall.

Contemplating a strategy for separating them and taking them out one by one, Noorim cringed when a loud crash came from the direction of the front desk. Noorim swiveled her head in a frenzy, aghast to see that Nibira, in an attempt to hide behind the desk, knocked over a stack of books.

The scuffle of movement as well as alarmed voices now emanated from the main room, followed by the sound of running feet, rapidly approaching.

In all her martial training Noorim had learned that in most instances the simplest moves often produced the best results. Sticking her leg out at the proper moment caused the first through the doorway to tumble to the floor on his face.

The second lunged toward her, reaching out to grab. The agile young Amarenian easily ducked below the grasping arms. Taking a hold of one of the flailing appendages, she tucked her hip in close and executed a throw. When the man slammed on the ground with a resounding thump, he gasped and then groaned.

The wily teen didn't relinquish her hold on the man's arm. Twisting it into a wrist lock, the thug screamed and she forced him to his feet directly into the path of henchman number three, in the process of drawing a dagger.

The knife wielder made several lunges at her, but Noorim managed to thwart each one with her human shield.

She heard Nibira scream when the one she tripped regained his footing and grabbed her.

Redati, burglar number four, pulled a pistol crossbow from his belt and pointed it at Noorim.

"Enough!" he loudly proclaimed. "Release him!"

Noorim did as ordered and the man stepped away nursing his wrist and arm.

"Well, it looks like we've got a few more *concerned* students on our hands," Redati said keeping the pistol trained on Noorim. "I know you had a map made of that barrister's back. Where is it?"

"I do not know," Noorim answered.

"You know what," Redati said with a nod of his head. "I believe you."

He then turned his attention to Nibira. "You're the one who knows."

The librarian, still being held, shook her head fearfully with tears streaming down her face.

"Release her," Noorim demanded. "She is no threat to you."

"The map first," Redati countered.

After a moment of a tension filled stand-off, Redati gave a frustrated huff. "Look I wasn't supposed to hurt anyone, but I'm not leaving without that map."

He then raised the pistol towards Noorim's head while staring at Nibira. "Give up the map or she dies. It's just that simple."

Nibira, distraught almost to the point of paralysis, blubbered away incoherently.

"Do not tell them!" Noorim said, brazenly leering at Redati.

"I wouldn't listen to her," the mobster said menacingly. "I don't think the color red would match the décor in here. Now, the map!"

"Top drawer," she croaked out through sobs, indicating a set of thin drawers acting as an endcap to the card catalogue.

Redati nodded towards the cabinet and two of his henchmen stepped over.

"It's locked boss," one reported.

"We do not possess the key," Noorim flatly stated to his questioning look.

"Break it open," he ordered.

The sound of wood cracking swiftly followed.

"Got it boss," one proclaimed holding the paper aloft.

The thug holding Nibira released her and she stood trembling watching the men head for the door.

"There, you see," Redati said, still keeping the weapon trained on Noorim. "We got what we came for and nobody got hurt. Let's keep it that way. My associates and I are now leaving. Any attempt to stop us and, well…"

The mobsters burst out the front doors and immediately turned to the left. Noorim stepped over to a still shaken up Nibira and sympathetically touched her arm.

"Are you alright?"

Nibira nodded, attempting to compose herself.

Noorim stepped back and reached into her pocket. She pulled out a palm sized shard of Larimar Etheria Crystal and held the white oblong gem with blue striations up in front of her face.

"Tally?" she said into the gem.

Taleeka's voice filled both their heads. "Is it done?"

"Yes."

"Are you both okay?"

"Yes, Nibira is a little shaken up, but we are unharmed."

"And the map?"

"They have it," Noorim said with a knowing grin. "All went according to plan."

Taleeka awoke to the sound of her mother's laughter from down the hall and it made her smile. In the seven grands she had been a part of the Konrad household she had mostly experienced Mal laughing at someone else's expense and seldom out of pure joy.

Rising and slipping on a robe, she padded down the hallway to the dining area where a lively conversation filled the room. Pausing at the doorless entry, she rubbed her eyes and yawned. The room, warm from the fireplace on the far wall contained a savory aroma in the air.

Mal and Alto, still dressed in their bed clothing, sat across from Karta and Nibira. Peshk stood off to the side, removing empty bowls from the table and they all looked over at Taleeka when she entered.

"Well good morning sunshine," Mal cheerfully greeted. "You're finally awake. Nibira's been here for a little over a deci."

"Why didn't you wake me?" she groggily asked, sliding into a chair at the head of the table.

"I figured you needed the rest,' Mal replied. "You've got a big day ahead of you."

"Besides, your mom's been telling us all kinds of great stories," Nibira said enthusiastically.

"I'm still amazed that you two know each other," Taleeka said to Karta and her mom.

Karta chuckled. "Yeah, back when your mom was an active Spice Rat, I defended her on the few occasions she managed to get caught."

Mal laughed and pointed at the handsome barrister. "This guy is a fucking legal genius! I remember once, probably twelve grands ago, there was this freak low tide, and I'm running a shit load of Lurdian Rubber, hauling ass into Narian Bay during the Kan. All of a sudden, the *Regis* goes aground, right between two, not just one, but two Quartermaster's Interceptors. Talk about bad fucking luck!

"So, needless to say they arrested me and the crew as well as confiscating my load. This guy manages to convince an Imperial Judge that I was on a humanitarian mission, delivering medical tubing to Clerria House. I swear to the Goddess, this guy's golden tongue could make a dead woman cum."

Upon hearing the lusty praise Nibira shot Karta an adoring side glance and blushed.

"Would you care for some breakfast Mz. Tally?" Peshk asked, placing a steaming mug of tea on the table before her. "There's still some of the pork stew left on the hearth."

Taleeka shook her head. "Nah, I'll eat later, thanks."

"You should eat," Mal said sounding very much like her doting navigator. "Like I said, it's going to be a big day. You'll need your strength. Peshk get her a bowl."

"Mom!"

"Don't 'mom' me, eat!"

Taleeka glanced over at Alto for sympathy but got nothing but a supportive smile.

"Just think," Mal said, sitting back in her chair. "Your first solo gig. This is exciting! I'd love to tag along to watch, but Joc' Valdur is dropping by later and I'm sure he's got a job for us."

"I'm not sure how I let you talk me into this, this weird treasure hunt," Karta said to Taleeka, just before a steaming bowl of stew appeared in front of her.

"Come on Karta," Taleeka said, picking up a spoon. "Where's your sense of adventure? You can't tell me that you're not the least bit curious as to where that map on your back leads."

"All I know is that I'm missing work," Karta said with a frustrated shake of his head. "I mean you've already kept me here for the last few cycles and now we're going to be taking off to who knows where, in search of who knows what."

"Awa," Nibira said sheepishly.

Karta spun in his chair facing the blushing teen who stared downward. "I beg your pardon?"

"We're going to the Island of Awa," she said glancing up briefly and then looking away. "It's one of the larger islands in the Tellasian Chain to the south."

"The barrister grinned at the smitten teen. "I know where Awa is."

This caused Nibira's face to flush again. "Sorry."

"Don't be sorry," Karta said gently. "There's nothing wrong with being smart. I happen to think smart is sexy."

Once she realized she had been complimented Nibira shifted nervously in her seat and then hastily stood, keeping her flushed gaze away from Karta.

"Well, I better go get my stuff ready," she said softly, while blushing. Then, while avoiding everyone's gaze, she hurried away.

"Look Karta, you're missing work and I'm missing school. I'm sorry for stashing you away," Taleeka said, peering up from the meal she ironically devoured. "That's for your protection after they tried to nab you. Whoever wanted the map, now thinks they've got it, so the heat should be off at least until they find out it's bogus."

Mal leaned forward and put her elbows on the table. "Those fuckers that tried to snatch Karta, you got a good look at them, right?"

"Oh yeah," Taleeka said definitively. "Mostly nondescript low-level thugs. Except the leader, who I managed to knock on his ass before the city guards arrived. He was tall and thin with a light reddish-brown complexion. Real angular face, with intense eyes and snow-white hair. He dressed nicely too."

"That sounds like the guy who led the burglars at the library, last Kan," Nibira enthusiastically added.

Mal gave a knowing grin and leaned back in her chair once more.

"Redati," Mal said with a touch of amusement. "So, the Antiquary's interested in the map. Huh, makes sense."

"Who's the Antiquary?" Taleeka asked, pushing her now empty bowl to the side.

"Yes, and how is it I have not heard of such a person?" Alto asked, searching his recollection.

"His name is Anak Bramoul," Mal began. "He owns one of the three largest shipping operations in Zor. He has ties to all the Silent Partner cabals operating in the various island chains of the Goyan Islands. The Silent Partner can't operate in Zor, so they funnel their goods and money through him. It's made him very rich and powerful. He has a sprawling estate to the west of town."

"And his moniker?" Alto inquired, still a bit perplexed.

"Just like the name suggests," Mal replied. "He collects shit. Rare shit. He's obsessed. Anything, as long as it is rare or one of a kind. I've done business with him a few times in my early days as captain of the *Regis*. Getting him the Bihira Vase solidified my reputation as a Spice Rat."

"The Bihira Vase was stolen almost twenty grands ago from the Aramos palace in Aris," Nibira said. "It's been missing ever since!"

"Only missing to some," Mal quipped.

Now, Taleeka gasped in astonishment. "Mom, wait, *you* stole the Bihira Vase?!"

"Nah, an associate of mine, a high-end thief by the name of Lopov did the actual stealing. I was the one who got it out of the city, off the island and into the hands of the Antiquary. Not sure why he wanted it. That is one fucking butt ugly piece of pottery."

"It's one of the few remaining artistic artifacts from the age of the first men," Nibira answered.

"Well, it looks like the Antiquary now wants whatever that map leads to," Mal said with a mischievous grin.

"This caused Taleeka to titter. "He's not going to find anything with the map he's got."

Anak Bramoul had a deserved reputation of fearlessness when confronting a challenge. He quickly rose from humble roots as a dockworker, on the Zorian wharf, to the owner of his own large shipping company. Command of such a far-reaching enterprise also required a healthy dose of ruthlessness. Many a time during his career, he dealt with the various cabals of the Silent Partner and had to garner their respect in order to do business with them. Not all of the encounters went smoothly and some confrontations turned quite violent.

Now, all notions of bravery and toughness were completely stripped away, negated by the airship *Metsik's* violent lurching from side to side.

Inside the main cabin, Anak sat holding onto the seat below him with a white knuckled grip. His terror-riddled face stared across the aisle to Redati, who shared his concerned demeanor. Beside them, sat their three henchmen. Two appeared just as unnerved as their employer, while one slept soundly, his slumber occasionally punctuated by the occasional snort.

"Yeeha, what a ride!" came a bellow from the front of the craft. "They don't call it the Sea of Storms for nothing!"

The voice belonged to their pilot and only other occupant of the beleaguered craft, Pagala de Atar.

The older human male stood controlling the giant ship's wheel directly behind two empty command chairs. His shoulder length greying brown hair swayed with each swerve of the ship and turn of the wheel.

"You're missing a great view," he said, peering quickly back at Anak in wide eyed exuberance. "I got a couple of empty seats up here if you want a better looksee."

The Antiquary stared past the eccentric airship captain to the driving rain pelting the windshield and silently shook his head.

"Suit yourself," he said, fighting a sudden lurch of the wheel. "I figure we'll be out of this storm in a few centis and we'll be coming up on Cupa Bay. From there, we take a left and head towards the mountains."

"You're sure you know where we're going?" Anak asked, in an attempt to distract himself from the tempest.

"Oh yeah!" Pagala heartily confirmed. "I knew that was a map of the Narrow Lands the minute you showed it to me. I used to run wine and other provisions to the Calden Ambassador here. He hated the local swill. Heh, what a prissy ass. Not sure what ever happened to him. Then there was the time I got caught between the two rival cities at the mouth of the bay. Wee-doggy, I thought they were gonna bring the whole dang ship down. They had to bring in the Calden Navy to keep the peace."

Anak and Redati shared a muddled glance at the pilot's monologue.

"Sir, are you sure about this?" Redati asked softly, his voice strained.

Anak threw a worried glance but remained silent.

"See, just like I said," Pagala announced when the rain stopped assaulting the craft and the skies cleared. "Looks like we avoided the Valdurian air traffic control balloon, and here's Cupa Bay. We're gonna just follow the river south, over Castor Lake and we'll be at that mountain trail head in no time."

"Does he ever shut up?" Redati whispered, just before Pagala launched into an off-key song in Valdur-Ya.

"He was supposedly one of the best Air Scouts in the whole Valdurian Air Service." Anak whispered back. "I think we can afford him a few eccentricities."

Redati shook his head in disbelief and sat back. With the weather finally cleared, the tension in the cabin noticeably diminished, evident by the relieved look on the passengers' faces. The rest of the trip went smoothly, with their quirky pilot chattering to himself and launching into an occasional song.

When they could see the peaks of the mountains ahead, Anak relocated to one of the command chairs in the front of the ship. Down below, the frozen tundra transformed from flat ground to rolling foothills.

"Won't be long now," Pagala said confidently, pointing out the windshield. "If memory serves, that trail head is right over there. Kinda hard to find, but then again, that's why you needed me. Am I right?"

He laughed boisterously at his own joke, then began a shallow descent. "I'll set us down right by the trail opening but we're gonna have to hump it the rest of the way."

"Just get us there," Anak said, keeping his eyes on the approaching mountains.

Pagala laughed. "It's what you're paying me for boss!"

The trail head itself appeared as little more than a rough-cut opening between two large boulders. The route itself consisted of a deep furrow through the mountainside sloping steeply upward. The pilot's assessment had proven correct, travelling on foot remained their only option.

Pagala had launched into another song, when he set the craft down and dropped the side hatch. A blast of cold air streamed into the cabin and everyone got to their feet.

"Here we are, boys!" the outlandish captain announced, buttoning his jacket. "I hope you all brought warm clothes and comfy boots."

Exiting the *Metsik,* they stared at the rocky terrain leading up the mountain with resignation. Anak started off in the lead, reflecting on how much he detested rural settings.

"Okay boys," Pagala said, "I'll be right with ya. Gotta park my ride."

He pulled a multi-colored Etheria shard from his coat pocket. The amber, bronze, black and green fob glittered in his hand. He pressed his thumb against the green portion while pointing it at the ship. The side ramp automatically closed. Then he pressed on the bronze section and the craft began to rise. They all watched the airship quickly ascend and disappear into a cloud high overhead.

"Yippee!" Pagala cheered enthusiastically, his long hair fluttering in the wind. "Up, up and away."

Redati leaned over to Anak and whispered, "This is going to be a long walk."

Vanir shuffled through the last of the reports just as the Grand Turine in the Zorian harbor rang out that the morning had almost passed. It had been a rare uneventful Kan for the most part. Petty thefts and drunken altercations were the bulk of the complaints.

The only incident of any note; a missing person, a wealthy businessman with the bespoke name of Egan Bosch. His wife originally reported him missing three cycles ago when he didn't come home from work. Vanir had made it a point to check the Kan reports every morning to see if his body had turned up. So far it hadn't.

The fact that Bosch was his confidential informant on the Zorian Monetary Council sent the lead investigator reaching for the whisky bottle on his desk. He had just taken his first gulp of the amber liquid, when a knock on his open office door caused him to spin in his chair and set the glass down.

A young man in his late teens stood in the doorway holding a small stack of papers. He stood only a little over five feet tall and a grey tunic covered a slightly pudgy frame. A head full of wild black hair adorned a chocolate brown, wide, youthful face which sported a short scraggly tuft of hair on his chin.

"Captain Vanir?" he said hesitantly. "Sorry to disturb you. I'm Talib de Bogat. Captain Gasata told me to report to you."

"Oh yes, the transfer!" Vanir said sitting up straight and extending a hand towards one of two chairs facing his desk. "Come in, have a seat. I imagine that paperwork you're carrying is for me?"

"Uh, yes, sir," the young man said, placing the papers on the desk and sitting down.

"Care for a drink?"

Talib hesitated, unsure if being tested. "Um, uh, sure."

Vanir pulled the papers in front of him and beamed at the response.

"Good lad!" he said, pouring a quarter inch worth of whiskey in a heavy bottomed tumbler and sliding it towards the nervous young man.

"Alright, let's see what we've got here," Vanir said taking another gulp, and then scrutinizing the reports before him.

Talib eyed the drink suspiciously. His nose wiggled and face scrunched when he smelled it. With a deep reluctant breath, he took a gulp, imitating the captain behind the desk. The moment the liquor hit the back of the youth's throat, his eyes bulged and he coughed loudly. A wave of gasping and sputtering immediately followed.

"Careful, that's got a kick," Vanir said calmly, not looking up from his reading.

"Three grands on patrol, I see."

"Yes, sir," Talib said, finally regaining his voice
Primarily in the Seven Sisters.

"That's a tough beat," Vanir conceded. "And Captain
Gasata gives you a glowing recommendation. That says
something. He hates to lose good patrolmen."

"I try sir."

The redheaded investigator finally peered up and took
another sip. "Looks like you do more than try. It says here
you were instrumental in breaking the Thelman case."

"Uh, yes, sir, that's why he recommended a transfer to
investigation."

Vanir nodded and shifted to another paper.

"Top of the class in Zekoff's Modern Policing and
Investigation course."

"Yes, sir, that was last grand, at Captain Gasata's
insistence."

"Actually, that was at my insistence," Vanir said,
shuffling another page to the top of the pile.

"Sir?"

"I've made it a new requirement to get into
investigation. Minimum of two grands patrolling the
streets, and then passing Zekoff's class."

"I see, sir."

Vanir gave a sympathetic smile. The kid seemed so
nervous he was practically vibrating.

"Okay, Talib, everything looks good. You're in,
congrats. Oh, and you can knock off the 'sir' business.
We're pretty informal around here. You can call me,
Captain."

Talib gave a taut grin at the humor. "Yes, Captain."

"Alright," Vanir said, coming to his feet and downing
the remainder of his drink. "You'll be tagging along with
me for a while until you get settled in. I'm heading over to
the Imperial Bank to do an interview with a person of
interest. I'll be looking forward to hearing your
observations."

"What's he a 'person of interest' in, Captain?"

Vanir chuckled while heading out the door. "A number of crimes, but for now it's a missing person."

"Yes, Captain."

"But first we have to stop by the armory. We're going to get you an upgrade from the standard pistol crossbow you're used to carrying."

Talib shifted uncomfortably when the hackney carriage came to a stop in front of the Imperial Bank. The pistol crossbow under his tunic dug into his side, making it difficult to concentrate.

"You get used to it," Vanir said once the hackney floated off down the busy street. "The Mark Six which we carry is a whole lot smaller than the older models. I hear there's a Mark Seven floating around out there, but it's too new for us to have. The only ones sporting that kind of hardware are Valdurian spooks and black market folks."

"So, Captain," Talib said, when they started up the bank's wide stairway. "What's the deal with this... What did you call him? Lord Banavor?"

"He's about your age," Vanir said, keeping his voice down. "He's a Senior Marassa at the university with his own school of economics named after him, as well as head of the Zorian Monetary Council. He's a full-blown financial whiz kid, I'll give him that. He's also a thief and a murderer."

"How is it he's still walking amongst us?"

They paused when they reached the portico and Vanir faced his protégé with an ominous expression.

"He's slick, that's why, and powerful, so be careful. In addition to everything else, he's got a serious seduction mojo working. I've got protection on me, but you don't, so watch yourself."

"Captain?"

"I'm serious, Talib. Don't let him touch you and if he starts to charm and seduce you, think of your grandmother."

"I will pray to Santi for strength," Talib said, making the ceremonial swirl in front of him with his forefinger.

"Santi, huh?" Vanir said, recognizing the noble sun deity. "Something else you should know. Banavor's a follower of Pa-Waga."

Talib inhaled sharply. "Servants of Pa-Waga have been known to persecute my religion. Especially the Piety Watch."

"Tell me something I don't know. Keep your religion to yourself. Especially when he starts going on about 'serving a mighty god' and the like."

"I cannot renounce my faith!"

"I'm not asking you to renounce anything. Just take any religious talk and tuck it up under your tunic next to your pistol. Can you do that?"

Talib weakly nodded.

"Good Lad!" Vanir said.

He pulled out his flask, took a swig and offered it to Talib, who silently declined.

"Alright, let's go see what slicky boy has to say," Vanir said, acknowledging the EEtah guards on either side of the double doors.

Once inside, they made their way across the lobby under suspicious stares from the bankers.

"I don't think we're very welcome here," Talib whispered apprehensively, when they reached the doors leading to the Zorian Monetary Council.

Vanir surveyed the sea of distrustful faces staring at them and scoffed.

"That's just tough," Vanir said, opening the doors. "Welcome or not, we've got a job to do and the authority to do it."

Once in the council's chambers they were led back to Banavor's office. As usual Banavor sat behind his desk looking over paperwork while the EEtah's Luft and Nagrada stood dutifully behind him.

"Why, Captain Vanir," Banavor said impatiently, coming to his feet. "You're here so often I'm tempted to assign you an office."

Vanir chuckled while Talib shuttered and shifted awkwardly at Banavor's manner of clothing, or lack thereof. The fledgling detective had become used to all manner of dress and undress in the cosmopolitan High Holy City, due to the individual inhabitance's varied cultures. This, however, in the young man's opinion, exceeded any cultural deviation he had ever encountered.

The comely young man was nude, save for an elaborate wire cage around his penis and scrotum. The painful looking enclosure resembled a dragon wrapping around his organ. The beast's ornately carved head rested just above the head of the economist's cock. A thin golden tongue emanated from the serpent's open mouth, which penetrated the Pa-Waga cleric's urethra.

"And I see you brought a friend along this time," Banavor continued. "Just who might *you* be?"

"This is Inspector Talib," Vanir replied stiffly. "He's new and here to observe."

"Ooh, fresh meat," Banavor gushed, coming from around the desk. "Well, *Inspector* Talib, allow me to give you a personal guided tour of the bank."

Vanir could sense the salacious influence Banavor emanated and considered its effect on his charge with every step forward. Moving in the way successfully halted his seductive advancement.

"I'm afraid our time is limited this cycle, Lord Banavor. I did want to ask you some questions."

Banavor halted and placed his hands defiantly on his hips.

"By the gods, what is it this time, Captain? Did someone's coin purse get pilfered or perhaps some random death that you think I might have something to do with? Why is it when something goes amiss in this city, you're in my office the next cycle? I could accept the visits if we were fucking, but *this* is becoming tedious."

Vanir ignored the outburst and remained calm.

"I'd like to ask you about Egan Bosch."

"What about him?"

"He's been missing for the last three cycles."

"I have no idea where my colleague might be. I last saw him at the council meeting."

"When exactly was that, Lord Banavor?" Talib asked somberly.

Banavor gave Talib a flirtatious glance. "Why inspector Talib. So, you really *can* speak."

"When?" Vanir reinforced the question.

Banavor sighed. "It was three cycles ago. I only see him at meetings. The next one is in a cluster from now."

"And you haven't seen him since?" Vanir pressed.

"No, he keeps an office in the building but he's seldom here. He has a business to run."

"May we see the office?" Talib hesitantly asked.

The seductive smile returned to Banavor's face. "Why Inspector Talib, I would be more than happy to oblige you in any way I can. My assistant will show you to his office."

Once in Bosch's spartan office, away from Banavor's licentious effects, Talib heaved a sigh of relief.

"I don't believe it," the young detective said, watching his superior search the missing economist's desk. "What in the name of the gods was that back there?! Thanks for intervening. I mean, the closer he got to me, the more I wanted to rip my clothes off and… and I don't know what. I'm not attracted to men. How come it didn't affect you?"

Vanir shook his head and closed a drawer. "I warned you, he's powerful. As for me," Vanir held up his left hand, displaying his pinky ring. "This Etheria trinket negates whatever he's got going on."

"Handy."

"You bet," Vanir sighed and looked around the office. "Well, I don't see anything obvious. I'll have an evidence team down here today to take a closer look at the papers he's got. Besides, I wouldn't know what I was looking at. So, what did you think about his story?"

"Well, I just met the man, but I could sense he's not telling us everything."

"Very perceptive. Good lad."

"I guess we're headed back, Captain?"

"Yep, you've got a report to write about this little incident." Vanir reached out and patted his protégé on the shoulder. "Well, how's your first day going so far?"

Taleeka watched the Kan fog slowly rise from the waters of the Shallow Sea below. Up ahead, the islands of the Tellasian Chain gradually disappeared from view in the thick enveloping mist.

"I thought pilots weren't supposed to fly during the Kan," Nibira said nervously, peering out the domed covering of the *Mala's* cockpit.

"Generally, no," Taleeka said, reaching into a small storage compartment on the dashboard. "Unless you've got the right equipment."

She retrieved, and then donned a set of round spectacles with blue glass. Attached to the outer corners, next to the lens, a delicate arm extended out containing an orange lens the exact size of the blue one.

"I got these from my mom when the Valdurians upgraded her stuff."

"Those things actually let you see through the fog?" Karta asked from the seat beside her.

"And in the dark, too," Taleeka replied, guiding her ship into the ever-growing mist around them. "The glass is treated with Etheria. Don't ask me how, but the blue lens reveals hidden things and allows you to see things as they really are."

She then flipped down the orange lenses. "The orange allows you to see any heat signature given off."

The barrister gave an impressed nod. "And you say your mom has even more advanced equipment?"

Taleeka smiled and banked the craft to the west. "Yeah, because of all the work she does for the Valdurians, they keep her outfitted with all the latest fun toys. I get the hand-me-downs."

Below, the sea gave way to the shore of Awa Island. They could make out the muted city lights of the capital, Awa-Ta, peeking through the dense clouds.

"There's your hometown," Taleeka said to Nibira. "Want to drop in and say hi to your folks?"

"Something tells me they wouldn't appreciate the intrusion," Nibira replied.

"No sense of humor," Taleeka cracked.

"That's an understatement," Nibira said with a nod. "According to the map, we should be heading for Awa-Ramos, a walled village at the base of the mountains."

Taleeka scanned the triple canopy jungle stretching outward in front of them and covering the small group of low mountains in the distance.

"From the look of that foliage down there, I'm gonna have to get creative as to where I put down."

"Doesn't it bother you that we don't know where we're going or what we're looking for?" Karta asked, watching the city lights quickly pass beneath them.

"We do know where we're going," Taleeka replied. "We've got a map. As for what we'll find, well let's just say I've got a good feeling about it."

"I wish I shared your optimism."

"You don't have to, Councilor. I've got enough for all of us."

When Awa-Ramos finally appeared from the mist as a round dark spot, Taleeka slowed the *Mala* and began a shallow descent.

Through her glasses, Taleeka could see the twelve-foot-high wooden fortifications surrounding the city, with guarded gates at both the east and west sides. The municipality itself seemed small, measuring no more than a mile across. Some lights twinkled in the various single-story structures but for the most part, the town had shut down for the Kan.

"Okay," Taleeka said, studying the terrain. "It looks like there's a small park on the northeastern side of town. That's where we get out."

"I can't see," Nibira said, peering into the fog. "Is there a really small building at one end flanked by two giant totems?"

"As a matter of fact, there is!" Taleeka said, sounding very impressed. "They look like bears."

"We might want to find a different spot," Nibira warned. "That's sacred ground. The local shaman lives in that building."

"Shaman?!"

"Yeah, healer, medicine man, whatever you want to call them. The members of the village must remove any clothing they're wearing, especially shoes when they gather on the lawn for an audience."

"Yeah, well it's a little too chilly to be running around naked." Taleeka said, settling the airship to the ground. "Besides, we're not going to be here that long."

Leaving the Etheria engines running, Taleeka popped the top hatch, grabbed her backpack and leapt out onto the ground. Nibira and Karta warily followed. Once outside the craft, Taleeka closed the top hatch, reached inside her pack and retrieved an amber, bronze, black Etheria fob.

Pointing it at the *Mala,* she pressed on the bronze end. The airship shuttered and then began to rise. Taleeka's outstretched hand followed the craft's ascension out of sight. When she saw the airship at a safe altitude, she pressed the black crystal in the center to hold it in position.

"Alright," Taleeka said, placing the shard back in her pack and slinging it onto her back. "Let's find a place to hole up until the Kan lifts. Then we can get some provisions and be on our way."

The others nodded and walked towards the nearest road. They had gone no more than a few steps when they heard shouting from the small building. Due to everyone's close proximity to the Larimar talking stone in Taleeka's coat, they could understand the hostile verbiage perfectly.

Everyone peered in the direction of the yelling, however only Taleeka with her Etheria spectacles, could see the source of the commotion.

"I knew this was a bad idea!" Nibira said, trying in vain to peer through the fog.

In the doorless entryway to the shack, Taleeka could clearly see a thin, middle-aged woman with dark black skin and short snow white hair. The shaman's only garment was a long necklace full of bear claws, which draped down to her patch of thick, white pubic hair.

"Defilers!" she screamed. "You desecrate sacred ground!"

Removing two claws from the necklace, she threw each one at the feet of the two bear totems. The moment the claw touched the base, rivulets of blue energy surged up the twelve-foot-tall wooden statues.

"Okay, this isn't good," Taleeka said anxiously.

"I hate to say I told you so," Nibira said when she saw the blue tendrils rising up through the fog.

"Then don't!" Tally snapped.

"These people take this sort of thing seriously!" Nibira continued, despite Taleeka's objection.

When the PSI lightning dissipated, both statues had converted into flesh and blood animals. Taleeka reached for her pistol when both went down on all fours and roared.

"Don't shoot," Nibira pleaded.

"What do you mean don't shoot? "Karta said in a panic, while backing away. "We're about to become bear snacks!"

"None of us are fast enough to outrun them," Nibira said, watching the bears aggressively approaching.

"I don't have to be faster than them," Karta replied fearfully, his voice cracking. "I just need to be faster than the two of you."

"Quick, take off your shoes," Nibira said, raising both hands in the air palms out.

"What?!" Karta asked incredulously.

"I'd just as soon not get into a dust up with the locals if we can help it," Taleeka said kicking off her shoes with pistol in hand. "Do it!"

"Peace to you," Nibira called out the traditional greeting of the region.

Upon hearing her own language, the shaman stopped yelling and the bears, now halfway towards them, paused but continued to growl.

"She's headed this way, get your damn shoes off," Taleeka hissed at Karta.

The barrister hesitated but then quickly complied.

"On your knees," Nibira whispered dropping to the ground.

"What?!" Karta protested.

Taleeka cocked her weapon and knelt down.

"Just in case," she assured the jittery lawyer.

Shaking his head in disbelief, Karta dropped down beside Taleeka.

"In the name of the great and powerful Ariu," Nibira said invoking the name of the local bear deity. "We humbly beg your forgiveness for trespassing. We are strangers to your land on a quest for the great Ariu."

Taleeka could see the shaman still heading their way flanked by the bears. Her face, however, had transformed from enraged, to cautiously curious.

"I saw you come from the sky," she said, finally coming into view of everyone. "What quest would the mighty Ariu entrust with strangers? I am Meshka, Priestess of the Great One. If any would be chosen for a quest, it would be me."

"Oh Meshka, we do not know why we were chosen," Nibira said humbly. "But Ariu has marked this man with a map that we follow."

Meshka's eyes narrowed at the explanation. "Show me."

"Karta," Taleeka said, not taking her eyes off the shaman.

The barrister quickly removed his shirt and respectfully bowed his head. Taleeka, pistol at the ready beside her, kept a watchful eye on Meshka, while she walked behind Karta and leaned over for a closer look.

The Ariu priestess slowly traced the lines on Karta's back with her finger and her entire demeanor changed. When she stood back up, she waved her hands at the bears. The two creatures lumbered back to their original positions beside the door and stood upright. The beasts stared at their feet and slowly reverted back to wooden totems.

"Rise," she ordered. "There can no longer be any doubt you were touched by the great Ariu, for this map leads to the Arcane Grotto, where Ariu slumbers. Your journey, however, is *not* a quest. The Great and Powerful Ariu has summoned you. Go in peace and haste, it is not good to keep the Great One waiting."

Zekoff saw the frustrated look on Vanir's face the moment he entered his office. When he silently sat down, the Marassa abandoned the papers he had been grading and pulled a whiskey bottle, along with a glass, from a desk drawer. Without a word, he sat both down in front of the investigator and reached for his pipe.

Checking the bowl, he then lit it while Vanir poured a healthy drink. The former commander of the city guards, turned college professor, watched his protégé sit back with the glass and sigh.

He really didn't mind him drinking so early in the day. Unlike almost everyone, Vanir actually performed better when under the influence of alcohol. It had been that way since he joined the Zorian Guards at fifteen. With as much liquor as the young man could put away, Zekoff had never seen him staggering or out of control.

He remembered back to the case Vanir insightfully helped crack, which got him promoted to Lieutenant. Patrol Captain Gasata had complained, calling Vanir a drunkard.

Zekoff replied, "Then send him a wagonload of whatever he's drinking."

He let the young man sit quietly for a moment sipping his drink. In the six grands since the now thirty-one grand old had assumed the role of Lead Investigator, his office at the university had always been a refuge.

"You know," Vanir finally said, "for the life of me, I can't figure out how that little shit keeps one step ahead of me."

Zekoff blew a column of evergreen scented smoke upward. "I take it you're referring to the illusive Lord Banavor?"

"Who else?"

"I thought you had someone on the inside of the Monetary Council?"

"I did," Vanir replied taking another sip. "He's gone missing. And, given who we're dealing with, he's probably dead."

"He is proving to be a slippery fellow."

Vanir scoffed. "He's only become more emboldened since we made that deal with him at the end of the Etheria war."

"You've turned one of his associates. I'm sure you can turn another."

"I'm not so certain," Vanir said skeptically. "Ever since my informant Bosch went missing, and the judge wanting an investigation into his business practices, he's really gotten paranoid."

"Bosch had been on the inside for quite a while," Zekoff noted, while examining his pipe which had gone out. "Surely he witnessed something you could act on."

"Apparently, he only uses the council as a rubber stamp for his policies. The shifty stuff only surfaces when he needs them to officially rule on something."

"I'd be willing to bet they all know what happened to your informant," Zekoff offered. "If you want to make an example of someone, the parties you want to intimidate would have to witness it."

Zekoff could feel the waves of exasperation radiating off the scruffy looking redhead. He knew he would eventually figure it out. It had always been this way, ever since he and his late wife took in the precocious nine grand old when his parents died. The old colonel had always made himself available as a sounding board and with a few well-placed questions the answer would come to him.

"Tell me about this investigation."

Vanir took another drink and shook his head. "My evidence team discovered some notes in his office. Nothing much, just vague references to improprieties at the Monetary Fund."

"Who was he going to use to conduct the investigation?"

Vanir gave a helpless look and shrugged. "It sure wasn't us."

"What about requesting an audit?"

Vanir gave a resigned smile. "Are you kidding. He's a golden boy to the Imperial Bank. They're not going to bite the hand that keeps feeding them gold."

"Looks like we've circled back around to turning one of the council members," Zekoff said, tapping out his pipe. "Remember, you're not a lone investigator anymore. You've got a whole department at your disposal, use them. Banavor may have become paranoid, but I'm thinking the rest of the council has gotten rather complacent. They're used to the law looking the other way from their activities."

Vanir nodded, deep in thought.

"Yeah," Vanir said, an idea finally percolating. "I bet each one of them has a crooked side hustle. I'll put tails on all of them. When one screws up, we'll bring them in and lean on them."

"That certainly sounds better than you running yourself ragged."

Vanir snickered at himself. "It sure does, doesn't it?"

"All it requires from you is a little patience."

The investigator downed the rest of his drink. "I just hope that if he's got some sinister plot brewing that we don't wait too long."

"If his intentions are that impactful, I would say that he would be in violation of your agreement."

Vanir nodded thoughtfully. The old man had done it again, bringing clarity to chaos.

"The trick is going to be catching him before whatever he's up to screws us all."

Vanir got to his feet and Zekoff moved the stack of papers back in front of him.

"Or you could always stay and help me grade papers."

"That's okay," Vanir said, heading for the door. "I've got a manipulative little bastard to catch."

Anak turned his collar up against the cold north wind and glowered at the bug-eyed man with wildly fluttering hair who now led them. Every now and then he would stop to consult the map but, through it all, he never stopped talking.

"Doesn't he *ever* shut up?" Anak whispered to Redati walking beside him.

"Apparently not," Redati replied, regretting his choice of a guide.

They had been climbing steadily for the better part of the morning. The narrowly-indented trail in the rock face became steeper and they had passed through quite a few covered portions of the route. Anak felt a small sense of relief that the bizarre pilot and scout had been correct in that an airship would not have been practical.

Pagala paused once again when the trail intersected another, which led off to the north. Consulting the map again, he brushed back swirls of long hair and surveyed the barren rocky terrain.

"I just love the Narrow Lands," he said with a sigh. "You know why? No snakes. Too cold. I hate snakes!"

Then, without waiting for a response, he took off again at a brisk pace.

Redati glanced back at the three, well-armed henchmen bringing up the rear and rolled his eyes. He could tell by the scowls under their beards that these city boys were miserable in this cold, inhospitable setting.

A loud screech from above suddenly wrenched everyone's attention skyward. A small herd of five wild Kells unexpectedly emerged from a nearby bank of swiftly moving clouds. Three of the long-necked, flying lizards did tight circles around the group, while two of them screeched and dove at them.

"Down!" Anak screamed.

All ducked into a cleft in the rock trail and the two sets of snapping jaws just missed them. The last henchman in line didn't move quickly enough and, although he missed being bitten, one of the Kell's tails raked along his back, ripping the pack off and slashing through his coat.

The man screamed and fell onto the ground. Blood immediately rushed from the long deep wound and the unfortunate henchman began convulsing on the cold stone.

From the relative safety of the furrowed trail, they all watched the contents of his ripped open backpack fly about the bleak mountainside, scattered by the chilled gusty wind.

"Oh yeah," Pagala said with an embarrassed face scrunch. "I forgot to mention the wild Kells. You know the Avions do a pretty good job of folding these bad boys into manageable herds, but every now and then..."

"Will you shut up!" Anak bellowed above the screeches of another diving lizard.

Undaunted by the rebuke, Pagala leapt up out of the trail, screaming and waving his short sword at the attacking creatures.

"Get down you fool!" Redati called out, not wanting to lose their guide to an insane act of bravado.

The call and warning went unheeded and Pagala dropped to the rocky ground just before the beast swooped mere feet over his prone body, jaws gnashing furiously.

When it passed just above him, he stuck out his sword and held on with both hands. The tip of the blade pierced the fast-moving creature just below the chest and its velocity drug the blade down the lower half of its body, slicing open the entire abdomen. The mortally wounded Kell screamed and flew over the group, drenching them in blood, severed body parts and foul-smelling fecal material.

The crazed pilot gave out a victory yell when the beast plummeted to the ground and bounced to a stop, dead. The other four, sensing this meal too costly, quickly banked away, their shrieks vanishing into the gusty winds.

Anak slowly stood, peering down at his dead henchman, and then over to a jubilant Pagala who rushed over to his kill.

"Whoo boy! Are we ever going to be eating good!" Pagala said excitedly, plunging his blade into the carcass and gleefully carving on the dead Kell.

"You ever had Kell steak?" he asked, totally oblivious to the gruesome scene around him. "Absolutely delicious! Of course, I'm partial to the wings, and in some parts, the eyeballs are considered a delicacy. Oh yeah, I'm definitely claiming the eyes…"

Redati, wiping away a bloody piece of unrecognizable internal organ from his head, scowled at the exuberant pilot. His boss, as well as all the others were completely soaked in blood and one of the remaining henchmen vomited next to his fallen comrade.

"I sure hope what's at the end of this map is worth it boss." Redati said, examining their blood-soaked clothes.

"Me too," Anak replied over Pagala, who now happily sang an off-key tune while carving away on the Kell body.

Inspector Talib ran a hand through his head of thick brown curls, set the pen down, and then exhaled loudly. *Ah, the unglamorous, behind the scenes part of the job.*

When back on patrol, his reports were few and far between. Now, as an inspector, he was well aware of a higher standard expected of him. He took time and care to make sure he accurately chronicled yesterday's encounter with Lord Banavor, even the embarrassing part of his arousal.

"Hey, new guy," a female voice called out from behind him. "I'm heading over to Maja's to get a bite. Wanna come or I could bring you back something?" Tantei de Bogat asked, getting up from her desk on the other side of the room.

"Is that the place with the mutton roll-ups?"

"Yep, so good, I'd fuck an EEtah to get one."

Talib snickered and shook his head, glad to have her as an office partner. Her dark, ribald, one of the boys sense of humor put him at ease right away. The more serious attributes impressed him even more, like investigative thoroughness and her being one of the guard's hand-to-hand combat instructors.

He watched the bald, athletically built detective slip on her jacket and noted how the form fitting garment did little to disguise the pistol bulge in the small of her back.

"Thanks," Talib said, "but I gotta get this filed."

"You do realize that you're passing up a golden opportunity to watch me eat one of those things?"

He sat back in his chair and raised an eyebrow at her pleasant, smiling features. "Yes, but can you fit the whole thing in your mouth?"

"You're just going to have to tag along to find out."

"As enticing as that sounds, I'm going to have to catch the next show. This is my first report for Captain Vanir and I want to make sure it's right."

"Suit yourself," she said, spinning towards the open door and glancing back over her shoulder. "I just want to mention, I like to eat slowly and play with my food."

"Looking forward to it," he said teasingly, before she disappeared down the hall.

Sitting forward, the young investigator sighed and picked up the first page when Vanir poked his head through the door.

"Young Talib, you're with me."

Talib glanced nervously down at the already tardy document and back at his boss.

"The report can wait," Vanir said reassuringly. "Right now, we gotta go see a woman about a body."

"Sir?" Talib said, standing and reaching for his jacket.

"Come on, let's see some hustle, I've got a meeting a little later today," the senior sleuth said, before heading down the hall in the same direction Tantei had gone.

"What's going on, Captain?" Talib inquired when he finally caught up, halfway across Judgement Square.

"I just got through talking with Colonel Zekoff and he had an interesting perspective on this case."

"You mean Professor Zekoff?"

Vanir chuckled. *The kid's quick.*

"Old habits die hard," he said, hailing a hackney.

Once seated in the warm cab, Vanir pulled the flask from his jacket pocket and took a quick slug. He then held it up, offering it to Talib, who shook his head.

"The woman we're going to talk to is a member of the Zorian Monetary Council named Hatya Sahid."

"As in Sahid Forge?"

"The same. See, I figure Bosch is as good as dead, which means the others have got to be a little nervous about the cost of displeasing Lord Banavor. I think Hatya saw, or at least knows something."

Talib nodded. "It's a safe bet that if the killing was disciplinary, he did it in front of the council for effect."

"That's what I'm thinking. It's time to exert a little pressure on Mz. Sahid."

A quick stop at the foundry revealed Mz. Sahid worked from her stately home in the upscale Hillcrest neighborhood of the Bogat Plat. It also revealed to the investigators, that if she did venture into the stifling and noisy metalworks, it usually meant trouble for some employee.

Talib watched the stately homes go by in awe. These were a far cry from the slums of the Seven Sisters he used to patrol. They pulled up in front of an elegant three-story home which spoke of luxury, yet fell well short of mansion status.

After instructing the driver to wait, both got out and paused at the front door.

"Okay," Vanir said, preparing to grab the oversized knocking ring. "We're going to play a little game with the lady of the house, invented by Colonel Zekoff, called friend and foe."

"Professor Zekoff," Talib quickly corrected under his breath.

Vanir bowed his head and grinned. "He *was* a colonel when he invented it, and don't be a smart ass."

"Sorry, Captain."

"Anyways, friend and foe. I'll be the hard ass and you play the nice guy. Just follow my lead."

"Got it."

A Picean servant answered the door and stared at them with an expectant gaze.

"Captain Vanir and Inspector Talib from the Zorian Guards to see Mz. Sahid."

The humanoid fish's gill flaps fluttered across her ear holes, translating Vanir's announcement.

"Do you have an appointment?" the Picean asked politely.

"We're from the Zorian Guards, we don't need an appointment."

"Mz. Sahid is very busy," the servant insisted. "She sees no one without an appointment."

The redheaded captain scoffed loudly and then sneered at the humanoid fish.

"Look, we can do this the easy way or the hard way," he said. "The easy way is, go tell your boss that we want to talk to her. It happens here and now. It's private, and over and done with quickly. The hard way is when we leave, I send a uniformed brute squad to forcibly bring her *to me* at headquarters. That's in public and it will probably take up the rest of the cycle. The decision is yours!"

The Picean's gill flaps now fluttered wildly and her face reflected the dilemma Vanir had just put her in.

"Wait here," she said, finally giving in.

"Smart," Vanir spat sarcastically.

"Damn, Captain, when you said hard ass, you weren't kidding."

"Practicing getting into character," the senior detective said, a devious smile crossing his face.

A few moments later, the door opened again and the Picean invited them in. The moderate sized, nicely appointed foyer with a totally feminine touch contained no hint of a man's presence in the décor. Off to their left, Hatya Sahid descended a wide staircase at a determined pace.

She stood at an average height for Goyan women, full figured with light brown skin and a head of shoulder length, gray hair. Her normally lovely facial features were now pulled taut with irritation.

"My maid says you want to see me," she said angrily, upon reaching the bottom of the stairs. "She also said you were rude and threatening."

"Lady, we're not some iron merchant here to sell you something," Vanir said commandingly. "When the guards want to talk, you comply, or face the consequences!"

"Do you have any idea who I am?!" she said, her blue eyes flashing with anger.

"I know exactly who you are! If you want to, you can file a formal complaint with the Head of the Investigation Division. Oh yeah, that's me!"

"Ma'am, we're truly sorry to bother you," Talib said placatingly. "We know you're busy. We'll try and be brief."

Hatya gave Vanir a final angry glance before focusing her attention on Talib. Her face relaxed slightly, but still maintained an annoyed scowl.

"Alright, you want to talk, so talk!" she said to Talib, completely ignoring Vanir.

"Ma'am, one of your colleagues on the council, Egan Bosch, is missing and presumed dead. I'm afraid we suspect foul play."

For the briefest moment Vanir detected a passing glance of panicked recognition upon hearing Bosch's name. Her defiant air quickly returned.

"Surely, you don't think I had anything to do with it?!"

"Maybe, maybe not," Vanir said accusingly, "but I'd be willing to bet you at least know something about it."

Just before giving out an indignant huff, Talib caught the tiniest look of panic on her face.

"I have no idea what you're talking about!" she asserted defiantly. "The last time I saw Egan was at the council meeting four cycles ago. We don't associate with each other outside of the council, so I didn't expect to see him until the next meeting a cluster from now."

"And you've had no contact since then?" Talib asked, continuing his calm line of questioning.

"None," she firmly stated.

The young detective amiably nodded his acceptance, but Vanir scoffed in disbelief.

"You know," he countered, "they say our job is dangerous, but right now, under your *current* leadership I'd say yours is more perilous. Bad things happen to people who displease Lord Banavor."

At the mention of Banavor's name, her resolve briefly cracked once again, but she instantly recovered.

"Lord Banavor is a financial genius," she said. "We're lucky to have him!"

"Until you piss him off," Vanir spat. "So, you gotta be asking yourself, how long before I'm on his bad side?"

"I don't know what you're referring to, but if there are no further questions, I must ask you to leave."

"Thank you for your time, ma'am," Talib said with a conciliatory smile. "We're sorry to disturb. If you think of anything that could be of help, please get in touch."

"Yes, I'll be sure to do just that," she replied sarcastically, her eyes firing daggers at Vanir. "Now, good day to you!"

Once outside Talib peered over at Vanir. "Well, what do you think?"

"Lad, I think you did great," Vanir said, opening the carriage door. "I also think we got to her."

"What now? Talib asked, settling into the back seat.

Vanir retrieved his flask and took a quick swig.

"Now we wait," he said, putting the cap back on the flask.

Tumuh de Bont watched the rooftops of Zor race past from her seat on the Valdurian Air Bus. The flight from the Spice Islands, at full capacity, contained twenty passengers, a pilot and an Air Marshal. The other travelers, all wealthy humans who could afford air travel, appeared quite comfortable with this relatively new mode of transportation. The majority of Annigan's other journeyers, as well as cargo shipments, relied upon the standard and decidedly more dangerous method of passage by sea.

Tumuh excitedly fidgeted with her small travel bag when the ship slowed and began its descent into the gaping maw of Air Station Three. Her mission had been a success and she couldn't wait to report her findings back to Lord Banavor.

These were exhilarating times. Ever since receiving his mark three grands ago, she had become smitten with the beautiful young man and priest of Pa-Waga.

She would always remember the first Kan when he initiated her and consecrated her body. There had been so much blood and semen all around her and the other six initiates, while Banavor defiled her every orifice. She still tingled at the recollection of the bodies writhing and her racking orgasm that was so intense she nearly passed out.

Since then, in all ways she strove to please him, knowing service to him also meant pleasing the mighty God they followed. Indeed, Pa-Waga had already rewarded her zeal for the faith, with money, expensive clothing and the best of everything. A far cry from her humble upbringing in the Seven Sisters Slums.

Thinking about her good fortune, she found herself playing with, and enjoying the feel of, her form-fitting blue silk dress which clung to her slender shape. Pursing her full lips, she closed her large green eyes and reveled in the sensual feeling of the garment against her body.

She opened her eyes when the craft settled into a slip and the passengers began getting to their feet. She purposefully remained seated, allowing all her fellow travelers to disembark first. She didn't like the idea of people behind her.

When she did finally step out of the hatch, the pilot, a skinny young man with blond hair and a bad complexion, followed her along, with the Air Marshal, who always exited the airship last.

The burley female marshal stood over six feet tall, with broad shoulders and large breasts filling out her official green jumpsuit. Tumuh also couldn't help but notice the sizeable bulge in her crotch, identifying her as an Amarenian Hill Sister.

The marshal's alabaster complexion, complete with freckles and red hair, contrasted greatly against Tumuh's own light brown skin common to the peoples of the Goyan Islands. If her size didn't make troublemakers think twice, the pistol at her side made for an added intimidation factor.

Air Marshals were drawn from the ranks of Valdurian Marines and had a reputation for their formidable abilities and no-nonsense attitude. By the serious look on this one's face, she definitely meant business.

The busy hangar was abuzz with flights arriving and departing and all the activities needed to facilitate those flights. She walked by the line of passengers waiting to board the ship's return flight through the Spice Islands, as well as past the relief pilot and marshal. When the two guards greeted each other, Tumuh overheard the marshal being told to report to Joc' Valdur's office.

Making her way through the crowded air station, she found herself on the equally busy streets of the capital city of the Goyan Islands. To her left on the side of the road, beside the walkway, a line of hackney carriages floated just off the ground, waiting.

Their drivers stood beside the hovering taxis, barking at passers-by, attempting to scare up business. Tumuh hopped into the nearest hackney and tossed her bag into the seat beside her.

"Imperial Bank," she ordered when the delighted driver got behind the wheel.

The trip took longer than expected because a lizard drawn cart and a hackney had collided, littering the street with produce, slowing traffic to a crawl. When the cab finally arrived at the bank, she felt her irritation at the delay melt away, replaced by a sense of excitement.

The anticipation in her continued to build while being led back to Banavor's office. When the door opened and she saw her lord and priest sitting at his desk, she felt her vulva twitch and moisten considerably. Stepping into the room, she rubbed her thighs against each other to wipe away a trail of her juices beginning to run down the inside of her leg.

"Tumuh," he greeted. "Glad to have you back. You brought good news I hope?"

His manor of dress, as well as his Etheria belly button jewel, increased her growing desire and she became aware of her slightly labored breath.

The attractive young man, dressed only in a black leather harness, which crossed his smooth hairless chest, stood upon her entrance. A thin strap extended from the bottom of the harness, tightly encircling the base of his bare cock before traveling between his legs and ass crack, attaching to the harness in back.

"Yes, lord," she replied stepping up and placing her bag on his desk.

"Do tell."

Reaching into her travel bag she pulled out a small leather sack, sinched at the top and placed it before him.

"This is the reason rubber production has been off the charts on Lurd Island. More specifically the Kenzie Plantation."

Banavor gave her a curious stare before opening the bag and peering inside. He maintained the questioning demeanor while dumping the contents of twelve small brown spheres onto the desktop.

"Those are Jabule Beans," she said, watching him pick one up and inspect it.

The soft, oval shaped beans were dark, almost black with a green tip where it had been separated from the stem. Sniffing it revealed a soothing odor of coco. Banavor then returned his attention to Tumuh and she continued her report.

"As you can imagine, rubber production smells horrible. Old man Kenzie discovered that placing one in each nostril of his workers completely masks the smell."

"I applaud Kenzie's ingenuity, but surely this can't be the sole reason production is up?"

"Only partly, sir, as you can tell the shell is soft and porous. Whatever is in that seed leaches out into the workers through their noses. Here's the good part. Whatever is in that nut makes the people cheerfully *want* to work, to the point of obsession. They gleefully perform even the most disgusting, menial or backbreaking labor. Many are so obsessed with their jobs they don't even want to rest.

They also get quite insistent about acquiring more beans. You see, Jabule Beans are highly addictive. Fortunately, they grow everywhere, like weeds. Until now they were considered nuisance plants. The nut is bitter and inedible."

Banavor's face glowed in a delighted greedy smile. Looking up from the beans, he took in his acolyte. Her round full eyes now squinted in exhilaration and she ran her hand through her head of short black hair.

"And you say they're everywhere?" Banavor clarified.

"Yes, lord, they grow all throughout the Spice Islands."

"You did well," Banavor said, returning the beans to the sack and coming from around the desk.

"We need these in a more useable form," he said, handing the bag back to her. "Get these over to Hemicar the Alchemist."

"Yes, lord," she said accepting the bag.

When his hand brushed against hers, she gasped and felt a flood from between her legs.

"You've been wanting more responsibility in serving the Lord," Banavor said seductively. "This is your chance. The project is yours. You will report directly to me."

"Thank you, lord, I won't let you down."

"If successful, besides the monetary compensation. The Lord will bestow a great blessing on you."

Tumuh could no longer contain the licentious grindings Banavor stirred up within her. Reaching down she lifted her skirt revealing a glistening pubic patch and wet inner thighs.

"Your seed will be the greatest blessing I could ever hope for, lord."

Banavor stared lecherously at the overly stimulated young woman and stepped in close.

"Come to my private temple during the Kan. We can talk about your blessing then. Right now, I need you to get those seeds to Hemicar."

Reaching down he slid his index finger through the soppy vaginal lips. When the tip of his finger brushed across her clitoris she orgasmed, shuttering as he slipped his finger deep inside her. When he pulled it free, she watched him through a post orgasmic haze, lift the digit to his mouth and slowly suck the juice off it.

"I hope you're this eager when you drop by later," he purred temptingly.

Sergeant Shurta de Ovora of the Valdurian Air Marshal Service left Air Station Three feeling a bit apprehensive at the thought of being called into Joc' Valdur's presence. With her propensity for trouble, she fully expected a demotion in rank or worse yet, expulsion from the service altogether.

She spent the entire walk to the Forum considering one unpleasant scenario after another. Standing outside the door to his office, she straightened her uniform, sighed deeply, and knocked.

A single "Come!" resounded from beyond.

Opening the door, she saw the Valdurian Ambassador to Zor and one of the most powerful people in the Annigan seated at his large but simple desk, busily reading a thick personnel file, hers. Several bookcases lined the walls and two chairs faced his desk.

She stepped inside and Joc' looked up smiling, which alleviated some of her concerns.

"Ah, Shurta, glad you could get here so quickly," he said, returning his attention to the papers in front of him. "Close the door and please have a seat."

Closing the door, Shurta stood at ease with her legs slightly spread and her hands clasped behind her. "The order did say immediately sir."

"Yes, I suppose it did," Joc' said distantly, while still reading.

He glanced up suddenly when he noticed her still standing formally by the door.

"Sergeant, seriously, have a seat," he said waving at the two chairs facing him.

Moving cautiously, she sat down, watching Joc' read with a puzzled look on her face.

"Well," he said, finally gazing up with the same friendly deportment. "I must say, *you* have quite the colorful past."

Shurta swallowed nervously.

"Eldorian father, Amarenian mother," he said referencing an individual sheet of paper. That's a story all by itself."

"I never knew my father. They say he was a gentle giant. He was a cook on an Eldorian merchant ship when Rayth raiders took it. He was taken as a breeding slave because of his physical attributes. My mom was an Amarenian noble scheduled to be bred. She fell in love with him and they escaped back to Ovora. She gave up everything for him."

"You were born in Ovora, a Hill Sister, is that correct?"

"Technically, no," Shurta replied. "I was born with the same physical attributes as Hill Sisters, but I wasn't given over to the Hill Sisters to be raised."

"Says here your father was lost at sea when you were two. That you practically raised yourself when your mother went into a tailspin. How is your mother by the way?"

The personal question took Shurta slightly aback.

"She has her good and bad days sir. Thank you for asking."

Joc' nodded sympathetically and then went back to the report.

"Looks like you had more than a few run-ins with the Ovora City Guards, brawling it says here."

"I don't like being pushed around, sir."

"I don't know too many people who do," Joc replied before continuing. "You had to leave Ovora, fearing retaliation, after crippling a local gang leader. So, you joined the Valdurian Marines. I'm curious, you were a subject of House Eldor. The logical choice for service would be the Eldorian Lancers. Why choose us?"

"I wanted to get as far away as I could sir. Besides, I don't like horses."

Joc' smiled at the answer, and then picked up her service record.

"This is where things really get interesting," he said, nodding towards the report. "You rose quickly to Squad

Leader after your actions in bringing down the Rayth Pirates in the War in the Darkness. That's when the trouble started. Insubordination mostly. Says here, you just finished up a two quinte stretch in the brig. Any comments?"

Shurta hesitated and Joc' dropped the paper onto the desk.

"You can relax sergeant. You're not in trouble."

Shurta took a moment to gage the ambassador's sincerity.

"Permission to speak freely sir?"

"I insist."

"After I got a few skirmishes under my belt and I wasn't so green, I realized a lot of the mid-level command were a bunch of fucking idiots."

Joc' chuckled at the assessment. "You know, there are times when I don't disagree."

"Sir, is that why I'm here, to review my record?"

"No, sergeant," he answered. "You're here because I want to offer you a job."

"Sir?" Shurta stammered, unable to mask her surprise.

"Yes, I'm offering you a position as a Valdurian Mechanic."

"You want me to be a fixer, sir?!"

Joc' shrugged. "You applied several grands ago and we're just now getting around to replacing our last one. By the way, we like to call them mechanics not fixers."

"Sir, that's my dream job. I thought I was passed by because of my discipline issues."

"No, I would say with your training and temperament, you're perfect for the job. And, as an added bonus, you'll be reporting directly to me. No more mid-level idiots."

"Well, yes, sir, of course sir, I'd be honored."

"Excellent, sergeant, welcome to the Society of Whispers."

"If I can ask sir. What happened to the agent I'm replacing?"

Joc' sighed and a sad expression descended on his face.

"Okawa was a good operative. She snapped during the Etheria War and went rogue, she had to be terminated. Like I said, we're just now getting around to replacing her."

After a moment's reflection, Joc' brightened up. "But, enough about the past. We're heading over to Judgement Square for a meeting with a handful of your contemporaries and possibly your first assignment."

"Oh?"

"Yeah," he confirmed. "Mal Konrad is back from a job in the Outer Zerians and has some intel for us."

"I'm going to be working with Mal Konrad?!" Shurta said in wide eyed delight. "She's a legend!"

"I'd get used to it if I were you," Joc' said, getting to his feet.

Shurta took the cue from her new boss and stood.

"Uh, sir?"

"Yes."

"If I'm now a *Mechanic*, what does that make you?"

Joc' chuckled again and started for the door. "I'm the one who tells you what's broken."

"Hurry up, I'm freezing!" Karta said with a shiver.

Taleeka, who had been surveying the intersection of three trails, each leading off into the dense jungle, peered back at the shirtless barrister. Nibira bent over behind him, standing close and straining to study the map through the light filtering through the dense foliage above. She snickered to herself watching her shy, bookish friend practically drooling over Karta's muscular body.

"Come on, it's not that cold," Taleeka said indifferently.

Karta gave her an irritated glance. "Are you kidding! My nipples could cut glass."

Nibira gave out an embarrassed giggle at the reference and then reached out and touched his lower back. The lawyer jumped at the initial touch then looked around at her.

"Tally, you should come see this," Nibira said, the timber in her voice shifting from beguiled to curious.

What?! What!?" Karta asked, frantically looking back over his shoulder.

"Relax, it's okay," Nibira said, placing a comforting hand on his back. "You wouldn't be able to see it, anyway."

"What am I looking at?" Taleeka asked, stepping over to her friend.

"This," Nibira replied, pointing to his bare lower back.

Taleeka cocked her head and recoiled slightly.

"Hey! What happened to that portion of the map?"

"Is it gone?" Karta asked with a touch of optimism.

"Partially," Taleeka replied. "What in the name of the Goddess is going on?"

"I think I know," Nibira said, taking another opportunity to run her hand along his beefy frame.

"Enlighten us," Taleeka said.

"Yeah, enlighten us," Karta parroted.

"This is the distance we've covered," she said, coyly tracing her fingertips up from the empty spot just above his buttocks to the route marked on his flesh. "Somehow it's showing us we're going the right way."

She then pointed down one of the intersecting trails.

"I'd be willing to bet that if we went in that direction the map wouldn't vanish."

"One way to find out," Taleeka replied. "Let's go."

"I can't put my shirt back on?" Karta whined. "I'm…"

"Yeah, yeah, I know, you're freezing," Taleeka acknowledged. "Put your shirt on backwards. That way we can see the map while saving your nipples."

The trio traveled fifty yards down the intersecting rock furrow and just as Nibira surmised, the map remained.

"Well, I'll be," Taleeka said, once they returned to the intersection. "Someone sure doesn't want us to get lost."

"I'm just happy this damn thing is going to be gone off my back," Karta said, in a mixture of relief and eagerness. "Let's go. The sooner we get to wherever this is leading us the better."

"Kan will be starting soon," Taleeka said, looking around. "It's already hard enough to see with this jungle on top of us. We'll need a place to set up camp. Preferably away from the trail."

They continued on, this time with Karta in the lead. Taleeka and Nibira followed close behind, keeping a watchful eye on the map. With every hundred yards traveled, that section of the cartography disappeared.

"Absolutely amazing!" Nibira marveled. "You would think…"

Karta abruptly halted and inhaled sharply, cutting short her appreciative ramble. Nibira looked up through the dim filtered light to see the trail slope downwards so that the walls on either side stretched upward about ten feet. The trail continued at that depth for twenty yards where they could vaguely see it sloped back up, returning to the three-foot sides they had grown accustomed to.

A rope, stained a ghastly shade of red, extended from trees over the indenture and through a dozen skulls gently rattling against each other in the autumn breeze. Nibira gasped in horror and stepped close behind Karta, unable to take her eyes off the gruesome spectacle waving before her.

"Looks like a warning to me," Taleeka said, making sure her club and knife were readily available. "Let's go."

"Wait," Karta said, pointing at the swaying skulls. "If you're right, and I believe you are, it's a warning for a reason, right?"

Taleeka shrugged. "Sure, but we really don't have a whole lot of choice. The map only leads in one direction."

"I don't know," Nibira said anxiously. "That looks dangerous."

"Probably," Taleeka confirmed. "I'll take the lead. You keep an eye on the map."

Nibira took a deep breath to calm herself, then nodded.

"You okay?" Taleeka asked the uneasy barrister.

He shrugged. "Like you said, 'we don't have a choice.'"

They passed under the skulls into the shadowed recess of the trail with Taleeka in the lead. Once the walls stretched up over their heads, the temperature dropped and they could now make out strange looking runes carved into the sides.

"I'm no linguist or runist," Nibira said, carefully examining the glyphs with a look of wonder etched on her face. "I've seen a bunch at the library, but nothing like these. They're so, I don't know, primal."

Taleeka had now deliberately slowed their pace so that Nibira could memorize the markings. When the trail sloped back up, Taleeka froze in mid stride.

Up ahead in the gloom, Nibira and Karta could make out several figures blocking the trail ahead. With the aid of her glasses, Taleeka saw them clearly. Six unclothed ape-men barred their path, armed with what appeared to be an assortment of pilfered weapons. Several more could be seen lurking in the jungle on both sides of the trail's stone walls.

"Okay," Taleeka said aloud to no one in particular. "This is where it gets interesting."

Shurta wasn't sure what to expect when she and Joc' Valdur climbed out of the hackney in Judgement Square. From the looks of things, it had been a fairly quiet Kan.

Most of the various torture and execution devices littering the plaza lay empty. A naked woman dangled from the gallows, the single word, *MURDERER*, scrawled on her bare chest. Shurta determined from the bloated tongue protruding from her mouth and the remains of her bowels and bladder just below her feet, that they must have hanged her promptly at the lifting of the Kan. Nearby, two teenage boys, obviously petty thieves, hung by their thumbs, sobbing and moaning. All the while a small crowd of curious onlookers murmured softly, excitedly soaking in the criminal's misery.

The headquarters of the Zorian Guards sat directly across the mall, nestled amongst the various Imperial Judges chambers and barrister's offices. The pair casually paraded through the double doors, nodded at the desk sergeant and made their way back to the office belonging to the head of the investigation division, Captain Vanir de Tuath.

Finding the spacious office filled with people took Shurta by surprise. The redheaded Captain Vanir sat behind his mentor's old desk, a glass of whiskey within easy grasp. The Zorian spymaster, Rafel, sat across from Vanir, looking especially sinister. Shurta found herself a bit starstruck when she recognized Mal Konrad seated next to Rafel. They had never met, but her reputation preceded her as an official bespoke hero of the realm. A tall handsome man, with short salt and pepper hair and neatly trimmed beard, stood behind Rafel. The quartet chatted amiably and looked up when they entered.

"Ah, good we can get started," Vanir said, waving them in. "Sorry I can't offer you a seat. We've got a full house today."

Joc' promptly introduced Shurta to everyone.

"I heard you don't take shit from anyone," Mal said with a a friendly nod. "You'll fit right in with this crowd."

They all laughed.

"Thanks for agreeing to meet," Mal said, getting straight down to business. "I'm pretty sure what I discovered is going to be at least moderately interesting to more than one of you. My team just finished a job up in the Outer Zerians. Lurd Island, to be exact. There was a little misunderstanding on the docks in Faul that we had to mediate.

"Anyways, one of my contacts in the Harbormaster's office passed along a piece of information about the Kenzie Plantation. Turns out someone there was getting paid a hefty commission to discreetly pass along preliminary information as to the plantation's performance to someone on the commodities exchange."

"Rubber, huh?" Vanir sat back and stroked his now trimmed red beard.

"Yep, Kenzie is the largest rubber plantation in the Annigan. Not only that, but my contact also said the arrangement had been going on for quite a while."

"Sounds like you're familiar with the subject."

"I've moved my fair share of Lurdian Rubber in the past," Mal said, smirking.

Vanir grinned back at his former adversary. "I'll bet you did. By any chance did your contact give you any names?"

Mal shook her head. "They said they didn't know. The initial contract was through a third party who conveniently turned up dead shortly after we made contact. All communications and payments went through a dead drop."

"Well, it sounds like this insider trading has been going on for a while, huh?" Mukavar said grimly. "So, I guess you've got to ask yourself, who's been making a killing in the rubber market lately?"

"We all know the answer to that, Lord Banavor," Rafel said, stroking his jaw line. "I couldn't help but notice you were speaking in the past tense."

Mal glanced over at the spymaster sitting next to her. "Yeah, I'd like to think this was simply a matter of passing along privileged information, but the dispatches have slowed to virtually nothing lately. I can tell you one thing, something fucking strange is going on over at Kenzie Plantation."

"Strange, how?" Vanir asked.

Mal's gaze shifted back to Vanir. "Rubber production is off the charts. That's why Banavor needs fewer reports. Rubber's a safe bet for anyone. It's *how* they got production up that's the strange part."

"How so?" Mukavar asked, understandably concerned about his house's responsibility in any manipulation in the commodities market.

"The workers," Mal replied shaking her head. "All of a sudden, they're obsessed with work. They don't want to stop and, from the intel I'm getting, some have literally worked themselves to death. To make things even stranger, they're happy to do it."

"Do you think old man Kenzie is dosing them with something?" Rafel asked.

"It wouldn't surprise me," Mal said. "I saw a couple of them delivering a wagon load to the docks. Both of the workers had dumb ass, blissed out looks on their faces."

"It sure would be nice to get some eyes on the Kenzie operation," Vanir said, peering around his desk. "Muuky and I are handling Banavor at this end and Rafel is dealing with all the rest of the nonsense this city has to offer."

A moment of silence descended on the office and all eyes found their way to Joc' and his new mechanic. The

Valdurian envoy snickered in recognition, and then patted Shurta on her shoulder.

"How're your jungle skills?"

"House Valdur paid quite a bit of money to have me train with the Zerian Rangers a few grands ago," the hulking redhead said, nodding contemplatively. "Let's see how much I picked up."

"We'll never outrun them," Nibira said fearfully, watching the ape-men warily approach.

"Besides, they're directly in our path," Karta added.

"Everybody stay calm," Taleeka said softly, before taking a step forward.

Smiling, Taleeka raised her hand, palm out.

"Hail, strangers," she called out cheerfully. "We wish to peacefully pass."

The humanoid apes remained silent and kept their weapons at the ready. Hearing a noise behind them, Nibira glanced back to see several more stepping out of the forest.

When they drew closer, all could finally get a better look at the sentients blocking their way. They all appeared to be male, with mostly human facial features. Short brown fur covered their bodies, and their arms and legs were gangly like Simeon's. Despite matching feet and hands, their gate remained very much human. Clearly this hybrid tribe of offspring derived itself from the union of humans and mountain apes.

"You do not belong here!" the lead one challenged in flawless common. "This is Kapik land!"

"We apologize for trespassing. We are only passing through," Taleeka explained still smiling. "We have business further up in the mountains."

"What business?" the leader asked suspiciously.

Taleeka quickly decided in this instance, much like their prior encounter, honesty would be the best course of action.

"We seek the Arcane Grotto," she declared.

This set off a nervous murmur in the crowd, and a high-pitched chattering argument, with flailing arms, between the three closest to them. The heated discussion moved so rapidly Taleeka's Larimar talking stone couldn't keep up.

When the dispute finally ended, the one she had been talking with faced her with a resolute stare. "We will take you to Mother. She will decide what to do with you."

"We really do need to be on our way," Taleeka said firmly.

"We take you to Mother!" he said, leaving no room for argument.

Taleeka glanced around at the force surrounding them.

"Mother it is, I guess."

The ape-men led them through the jungle until they came to a small clearing. The Kan fog now extended up to their ankles and everyone knew it wouldn't be long before the entire forest would be consumed in the dense haze.

Six female ape people and several elderly males squatted about in a clearing. Two naked human females also crouched among the group. An elderly human woman with shoulder length matted gray hair sat on her haunches behind one of the ape females, picking bugs out of her fur and popping them into her mouth. A younger, very pregnant human girl cowered, loosely bound to a tree by a rope around her neck, at the clearing's edge.

The old crone rose from her grooming and stepped over to them. The male who led the captives nodded his greeting at the woman's questioning gaze.

"We found them on the trail, Mother" he reported. "They claim to be heading for the Arcane Grotto."

Mother silently examined each of them up and down with a stern scrutinizing gaze. First Taleeka, then Nibira beside her and then Karta. When finished, she addressed the young leader.

"Kill the male. Breed the females," she curtly ordered, and then turned to go.

Nibira, seized from behind, screamed in surprise. The ape-man holding her arms joined in with her, screeching in delight. The one in front of her started to advance towards the terrified librarian with his pointed pink penis already rising from its furry sheath.

"You'll make good babies," he proclaimed lustfully.

Taleeka shot both arms over her head, reached for the side holsters on her backpack and pulled both blade and cudgel at the same time, she sent the foot long Eldorian steel dagger down on the exposed erection, severing the member. The ape-man screamed and grabbed his crotch, attempting to quell the geyser of blood erupting from between his fingers onto the ground in front of him.

She simultaneously launched the club at the next, nearest one to the full length of the lanyard. The Ukko wood impacted on the lunging sentient's chest, sending him flying backwards into several of the others.

Karta quickly spun and connected with a hard right hook to the nose of the one who held Nibira. Blood exploded from the impact point and the ape-man dropped unconscious to the ground.

The clearing descended into complete pandemonium, with enraged members of the Kapik tribe squealing and shrieking in rage. Taleeka wasted no time in taking advantage of the confusion. Leaping over to the old woman, she grabbed her from behind and held the knife to her throat.

"STOP!" she screamed.

It took a moment for the tribe to calm themselves enough to take in their situation; Nibira now cowered behind Karta who had his fists raised. Taleeka stood defiantly with a foot long blade at their mother's neck.

The enraged males growled and inched forward aggressively causing Taleeka to press the blade tighter against her wrinkled skin.

"I don't want to hurt her," Taleeka said forcefully. "But if we're going to die, she goes first."

The mob froze, unsure as to what to do.

"Now, we came in peace and that's the way we're going to leave."

Taleeka then led the old woman to the edge of the clearing with Karta and Nibira close behind. Along the way, Karta reached down to retrieve a fallen short sword off the ground.

When they passed the bound woman, Taleeka quickly removed the knife from Mother's throat and severed the rope holding the captive.

"Leave if you want, but you can't come with us," she said, before shoving the old crone into her frustrated children and escaping with her companions into the fog shrouded forest.

"Why didn't they chase us?" Nibira asked when they finally reached the trail.

"They can't see through the fog any more than you can." Taleeka lightly tapped the sides of her orange spectacles. "It pays to have the right equipment."

A feeling of profound exhaustion swept over Hatya Sahid when the hackney she rode in pulled up in front of her well-appointed home. Earlier that cycle, she had been called to her forge operation to placate an irate client whose very large order had been completely bungled.

Now, with the Kan fog all about and the pervasive autumn chill numbing her limbs, all she wanted was to sit quietly by her fireplace with a glass of wine. She knew her Picean maid would have prepared her a meal before she went home, but she wasn't even hungry.

The iron baroness knew something to be amiss when she found the front door unlocked. At first, she thought the maid forgot to lock-up when she left, but when she saw a robust fire in the hearth, she felt her stomach knot up.

She cautiously, with trembling limbs, headed towards the entrance to the living room, when she caught a familiar fishy odor. Anxiously peering around the corner, she screamed.

The blazing fire illuminated the room, revealing a very relaxed Banavor sitting in her favorite wing-backed chair. His EEtah bodyguards, Luft and Nagrada, stood flanking either side of him. A black and fawn colored Mawl mongrel sat cross-legged beside a nearby wall. Its hands, bloody from the gory mess in front of it.

Her beloved cat, Tootsie, stared lifelessly outward, nailed spread eagle on the wall beside the mongrel. They had completely opened up the front of the dead pet and artfully arranged the creature's intestines in geometric patterns on a field of its blood across the floor. The cat's guts stained the entire wall a ghoulish shade of crimson directly below the impaled animal.

"Oh good, you're back," Banavor said jovially, despite Hatya's traumatized screams.

"I do apologize for the mess, but it was unfortunately necessary."

Hatya, now sobbing, found herself unable to take her eyes off the body of her sole companion and confidant. Her late husband got it for her shortly before he died, ten grands ago. Often away on business, he thought the adorable ball of fur would be good company. He had been right. The two immediately bonded and when at home, Tootsie rarely left her side. Her precious Tootsie was not just dead but had been eviscerated and desecrated.

"I received a disturbing report the other cycle that the city guards paid you a visit. My new associate from Nocturn confirmed that with the assistance of your pet."

Banavor's look then went from friendly, to icy.

"Let's discuss that conversation, shall we?"

Shurta squirmed in the gray skintight ghost suit and wondered if she would ever get used to its clinginess. Unlike her standard issue green jumpsuit, this single piece outfit clung to her every curve and left little of her ample attributes to the imagination.

The airship rocked slightly when it caught an unexpected updraft from the Zerian Reef several thousand feet below. Shurta waited for the rocking to pass before putting on her gun belt. She decided she liked being a mechanic because all the latest gadgets were now hers to play with, like the new Mark Seven pistol resting on her thigh.

"We're getting close to the drop point," the pilot called back.

"Roger that," Shurta said, strapping the wing pack onto her back and attaching the underside of the wings to her arms. Donning her Etheria goggles, she made sure the mechanism to change lenses operated quickly and properly.

Ready to go, she silently reassured herself.

"Ten ellipses," the pilot warned.

She opened the side hatch and stood in the doorway. Her red hair fluttered wildly in the cold rushing air and she became aware of her nipples stiffening. Down at her crotch, her cock twitched and strained at the suit's material.

She wasn't sure what caused this reaction. Perhaps because of the chilly autumn gusts, or the exhilaration she experienced every time she jumped. It didn't matter in the end. This had become her favorite pastime sport and she felt happy that it fit in perfectly with the mission.

Hearing the order, "Go!" over the rushing wind, she quickly double checked to see if her equipment bag remained secure, and then stepped out into space. Falling rapidly, she angled her body downward and opened her wings. The moment the air caught the wings and she began her flying decent, she felt an intense tingling between her legs. She had never been with a man before, but wondered if this was what it felt like.

Down below, under the thick layer of Kan fog, Lurd Island stretched out before her. At her rate of descent, she swiftly entered the fog bank at a thousand feet. Pulling her wings in caused her to drop rapidly. Fortunately, she only needed a brief moment to slide her goggle's orange lenses over the blue ones. Keeping her body angled down allowed her to deploy the wings once more and continue her controlled glide.

Now, with the aid of the Trinilic tinted lenses, the entire island's outline and heat signatures became visible. Banking slightly to the left, she aimed for the northern part of the mountain range running diagonally across the island just above the Kenzie Plantation.

Just as with most mountains in the Spice Islands, they rose to a relatively low height, with vegetation and jungle covering them. In the case of Lurd Island, the prevalent flora, rubber trees, grew abundantly but only on their slopes.

Shurta came in several hundred feet above the plantation and noticed considerable activity still going on at a time when most would be resting.

She rapidly came up on the mountainside, located a small clearing and used the ratchet assist to tilt the wings at a forty-five-degree angle. The Valdurian mechanic glided into the opening in the trees in almost a seated position, with legs out in front of her and knees bent.

The landing could have gone smoother. She slightly misjudged the size of her target verses the angle of descent. Once her feet touched the ground, she found herself running to a stop, barely missing a tree.

She folded back her wings, unstrapped her hands and removed the wing pack. Making sure to secure all moving parts, she removed a two-part amber Etheria tracker from her equipment bag. She separated the two, placing one half on the wings and pocketing the other, before hiding the device in a thicket.

Pulling a spyglass from her equipment kit, she positioned herself beside a rubber tree on a slope which overlooked the plantation. The large unfortified estate contained over two dozen buildings and a sizeable triangular courtyard in the middle. Four roads cut through surrounding agricultural fields into the plaza. Lights were on in many of the buildings and people scurried about.

However, besides the unnatural bustle below, the whole area reeked of a rancorous odor Shurta never encountered before which made her eyes water.

Taleeka watched the trail ahead grow steadily steeper and more overgrown. She could tell by the thinning mist all around that the Kan fog would soon be lifting. She peered back at Karta and Nibira and could see the fatigue on their faces.

"The Kan's almost over," she said, surveying the area around them. "We're all tired, so let's find a place to hold up until we get some more cover to move in."

"How far do we have to go?" Nibira asked.

"Good question," Taleeka replied, glancing past her friend to the barrister bringing up the rear. "Okay, 'stud muffin,' let's have a look."

Karta rolled his eyes and Nibira blushed at the reference. Since he took Taleeka's advice and now wore his shirt backwards, accessing the map became just a matter of releasing a few buttons.

"Wow, we actually don't have that far to go," the librarian noted, scrutinizing the last remaining segment of the mysterious map.

"We should be there by next cycle," Taleeka concluded. "In the meantime, let's get off trail and find some cover."

"Do you think those ape people will be looking for us?" Nibira asked, following Taleeka into the jungle.

"No telling, but just to be on the safe side, we'll continue traveling during the Kan."

"But they know where we're going," Nibira added anxiously.

Taleeka shrugged. "We'll jump off that bridge when we come to it."

They had traveled about a hundred yards through thick underbrush and the fog diminished to knee high when Taleeka saw the small cave entrance.

"Alright, we may have something here," she said drawing her knife. "Karta, give me a hand clearing that entrance."

The two hacked away at the foliage until they could clearly see a four-foot, round opening in the mountainside.

"Finally," Karta said triumphantly, starting forward. "My feet are killing me."

Taleeka's arm shot out, barring his way.

"Not so fast," she warned. "I doubt if humans have ever seen the inside, so who knows what kind of creepy-crawlies are in there."

The teen unslung her backpack and opened it. She fished around inside and pulled out something, that at first glance, resembled a palm sized orange ball. Closer examination revealed it was cut into two distinct haves separated by a half inch divide. Six small dowels and a thin balsa wood membrane kept the halves suspended apart from each other.

"Let's cleanse the place, what say," Taleeka said holding the Etheria grenade up for all to see.

She then pressed down on both orange Trinilic halves. The dowels crumbled under the pressure, uniting the sections. The balsa wood film, now the only thing separating the volatile crystals, began to smoke.

"We might want to step back," Taleeka advised, tossing the grenade into the cave mouth.

A brief moment later, a brilliant, silent flash erupted from the opening.

"Alright," Taleeka said, picking up her pack and drawing her knife once more. "Let's check out our new digs."

The small cavern, barely twenty feet across, had an inhospitable looking, rough, rocky floor and walls.

"Well," Taleeka said, examining the interior. "Pick out your least uncomfortable spot and try to get some rest."

"I'm kinda hungry," Nibira said, upon hearing her stomach growl.

"Now that you mention it," Taleeka said reaching into her pack and pulling out three meat sticks wrapped in butcher's paper. "I got us covered."

Karta stared warily at Taleeka's pack. "That's a pretty small backpack. How do you get all that stuff in there?"

Taleeka handed the food to Nibira and then pointed to a row of green and pink crystal beadwork running horizontally around the pack.

"This is the Etheria crystal Cavernite," she explained with a smile. "When placed on the surrounding walls of a structure, it increases the internal space beyond the external boundaries."

"You mean the inside of the pack is bigger than the outside looks?" Karta asked, unable to contain his astonishment.

"Pretty much!" Taleeka replied. "There's just one catch. The Cavernite needs a constant supply of PSI power to keep operating. I've got an Obsidian PSI battery in the bottom of the pack powering them. If you let the battery run dry, then the interior reverts back to its original size. If there's anything big inside when that happens, it could get messy."

"How in the name of the gods do you come up with all these things?"

Taleeka gave a wry chuckle. "You forget who my parents are. We worked very closely as troubleshooters for House Valdur. The same house at the forefront of Etheria research, thanks to a sentient we extracted from the Dark Waste about seven grands ago."

"And they keep you supplied with the latest gadgets?" Karta said, accepting a meat stick from Nibira.

"Yeah, well, my mom's team is pretty small in comparison to the size and lethality of the jobs she takes on. We need all the help we can get."

When Nibira offered her a stick Taleeka held her hand up, declining the offer.

"Thanks. You two go ahead. I'll eat later. Right now, I'm going to park myself over there and get some rest, but first I'm going to ensure our repose goes undisturbed."

Karta and Nibira munched on their meal while watching Taleeka reach into her bag once more and pullout a small rubber bulb with a three-inch nozzle attached to one end. She placed the tip of the nozzle against the top of the cave opening and gently squeezed the bulb while tracing a line across the cave's mouth. The nozzle deposited a thin white strand diagonally across the opening. She repeated the process several more times until the path to the outside became covered in a network of webbing.

"Should I even ask?" Karta said, before popping another chunk of dried meat into his mouth.

Taleeka gave a sly grin and walked to the other side of the cave to sit down against the far wall.

"Cevot spider silk," she said. "Very tough. If anyone, or thing tries to get through, it'll take them awhile and we'll know about it."

Reaching back into her pack she retrieved her Mark Seven pistol and placed it in her lap. "Just in case they *do* get through. Alright, Time for me to perform an inspection on the back of my eye lids."

Taleeka found herself pulled from her slumber by the sound of soft moaning. Half opening her eyes, she saw Karta and Nibira passionately kissing.

Smiling to herself she rejoiced that her friend had landed her "muffin" and virginity would no longer be an issue for her. When Taleeka saw pants being pulled down, she closed her eyes again.

They needed privacy and she needed sleep.

Taleeka didn't know how long she had slept, but two blue flashes on the cave wall next to her woke her. She bolted to her feet and scanned the room, pistol aimed outward.

Karta and Nibira slept in each other's arms on the other side of the cave., A young man, who appeared to be in his twenties, stood next to her. She clearly saw his gaunt, pale body and disheveled dark hair. Streaks of grime covered his pasty face and his eyes sunk into the wide dark rings around them. When she pointed the barrel his way, he raised his hand in a nonthreatening gesture.

"Taleeka Konrad, I mean you no harm."

"Who are you and how did you get in here?!"

"I am known by many names, but I am most recognized by the name Bezsunni, the sleepless one. I am a Harbinger of Balance constantly watching the realms between the gods of dream and nightmare."

"Are you human?" Taleeka asked, lowering her weapon.

"Yes, you could shoot me right now and I *would* die. Some might consider death a blessing, for you see, I have not slept in two thousand grands."

"Why?!"

"I, along with the other Harbingers, must constantly watch for imbalance in the Annigan. This is why I sought you out, to warn you of a *great imbalance*. A single event so great, the Black Mural teeters once more. It was your family who restored the balance last time, so to you I come."

Taleeka nervously looked over at the sleeping couple.

Bezsunni shook his head. "You need not worry. Your friends cannot hear us. I have them slumbering soundly on the Dream Plain of the Middle Realms. They are safe, and we may talk freely."

"Good, because I've only got a few hundred questions," Taleeka said, putting the pistol down. "Let's start with, what are the Harbingers of Balance and the Black Mural?"

"The Black Mural inhabits the deepest oceans of Nocturn. It records every act of imbalance no matter how large or small. As it grows to accommodate the records, it plunges ever closer to your world's core and its destruction. We, of the Harbingers, are tasked with issuing a warning, when this happens, to the ones most likely to be able to do something to rectify it."

"So, what's the '*it*?'" Tally asked, grasping the weight of the matter. "What imbalance pushes the Black Mural?"

"One of the gods has passed over from the Middle Realms into your plain, the Corporal Reach. This angered the other gods, for his power is unmatched while he resides on this plain. This caused the greatest imbalance which could spell the destruction of everything."

"Even the gods?"

"The only way gods die is when there is no one to believe in them. If the Annigan dies, so do its gods."

Taleeka tried to make sense of what she had just heard.

"You said my family helped out before," she said after a moment. "Is that the reason you chose to visit me?"

"Partially, you were also chosen because you have dutifully followed the map the gods provided you. The Arcane Grotto contains the answers to what must be done to restore the balance to the world."

"You're putting a lot of faith in a couple of teenagers and a lawyer."

"We do not call upon the unworthy or the unwilling. You have all the skills necessary. Now sleep, Taleeka

Konrad. Your fog cycle will soon begin and you are close to your destination."

With the suggestion of sleep Taleeka felt her eyelids growing heavy. She vaguely remembered seeing Bezsunni stepping through a swirling blue portal which appeared beside him on the cave wall.

Over the past grand, Talib had developed a love/hate relationship with Clerria House. The healing institution and the sisters who ran it had always been kind to him. However, as the street level branch of the Isiod School of Medicine at the University of Marassa, their abilities were the most basic.

"How ya feeling today, Pops?" he asked, staring down at the unconscious man in the bed. "Sorry, I haven't come for a few cycles. Work's kept me pretty busy. I've been promoted. I'm an inspector now. My first case is a big one."

The man remained unresponsive and Talib felt a tear well up. Raalf de Zor had been the only parent he had ever known. Talib's mother died in childbirth, leaving Raalf to raise him alone. Life had been hard, but the simple cobbler always managed to provide for the small family.

Talib remembered playing around the shop when very young, and then eventually working there under his father's tutelage. The life of a shoemaker, however, did not fulfil him like it did his father. He remembered the look of disappointment on his father's face when he told him he had joined the Zorian Guards. Even then, Raalf still supported his son's decision.

A grand ago, Pops had gotten sick from a mysterious disease carried by their newly acquired Cheepa pet. The Nocturn based illness only affected a rare few and it had passed Talib by. Now, his father lingered on the edge of unconsciousness, waiting for his turn on the list to be seen by the Etheria Healers of the Isiod School.

Talib didn't know if he could sense his presence, or if he would ever wake up, but he would visit every day and talk to him just in case he could hear. He wiped away a tear, reached out and gently touched his father's arm, before making the swirling sign of the sun god, Santi.

"May Santi watch over and protect you," he said dolefully. "Well, Pops, I gotta get to work. I'll be back soon."

Talib spent the carriage ride to headquarters in silent melancholy, staring out the window at the passing city. Once inside the Command Center for the Zorian Guards, he tried to lose himself in the fast-paced activity there.

"Hey, new guy," Tantei said, getting up from her desk and reaching for her jacket. "Keeping bankers' hours, I see."

"Sorry," he said sadly, making his way to his desk. "I was visiting Pops over at Clerria House."

The female detective gave a good-natured scoff. "Ah, I'm just busting your balls. Don't get too comfortable, the boss wants to see us."

"Both of us?"

"That's what he said, so drop your cock and grab your socks," she said, patting him on the arm as she passed. "Let's go."

In the hall, Tantei glanced over at Talib. "So Clerria House; is your Pops okay?"

"He's been unconscious for almost a grand now."

Tantei gave a shocked whistle. "That sucks, what's wrong?"

"They're not entirely sure. He's on a list to see an Etheria healer, but, as you can imagine, it's a long list."

"Damn, I had no idea. Sorry about the crack back there."

Talib gave a weak smile. "It's okay. When I was in Patrol Division, I could visit him every day because I had a set schedule. Now, not so much."

"Yeah," she agreed, "the life of an inspector is unpredictable, to say the least."

"That is quickly becoming all too clear. Speaking of which, how long have you been sleuthing it?"

"Since they started Investigation Division six grands ago. I was in Zekoff's first class."

They paused outside Vanir's open office door and Talib leaned in close. "Any idea what this is about?"

"Beats the shit outta me. I say we go find out," she whispered back.

"The meeting is not out in the hall, you two," Vanir called out. "Come on in and close the door."

Once inside, Vanir pulled the bottle and a glass off the shelf behind him.

"Drink?" he offered before turning around.

"No, thanks," Talib said scrunching up his face.

"I'll take a snort boss," Tantei replied. "If you're offering, you must think I'm going to need it."

The detective captain chuckled, poured two glasses and handed one to her. Taking a sip, Vanir sat down and peered up at his senior investigator.

"Tantei, you closed your last case a few cycles ago, so I'm folding you in on this investigation. You two will be working together. You're lead on this case."

Talib saw Tantei freeze in surprise. Her jovial nature evaporated and her eyes narrowed. Downing her drink in one gulp, she glowered at her captain.

"Boss, you know I like to work alone! I don't have time to babysit the new guy, no offense."

"None taken," Talib casually replied, enjoying his new partner's reaction.

"Unfortunately, you don't have that kind of luxury," Vanir said, pouring her another drink. "This is big. You'll be working with several mechanics from 'The Society' while I coordinate. It turns out Banavor's got his grubby fingers in quite a few pies these days and we stand a good chance of bringing him down this time."

"They're bringing in fixers, huh?" Tantei said with an appreciative nod. "That's badass!"

"House Valdur have commissioned a former Air Marshal, named Shurta, to monitor Lord Banavor's drug operation and House Calden just assigned a former naval lieutenant, named Mukavar, to investigate his market manipulations. You may not be working with them directly, but your paths are sure to cross. Don't be afraid to share information with them. You know how slippery Banavor is, it's going to take team work to bring this guy down."

"I had no idea it was this big," Tantei said, finally grasping the gravity of the situation.

"Pick up the case where we left off. Finish interviewing the rest of the monetary council. Rattle some cages."

"I like the sound of that boss," Tantei said enthusiastically, and then downed the second drink. "Come on, new guy, let's go lean on some bankers."

Cakara de Tor gathered the last of the breakfast plates from the table, and then straightened up to stretch her back. The thin framed brunette with pleasant features took a moment to reflect on just how much her life had changed as of late. At just a little under one grand of servitude, in a five grand contract, she felt fortunate to have been purchased as a domestic indenture by the Kenzie family. Her fate could have been so much worse. She could have been assigned to back breaking field work, or worse yet, a pleasure slave for the field hands. Instead, she cooked, cleaned and looked after things inside the family's rustic yet regal manor.

Already she had found favor in the eyes and the bed of the family patriarch, Anatol Kenzie. The elder Kenzie had grown so lonely since his wife's death, several grands ago, and she truly felt honored to have been chosen to give her kindly benefactor the affection he deserved.

His words were kind, his touch, gentle and now she felt doubly blessed. Four quintes ago, she had stopped her monthly bleeding and her normally small breasts grew larger and tender to the touch. Her heartburn and morning sickness, while still present, thankfully abated.

Yes, she carried his child. She just knew it. It excited her to think that she would bear the next in the Kenzie line and she began humming a happy tune while taking the plates to the sink. She so hoped it to be a boy. Presenting him with another heir, watching him grow up by her lover, and dare she even consider it, *husband's* side, would be a dream come true; a real-life rags-to-riches fantasy with her as the lady of the manor.

"Cakara," a soft feminine voice came from behind, breaking her out of her romantic daydream.

Lifting her hands from the soapy water she smiled at her friend Jaque's approach. The short squat blond and fellow domestic shared the same age but couldn't have been more different in temperament. Where she had always been open, forgiving and a bit naive, Jacque's more reserved and worldly demeanor came across as the exact opposite. The two forged an admittedly unlikely friendship, but it worked.

"Lord Adok and Erek want to see you immediately in the study," Jacque said with a pensive look.

"Did they say why?"

"No, but it sounded serious."

Drying her hands, she nodded her thanks and then quickly headed for the family's large studio. She didn't know what it concerned and hoped she wasn't in any trouble.

Adok and Erek were Lord Anatol's sons and known for their tempers. The Kenzie patriarch was a soft-spoken thoughtful man, whose devotion to his craft consumed him. His sons, however, ran the plantation's day to day operations, sometimes with a heavy hand. She dreaded the younger Erek, who had slapped her around shortly after her arrival for spilling wine.

After a brief knock, she opened the wide double doors and stepped into the spacious room. On the far wall, a series of floor-to-ceiling windows bathed the room in warm sunlight. Bookshelves, desks, overstuffed chairs, along with a couch filled the space, and several faces sternly watched her enter.

Cakara peered around apprehensively and closed the door. As reported, both sons stood in the middle of the room, staring coldly at her. They very much resembled younger versions of their father. Both were larger and more muscular with shoulder length brown hair. Adok's beard had already begun to show touches of gray while Erek's moustache still remained dark.

Next to them, holding a folded blanket in front of her, stood Qabila, the family's medicine woman. In her late thirties, with long brown hair, Qabila always carried a dour expression. Two mysterious red runes adorned the center of her forehead, which significantly contrasted against her dark brown skin. On either side of the couch, two of the lord's stern-faced personal guards stood imposingly.

"You sent for me, my lords?" she said meekly, coming to a stop in the middle of the room and bowing her head.

"We did," Adok curtly replied before glancing at the medicine woman. "Qabila, you may begin."

Qabila gave Cakara a supportive, yet forlorn look and then spread the blanket on the couch.

"Come child," she said, indicating the covering. "Get undressed and lay down."

Cakara glanced shyly at the men staring at her and froze.

"You heard her, wench!" Erek snapped. "Get on with it! We don't have all day!"

With the stern rebuke, fear of retribution overcame any uneasiness over modesty and she quickly slipped out of her dress and underclothing. She could feel the men's leering gazes follow her naked body to the couch.

"You believe yourself to be with child?" Qabila asked, watching her lie down and placing the back of her head on the armrest.

The young woman gave a warm smile and nodded upward enthusiastically.

"We shall see," the medicine woman said, reaching into a small pouch attached to her rope belt.

"Now, spread your legs," she said pulling out a small white leaf.

Cakara did as requested, and then attentively watched Qablia place the leaf between her legs, nestling it deep between the folds of her vagina. She held it there in place for a long moment, and then lifted it up for all to see.

The leaf had now turned blue.

Upon seeing the confirmation, Cakara broke into a satisfied grin while everyone else in the room grimaced and groaned.

"I'm so happy!" Cakara gushed. "Lord Anatol will be so thrilled. Can you tell if it's a boy or a..."

She abruptly halted when she saw the mood in the room becoming anything but festive.

"Quick, run and fetch Namla," Adok ordered one of the guards, who immediately complied.

The eldest son then nodded at the others. Erek immediately pinned her shoulders down while the remaining guard held her legs open.

"Wait, what are you doing?!" Cakara asked in a panic. "I carry Lord Anatol's baby. Unhand me."

"We know whose child you bare," Adok said dispassionately. "And we will never allow that to happen."

Cakara could now feel dread begin to rise in her like an ominous tide. She then began to thrash against her bonds, searching in vain for a compassionate face.

"What! Why?!" she asked between the choking tears. "Lord Anatol favored me!"

"Stop your wailing and struggling!" Erek growled, peering angrily down at her. "Don't make this any harder than it has to be!"

Cakara choked back the sobs and stared fearfully around at her captors. Qabila now pulled a teardrop shaped Etheria shard from her pouch. The top consisted of a bright bronze color, while the bottom hue blended into an ominous brownish yellow.

"A slave girl will never be allowed to carry a baby with the Kenzie name, much less give birth to it!" Adok said with a sneer.

The door suddenly opened and the guard returned with a tall, thin older man. His filthy naked skin and face were severely wrinkled and weather-beaten. His virtually bald head seemed to macabrely complement the hideously scarred left side of his face.

"Ah, just in time, Namla," Adok greeted. "We should have an offering for your children any time now."

The old man smiled and bowed his head. "You honor me, Lord Adok."

Cakara silently sobbed and uncontrollably trembled when the medicine woman touched the rounded edge of the shard on her abdomen, just below her navel. Qabila then slowly ran the stone down her abdomen to her vulva.

The Abortion Stone, a compound of two Etheria Crystals proved gruesomely effective. Ukkonite for repelling combined with Xenoti, which traditionally removed parasites and poisons, became a staple in almost every midwife's bag of tricks.

With the twin crystals working together, Cakara could feel a tingling deep within her when the crystal passed over her. A loosening and then flushing feeling, much like a badly needed trip to the privy soon followed.

She cried out when her vagina suddenly dilated, expelling the fetus and afterbirth in one giant ejection onto the blanket with a loud wet plop. Even though the physical pain had quickly subsided, she knew her baby had been expelled and began to sob uncontrollably.

Qabila quickly wrapped the gruesome remains in the blanket and handed it to Namla, who silently nodded and promptly left. Releasing her shoulders, Erek stood and gazed down contemptuously.

"Now, get back to work!"

"She can't go back to work today!" Qabila said defiantly. "She could bleed to death."

"I don't care," Erek's cold, unfeeling attitude angered the medicine woman and her eyes narrowed at the pitiless young man. "Well, I'm certainly glad your family can afford an expensive indenture, only to let her die."

Erek's eyes bore angrily at the only person on the plantation beside family that would dare talk to him in such a manner. He snapped his head away in defeat.

"Fix her up and have her back at work by next cycle."

Erek then brought his scowling face within inches of the terrified Cakara. "We went easy on you this time because you're new. If this happens again, expensive or not, I'll cut it from you and leave you to your own devices."

By midmorning, from her perch on the mountainside, Shurta decided she had already learned more about rubber production than she ever wanted to know. By far the most interesting and unusual process involved the raw latex when taken from the trees. The raw product, poured on top of three massive, interconnected bins, produced a fascinating result.

Each bin contained an ant super colony. She watched the large yellow ants swarm in seemingly chaotic patterns all over the thick liquid. When they were brushed away, a sheet of rubber could be peeled off the mound and taken for further processing.

The one the others called Namla, completely impervious to the ants, supervised the entire process. He, alone, dealt directly with the insects, moving about on top of the hive, inspecting the process at every stage. His four assistants all kept their distance and used a variety of long handled tools to manipulate the curing latex.

He had been called away a few centis ago and production all but came to a halt. When he returned, he carried a small object wrapped in a blanket.

Shurta thought it odd that even after he rejoined his subordinates, work did not resume. Instead, he unwrapped what he had been carrying and stepped directly into the ant hill. He took three labored steps towards the center of the bin. With each footfall he sank lower, knee deep in the dirt and wood pulp mixture.

Immediately, thousands of the inch-long, brightly colored ants swarmed up his body. Showing no signs of succumbing to what would normally be considered a lethal dose of bites, he held the dripping object outward at arm's length.

Just before everything became covered in teeming layers of marauding insects, Shurta saw what it was he held. The Valdurian agent gasped in shock. She recognized that the pasty looking rope in his hand, with fleshy objects dangling from each end, was an umbilical cord with a fetus and afterbirth still attached.

He stood motionless while the ants covered the gruesome offering and continued to pile on without stopping. Slowly, the overflow of the small creatures began to trail off the man's hands, appearing almost like dripping liquid. They continued their steady descent, adding to the length of the undulating chain, until it reached the top of the anthill by creating a two-inch thick, living ladder. Now, a greater number of the voracious insects could freely move to and from the elevated meal.

Shurta jumped slightly when she saw the aborted remains twitch in his hands, which remained stationary. Hundreds of ants worked together, with methodical precision, moving the entire fetus, placenta and umbilical cord down their ladder to the nest below. Once on the surface of the mound, more of the hungry brood joined the fray, quickly ripping it apart and bringing it below.

Shurta, so captivated by the disturbing spectacle, became startled when she heard commotion fifty yards to her right. Peering from her hiding place, she saw a small harvest team get off their cart with pails in hand, making their way towards a small stand of trees in the opposite direction. Another group of four headed towards her, carrying empty fruit baskets.

Taking no chances at being spotted she tapped the Etheria shrouding stone on the upper sleeve of her ghost suit which bent the light around her, causing her to disappear from view. The group stopped just on the other side of the very bushes she was hiding behind. Seeing how she no longer needed cover, she stepped out to view their activity.

Before beginning, two of the workers, a pair of large males, removed small round objects from their noses and tossed them to the ground. Mentioning the smell, they then picked two beans off the very bush they were about to harvest and deposited them up each nostril. The two then happily went about filling the baskets with the beans and placed them in the cart.

Shurta thought the worker's attitudes odd. Unlike with normal field hands, she didn't hear the ubiquitous constant complaining or any type of cadence singing. All the workers she moved in and around displayed pacified smiles while silently working without stopping.

Moving further away and acquiring cover, she turned off the Shrouding Stone to preserve her PSI battery. She ultimately decided to wait and watch. When the work shift broke for the cycle, she would follow the mysterious beans to their destination.

The stream which ran so cold that Anak felt a burning sensation wherever the water touched, turned out to be the only place available to wash up. At least it resided right where Pagala said it would.

He watched a chunk of ice flow past them from further up the mountain where the completely iced over sixteen-foot-wide waterway stretched up the rocky incline. The bleak slope stretched out in simple solitude in either direction. Beneath them, they could follow the water's journey down the gradient, diminishing gradually until finally integrating with the tundra, where they began their journey.

Anak, Redati and their two remaining henchmen had managed to get most of the Kell blood off their garments and themselves. Their clothing, now damp, sent the mobsters into spasms of severe shivering.

Pagala sat naked twenty feet upstream, in water up to his waist, casually bathing. He cheerfully hummed while he scrubbed away, seemingly immune to the frigid temperatures all around.

"All clean behind the ears?!" he jovially asked, standing in the knee-deep water.

"We gotta get warm," Anak said through chattering teeth, watching the eccentric scout casually wade to the shore and climb out.

Pagala, still not dressed, with his wet long hair plastered to his head and shoulders, gave Anak an innocent questioning look. Pausing for a moment, he genuinely struggled to grasp the concept of their discomfort.

"Heh, keep forgetting you're city boys," he said, picking up his clothes beside the stream's bank. "Don't you worry. Somebody's running a hot camp just over that ridge."

They all followed his gnarled pointing finger to a spot in the distance where a sparsely foliated mountainside met the sky full of racing clouds.

"I don't see anything," Anak said, shaking his head.

"Hard to see the smoke because of the wind and clouds, but trust me, it's there. I can smell it! Can't ya smell it?!"

Anak and Redati shared confused glances but now felt a bit more confident in their guide.

"If there is a camp what makes you think they'll help us?" Redati asked while watching Pagala put on the rest of his damp apparel.

Pagala chuckled and shook his head. "You fellas *really are* city boys. Out in the wilderness, the rules are quite different. Unless it's an enemy, hospitality is the rule out here, not the exception. Besides, we got Kell meat to trade."

They nodded their acceptance of his explanation and set out once again following the frozen stream steadily upward. The further they progressed, the more they began to catch the whiffs of smoke and the clinging smell of burning wood.

Just as their curious docent indicated, once over the blunt ridge they found the campfire fifty feet from the iced over stream. Six short and squat people, with blue skin and heads tapered at the top and bottom, sat around the fire.

Several caribou carcasses hung suspended from the branches of a dead tree off to their right. Along with four spears neatly stacked against each other at the base of the tree with their tips pointing upward.

"Yep, just like I thought," Pagala said, obviously pleased with himself. "A Yupik hunting party."

"Are they hostile?" Redati asked apprehensively.

"They sure can be. By the markings on them and those spear tips, they're Lovac Clan. They can get kinda testy especially when it comes to protecting their kills."

When the clansmen saw them approaching, they halted their conversation and stared intriguingly at the strangers.

"Alright, no hint of aggression. This is a good sign," Pagala said softly, raising his hand in a peaceful gesture. "You just let me do the talking. I'm familiar with all hundred sixty-eight Yupik dialects and the one thing they all have in common is their three-word greeting of friendship."

When they got within a few yards of the campsite two of the Yupik stood to greet them with curious expressions.

"Jebi svoju majku!" Pagala said cheerfully, stepping forward and extending his arms.

Pagala's words, no matter how merrily spoken, had an immediate deleterious effect on those around the fire. Neutral faces became scowls of anger and eyes narrowed menacingly. Two of the ones seated began a torrent of harsh words and wildly waving hands.

"What did you say?!" Anak demanded in a low growl.

Pagala stood frozen with a dumbfounded expression. "I might have accidentally said something about their mothers."

"Well, fix it!"

The angry group, now all on their feet, aggressively advanced on them, screaming and brandishing weapons.

"We may be beyond that," Pagala said calmly. "I have a new strategy, RUN!"

Without waiting, the errant scout spun and took off running, following the stream back down the mountain. Anak and Redati shared a quick frustrated glance before taking off behind their pilot, calling for the rest of their team.

They heard the Yupik in pursuit behind them. The sound of arrows whistling punctuated their angry screams.

"Whoo-wee boys!" Pagala shouted. "They sure are touchy. Good thing they can't run fast."

Pagala's statement preceded a dull thud to their rear followed by an anguished cry. No one stopped to check on one of Anak's unfortunate men who took an arrow to his back and toppled to the cold hard ground.

They weren't sure of the significance of the ram's horn being blown behind them, but when the ice started to crack in the water next to them, they knew it wasn't good.

"Something's under that ice!" Redati screamed not breaking stride.

The surface ice now exploded twenty yards in front of them and something rose from the water.

"Of all the hunting parties we could come across, you had to pick one with a shaman!" Anak said, stingingly pointing away from the river. "This way!"

The blueish green creature rose completely out of the water. Dozens of short legs rapidly propelled its twenty-foot-long, two-foot-thick, snake-like body. It reared the head of a viper with glowing green eyes and a snout pushed upward. Easily slipping in front of their path, it hissed, revealing rows of sharp teeth and a long, barbed tongue.

"Something tells me that thing can keep up with us," Anak said, coming to a halt.

The remaining quartet found themselves trapped by the Yupik who were rapidly catching up and the ice serpent glowering malevolently in front of them.

"I don't like our odds," Redati said, hope draining from his voice.

"I can fix this!" Pagala said optimistically raising a forefinger.

"You've already done enough!" Anak barked, and then turned towards the Yupik who had almost caught up to them.

"Enough!" he yelled, raising his hands.

Surprisingly, the irate group paused.

"Look, I don't know if you understand me or not. But I apologize for anything this idiot might have accidentally said. He was just trying to be friendly in your language."

By their still angry expressions he could tell they didn't understand. Then, one of their faces softened and he stepped forward.

"He said that he 'fucked our mothers,'" the Yupik said in fluent common.

"Drat!" Pagala said, chastising himself. "The words were so close."

Anak shot him an irritated glance before returning his attention to the Yupik.

"You speak the common tongue, good!" Anak said, feeling relieved.

"Yes, I speak your language. Lately, we have had quite a few of your people visit our mountains." He suddenly became grim once more. "And I've heard you apologize for the grave insult, but not the one who gave it."

All eyes turned to Pagala, who straightened up and smiled at the attention. "I most humbly and sincerely do apologize for my grievous error. I beg your forgiveness. It shall not happen again."

He ended his grandiose penance with an exaggerated bow and flourish of the arm. The Yupik traded perplexed expressions before settling on Anak, who nodded in confirmation. The leader then spoke a few rapid, guttural words and the group settled down, but remained wary, especially towards Pagala.

"We were only hoping to share your fire and get warm," Anak explained. "We have things to trade for it."

"What things?"

"Kell meat!" Pagala answered enthusiastically.

When translated, the Yupik seemed to get genuinely excited at the notion of such a gourmet addition to their diet.

"And, as a further token of my sincerity I offer you the eyes," Pagala said, opening his backpack and producing the two handful-sized orbs.

Upon seeing the Kell eyes, the group's mood suddenly transformed from guarded to giddy. They cried out joyously and accepted the treats from Pagala.

"All is forgiven," the leader said, nodding back towards their camp. "Come share our fire."

On their way back up the mountain, Anak heard the serpent returning to its watery home and wondered how much more he could take of this very loose spoke who guided them.

Undeterred, Pagala leaned over to Anak and whispered, "See, didn't I tell ya that they're a delicacy to some?"

Vanir looked up from his paperwork to see a very excited Talib enter his office with Tantei following close behind.

"You called it, Captain, that 'friend and foe' routine worked. I just talked with Mz. Sahid and she wants to talk."

Vanir sat back and nodded while assessing the time it took for her resolve to break.

"Two cycles, that's about right. When?"

"Now, at her place. Get this, she admitted Banavor killed Bosch himself. In fact, she sat next to Bosch when Banavor blew his head off. She said his body actually fell over into her lap."

"That had to be traumatic," Vanir said grimly.

"And get this, being on the council, she knows almost all the details of Banavor's shady financial dealing, especially with the Calden Commodities Exchange."

"And she'll tell all of this to an imperial judge?"

"She says so."

"We just might have Witness Zero here. The one person who can bring down Banavor's complete operation. What do you know, it worked."

"Partially," Talib countered. "Banavor paid her a visit the cycle after we did. He wanted to know what she said to us. He's got some sort of Mawl with him who killed her cat. Turns out, she really loved her cat. That was the thing that gave her the final nudge to cooperate."

"This just entered a new dimension of weirdness," Vanir said, picking up a half full glass of whisky and thoughtfully taking a sip.

"She did have one demand, Captain."

Vanir's attention snapped back to his inspector.

"What's that?"

"Friend and foe worked a little too well. She doesn't want to deal with you."

"Can't say as I blame her," the detective captain said with a knowing grin. "You two get over there before she changes her mind. On your way, stop by the Forum and get Mukavar, the Calden Mechanic I told you about. He'll want to be in on it. If the three of you like what you hear, get her ass in front of an imperial judge fast. If they issue an arrest warrant, we can have Lord Banavor in custody by close of business."

Talib felt his stomach knot up and throat go dry when they pulled up in front of Sahid's home at the same time as a patrol of two city guards arrived on foot. Someone had smashed open the front door and what remained, hung precariously by a single top hinge.

"No, no, no!" Talib cried out, bounding from the cab and drawing his pistol. Tantei and Mukavar followed, joining the two patrolmen racing for the decimated door. Beyond the foyer in the living room, they could see a body and everyone cautiously entered with weapons ready.

"Sweep the house," Tantei ordered. "You two take the top floors."

The two patrol guards hurried up the stairs, while Mukavar and Tantei went room by room on the first floor.

Talib slowly walked over to Hatya Sahid's contorted, naked body. Her shredded clothing lay littered about her. They had bent the metalworks magnate over backwards, with her forearms bound to her ankles and she died with her eyes open wide in fear and agony. Blood filled her gaping mouth from them cutting out her tongue.

He continued sadly examining the gruesome scene but put his pistol away when he heard the reports of 'clear' resounding through the house.

"Tongue removed," Tantei said coming up beside him, "classic punishment for snitches."

"It wasn't a quick death either," Talib said sorrowfully. "She drowned in her own blood."

"And it happened recently," Mukavar said, pointing at the grisly spectacle. "The blood hasn't even had a chance to dry."

"I just talked with her less than a deci ago!" Talib said in frustration. "How in the name of the gods is he staying one step ahead of us?!"

Much to Shurta's dismay, work didn't stop, it only slowed its pace on the Kenzie Plantation during the Kan. In the central plaza, they loaded several long wagons with the finished rubber, which took the form of ten-foot-long round strips. In one wagon, separated from the others, they packed four large bins filled with the mysterious Jabule beans.

The Valdurian agent moved methodically down the mountainside and out of the rubber tree groves on its slopes. Keeping low, she slipped across the vacant agricultural fields to the outskirts of the plantation itself. Steering clear of any lit windows, she navigated between the plantation's various buildings, avoiding the estate's busy thoroughfares.

Pausing in the shadows just outside the main square, she eyed the wagons due for morning departure. They were stacking the last strands of rubber under the watchful eye of Namla, the Itori insect shaman, and a person of authority referred to as Lord Kenzie. Too young to be Anatol Kenzie, because of his youthful appearance and scraggly moustache, she surmised he must be one of the patriarch's two sons.

Her orange lenses cut through the fog and she observed one of the workers teetering when he hefted several of the rubber sections. He made no attempt to stop and the cheerful smile on his face directly conflicted with the way his body performed. The man took two more steps, still maintaining his blissful expression, when his eyes crossed and he toppled to the ground, dropping the rubber.

The younger Kenzie and Namla just stood watching while the single guard and the man's six co-workers rushed over to offer their assistance.

Seizing the opportunity the distraction offered, Shurta engaged the shrouding stone and cautiously made her way over to the wagon containing the enigmatic beans. Using her dagger, she popped the top of the nearest bushel basket and made sure of its contents.

She retrieved another of the small, two-piece, amber Etheria trackers from a utility pocket on her ghost suit. Pulling it apart, she buried the male end deep in the beans to avoid discovery and then pocketed the female part, as well as a few of the beans themselves.

Shurta listened to the workers who knelt over their fallen comrade talk about exhaustion. The younger Kenzie shouted at them angrily, his harsh words reverberating off the plaza.

"Why isn't that basket properly secured?!"

"But sir..." one of the kneeling workers administrating aid protested.

"'But' nothing, he'll be fine. Move him off to the side and get back to work! And secure that damn basket!"

Shurta jumped back just before two frantic workers rushed over to her position. Her quick action, however, failed to prevent one of the female workers from colliding with the invisible agent, sending her to the ground with a perplexed look.

"Hey, what's going on?!" she said, rubbing her sore backside while getting back up.

Erek Kenzie and Namla now looked around suspiciously while Shurta attempted to creep away.

"Everybody, stop moving," Namla commanded gruffly.

The confused laborers froze as ordered, while Shurta put as much distance as she could between her and the wagons. The old insect shaman squinted his eyes and concentrated while his ant-like abilities sensed the vibration of movement on the ground.

"Over there!" he called out, pointing in Shurta's direction. "Whatever it is, it's right there."

"I don't see anything," an anxious worker declared staring where the shaman pointed.

"It must be invisible!" Namla said impatiently. "Just go where I tell you."

Shurta's heart thundered in her chest and the palms of her hands moistened. She knew movement betrayed her position, but couldn't just stand around, waiting for her PSI battery to die. With no good choices, she bolted for the agricultural fields and the mountainside beyond.

Rushing through the rows of crops she could hear Namla rallying her pursuers, "It's heading off the estate. Over there! Over there!"

Shurta reached the mountainside's incline and the first row of trees. She disabled the shrouding stone and relied on her ghost suit for camouflage.

Catching her breath, she watched Namla stop before the mountainside looming ahead of him in the fog. He paused and let the ten men in his charge run past him. The insect shaman cupped both hands around his mouth and made a loud clattering noise which echoed across the treetops.

Shurta's relief at having finally reached cover turned out to be short lived. From all around her, the deafening sound of insect wings dogged her every step.

"Follow the cicada," Namla yelled, before watching the pursuers disappear into the tree line.

Just beneath her, she could hear the mob noisily following her through the orchard and up the mountainside. She didn't know how many pursued her, but she knew she wouldn't be able to engage all of them. Nor did she want to, reconnaissance missions required stealth and anonymity, not a firefight. With the bugs in the trees betraying her location, she would have to keep a substantial lead to be able to get to her wing pack in time.

She had to do something to slow them down.

The answer came to her when she leapt over a three-foot-wide irrigation trench.

They can hear where I am, she thought surveying the loose foliage on the forest floor. *Nothing I can do about that, but they're still blind in this fog.*

Grabbing two medium sized dead branches, she suspended them across the ditch. She then spread a thin carpet of smaller green foliage over them and positioned herself just inside the trees where she could be easily seen.

It only took moments before her pursuers came crashing through the underbrush in hot pursuit. When she was certain she was in their vantage point, she broke from behind the tree where she hid.

"There!" one called out and several more grunted in agreement.

Shurta could hear them giving chase just behind her over the cacophony of insect noise. A satisfied smile played at her lips when she heard the crash of branches giving way, followed by swearing and cries of painful surprise. Reaching into her pocket, Shurta grabbed the amber tracking gem to lead her to her hidden pack.

When the much older Namla caught up with his men, he sighed in disgust, watching them climb wet and banged up out of the trench. One lay dead staring lifelessly outward, his neck broken by a large tree root.

"Get up," he admonished, pointing in the direction of the cicada sound fading off up the mountain.

Several of the men broke their legs, but for most, the only thing damaged had been their pride. They hobbled off, following the insects' audible trail. The path abruptly ended at a cliff with a sheer drop of several hundred feet to the next tier of rubber trees below.

With the Kan fog now well below them, they cried out in frustration watching Shurta, wings fully extended, catch an updraft and soar away into the bright Lumina sunlight.

Banavor lifted a finger for silence and went into a contemplative trance. After several uncomfortable hushed moments, Stovle began nervously rocking on his feet, while Luft and Nagrada stood stoically behind their boss, unaffected by his mood.

Finally, he returned to the present and locked eyes with his assistant. "And you're certain this is accurate?"

"Yes, my lord," Stovle said, bowing his head slightly. "Our people in the Zorian Guards tell me that Maluria Konrad returned from Lurd Island with information about your latest endeavor and shared it with the local branch of the Society of Whispers.

"Their meeting took place several cycles ago. Since then, our people nearly apprehended a Valdurian reconnaissance personnel snooping around the Kenzie Plantation."

"Nearly?"

"Yes, my lord. They escaped using some pretty impressive equipment, so we suspect they're probably Valdurian. In addition to that, when the shipment of Jabule beans arrived at Hemicar the alchemist this morning, they found *this* in one of the bins."

He placed Shurta's amber tracker on Banavor's desk and stepped back. The comely youth picked up the small Etheria bauble and stared at it.

"What *is* this?"

"It's Etheria. Hemicar thinks it might have been used to somehow track the shipment."

Stovle had been with his boss long enough to know when he grew angry. He never succumbed to outbursts and seemed to take bad news in stride, but there were always tell-tale signs, the twitch of his left eye with a calculating stare seemed to be the most common.

"Well," Banavor said, left eye twitching, "I think this matter requires some immediate attention before it gets out of hand."

"Should we consider having the Konrad woman eliminated?"

"With her reputation, I think that will be easier said than done." Banavor gave a calculating stare into space. "No, I've got a better idea."

The trail abruptly ended before a large outcropping of boulders extending over both sides of the path into the forest and fog. Thanks to her glasses, Taleeka could see the house-sized rocks, overgrown by the relentless jungle. Massive tree trunks jutted from between the stones and thick exposed roots rose up like arches from the entangled flora.

"This must be the place," Taleeka said, examining Karta's now almost completely unmarked back. "All that's left is this one line of runes."

"It's really gone?!" Karta asked cheerfully.

"Yep," Taleeka confirmed.

"But where is here?" Nibira pondered, straining to see through the fog.

"I don't know," Taleeka said, watching the edifice of wood and stone slowly grow more visible with the receding Kan fog, "but someone or something went to a lot of trouble to lead us here."

"I'm intrigued," Karta said.

The barrister surveyed the crag, with hands on his hips. So consumed with taking in every detail, he failed to notice the clandestine, loving glances Nibira sent his way.

"The fog's cleared enough," Taleeka said, watching the fading mist reveal more of their mysterious destination. "Let's spread out and see what we can find."

Each headed in a different location along the rock face and searched for any clue as to why they might have been led here in such a cryptic fashion.

"I can feel cool air," Nibira said, running her hand over the gap between two boulders.

"Same here," Karta confirmed from the across the trail.

"There's definitely something back there," Taleeka said.

She put her face up to the cleft in the rocks and felt the cool air on her face but saw nothing beyond. "The rocks aren't far enough apart to get through. I'm not seeing anything back there."

"Maybe there's something over here," Karta said, clearing vines and underbrush from the rock face.

The Kan had now officially lifted and streams of sunlight filtered through the treetops causing Taleeka to lift her orange lens and inspect the area with her blue ones.

"I'm still not seeing anything…" she said defeatedly, before being cut off by Karta.

149

"I've got something here," the lawyer said, pulling back a large tangle of vegetation in front of him.

Both teens rushed to his side and Nibira gasped, holding both hands over her mouth.

A large, flat, oblong rock listed slightly to one side against the mountainside, resting on what appeared to be a stout wooden pin jutting from a precisely bored hole. The dowl spanned four inches in diameter with a round circular handle. A line of runes could clearly be seen running diagonally above the pin.

Nibira gasped. "Those are the exact same runes that are on Karta's back!"

"Really?!" Taleeka asked, stepping around behind the burly lawyer and opening the shirt. "They're gone!"

"Just like the map itself," Karta said, with a look of relief on his face. "This must be the place."

Nibira took the opportunity to sensuously run her hand down his back. "Yes, all gone."

Taleeka smiled at her lovestruck friend. The affectionate glance the much older Karta gave back is what surprised her.

"Alright, I'm guessing that's the way in," Karta assessed aloud, reaching for the dowl. "So, all we have to do is pull that ring and it opens."

"Woah there, hard charger!" Taleeka said, grabbing his arm. "If there's anything I learned from grands of traveling around breaking into places, it's 'always check for traps'. In fact, you two might just want to go stand over there."

Karta and Nibira exchanged anxious glances and then moved twenty feet away, just off the trail.

"Yeah, when you're probably the first to open an ancient doorway like this," Taleeka said aloud, while carefully examining the entire area on and around the door, "it might just have a real killer attached. I remember one time in the Dark Waste with my mom and dad. We came across this hidden door that shot Etheria fire thirty feet out when opened. It burned so hot it turned the sand into glass."

Taleeka finished her inspection and smiled at her companions.

"I think we're clear," Taleeka said, reaching for a hanging vine, "but just in case."

She cut off a long section and tied it to the wooden ring, before walking out to the full extent of the rope. She winked at Karta and Nibira, before giving a tug on the vine.

The wooden rod creaked in protest but eventually came sliding out and dropped to the ground. The flat rock remained stationary for a brief moment, before shuttering and then falling to the side with a crash. All could feel an immediate rush of cool, stale air washing over them.

The dark interior revealed little, but the floor just inside the illuminated doorway looked flat and smooth.

"Well, there it is," Taleeka said, dropping the vine and stepping towards the open doorway. "Let's go see what's so all fired important."

"Wait a minute," Karta said, his voice strained. "You're just going to march in there?!"

Taleeka reached into her backpack and pulled out a foot long orange rod and handed it to Karta.

"I seriously doubt whoever is responsible for all this did it just to kill us. There are a lot more effective ways to accomplish that. But, if it makes you feel any better, you carry the torch so I can get to my weapons quickly."

Karta begrudgingly accepted the rod and, along with Nibira, followed Taleeka to the entrance.

The moment the trio entered the cavern, lights in the ceiling twenty feet above began glowing, filling the room with warm orange light. Unlike the floors, the walls of the thirty-foot square enclosure were rough-hewn and plain. A ramp sloped gently downward through a ten-foot-wide opening on the far wall.

"Alright, no torch needed," Taleeka said appreciatively, taking the rod back and slipping it into her pack. "We're off to a good start."

When they stood at the head of the ramp, it triggered the lights again, they flickered on down its considerable length to a wide landing framed against the darkness. They felt cool air flowing up towards them. Taleeka strained to make out a noise coming from the blackness beyond the landing.

"Do you hear that?" Taleeka asked, concentrating.

"It's a low hum that's more of a sensation than a sound," Nibira replied, tilting her head.

"I don't hear anything," Karta announced. "And what's with the ramp? It's a little too steep for carts. You would think stairs would be more efficient."

"Something tells me this place wasn't designed for humans," Nibira said, peering down the incline.

"Maybe not," Taleeka said, starting down, "but we're here now. Let's go."

The angle of the declination proved easy to traverse, although Taleeka noted that Karta was right. It seemed too steep for cart traffic.

When they reached the landing, the lights came on from hundreds of feet overhead, illuminating their surroundings.

They gasped in surprise.

The cavernous expanse extended for miles, fading from view in either direction. Massive pillars of giant interlocked Etheria blocks filled the vast enclosure in orderly rows. They slowly strobed muted colors and softly pulsed the vibrations felt upon entering the cave. Thick diamond rods connected the pillars and each pillar seemed to be covered in countless, identical, rectangular indentures about five feet in length.

A wide stone catwalk extended out from the landing allowing access to the Etheria monoliths.

"What is this place?!" Nibira stammered, gazing about in wonder.

"I don't know," Taleeka replied, "but someone *wanted* us to find this."

"Yeah, but why?" Karta asked, watching a slow surge of blue energy flow from one pillar into the next through a diamond connecting rod.

"I have a feeling the answer to that question is out there," Taleeka said, indicating the rows of megaliths. "This is a big place. We better stick together, but just in case we get lost..."

She reached into a side pocket on her backpack and removed a two-part amber Etheria tracker. Pulling it apart she placed the male end on the floor of the landing and pocketed the female end.

"Where do we start?" Nibira asked inquisitively.

"Pick a direction," Taleeka said, looking up and down the catwalk. "I'm not sure it matters."

"We're here!" Pagala jubilantly announced, dramatically throwing his hands into the air.

Anak peered out over the barren windswept cliff to the tundra of the Narrow Lands far below and scoffed loudly.

"Alright boys," he said, sounding quite defeated. "The map's bogus. Pack it up. We're going home."

Pagala's face fell at the news, shifting from accomplishment to disbelief.

"What, wait no!" he protested, animatedly pacing on the edge of the cliff, his long hair flying all about, wildly gesticulating while making his case. "This *is* a holy mountain to the Yupik. This *very* cliff is where they come to fast, pray and receive visions! Whatever you're seeking *has* to be here!"

The Antiquary watched the eccentric pilot and guide's antics with a bored expression which slowly turned to one of irritation. With a disgusted huff, he drew the pistol crossbow from under his jacket and fired at the deranged guide.

The subsonic, Na-Kab carbon bolt blew a gaping hole in his chest cavity, propelling his still rambling corpse over the cliff's edge and out of sight.

"I guess that's one way to finally shut him up," Redati said with an amused smirk. "But, uh, boss, how are we gonna get home?"

A superior smile crossed the Antiquary's face. From his coat pocket he retrieved the dead pilot's Etheria remote control fob.

"I lifted it off him a while ago," he said, pointing it upward and pressing on the amber end.

"But boss, none of us know how to fly an airship," Redati protested, watching the craft descend from a cloud bank and head their way.

"We don't have to do anything fancy with her," Anak said, guiding the ship gently to the ground. "We'll fly her low and slow till we get her and us home. I've always wanted another airship."

They had been walking for some time now and Taleeka began to feel a little disheartened. For the most part, the massive monoliths of Etheria towering over both sides of the walkway looked and acted similarly. Each appeared to be active but awaiting something to fully bring them to life. For what purpose, she had no idea.

Several times they came upon an intersection which led away for miles, however Taleeka had made the decision to continue straight on. She definitely didn't want to get lost down here.

Nibira on the other hand, felt completely enthralled in academic wonder. She closely examined every one of the intricate crystal apparatuses as they passed them, sometimes stopping for a more detailed assessment.

Taleeka started doubting her choice of directions when the sound of crackling energy emanated up from beyond the crossroad just ahead. The sharp noise cut above the gentle constant pulsing to which they had grown accustomed.

Approaching the crosswalk cautiously, they were surprised to see the walkway to their right extended only about a hundred feet. It ended at a large sheet of Larimar Etheria suspended between two obsidian pillars. Rivulets of iridescent blue lightning arced between Aur-Quaz crystal globes on top of the pillars.

"Finally, something different to look at," Taleeka said, standing in the middle of the intersection.

Nibira, fixated on the sheet of pale white Larimar Etheria with blue striations and found herself walking towards it.

"That's the same kind of crystal they use to make our talking stones," she said in awe. "I wonder what it does?"

Without another word the curious librarian began walking trance-like, towards the intriguing object.

"Are you sure this is safe?" Karta asked, stepping up beside Taleeka.

"Beats me," Taleeka said, watching her friend approach the pale crystal sheet. "We probably shouldn't leave her alone down there. Besides, it's really the only different thing we've seen. Maybe this is what we're supposed to find."

Karta nodded and the pair started off to join a very enthralled Nibira, dwarfed by the Etheria wall before her. Taleeka gasped then took off running when she saw Nibira reaching out for it.

"Nibira, no, don't touch it!"

The warning went unheeded and the captivated teen placed the palm of her hand against the smooth surface. Immediately, the iridescent lightning stopped dancing between the globes. Taleeka and Karta ran up to Nibira just as the Larimar sheet flickered to life.

Taleeka stood beside her friend watching the crystal fill with the same runes they saw outside the cave and on the trail. What looked like mathematical formulas punctuated the unknown glyphs.

"Well, we're in it now," Taleeka said, when the text started scrolling.

Nibira remained silent, her eyes skimming across the text, memorizing it. The motion of the script picked up, moving faster with each passing moment. When it became too swift for them to make out, Karta and Taleeka focused their attention on the mesmerized Nibira taking in whatever the mysterious device showed her.

After a deci of watching their friend absorbing the frantic stream of data, the rate of the flowing text slowed. When it finally stopped, the screen went blank and the lightning resumed overhead.

Nibira wearily shook her head, just before her knees gave way. Karta quickly reached out and caught her. The shaken teen peered up at both of them with a fearful look.

"What?!" Taleeka asked worriedly, after seeing the expression on her face.

"We have to go, *now*!" Nibira said, peering around in a panic. "It knows we're here!"

Shurta had successfully tracked the shipment of Jabule beans to its final destination, Zor. That turned out to be the easy part. Her map pad saw to that. The Etheria composite piece of Magitech had no problem keeping up with the amber tracker on its nautical voyage.

When the cargo hit the docks of the High Holy City, things got tricky. Once they unloaded the four-bushel baskets containing the beans, she had to follow on foot, maintaining visual contact. In keeping with her undercover status, she wore no uniform, just a coat protecting her from the autumn chill and concealing her pistol. The messenger bag on her shoulder remained safely tucked beneath a hooded cloak.

From a busy street corner just off the docks, she watched them place the baskets in a private cargo vehicle. Once loaded with the singular shipment, it set off for the outskirts of the Kampo Plat near the university. Because of the strict speed limitations built into all urban vehicles, following on foot did not present a challenge either. When they reached their destination, things became problematic.

The building they were eventually delivered to turned out to be an unattached, three-story structure with main thoroughfares in front and back. Narrow alleys flanked either side of the establishment. From all appearances, an independent artisan occupied each floor.

Walking past the front of the property, safely tucked away in a crowd of passers-by, she read the shingles beside the front door.

The ground floor belonged to a garment maker. The second story contained a jeweler. The third story shingle eventually caught her attention.

"Hemicar de Kampo

Potions, Powders and Elixirs"

An alchemist, that had to be their destination, she thought. *It only made sense.*

Now, at least she had an idea what floor she needed to be concerned with. The strapping redhead had no time to congratulate herself before she saw the petite form of Tumuh enter the building, she also carried a messenger bag across her shoulder.

Shurta recognized her from the airbus ride to Zor almost two clusters ago. The former air marshal rarely forgot passengers' faces and definitely didn't believe in coincidence. She had to attempt to follow her.

Shurta found the front door to the artisan collective unlocked and she stepped inside. The interior was quiet and the clothier's door on her right was closed. She approached a staircase at the back of the foyer leading upward. With the noise of the street gone, she could hear Tumuh stepping onto the second landing.

Padding as softly as possible, she gave herself a satisfied smile when Tumuh's echoing footsteps headed for the third floor. When she started up from the second story landing, she heard a knock on a door and a muffled greeting.

Entering the third floor, she slowed to a more cautious pace. Peeking over the edge of the landing, she saw the solitary door and no one around.

Creeping up to the door, she opened her bag and pulled out a two-foot length of tubing, with a large funnel on one end and a smaller one on the other. The rim of each funnel had a lining of different colored Etheria.

Placing the large end against the door and the smaller one to her ear, she listened to the conversation already in progress. A male and a female voice both talked in normal tones. She easily distinguished the female as the dominate of the two.

"...yes, they arrived a short while ago," the male was saying enthusiastically. "I got right to work breaking them down and I have to say, these beans' placation and suggestive properties are amazing."

"Glad to hear it," the female replied. "I have your payment. One thousand secors as agreed."

"Good, good, just set it down over there."

"How soon before we have something we can use?"

"That's the good part," the man said giddily. "If I'm correct, and I'm always correct, very little needs to be done to process the fruit. The most time-consuming part of working with these will be shelling them. I've sent for my assistant to handle that. You can tell Lord Banavor that I will have him a useable sample soon."

Shurta perked up at Banavor's name remembering it from her meeting with the society in Vanir's office.

"How soon?" the female pressed.

"Soon, soon," the man said flippantly.

Shurta broke away from her eavesdropping when she heard footsteps on the stairs headed her way. Stepping well away from the door, she activated her shrouding stone and waited. Moments later a studious young man in a full-length apron stepped onto the floor and, without knocking, entered the alchemist's studio.

Shurta ran over the conversation in her mind. It sounded like Banavor was concocting a new drug to flood the streets with. Even though the recreational use of drugs violated no laws, she had a bad feeling about this one.

Talib stepped out into the streets of Zor's Kampo Plat from the warmth and serenity of Clerria House and pulled his jacket tighter against a stiff autumn breeze from the north. The visits to see his father had grown tougher of late. Cycle after cycle of no change in his condition, combined with the seemingly endless wait to get the help he needed, drained him emotionally more than anything else.

Needing to clear his head, the junior investigator chose to walk to work despite the chill. He cut across the neighboring campus of the University of Marassa and decided to take advantage of the many parks and plazas the grounds provided. Finding a bench across from the library, he surrendered to solitude and stared off, contemplating his current station in life.

As with most chilly days, loitering on the lush lawns proved too uncomfortable. He watched bundled up students hurry from one building to another, attempting to minimize their discomfort, when Talib became aware of someone sitting on the other end of the bench. He remained absorbed in his somber thoughts and paid no attention.

"How's your father?" the lone figure asked.

The question snapped Talib out of his disheartened trance and he stared quizzically at a man he didn't recognize. The sleuth studied the man's features, searching his recollection. The well-dressed man stood about his same height, thin, with an angular face and a dark receding hairline. From what Talib could make out from his profile, he had minimal facial hair.

"I'm sorry, have we met?"

"No," Stovle said, still facing forward. "I represent someone who might be able to help."

"Who, and help with what, exactly?"

"Oh, the person I'm referring to would rather remain anonymous."

Stovle then faced the curious detective and smiled. "The question remains. How's your father?"

"The same," Talib replied skeptically, which rapidly became inquisitive. "Help, how?"

"Your father is on quite a lengthy waiting list to see a specialized healer."

"How in the name of the gods did you know that?!"

Stovle shook his head, shrugging off the question. "The person I represent can make it possible for your father to go to the top of the list."

Talib blinked in astonishment. "How?!"

"The details are unimportant," Stovle said with another dismissive nod.

The stranger's vague deportment and lack of details now made Talib suspicious. "And exactly what would this anonymous person you represent want in return?"

Stovle stared forward and took a deep breath.

"The investigation you are currently working on is... *misguided*," he said, exhaling. "If you could see that it's steered in another direction, you can rest assured that your father will receive the very *best* medical care."

Upon hearing the offer Talib broke out into laughter, prompting a bewildered look on Stovle.

"Wow! This is something," the detective said after calming down. "My first actual bribe! You know in all the grands I patrolled the sisters no one ever tried to bribe me. This is *really* something!"

Stovle remained serious, staring at the amused young man. "Bribe is such an ugly word. I'd like to think of it as two people assisting each other in a mutually beneficial arrangement."

Stovle's description caused Talib to laugh even more.

"Call it what you will," he said, "a bribe, by any other name, is still a bribe, and I'm going to say no for a couple of reasons. First, I'm the junior partner on the case. I can't steer it anywhere. Second, my father would lose all respect for me if he found out how he got the treatment. And lastly, I couldn't respect myself. So, the answer is no, and, if this wasn't my first time, I'd be taking you into custody for attempting it. You can tell Lord Banavor, nice try."

"That's unfortunate," Stovle said expressionlessly, before getting up and calmly walking away.

Talib sat back with an amused grin. One good thing about the incident, it completely lifted him out of his funk.

○ ○ ○

"What are you talking about?!" Taleeka asked, still holding on to Nibira's shoulders. "Who knows we're here?!"

"Not who, *what*," Nibira said, teetering on the verge of panic and looking wildly around. "We've got to get out of here, it may already be too late!"

"Too late? Nibira…"

"I'll explain while we leave," Nibira said, breaking away from Taleeka's grip, "but we've got to go, *now*!"

Not waiting, Nibira took off at a trot towards the intersection with the main catwalk. Karta and Taleeka shared a quick concerned glance before following.

"Alright," Taleeka said, catching up to her friend, "we're leaving. Now, what's going on?"

"This, this thing we're in, it's kind of a machine made out of Etheria."

"What kind of a machine?" Karta asked. "What does it do?"

"I don't know. But it's on automatic right now, waiting for its creators to return."

"Is it alive?" Taleeka questioned.

"Not life as we know it. It's crystalline based, very different. This place has been designed to keep itself running, repairing and defending itself against anything that might compromise it."

"Like us," Karta said, finally comprehending.

Nibira nodded, her eyes welling up. "When I activated that screen, it detected us. Now, we're the infestation."

The trio had no sooner made it to the intersection than blue lightning bolts erupted from the crystal edifices on either side and consumed the hundred feet of walkway in front of the Etheria screen. The light show lasted mere moments, but it managed to frizz everyone's hair and leave a cloying metallic taste in their mouths. It left no doubt in anyone's mind that if they had been caught in that lightning storm, it would have meant certain death.

"This way!" Taleeka said, leading them at a brisk pace back down the catwalk, the way they came.

"Did you learn anything about this machine from what we saw displayed on the screen?" Karta asked, anxiously looking around.

"No, I couldn't understand what I was looking at. I just memorized the characters. I got just an inkling about this thing when I briefly touched the surface."

They traveled several hundred yards with no further attacks. Taleeka heard Nibira's labored breaths and slowed her pace.

"Maybe it assumed it got us?" Karta offered.

"Maybe," Taleeka said optimistically. "In the meantime, just don't touch anything crystal."

Karta all of a sudden began looking around frantically.

"What's that sound?"

All paused to hear a high pitched whining drawing closer.

"What is it?" Nibira asked.

"There!" the barrister said, pointing back down the walkway where they had just come.

A flat circular diamond disk, the width of the path, streaked their way, leaving no room on the sides of the walkway for escape. A round bronze colored ball hovered and skimmed inches above the floor, dividing the center of the disk. The edges of the disk appeared razor sharp and spun around the ball, giving off its ominous whine.

"Get behind me!" Taleeka called out authoritatively, reaching for her backpack.

Both companions did as they were told and Taleeka pulled out her cudgel. Grabbing the end of her two-foot lanyard, she spun the club in front of her, propeller style. The Ukko wood cudgel sliced through the air humming softly.

"Let's hope this works," Taleeka said, just before the crystal buzz saw collided with the spinning club.

The velocity of the collision rocked the teenager, but the repellant properties of the Ukko wood sent the wildly spinning disk off at a sharp right angle with a crisp screeching report. It crashed loudly into one of the monoliths and a network of thin blue strands of lightning surrounded the embedded weapon.

RUN!" Taleeka screamed, bolting for the landing she saw in the distance.

The massive crystal machinery on both sides of the escaping trio came to life. Their gently pulsing colors now turned more vibrant and rapid. A persistent rumble replaced the soothing hum.

Fifty feet from the landing, Taleeka felt the first glimmer of hope that they might just make it out in one piece. She heard Karta's footsteps right behind her, but Nibira's sudden scream caused them to stop and spin around.

"What the..." Karta called out in shock.

A long tentacle, comprised of thousands of tiny crystals, extended from a nearby Etheria monolith. The multifaceted arm held her friend by the ankle, attempting to pull her off the catwalk. Nibira frantically clawed at the stone walkway, shrieking, not only in fear, but in pain. Just above the tentacle's grasp, Taleeka could see the compound fracture Nibira's shin bone protruding from the flesh of her ankle.

Behind her, Taleeka heard a roar and felt a burst of heat. Peering back over her shoulder, she saw Trinilic panels, in the Etheria just opposite the landing, belching tongues of fire across their only escape route.

Karta had now made it to Nibira and grabbed onto her hands. Leaning back and putting his entire weight into it, he struggled to keep her from being pulled away.

With the lanyard still around her wrist, Taleeka propelled her cudgel at the appendage. The Ukko wood club struck the crystal arm a foot from its grip on Nibira's ankle. The Ukko wood's resistant assets combined with the velocity smashed the limb into its many individual parts. This allowed Karta to pull the screaming teen fully back away from the edge. The cudgel had no sooner returned to her hand than the tentacle reformed, grabbed Nibira and continued its deadly tug of war with Karta.

Taleeka had enough. Reaching into her pack, she retrieved her Mark Seven pistol and fired it at where the base of the arm connected with the massive Etheria machine. The impact of the Na-Kab carbon bolt exploded the area in a multi-colored shower of crystal shards. The assaulting limb disintegrated into the thousands of tiny components and dropped out of sight.

"That leg's pretty badly broken," Taleeka said, holstering her club. "Can you carry her?"

The barrister nodded.

"What about that?" he asked, indicating the fire spitting Trinilic.

"As my mom would say, 'fuck this shit, we're leaving!'"

Raising the pistol once more, she fired at the rectangular orange panel. The carbon bolt, forged in the fires of Mount Goya, passed harmlessly through the belching magical flames. It hit with a loud crash and the erupting blaze ceased.

Taleeka watched a large crack form in the panel while Karta picked up Nibira. When the group finally started up the exit ramp, they heard the loud crash of the damaged Trinilic, breaking loose and falling.

They had made it into the entrance cave when everything started rumbling and shaking. Dirt and small pieces of debris fell from the ceiling and it felt like the whole mountain shifted on top of them. Outside the cave mouth, they could see trees and rocks falling from higher on the mountainside.

"Keep going once you get outside!" Taleeka yelled, over the chaotic thundering.

When halfway across the entrance cave, another clamor and tremor sent a large tree toppling across the opening, blocking any way out. They abruptly halted and Karta cried out in frustration.

"Get down," Taleeka said with a determined scowl.

Karta set a whimpering Nibira down on the smooth floor and shielded her with his body.

Taleeka fired at the arboreal barrier. The powerful subsonic projectile blasted the wooden obstruction into kindling, showering the forest beyond with fibrous shrapnel.

"Now, let's go!" Taleeka yelled.

Karta picked up Nibira and they rushed through the now open egress. Forty feet down the trail, they heard an even louder pounding coming from above the cave.

They stopped and turned to see the landslide completely cover the cave mouth with barren rocks, giant boulders and trees, disguising any hint an opening existed. An eerie quiet settled on the mountainside occasionally punctured by the sounds of birds squawking.

Karta set Nibira down against a log and gently stroked her cheek. "Don't you worry," he said tenderly. "We're gonna get you taken care of."

He then sat down next to her and sighed, while Taleeka put her pistol away.

"I gotta rest for a few," he said wearily. "It's gonna be a long walk back."

"Nah," Taleeka said, pulling the remote-control fob from her pocket. "One of the few bright spots today. We've now got an open spot in the jungle canopy for the *Mala* to come to us."

Pointing the fob skyward, she pressed the amber end and all watched a small dot, high above, begin descending towards them.

Mal pushed the plate away, sat back and gave a contented sigh.

"Well?" Alto asked, looking up from his lunch.

"Yeah, well?" came a feminine sounding male voice to her left.

Mal peered up at the expectant face of Pronari de Bogat, owner of the Dokana Pub. His lanky, well-dressed frame appeared tense with anticipation, his hands nervously covering his mouth.

"That," she said pointing at her empty plate, "was fucking awesome!"

Upon hearing the positive review, Pronari's body uncoiled and he heaved a deep sigh.

"Oh, thank the Goddess!" he squealed, pulling his hands away revealing a broad grin. "I'm going to send one of the girls down to the market to stock up on the ingredients. It goes on tonight's menu!"

Mal gave a satisfied grin at Pronari's reaction. As an anonymous benefactor in the Dokana Pub, the owner/head chef had always used her as one of his taste testers and his reaction to her critiques seemed to be always the same.

Mal considered it one of the perks from having loaned Pronari the money to buy the place over ten grands ago. She also considered the private alcove a nice perk too, but the food was the real star. Pronari was a culinary genius and Mal was happy to be his test subject.

"Mal, you're the best," he excitedly said, leaning over and hugging her neck.

He then just as quickly stood and looked around, "Okay, I've got to scoot, million things to do you know."

"Debut menu item!" He could be heard saying while passing through the beaded curtain into the main dining room.

"I am glad your appetite has returned, my love," Alto said putting his fork down. "The notice this morning from Taleeka certainly perked you up."

"You can't blame me for being too nervous to eat. I mean it was our little Tally's first solo gig."

"Yes, the little one is not so little anymore," Alto noted solemnly.

"She should be back by dinner time," Mal said, unable to contain her anticipation. "I can't wait to hear all the juicy fucking details!"

From just outside the curtain there came a knock on the door jamb and a long thin face neither recognized poked through the beads.

"Excuse me," he said politely. "I apologize for interrupting your lunch. Are you, by any chance, Maluria Konrad?"

"Who wants to know?"

"Uh, yes," he said, stepping fully into the tiny room. "My name is Mashtrim. A rather excited gentleman out in the dining room said I could find her here." He paused and shyly bobbed his head. "I presume that's you?"

Mal gave a slight grin assessing the timid gentleman. He stood of average height and build with very short dark hair revealing a receding hairline. His narrow chin sported a tuft of hair unconnected to a scraggly moustache. The only thing about him which did not scream "ordinary" turned out to be his clothing. She made note of his expensive silk long-tailed white shirt and dark blue pants.

"I'm her. What can I do for you?"

"Well, um, I represent the auditing division of the Imperial Bank."

"Auditing huh," Mal quickly adopted a defensive bearing. "Look, the Dokana is a legitimate operation! Besides, Pronari runs the place and he's a stand-up kinda guy. I'm just the bank."

Mashtrim nervously cleared his throat. "Uh, Mz. Konrad, I'm not here to talk to you about your pub."

"It's not my fucking pub!" Mal said emphatically.

"Yes, yes, of course," he said meekly, lowering his eyes. "It's not about that."

The Spice Rat's eyes narrowed. "What then?"

"Well, simply put, the Imperial Bank wishes to hire you."

A moment of genuinely stunned silence descended on the table, just before Mal broke into a wide grin.

"You're shitting me?!"

Alto could also not contain his amusement. "Quite the reversal of opinion."

"Yeah, no shit!" Mal said, her face alight with amusement. "Usually, the Imperial Bank and I don't share the same side on just about everything. So why me?"

"Reputation and mobility, in other words your airship. Time could be a critical factor."

Mal nodded at the explanation. "Fair enough."

"Um, you, I mean, would you care to hear the proposal?"

"Are you fucking kidding me? I'm all ears!"

Mashtrim cleared his throat once again and stepped up to the table. "A cluster ago we sent an auditor, a woman by the name of Shenji de Warton, to the Dahia Plantation on Wou-Late' Island. Rolf Dahia runs the largest and finest grain and livestock operations on the island, or for that matter, the whole Wouvian Island Chain."

"Yeah," Mal agreed. "Pronari's got Dahia beef on the menu. It's expensive as shit."

"Yes, well, tensions have been high between the bank and the Dahia family ever since the Unification War."

Mal nodded. "Yeah, those Valdurian Plantation owners didn't take a liking to the Eldorian land grab."

"And we've had some rather unpleasant dealings just recently," Mashtrim continued. "Hence the reason for the audit. We greatly fear that our auditor has either been taken or killed outright."

"And you want me to go and find out?"

"Exactly! You have the bank's authorization to use any means necessary."

Mashtrim leaned forward onto the tabletop and stared intently. "Extreme measures with extreme prejudice."

Mal scoffed. "Damn, it sounds like those dealings with the Dahia family really were *unpleasant*. Sorry, my people and I aren't assassins. Death is just, more or less, a byproduct of our jobs. If you want people gone, the Hand of the Wind is who you need to see."

Mashtrim's demeanor quickly became conciliatory. "Yes... yes, of course. Our main concern is for our auditor."

"Sounds simple enough," Mal said with a nod.

"Then you'll take the job?"

"Sure, give me a cycle or so to put things together. My fee is six, one-hundred-secor, Imperial gold notes in advance and non-refundable."

The banker shifted nervously. He well knew that equaled a whopping six thousand struck gold coins, a hefty fee.

Mal noted his discomfort and smiled. "That's one hundred for each member of my team and two hundred for me as captain. Hiring the best isn't cheap."

Mashtrim sighed in defeat, before pulling six oblong Ukko wood wafers from his messenger bag and set them on the table."

"A pleasure doing business with you," Mal said, scooping up the bank notes. "I imagine I can contact you at the bank when we're done?"

"No, no, please, the bank wishes that the greatest discretion be used. Send a gull to me personally and I'll meet you back here."

Mal shrugged. "Suit yourself."

"Very well," Mashtrim said, visibly relieved. "If our business is complete…"

"I'll be in touch," Mal said, watching the banker step back and turn to leave.

"What do you think my love?" Alto asked, once their newest client had gone.

"Not sure," Mal replied, deep in thought. "Tally should be back this evening. I'll have her tail him and see what that turns up."

"Tell me again why we are venturing into this unsavory locale?" Alto asked, peering out the window from the back seat of the hackney. The streets of the Seven Sisters Slums came to life all around the slow-moving cab with the arrival of the Kan fog.

"The Tom-Tom Room?" Alto clarified. "I believe that is what you called it."

"I gotta see a guy," Mal replied, watching a drug transaction taking place between an Outer Clan EEtah and a human on the street corner. "We're probably gonna need some muscle on this upcoming job and I've got someone in mind."

"Oh?"

Mal chortled and looked over at the swordmaster. "You're gonna love this place. The locals sure do. It's a big, kinda wanna-be classy dive bar, which is supposed to have decent entertainment."

"And the person you seek frequents this establishment?"

"You could put it that way. His name is Larzz and he's the bouncer."

"You are certain you can lure him away? How will the proprietors feel about that?"

The question caused Mal to laugh. "Jabea and his wife Sonja own the place. Two of the most butt ugly fuckers I have ever laid eyes on. I sure am glad they found each other, because the only other way either of them gets laid is by paying for it."

"I fail to see what being aesthetically challenged has to do with this."

Mal sighed, disappointed at not being able to tell her story. "Basically, being a bouncer at the Tom-Tom is a potentially dangerous job that doesn't pay shit. I just hope he's up for it. I haven't seen him in quite a few grands."

"Are you sure you will be able to recognize him after all this time?" Alto inquired when the carriage came to a stop in front of a large well-lit establishment.

Out front, a line of ten patrons waited to get in the door and they glanced over at the duo exiting the cab. A thin Picean, in a ludicrous red tunic, stood directly in front of the wide double doors collecting a single silver piece from each person in line before allowing admittance.

Standing beside him, a seven-foot-tall human/EEtah hybrid loomed. The immense figure possessed mostly unkempt human features. He had a bald head, but his face contained a permanent shadow of facial hair framing a bored expression. He wore a thin, white, tank top tee-shirt stretched tightly over an enormous pot belly and random patches of hair poked out of the garment's edges.

"That won't be a problem," Mal said, walking over to the mixed-race sentry.

His face lit up the moment he saw her. His lips pulled back in a smile and Alto noted the mouth full of sharp teeth.

"Mal!" he greeted boisterously. "Long time no see!"

"How ya doing, Larzz?"

"Eh, you know," Larzz said, keeping one eye on the steadily moving line of humans. "The same old same old. I heard you set up shop here in Zor, now that you got your fancy bespoke name and been branded heroes of the realm."

He looked over at Alto. "And you must be Alto, the sword guy everyone's talking about."

The swordmaster smiled and nodded with a slight bow. "Alto Konrad, at your service."

Larzz's eyes curiously shifted back to Mal. "Does he always talk like that?"

Closing her eyes, she nodded with a smirk. "All the fucking time."

The half EEtah nodded his acceptance. "So, what brings you to my little corner of the Annigan? I sure hope it's not for the entertainment. This group played here last Kan and they sound like crap. I don't know how they draw this kind of crowd."

"Nah, actually I'm here to see you…"

Suddenly the raucous sound of three human/Cul-Tahs attempting to cut in the front of the line interrupted Mal's explanation. The five-foot-tall hybrids appeared mostly human with the exception of a short snout and whiskers. A thick head of dark hair appeared to run all the way down their back in a wide strip. All three had exactly the same facial features and spindly frames. Were it not for their different attire of expensive looking tunics, they would have been indistinguishable.

"Excuse me," Larzz said resignedly, "but I gotta go to work."

"Alright you three," he admonished over the protests of the others in line. "There's no cutting in line! Besides I ain't letting you in anyways. I told you not to come back after I threw you out last time."

"That wasn't us!" one protested squeakily. "That was our brothers."

"I don't care!" Larzz replied, rapidly losing patience. "You all look alike and you're nothing but trouble, so beat it!"

"It's not fair! My money is just as good as theirs!" he rationalized, pointing back at the growing line of humans who became more heated by the moment.

Mal, standing off to the side with Alto, mischievously grinned at the amusing altercation.

One of the other brothers looked over at Mal with a contemptuous sneer. "What are you laughing at, *quim*?!"

Before any could react, Mal's arm shot out from her side, viciously backhanding the humanoid in the face. He reeled from the blow and his snout erupted in blood. Screaming, he covered his nose and staggered about.

"Talking about quims," Mal spat. "What self-respecting woman lets a Cul-Ta fuck her, much less bear his whelps?!"

The two others turned aggressively towards the Spice Rat, who defiantly stood her ground. Larzz stepped between them to quell any further hostilities.

"I told you to get out of here," he growled, displaying his sharpened teeth.

Humiliated, the three ran off chattering loudly and the crowd cheered their retreat.

"I kinda wish you hadn't done that," Larzz said sorrowfully with a shake of his head.

"Why?" Mal asked skeptically. "The little fuckers didn't put up much of a fight and ran off like a bunch of pussies."

"Yeah, it's not that simple," Larzz explained. "Those kids belonged to this four-hundred-pound woman known only as 'Big Mama.' All she does is eat, fuck Cul-Ta and spit out their babies."

Alto's face soured. "Well, I guess there is indeed no accounting for taste."

"Yeah, and every one of them looks alike. They're…"

A chorus of angry Cul-Ta chattering cut short the bouncer's explanation when a dozen of the brothers appeared out of the Kan fog. They rushed through the line of patrons which dispersed in a panic.

"There's a lot of them," Larzz said, stepping between his two guests and the angry mob of hybrid rat-men.

"That's her! That's the one!" came an angry call from the throng before they charged.

Immediately Mal's hand went to her pistol and Alto partially drew Defari from her sheath. The blade instantly began growling.

"I got this," Larzz said confidently, stepping forward to greet the incensed sentients.

"Knock it off," he bellowed, grabbing the nearest one by the throat and tossing him back into the advancing mob.

The command went unheeded and they swarmed him trying to get around to Mal.

The half EEtah easily absorbed their ineffectual blows but struggled with being outnumbered. Mal grinned and nodded approvingly, impressed at his non-lethal method of crowd control. If any made it past him, she would not be so lenient.

Still maintaining her defensive position, she found herself grinning at the confrontation. Larzz had his foot on one's back pinning him to the ground. Another frantically squirmed under one arm while he held one aloft by one leg in his other hand.

"I SAID KNOCK IT OFF!" he screamed to the group, before lifting the one he held by the leg until he faced him. "I'm saving you little bastards' lives!"

The statement had a sobering effect on the group, but Larzz continued to lay it on. "The only reason I don't get out of the way and let you tangle with these two is that all your dead bodies in front of this place would be bad for business!"

Twelve identical faces anxiously peered past Larzz at two calm, confident expressions staring them down. The man's hand rested on the hilt of a partially drawn, growling sword, while the female's hand gripped the handle of an extremely advanced looking pistol.

From down the street the shrill whistle of the city guards coincided with the front doors of the Tom-Tom Room flying open. A short older man with a receding, gray hairline and a deeply furrowed face, more resembling a map of mountainous topography then human features, came storming through the entrance and out onto the sidewalk. Right now, those features were contorted in rage.

"What in the name of the gods is going on here?!" Jabea de Zor demanded.

Larzz self-consciously bowed his head and released his captives, who wasted no time in fleeing before the imminent arrival of the Zorian Guards.

"Sorry, boss but…"

"Sorry nothing! I hired you to keep things peaceful. Instead, I find you brawling in the street, driving off customers, as well as attracting the attention of the city guards! You're fired!"

"He didn't drive anyone off," Mal said, aggressively stepping forward. "It was those little fucking rat-men. Larzz was containing the situation!"

"I wasn't talking to you!" Jabea angrily snapped.

"Well maybe you should," Mal countered stubbornly, "because I saw the whole fucking thing, you didn't!"

Jabea ignored the Spice Rat's defense.

"I want you gone," he said, scowling up at Larzz.

Mal gave a sarcastic chuckle. "Well ass-wipe, you just did me a favor. I was coming here to offer him a job."

"Really?!" Larzz said, his mood instantly brightening.

"Yeah," Mal confirmed, pulling the hundred secor commodity note from her vest, "and I guarantee it pays a whole lot better than this jerk-off job."

Taleeka had only been back in Zor a few deci before Mal had put her to work. She had arrived back from Awa just before the Kan. After dropping off Nibira and Karta at Clerria House to tend to her friend's broken leg, she finally made it home to a hot meal where she regaled her parents with her exploits in the crystal caves of the Awa Mountains. She rose with the lifting of the Kan and waited in front of the Imperial Bank for the auditor her mom described.

She didn't have long to wait. After procuring a breakfast roll-up from a street vendor, she contentedly munched away with several other diners while the morning rush of the High Holy City clattered around them.

The teenager became intrigued when the auditor arrived in a large private street ship that emerged from the constant flow of hackney carriages and lizard drawn carts. Private vehicles were rare in Zor, owned exclusively by the elite. When the four-door, Ukko wood craft pulled up to the curb and hovered inches from the street, she understood.

The man who introduced himself to her mom as "Mashtrim" got out first from one of the rear doors. Dressed formally with white high collared shirt and black slacks, he looked like any other banker. He carried a messenger bag draped over his shoulder and balanced a stack of file folders in one arm. Briskly walking around to the rear door on the other side, he opened it and Lord Banavor stepped regally onto the sidewalk. Two EEtahs met them and escorted them into the bank.

Taleeka knew of Lord Banavor—few didn't—she just had not met him. His appearance caused a curious smile to creep over her face. The attractive young man, with honey brown skin and short curly hair, gave more the appearance of a male prostitute than the financial genius everyone claimed him to be. She also found it strange that Mashtrim behaved more like a toady to the head of the Monetary Council than a senior bank auditor.

Popping the last piece of the meal into her mouth, she followed the humans and EEtah's into the bank. All four passed through the lobby into the doors of the Zorian Monetary Council.

Not wanting to appear suspicious, she approached a banker's desk and arranged a small withdrawal of six struck gold coins from her family's account, then returned to the food vendor. On this occasion, she actually had a chance to finish a steaming bowl of yugo, before she saw the private car pull back up front and Mashtrim, still sporting the messenger bag, got in it.

Fortunately for Taleeka, private vehicles were subject to the same speed laws as the public hackneys, so following on foot proved easy. The opulent vehicle coursed its way across town to the southern docks. It pulled up to a hundred-foot transport ship being loaded on dock three, sitting with cargo holds open, ready to receive. Mashtrim approached someone who appeared to be the foreman, who proceeded to give him a tour.

Deciding she needed a better look, Taleeka found a stack of crates for cover and pulled a small spyglass from her backpack. Nestling herself between two of the large shipping containers, she opened the glass and studied the shipboard activity. She could see the ship's deckhands definitely preparing for sea, while dock workers loaded racks of mining equipment and several large screw pumps.

Taleeka had to look twice when a winch lowered two excavating wagons into the hold. From the blades beneath them, these super plows could easily churn up then move massive amounts of soil.

Once Mashtrim and the supervisor watched the wagons winched below deck, the banker seemed satisfied and they said their goodbyes.

When they returned to the bank, Taleeka watched from the opposite side of the street as a thin, dark-skinned woman with short hair greeted him on the steps. They talked for a moment and then entered together.

Taleeka scanned the area and saw something that greatly piqued her interest, a tall, stout, redheaded Amarenian hill sister, with pale skin and freckles, standing fifty feet away also intently watching the duo's meeting before they disappeared inside.

Crossing the street and flanking around behind her, Taleeka could see the tell-tale bulge of a pistol under her light jacket in the small of her back.

"Joc' Valdur sends his regards," she said softly, stepping up beside her.

The Valdurian agent's head whipped toward Taleeka, her eyes wide in surprise.

"Relax," Taleeka said, holding up her hands. "My mom told me about you. You're Okawa's replacement, right?"

Shurta eyed the teenager suspiciously but said nothing.

"Taleeka Konrad," she said, eyeing the front of the bank.

"Konrad!" Shurta said in surprised revelation. "You're Mal's kid."

"Yep, are you following that guy, too?"

"No, I'm following the woman. Her name's Tumuh and she's been dealing with an alchemist on Banavor's behalf. Beyond that, I'm not sure what's going on. You?"

"The guy hired my mom last cycle to do a job for the bank. She asked me to keep an eye on him. He arrived with Banavor this morning. Other than that, and inspecting a freighter being loaded with mining supplies, nada."

"You can bet if Lord Banavor has anything to do with it, it's shady." Shurta said direly.

Taleeka scoffed. "I got my first look at him today. He's a prissy little thing, don't you think?"

"Don't underestimate him," Shurta warned. "I may be new on this detail, but I've read the reports. He's an utterly ruthless man with ice water running through him."

Multicolored light bathed the inside of the *Haraka* as it streaked northeastward toward the Wouvian Island Chain, specifically the island continent of Wou-Late'. Zau's phantasmal globe, projected from her eye, set the command chairs in the bow awash in blue. The orange glow from the Karabite Etheria Crystal overhead lit the seating area.

Larzz stared around the airship's interior and nodded approvingly. "This is nice, Captain! Sure beats that old tub you used to sail around in."

Mal smiled sadly from the captain's chair. "She was called the *Regis* and she burnt down to the waterline eleven grands ago."

"Looks like you traded up real nice."

Mal, too busy to respond to the compliment, conferred with Zau about their destination. Both peered out the orange tinted windshield into the Kan fog and then back at Zau's globe. They pointed to various positions on the projected sphere and the Singa navigator zoomed in on the eastern half of the island.

"Alright," Mal said, finally addressing everyone. "We're almost there. According to the Imperial Bank, we're headed towards the Dahia plantation. The damn thing is immense. It takes up practically the entire eastern half of the island. It's run by a guy named Rolf Dahia.

"Usually, these kinds of rural, family run operations have multiple children to bear the burden of keeping up with the day to day, as well as providing an heir, not so in this case. Rolf's newlywed wife died in the Unification War before they had children."

"I can only imagine that he has no love for House Eldor," Alto said solemnly.

"Yeah, no shit!" Mal replied. "He still considers himself a loyal Valdurian subject, even though he now pays his taxes to House Eldor.

"The person we're looking for is a female auditor by the name of Shenji de Warton. She's been missing now for a little over a cluster. She's presumed taken prisoner and I just pray to the Goddess she hasn't been killed."

"Sounds like a lot of territory to search, Captain," Larzz said, moving forward in his seat.

"Yeah," Mal confirmed. "To further complicate things, Dahia's got offices in the island's central city of Basone and in Leem on the far eastern coast. I'm betting she's on the plantation proper. If not, it's a good place to start."

Everyone nodded and Mal continued, her manner transforming from informative to stern, "One last thing, remember, despite a few armed guards, these are farmers not fighters. We can't just go barging in there kicking ass. Our job is to bring this auditor back in one piece, that's it! We'll leave the punishment for nabbing her up to House Eldor. This plantation produces *the finest* meats, grains and produce in *all* of Lumina. We can't go in raining death and destruction down on it. Besides, this could be the actions of a rogue group. We just don't know. So, save the aggression for when it's needed. Are we clear?"

Everyone nodded once again.

"We're coming up on the plantation house," Zau said, looking out her side window. "Looks like we've got a lone sentry with spear by the front door. Oy, that place is big."

Mal stared down at the three-story structure nestled in the middle of perfectly manicured grounds. As usual, there appeared to be little activity, due to the thick Kan fog.

"Alright, we've got to do a little recon before we go crashing the party," Mal said, facing her pilot. "Since Tally isn't here, that's going to fall to you, Kumo. Take us up to the roof and hover just above it. Zau will hold the ship steady. You go out the bottom hatch and check inside each of those windows then report back."

"Yes, Captain," the spider-woman replied meekly.

"And for the love of the Goddess don't let anyone see you!"

"Yes, Captain."

Mal watched her pilot nimbly scurry down the roof and over the side. Several long, tense moments later, she climbed back up onto the ship and relieved Zau at the wheel.

"Well?" Mal asked expectantly.

"All are sleeping except two in dining room," she reported softly.

"What are they doing?"

"Eating."

"Looks like we've got the element of surprise, kids," Mal said optimistically. "Alto and Larzz, you're with me. Kumo, drop us off on the side of the house. Once we take care of the guard and breach the door, bring the ship around the front and lower the side hatch.

"Alright, let's do this hard and fast. I want to be gone with our target before the fucking cavalry arrives."

The lone candle on the table cast soft shadows on the couple's nude bodies. Gazing into her eyes, the man picked up a grape from the plate between them, softly kissed her, and then fed her the morsel. Swallowing the treat the woman sighed and gazed lovingly at the man.

"I could get used to this," she purred.

The man smiled lovingly, his youthful face deceptively matched with greying hair and beard crinkled with delight. He reached over and tenderly stroked her shoulder length gray hair.

"I hope you'll give me the chance to spoil you…"

The front door smashed open and Larzz's massive frame crashing in, raucously interrupting the romantic moment. Mal immediately followed with pistol drawn and Alto brought up the rear.

The love-struck couple spun towards the disruption in stunned surprise. The woman screamed covering her breasts and the man immodestly rose to his feet in a rage.

"What in the world do you think you're doing?!" he shouted. "How dare you!"

Mal ignored the outburst. "Larzz, watch the door. Alto, watch the stairs."

She then spun and faced the naked couple. A look of bewilderment crossed her face when she fully took in the intimate moment, now broken... much like the front door.

"Shenji de Warton?" Mal asked, clearly confused.

The woman meekly nodded.

"We're here to... rescue you?"

"She doesn't need rescuing!" the man said emphatically. "You are trespassing in my home! Who are you?!"

Mal slowly lowered the pistol and shared a bewildered look with Alto before returning her attention to the couple.

"We're the people hired by the bank to rescue Shenji," Mal explained. "It's been over a cluster since they heard from you and, given their contentious relationship with Si. Dahia they thought you had been either snatched or killed."

Shenji locked eyes with Mal.

"The reason they didn't hear from me is, *I'm not coming back*. I've accepted Lord Dahia's proposal of marriage. I drafted a letter of resignation..." The auditor paused. "Could I please have my robe over there?"

Alto retrieved it from the back of a chair and handed it to her and Mal put her pistol away.

"It's very unusual that the bank would be concerned," Shenji said, tying the front of the robe closed. "I've been gone this long before and they didn't worry."

The lord of the plantation nodded at his fiancé's statement. His hand shook as he contentiously pointed a finger at Mal and Alto.

"I don't know who you are but I want you gone now!"

"Alto and Maluria Konrad," Mal introduced sheepishly, "and we're truly sorry for the intrusion."

At the mention of their names Lord Dahia's attitude completely changed to that of wonderment. "*The* Maluria and Alto Konrad?"

"Yeah,"

"I don't believe it! I just don't believe it," he happily beamed. "Maluria and Alto Konrad, Heroes of the Realm, here in *my* home. This is exciting! Isn't this exciting, dear?

"Thrilling," Shenji answered irritably.

Dahia shyly looked back at Mal and Alto. "I even have renderings of you in my collection."

"Renderings?" Mal asked quizzically, tilting her head.

"Oh yes!" Dahia said excitedly. "Let me show you!"

They watched him bound over to a tall thin cabinet with ten shallow drawers. He opened one, pulled out two rectangular, ultra-thin, Larimar sheets and held them up. Sure enough Alto's face graced one and Mal's the other.

"Where did you get these?!" Mal asked in astonishment.

"They sell them in various shops," Dahia explained, then meekly lowered his face. "I don't suppose I could ask you to sign them for me?"

Mal and Alto traded confused glances.

"You want us to sign them?" Mal asked in disbelief, watching him nod his head hopefully. "Uh, sure."

"Oh, thank you, thank you!" he gushed, setting the pictures on the table and handing Mal a pen.

"It would mean so much to me!"

After signing their likenesses, Alto set the pen down and watched a very happy Dahia running his hand over his new treasures.

"Tell me Lord Dahia, why is the bank being so combative?"

"The reason my relationship with the Imperial Bank is *'combative,'* as you put it?" he asked wearily, "Because they've been trying to secure a hold on the mineral rights on my land for a while now."

Mal's eyes narrowed suspiciously. "Mineral rights?"

"Yes," Dahia explained, "we discovered a thick sheet of multi-colored crystal about ten feet underground when digging a new well."

Etheria. The thought thundered across Mal's brain. *Well, that solves the mystery of this plantation's superior output.*

"And how long has the bank been trying to strong-arm you?" Mal asked, a theory forming.

"A little over six grands now," Dahia replied. "The crystals are too close to the surface for them to tunnel to it. They would have to strip-mine my land. It would ruin me. The last time they tried it I got a barrister and brought them in front of an Imperial Judge. I won."

Mal recalled her conversation with Tally before they left. The ship being loaded with mining equipment at the time seemed innocent enough, but now.

"That certainly explains why the person who hired us gave us the go-ahead to kill you," Mal continued. "With you out of the way, and with no heirs, the fuckers could waltz right in and do whatever they wanted."

Shenji sat down next to her still naked fiancé with a troubled expression. "May I ask, who exactly at the bank hired you?"

"A guy named Mashtrim," Mal replied. "He said he was your boss."

Shenji 'shook her head and seemed perplexed. "I've been with the bank for over ten grands. There is no one by that name there, much less my boss. What did he look like?"

"A little taller than me, thin, short brown hair with a receding hairline, sharp chin with a disconnected moustache and goatee."

The auditor appeared stunned. "You've just described Lord Banavor's assistant Stovle."

Upon hearing Banavor's name, Mal could feel her stomach tightening in anger. *That greedy little fucker was trying to get us to do his dirty work!*

"It's good that you're getting married Lord Dahia. Now there will be someone other than the bank for your estate to go to," Mal said calculatingly. "I'd tie the knot as soon as possible."

"We plan to," Lord Dahia said with an adoring look at Shenji.

"We humbly apologize for the intrusion," Alto said with a conciliatory nod of his head.

"Yeah," Mal agreed. "Sorry about the door, and your guard's probably gonna have a headache tomorrow.

She gave a sly, cruel grin. "Tell ya what. That resignation letter? You can give it to me. I want to deliver it personally."

Taleeka could hear the bickering through the door of one of the libraries several conference rooms. Closing her eyes, she gave a frustrated sigh.

It had been four cycles since they returned from Awa. Nibira went straight to work copying the numerous runes she had been exposed to in the Etheria cave. The University of Marassa, theoretically, should have been the perfect place to have them studied. Now, in true academic fashion, the various schools battled over seniority as to who would lead the research.

She dreaded entering the room, but Nibira promised they had made some sort of breakthrough when she saw her earlier that morning in Zekoff's class. Knocking softly, she opened the door without waiting for a reply.

The spartan room contained a long table dominating the center and surrounded on all sides by ten uncomfortable looking chairs. Three of the four walls contained chalkboards filled with the runes and Nibira's drawings littered the table.

Nibira sat placidly at the head of the table watching two women and one man in red robes contentiously argue. Taleeka immediately recognized them as the head of their various departments. Marassa Osius, the lone, clean-shaven man to her right, like all Marassa's of the Oysa School of Rune Magic, the crown of his bald head contained a blue tinted set of runes in a circular pattern resembling a skull cap. He indicated a grouping of three runes on the board while trying to make a point.

Two women on the opposite side of the table appeared around the same age and both had shoulder length white hair, but the similarities ended there. Marassa Keel from the School of Language Arts had large eyes and pleasant features. Marassa Kioo of the School of Etheria Studies had a long, disfigured face with a scar running vertically down her left cheek.

They all halted their animated conversation and gave Taleeka an annoyed stare when she stepped into the room.

"Who are you and what are you doing here?!" Osius snapped, his eyes flashing angrily.

Unintimidated, Taleeka gave an amused grin. "I was invited," she stated calmly.

"Learned ones this is Taleeka Konrad," Nibira said, finally standing. "She is the one responsible for getting me to the runes."

"And back to the university with those mysterious glyphs safely stored in her head." Taleeka added.

Marassa Kioo scoffed loudly. "While we acknowledge and appreciate your effort, this is no place for you. The runes are now our responsibility."

"I asked her to be here," Nibira said firmly.

Kioo's face contorted in anger which caused her scar to appear to quiver. "You have no authority to do that! You're just a student librarian!"

"Wow," Taleeka said, gazing at the bellicose group. "The way you bicker like fish wives on the docks, it's a wonder you've gotten anything done!"

The two argumentative Marassas' eyes widened and they sputtered in outraged disbelief at the teen's audacity. Marassa Keel lowered her head and smiled at her combative colleagues being taken down a peg.

"Are you sure you could understand?" she calmly asked.

"The details, probably not," Taleeka replied pulling out a chair and sitting down without invitation, "but Nibira said you had some sort of breakthrough. All I need is the big picture. Then I'll leave all of you to get back to your academic blood sport."

Keel smiled again at Taleeka's description then pointed at the papers on the table.

"Basically," she patiently began. "The single runes are an alphabet which predates anything I have ever seen."

"Runes that deal directly with Etheria!" Kioo said, irritated at her colleague humoring the teen. "Which is why the Etheria Studies Department should be leading the research."

"Except they are runes, which falls under my department!" Osius quickly countered.

Keel pointed to various groupings of runes. "We're unsure of their couplings, which is why my Language Arts Department was brought in."

"I see," Taleeka said, studying the various markings.

"I doubt that," Osius said demeaningly.

At that point, Taleeka decided that, as elitist and condescending as the Marassa had been, he had been right. She also knew someone else who could help her and benefit from access to the runes. She now silently applauded her decision to have Nibira make a second set for her.

Mal marched up the wide stairs to the Imperial Bank with fists clenched and lips drawn taut. Alto and Larzz followed just behind her, unsure what the incensed Spice Rat would do. Both, however, knew well what she was capable of.

She kept her eyes straight ahead, leading the parade through the lobby. When she passed through the doors of the Zorian Monetary Council, a bright-eyed young clerk greeted her, delivering papers between offices.

"Good morning, ma'am, can I help you?"

"Fuck off!" Mal growled in response, focusing on Banavor's office.

"Alright," she snarled, just outside the closed door. "I'm gonna have a little chat with Lord Banavor. You two make sure we're not disturbed."

She then nodded her head at the door. "Larzz."

The half EEtah gave a grateful, mischievous smile. "Thanks, Captain!"

"It's only fair," Mal replied grimly. "We did it to the Dahias."

With a look of brutal joyousness, Larzz lashed out with his heavy boot at the wooden barrier. It flew open in a resounding crash with Mal right behind it.

"YOU LITTLE FUCKING PIECE OF SHIT!" she screamed pointing at the seated head of the Monetary Fund.

Both Banavor and Stovle, conferring over some paperwork, looked up with startled expressions. Nagrada growled and he and Luft lunged forward.

With a resilient scowl, Mal unhesitatingly drew her Mark Seven pistol and fired at Nagrada after only one step. The Na-Kab Carbon bolt blasted into the EEtah's chest propelling him back into the wall, showering it in crimson and pulverized internal organs.

Luft had made it to the corner of his boss' desk when Mal fired again. A significant portion of the EEtah's upper body blew out his back, completely spraying the rear half of the office red. Banavor and Stovle stood staring in stunned disbelief while unidentifiable clumps of gore dripped off them. Banavor, however, recovered quickly.

"Why, Mz. Konrad, you seem upset," Banavor said, calmly wiping a bloody clump off his cheek and flicking it to the floor.

Mal scowled and aimed her pistol squarely at the blood-spattered young man. "Your little fucking plan didn't work, motherfucker! Dahia is still alive and married by now, so you're never gonna get that Etheria field. You fucking wanted my people to do your fucking dirty work for you! I should fucking kill you where you stand!"

She then looked over at Stovle. "You too Si. Stovle or Mashtrim, or whatever the fuck you're calling yourself!"

"That's quite a mouth you've got there," Banavor said with a raised eyebrow.

"Choose your next fucking words carefully," Mal growled centering the pistol on his chest.

Banavor gave a bored sigh. "So, you would kill me and my assistant right here, in broad daylight, with all these witnesses present?"

He then glanced down at Luft's still oozing body. "You know, killing EEtahs isn't against the law, but killing humans, that's an entirely different matter. Just know that I'll be looking down from wherever realm my essence lands at your body swinging from the gallows in Judgement Square." He ended his monologue with a confident smile and Alto poked his head through the doorway.

"My love, as much as I hate to admit it, the man does make a point."

A seething Mal continued staring into Banavor's confident face while she slowly lowered her weapon.

"Fine!" she frustratingly snapped. "Sorry you had to buy all that mining equipment for nothing. I'll bet it was expensive."

She then reached inside her vest, pulled out a folded piece of paper then tossed it onto the blood-soaked floor.

"Oh, yeah, I almost forgot," she added. "There's the resignation letter from your auditor, the new Lady Dahia."

When Mal turned to go, she saw that a small crowd had gathered in the outer office. They murmured nervously, keeping their distance from Larzz's intimidating frame.

"This isn't over, motherfucker," she added. "By the way, my fee is still nonrefundable."

"Indeed, it isn't over by a long shot." Banavor said faintly to himself, watching Mal push her way through the stunned bank employees.

He then turned to Stovle. "Get this place cleaned up and then put a wet team together."

Mal looked up at Alto from her half eaten Dahia steak with a pensive frown and sighed loudly.

"Blade slinger, I don't mind saying, this last gig has left a bad taste in my mouth and I'm getting really fucking tired."

Outside their private alcove in the Dokana Pub the dinner rush had just gotten started. The Spice Rat found it only fitting they splurge for dinner with the bounty of the plantation they had just saved.

She listened to the Grand Turine in the harbor ring out seven bells before continuing. "I mean, we've got more than enough money to live well for the rest of our lives. We still keep beating our heads against the wall. Recently, I've been asking myself, what's the fucking point?"

Alto, who had been patiently listening, dabbed his mouth with a napkin and gazed tenderly at his partner of the last eleven grands.

"I agree my love. We certainly have experienced much together. What do you propose?"

Mal set her fork down and slowly shook her head. "I don't know, I'm just talking."

Her demeanor suddenly turned from wistful to playful with a mischievous grin. "In the short term, I say we go home and fuck. Tally's studying with her friends over at Nibira's so we'll have the place all to ourselves."

The swordmaster pursed his lips and appeared deep in thought considering Mal's salacious proposal. She rolled her eyes, reached out and swatted his arm.

"Asshole!"

Alto grinned broadly. "I'll call for the check."

After saying their goodbyes to the owner, Pronari, they stepped out into the cool, murky Kan fog.

"We're gonna have a bitch of a time finding a hackney in this fog," Mal said pessimistically.

She knew better though, in the past six grands since the Etheria War, Zor became a city that didn't sleep. Thanks to Etheria navigation shards, traveling during the Kan had become much less treacherous.

They stood on the curb with their arms around each other's waists. Alto raised his hand and waved. To Mal's delight a six-seater cab pulled away from the thinning traffic and halted right in front of them.

"Now that's what I *fucking* call service!" Mal said exuberantly, opening the door to the last row of seats.

"Twenty-three hundred Kasada Drive," Mal instructed as soon as they got settled.

The driver wordlessly nodded and the hackney took off at its lethargic pace back into traffic. Alto slipped his arm around Mal, pulling her close and kissing her neck.

"I would ask if this thing could go any faster, but I know the answer," Mal whispered in Alto's ear before sliding her hand down into his robes and between his legs.

"Why, Si. Konrad," she seductively purred while rubbing his growing erection, "I think you like me."

"Most astute, Mz. Konrad," he whispered back before leaning in and brushing his lips with hers.

With a gentle yet firm grip on his now rigid member, she leaned in, locking lips, while their tongues passionately danced. When they broke, Mal breathlessly looked around in confusion while Alto continued nibbling on her neck.

"Hey, why are we going this way?" Mal asked huskily.

The driver rotated his head to the side. "When I dropped off my last fare, I saw that the city guards were closing off a good-sized section of Meridian Street. We're going to have to go around."

Mal accepted the explanation and considered lowering her head into Alto's lap when the vehicle turned down a narrow, vacant side street.

Through a lusty haze she saw the driver make a slight erratic jerk to his left and her survival instincts kicked in.

"Down!" she yelled, shoving the aroused swordmaster to the floorboard and falling on top of him.

The driver ducked to his left, but not fast enough. The windshield of the cab exploded along with his head, which showered the interior of the hackney with blood and brain matter.

Three more crossbow bolts destroyed the rest of the windows, sending shards of glass spraying everywhere. They could hear the ringing of bolts bouncing off the Ukko wood body of the cab and both attempted to count the rounds fired to gauge the direction and number of attackers.

As suddenly as it began, it stopped and Banavor's voice rose above the tense stillness, "Mz. Konrad, we can avoid any more unpleasantries this evening if you will only take the deal I'm offering you."

Inside the back of the cab, Mal and Alto peered into each other's scratched up and bleeding faces.

"You're hit," Mal said, noting the shard of glass embedded in his left shoulder.

"It is nothing," the swordmaster replied seriously. "How many did you count?"

"At least three," Mal replied, readying her pistol and making sure she had her spare magazine close at hand.

"Four," Alto confirmed. "Two behind us and two up front with Banavor."

"They're using older model pistols, probably Mark four's and firing in volleys to give the others time to reload."

"So, it is going to come down to timing," Alto said, picking up several large shards of glass.

"I'll take the front," Mal said with a determined sneer. "I want a shot at that little drama queen."

"My proposal is really quite simple," Banavor continued confidently. "Your life for your daughter's life. You can come out now and we can get this over with quickly and painlessly. Then, I will leave your daughter alone. Or we can kill the both of you and then kill your daughter too. The choice is up to you. I give you to the count of three to choose…One…two."

The second of the count had no sooner left his lips when Mal and Alto sprung up in the seat catching the assailants, who were waiting for their boss' count, completely off guard.

Just as Alto had assessed, Banavor with two thugs stood ten feet away from the hood of the cab and two more stood at the entrance of the side street.

Mal got off two quick shots at the henchmen flanking Banavor. Their torsos exploded, one quickly after the other, showering the young man with blood from both sides.

Alto hurled the two broken pieces of windshield glass at the henchmen behind them. One shard embedded in the forehead of one, but the second fragment struck the other in the upper arm. The one struck in the head teetered, and then dropped to the street. The second winced in pain but quickly recovered and started to raise his pistol.

Alto had no time to pick up another piece. Reaching around to his wounded arm, he yanked the piece of glass lodged there free and flung it at him with deadly precision. The jagged edge struck the aiming mobster's mid chest. A shocked look crossed the man's grizzled face, just before dropping the pistol and following it to the ground.

Alto spun when he heard the explosion behind him. Mal missed a shot at a fleeing Banavor. The round connected with the corner of a building he disappeared behind, blowing out a large chunk of the wall and sending fragments in every direction. From the cry of pain just out of sight, Mal assumed some concrete shrapnel found their mark.

Once certain the danger had passed, both slumped back in the carriage backseat, their ragged breaths punctuated by the shrill whistles of city guards headed their way.

"If I wasn't sure before, I am now," Mal wearily said, staring straight ahead. "I'm sick of this shit. I really think it's time to hang it up before our luck runs out."

"After recent events, I would be inclined to agree." Alto replied, equally as weary.

Yeah, but not around here. Maybe we can find a nice quiet spot where we can spend some of that money we've made."

"Do you have any ideas as to where?"

Mal gave an exhausted sigh and finally looked over at Alto. "Some place fucking far from here."

Captain Vanir set the report down on the stack of papers and gave a frustrated glance up at Talib and Tantei.

"Nothing?!"

"Not since he tried to bribe me," Talib replied.

"That was six cycles ago."

Talib gave a shrug with a look that said, *what can I do?*

"Boss, we've got tails on Banavor, as well as the whole monetary council, so far, nothing." Tantei said in disbelief.

"He's been visiting that alchemist but that's about it," Talib reported.

The captain's eyes stared off into space and he shook his head. "An operation the size of Banavor's doesn't just go quiet. Somethings going on."

"Captain? Inspectors?" came a voice from the doorway.

All turned to see the desk sergeant leaning into the room.

"One of our patrols just reported in," he said gruffly. "There's been an altercation just off Meridian Street by the Northern Docks. The Konrad woman was involved with some of Banavor's men. There are casualties."

Vanir exhaled loudly. "If Mal and company were involved, I have no doubt there *are* casualties. Inspectors, I believe this is where you come in."

"Well, so much for quiet," Tantei said, heading for the door. "Come on, new guy, let's go."

Shurta stood close to the relative warmth of a food vendor's stall on a chilly autumn morning. She had followed the transport vehicle for the past four deci, while it plodded through the congested streets of Zor, carrying the small flat boxes loaded from the lab of Hemicar the Alchemist.

The vehicle stopped at three apothecary shops throughout Zor. They unloaded a dozen boxes at each stop before the floating box truck lumbered off to the next potions dealer. Shurta followed the delivery man, certain this had to be Banavor's final product, because of the burly, bull-necked guard in back, armed with a medium crossbow.

At shop number four on the southern docks, she recognized the proprietor who came out to greet his latest shipment. Denuar de Aris, a man of medium build with long brown hair and a thin beard with touches of gray, stepped out the front door of his shop. His squinty eyes and constant dour expression disguised his cunning nature with the appearance of a common thug—he, however, was anything but that.

He had been Shurta's first arrest upon entering the Air Marshal's Service. The unassuming man devised a brilliant smuggling operation using the Valdurian's own transport airships. After she turned him over to the Quartermasters, the Whitmar slavers sold him into ten grands of punishment slavery, performing heavy labor in a Zorian apothecary's warehouse. Now, with his sentence served, Shurta figured he must have picked up a few skills while being around all those potions and powders.

The Valdurian agent waited for them to unload the last box and pull the truck back into traffic before heading for the shop's entrance. A tiny bell on the glass door signaled her arrival and the stout redhead took in her surroundings.

The business measured approximately thirty-feet-square with shelves lining the walls. Partially filled glass bottles rested on every crowded shelf. The owner stood behind a long, cluttered counter in the rear of the shop.

Shurta found it odd that it was already mid-morning and the business had no customers. Opening her jacket, she welcomed the warmth of the interior but winced slightly at the cloyingly acidic odor hanging in the air.

"I'll be right with you," Denuar said, not taking his attention from inspecting the boxes' contents.

Approaching the counter, Shurta could see into the hurriedly opened top box. Dozens of tiny glass vials filled the container, each in their own individual compartment. When Denuar finally looked up, his face fell upon seeing who had walked through the door.

"What do you want?" he asked suspiciously, not bothering to conceal his contempt.

Shurta maintained her pleasant disposition. "Relax Denuar, what's with all the hostility?"

"Ten grands of hard labor. That's what!"

Shurta casually peered around the well-stocked interior. "Well, for someone who just went free, you seem to be doing pretty well for yourself," she said calmly, before chuckling. "The way I see it you should be thanking me for setting you on a new *legal* career path. That is what you're doing, right?"

"Yeah, thanks a fucking lot. And yeah, selling this stuff isn't illegal. Now, what do you want, I'm busy?"

"I want to be your first customer for that new shipment you just got in."

Denuar shifted his attention warily down to the box, then back to the Valdurian. "It's not for sale yet."

Shurta gave a weary sigh. "Look, Denuar, I could just confiscate one, but I'd rather purchase it. What do you say?"

Reluctantly, Denuar pulled out one of the inch long tubes containing a clear liquid and placed it on the counter.

"That'll be one copper."

Upon hearing the price, Shurta's face scrunched suspiciously at the apothecary. "Why so cheap?"

"Manufacturer's orders."

"And who might that be?"

"None of your fucking business. Now, are you buying it or not?"

Shurta placed a copper coin on the counter, with a sly smile and placating nod, before pocketing the vial.

"Good doing business with you, Denuar," she said, moving towards the door. "I'll see you around."

"Anytime will be too soon, *bitch!*"

She let the insult pass, stepping out into the chilled air. Her next stop, the School of Alchemic Studies at the University of Marassa to get her latest acquisition analyzed.

Taleeka stared down at the page, then back up at Nibira with a perplexed look.

"What in the name of the Goddess does 'Terry Stop' mean again?"

Nibira smiled at her friend and looked thoughtfully into space while she searched her memory. "A Terry Stop is an Investigative detention of a person by a law enforcement officer, named for the 6 P.A. Imperial Court decision in Terry v. Zor."

Taleeka shook her head in amazement. "You really never forget anything, do you?"

The stout brunette blushed from the compliment and glanced shyly downward. "Most say it's a blessing, but sometimes I think it's a curse."

Taleeka smiled at her friend's assessment, then peered around at the sparce morning activity in the university library. "Well, it sure came in handy with those runes. Thanks for my own set. And I bet Karta finds that memory of yours comes in handy.

"How's it going with him by the way? You two have been spending quite a bit of time together."

Nibira continued to blush. "I've been staying at his place since we returned. I stayed there that first night back after the Clerrias healed my leg and neither one of us wanted me to leave. We really get along."

"That's great!" Taleeka congratulated, genuinely happy for her. "The age difference isn't an issue? I mean, he's got a good ten grands on you."

Nibira shook her head. "So far no, it's a real benefit having a man that knows how to treat a woman, especially... you know."

Taleeka gave a single salacious chuckle. "Yeah, from the college boys I've met, I'd be willing to bet they're real bumblers between the sheets."

Nibira blushed yet again. "He sure knows how to make me happy."

"Hang on to that as long as you can. Screw the age difference." Taleeka returned her attention to the textbook on the table in front of her. "I really appreciate you helping me out playing catch-up with Zekoff's class. It's starting to get complicated."

"Glad to help, I..."

"Hi Nibira," a timid male voice interrupted.

Both looked up at a gangly young man with pleasant features, reddish brown hair and a goofy smile. He wore a soiled white apron that smelled of grease.

"Oh, hi Kuvati," she greeted warmly. "With your class load, I didn't think they'd have you working today."

"Yeah, some people didn't show this morning, so they called me," he said, nervously bobbing his head. "Uh... I just wanted to let you know that I just got through making a batch of braised goose. Um... Well, it goes pretty fast and... Well, I know it's one of your favorites, so I... um... set some aside for you. If that's okay?"

"Why Kuvati," Nibira beamed, "that is so sweet. Thank you!"

The student cook shifted nervously back and forth on his feet with his head lowered. "Oh, you're welcome. Um... Like I said, I knew you liked it and...well, I better get back."

"Thank you again, Kuvati. That was very sweet."

Meekly smiling, he quickly exited the library, heading back to the kitchen.

Taleeka grinned at her friend's popularity. "Look at you! You're getting more action than any three people I know."

Nibira's face flushed once more and she peered down at the table. "It's not like that. He's just a friend."

Taleeka wryly scoffed. "Yeah, well someone needs to tell him that. He's got it bad for you."

"You think so?"

Taleeka's face scrunched in surprise. "You can't see it?!"

"I guess I can't. I mean, I've got Karta so I'm just not looking."

"Sure," Taleeka said with a shrug. "Why eat meatloaf when you can have steak? Speaking of which..."

Taleeka nodded towards the library's open double doors and the well-dressed barrister walking through them. Taleeka smiled in delight when Nibira spun in her chair and her face lit up.

"Karta, what are you doing here?!" she asked exuberantly, bounding to her feet and hugging him.

"What, I can't drop by for a visit?" he teased.

"Of course," she said demurely, stepping back.

"Actually, the reason I'm here is because I knew this was the place that I'd more than likely find both of you."

"Oh?" Taleeka said, sharing a curious glance with Nibira.

"I just wanted to thank both of you for helping me out. I mean, you literally got that thing off my back at considerable peril to yourselves. I was wondering if I might be able to offer you some compensation for your efforts?"

"Take me out to dinner tonight," Nibira offered with a love-struck grin.

"Sure, but I can't help but get the feeling I'm getting the better end of the deal."

Nibira giggled and he inquisitively peered over at Taleeka. "And you?"

"Nah," Taleeka said glibly. "I got plenty of money. Let's just say, you owe me one."

○   ○   ○

For Taleeka, the dinner table at home had always been a place of comfort. A time and location where she and her parents could connect during their very busy lives. This time however, the mood was decidedly different.

"Alright, you two," Taleeka said, putting down her fork, "what's going on?!"

Mal and Alto shot each other a quick nervous glance before Mal gave out a sigh and set her utensil down.

"Tally, sweety, your dad and I have something to tell you."

Taleeka eyed her parents suspiciously. "Does this have anything to do with you getting ambushed last Kan?"

"Kinda," Mal replied, nodding. "Tally, your dad and I have decided to retire."

"Retire?"

"Yeah, we've been talking about it for a while now. The events of the last Kan pushed that decision over the edge."

"Retire," Taleeka repeated hollowly.

Mal could see her daughter wrestling with the concept in her head and decided to continue.

"We don't need the money. We already couldn't spend it all in our lifetimes. All we're doing is taking unnecessary risks. And let's face it, I'm getting fucking tired. So, we've got some land in Amarenia…"

"You're leaving?!"

"We must, little one. We would have no peace living here," Alto explained patiently.

"Yeah," Mal agreed. "There would always be some fucker from our past showing up looking for a fight. Or our current clients would always be trying to drag us back in. We gotta go where no one really knows us."

"I suppose," Taleeka said, still coming to terms with the idea. "What about me?"

"Of course, we would love to have you accompany us," Alto replied. "However, you have already taken the first steps in your new life. You have your friends. You are attending the university."

"And you just did your first solo gig," Mal chimed in. "So, we know you can handle yourself. You've got a bright future as an independent fixer if that's what you want to do."

"It just won't be the same without you," Taleeka said sorrowfully.

I know, little one," Alto said, his voice calm and measured. "Change is the only constant in the multiverse. Your mother and I are entering a new phase in our lives while you are just beginning yours."

"I guess," Taleeka said, staring down at the table.

"We're not kicking ya to the curb," Mal attempted to reason. "We've set up a fund through Pierce Calden in their commodities exchange. You'll have all the money you will ever need. The house is yours. Peshk will stay on if you want her to and you'll have full use of the network we've built. Shit, over the last six grands of running around with us, most of them are already well acquainted with you."

"I don't want any of that stuff. I want you," Taleeka said, sighing deeply and looking up from the table into her parents loving gaze, "but I think I understand."

"We also both possess talking stones," Alto offered. "So, we can communicate any time you wish."

"And if you need to visit, we're just an airship ride away," Mal added. "One thing though."

A questioning gaze crossed the teenager's face and her mother's tone became somber.

"You can't tell anyone where we are. I mean *nobody*, not your friends, not our clients, nobody! Swear it."

"I swear," she said, now resigned to the finality of the situation.

"Good girl. Now come give me a hug."

ACT TWO

You Owe Me One

The murky Kan fog cloaking the Aramos capital city of Aris amplified the autumn chill. Taleeka, however, felt ready to break into a sweat under her Valdurian ghost suit. The very spot on the wall she deftly scaled, disappeared into the gently swirling vapors in all directions.

Taleeka loved climbing and the challenge of a steep incline so much so, that her mom jokingly called her part mountain goat. Right now, she needed a challenge and a distraction. Tomorrow her parents, the ones she spent the last seven grands inseparable from, were moving away.

She never had time to reflect on how they rescued her from the horrors and abject poverty in the streets of Toriss or even reminisce about how they swept her into the life of adventure, wealth and honor. For no matter how dangerous a position her family found themselves, they always made her feel loved and nurtured.

Right now, climbing the wall of the Aramos represented all that mattered. The climb fulfilled just what she wanted and even needed. One hand over the other, fingers and toes searching for a foothold to exploit, no matter how tiny or seemingly insignificant.

Reaching the roofline of the four-story structure, the teen grabbed onto the roof's edge and pulled herself horizontally along the rear of the building, legs dangling precariously in mid-air.

When she reached the large picture window, she peered inside the dark room. The orange Trinilic treated lenses revealed no organic heat sources. The distinct orange dots, on either side of the glass cases lining the wall, told her all she needed to know. They were alarmed and booby-trapped.

She pulled herself onto the thin sill and balanced while reaching into her backpack. Fishing around inside the sack, she finally pulled out a four-inch, oblong, green Etheria shard with one end honed to a point. She reached out to place the tip against the glass when her Trinilic lenses detected a heat source heading through the doorless archway from the next room.

She quickly placed the crystal between her teeth and slipped off the ledge, catching hold of the edge with her fingertips. Holding on tightly, she quietly dangled against the side of the building while the guard passed through the room. Taleeka even saw him pause to look out the window she hung from, oblivious to her presence.

Once she felt a sufficient amount of time passed, she pulled herself back up, and then double checked to make sure she would be entering a vacant room. Satisfied, she placed the tip of the Agress Etheria Crystal against the bottom corner of the window and scratched out an arch across the window's bottom half. She gave the segregated area of glass a gentle push and felt it give way. Slipping her hand along the top edge, she lifted section from the rest of the windowpane and set it carefully on the floor inside.

Once she determined the semicircular hole in the glass was large enough for her to crawl through, she slipped inside. Allowing herself a brief moment to enjoy the room's warmth, Taleeka scanned her surroundings.

With no time to lose, she bounded over to the third case from the door. She peered through the glass and saw three small, glowing crystal medallions lying on either side of the case's interior. Thin beams of blue light connected them in crisscross patterns surrounding the small artifacts on display there. She didn't know exactly what would happen if she broke the beams and she sure didn't want to find out.

The small gold statue sat just where Taleeka spotted it while casing the establishment two cycles ago. They had placed the crudely crafted ancient depiction of the ape god Konga third article from the end. Despite its unappealing looks, the statue commanded a king's ransom, if the priceless relic ever sold.

Reaching under the cabinet's base, she used the Agress' tip to trace a hole directly under the figurine. The artifact dropped between the surrounding light beams, into her hand. She looked it over and shook her head, before slipping it into her pack and crawling back out the window.

Unlike in her younger days on the streets, Taleeka didn't normally engage in larceny. She had more than enough money to sustain herself in luxury for the rest of her life. No, she had plans for this invaluable token as a peace offering and bargaining chip.

Hemicar's lab buzzed with activity when Banavor and Tumuh arrived. They converted all the empty space to a mass production area. Off to the left, several cauldrons bubbled away. Their aromatic smoke had a fruity, but not unpleasant, smell that filled the room, eventually filtering out the three open windows to the rear. Two large baskets full of Jabule Beans sat beside the cauldrons.

A dozen Cul-Ta stood on boxes around two long tables in the center of the room and filled the small vials with a clear liquid. The humanoid rats chattered away amongst themselves and worked at a feverish pace.

A stocky young man with dark brown skin, a bald head, a thick, bushy, jet black beard and dressed in a soiled white apron, tended the cauldrons and supplied the liquid.

"Hemicar, I would like to introduce you to the benefactor of this operation, Lord Banavor," Tumuh said when the alchemist came over to greet them.

When Hemicar took Banavor's limp hand to shake it, he winced from its cold touch and the lecherous look that crossed his face.

"Most happy to finally meet you, Lord Banavor," he said, suddenly enraptured by the attractive young man in the tight blue Kell skin bodysuit. "As you can see, we are already well under way."

Banavor smiled and silently gazed around at the activity.

"Yes, Tumuh said, speaking for her boss. "Now that the first shipments have gone out. I just had to see for myself."

Banavor then took one of Hemicar's thickly muscled arms and stepped in close. "You must give me a tour."

Tumuh grinned watching the alchemist attempt to compose himself. From the massive bulge in the front of his pants, she knew that if Banavor hadn't distracted him with conversation, he would have already blown his load.

"Well, sir, you're pretty much looking at it," Hemicar said, nervously clearing his throat. "I measure the crushed beans into the boiling liquid. Turns out you don't even have to shell them, so that saves time. Then, you let it cool and filter out the beans. The remaining liquid goes into the individual vials."

"I've heard the liquid is very effective."

"Oh yes," Hemicar confirmed, proudly smiling. "I call it Dawa. One vial, once a day and it turns anyone into a happy, productive worker. It doesn't matter how shitty the job is, one dose of this, and they *want* to do it. You actually have to make them stop working."

"Excellent," Banavor said, noting the Cul-Ta. "Most unusual work force you've got there. How in the name of the gods did you lure them out of the sewers to actually do work? I mean they're hardly the ambitious lot."

"I've got them dosed," Hemicar replied. "The little fellas only need half, but it works great, even on them."

"Very good," Banavor said admiringly. "I predict productivity and profits on the rise in the very near future."

"Just one thing," Hemicar said, his voice trailing off causing Banavor to raise a questioning eyebrow.

One of the Cul-Ta screeched, just before attacking another working beside him, and cut off the reply. The two tumbled off their perches and rolled around on the floor clawing and biting, all the while making a horrendous racket. The others immediately jumped down, separated them and restrained the attacker. The alchemist rolled his eyes, sighed heavily and picked up a wooden mallet from the table next to him.

"Excuse me please," he said to Banavor, before stepping over to the captured aggressor struggling against the two holding his arms.

"What did I tell you little bastards about double dosing?!" Hemicar admonished angrily, before bringing the hammer down on the struggling rat-man's head.

The wooden cudgel made a loud crack when it crushed his skull and the Cul-Ta went silently limp in his captors' arms. Hemicar nodded towards the door and they dragged the body away. Coming back to an amused Banavor, he set the mallet back down and gave a resigned shake of his head.

"I lose about two of them every cluster. That's what I was about to tell you. One dose a day is all the average human can take. If they overdose, they get violent and paranoid. That's the reason for the size of the vials. They're premeasured for one human size dose."

"That shouldn't be too hard to remember," Banavor said confidently.

"Easier said than done," the alchemist replied. "This stuff is *very* addictive."

"That, my dear Hemicar, is not my problem," Banavor proclaimed glibly. "The lord delights in personal choice and the free market. The consequences are to be borne by those making the choice."

Shurta de Ovora guided her intimidating six-foot-four frame through the busy corridors of the Zorian Guard's Headquarters. Her hands tightly gripped the three sheets of paper, giving her a grim expression.

She turned down the hall leading to Captain Rafel's office, still organizing her thoughts, and saw Mukavar leaving the spymaster's office. When he closed the door behind him, she couldn't help but notice him putting his belt back on and his face looking slightly flushed.

"Shurta," he greeted with a nod when he passed.

"Muuky," she replied with an amusingly perplexed look.

Stepping up to the door and knocking, she waited for a reply before entering. The call to enter happened immediately and the Valdurian agent breathed a sigh of relief she wasn't walking in on a compromising situation. Rafel stood behind his desk organizing a very disheveled group of papers, scattered about haphazardly.

"Shurta," he said with a pleasant grin, not bothering to stop his arranging. "What brings you by my mess?"

"I've got a few more papers to add to your collection there." Shurta replied, extending the leaves at him. "I just got the report from the Alchemists over at the university. I purchased one of those vials of Dawa from an apothecary three cycles ago and had the Marassa's break it down."

Rafel took the papers and sat down. "I take it by the look on your face that the news isn't good?"

"Troubling to say the least," she said.

Shurta noticed Rafel wince in pain when his seat and back touched the chair. She now felt certain she understood why Mukavar had his belt off.

"Okay," Rafel said, reading only a few lines. "There's a lot of technical jargon here. What's your take on it?"

Shurta gave a sympathetic smile. "Yeah, I had to have them go over it with me too. Basically, it's mostly the concentrated extract from the Jabule Beans. We already know about the beans and how they turn the user into happy workers. These doses are *really* condensed but that's not the truly disturbing part."

Rafel peered up from the paper. "Well good, because I was hoping for a truly disturbing part."

"The liquid they're using to infuse the beans is unstable."

"Unstable how?"

"It's used to prevent the bean's potency from breaking down too quickly. In a single dose or smaller, you're fine, but two doses within a cycle will probably lead to a violent paranoid episode."

Rafel sat staring in disbelief at the Valdurian mechanic, attempting to process what he had just heard.

"The Marassas are certain?"

Shurta nodded. "It's not illegal and it's cheap. One dose is only a copper piece."

Rafel exhaled loudly and rolled his eyes.

"Well," he said standing. "That puts a whole new spin on things. I've got the regular morning cross division briefing in a few centis. I want you to bring the rest of them up to speed. Patrol Division's going to have a field day with this."

"And, here we go," Taleeka whispered to Noorim when the first of the Antiquary's henchmen entered the pub.

He stood well over six feet tall, with broad shoulders and a muscular physique stuffed into an expensive looking shirt, slacks and jacket. Another henchman, who could have been his twin, followed him.

"Think they use the same tailor?" Taleeka quipped, watching them warily survey the interior.

The bodyguards locked onto the two teens standing at the bar and then one left.

"Are you sure this is a good idea?" Noorim asked in her usual deadpan.

"Too late now," Taleeka replied when the second thug returned with Anak Bramoul and yet another guard who looked amazingly like the other two.

"You were supposed to come alone," a henchmen said aggressively when he approached. "We might just have to throw your friend out to show we mean what we say."

Taleeka glanced over at Noorim defiantly staring the much larger man down, and then back over to the gangster.

"Having your asses handed to you by a teenage girl in a public place would be embarrassing," Taleeka said serenely, "So, why don't your boss and I have a private conversation at that secluded table over there. That way, you all can continue your staring contest."

The mobster reluctantly broke his concentration on the Amarenian, gave a defiant glance at Taleeka and then returned to his boss still standing by the door. He whispered something and indicated the table Taleeka already headed towards. The Antiquary left his entourage and cautiously made his way over to the table and a smiling Taleeka.

"Your message said we should talk and that you had something that might interest me," Anak said, taking the seat across from her.

"I think I do," she confirmed, reaching into her backpack placed in the chair beside her.

When her hand disappeared inside the tote, the Antiquary tensed briefly, causing Taleeka to snicker.

"Relax," she said, pulling out a small object wrapped in cloth. "Think of this as a peace offering and a 'no hard feelings' gift."

She placed it on the table in front of Anak. The Antiquary eyed the package and his attitude slowly shifted from cautious to curious.

"Go ahead," Taleeka prompted, nodding at the gift.

He slid it over directly before him and slowly unfolded the cloth, all the while casting brief glances at the teen across from him. When finally opened, he stared at the crude golden ape statue and his eyes went wide.

"The Konga Relic!" he sputtered.

"Yep," Taleeka said nonchalantly.

"The original?!" Anak asked in wonder, picking it up and reverently examining it.

Taleeka gave an amused grin at the question.

"But this is supposed to be locked in the Aramos Archives up in Aris!" he exclaimed.

"It was, up until last Kan."

"You?"

Taleeka gave a shallow shrug. "I got skills."

With a flash of realization about being in a public location, Anak quickly covered the artifact and then looked around. Gazing back up at Taleeka, his cruel features relaxed a bit and his pencil thin moustache curled upwards in a smile.

"I've had my eye on this for quite a while," Anak said appreciatively.

"I know."

"How could you possibly have known?"

"Like I said, 'I've got skills.'"

Anak sighed and sat back in his chair. "Well, nothing says forgiveness like a priceless antiquity. All right, no hard feelings."

Taleeka leaned forward on the table and put on her best diplomatic attitude. "I figured, we don't have to be friends, and though we may be adversaries from time to time, we don't have to be enemies either. Who knows, we might even find ourselves on the same side in the future."

"Sure," Anak conceded. "Well, now that we're all buddy-buddy, tell me about that map. The one I got was fake and I lost three good men following it."

Taleeka gave a sly grin. "All the maps were no good."

Anak now sat forward attentively. "All?"

"Yeah, we had a half dozen drawn up directly from the barrister's back. Each one of them turned out different. The map couldn't be copied. If you were going to follow it, you'd have to work off the original. That's why we let you steal it so easily. You could have taken any one of them and it still wouldn't have mattered."

"The original? You're talking about the one on his back?"

"Yep."

"Did you follow it?"

"Yeah, it was a real pain in the ass."

"Where did it lead?"

Taleeka shook her head indifferently. "Some musty old cave up in the mountains. Nothing of value, just a bunch of glyphs on the wall."

"Looks like we both got taken on that one," Anak said.

Taleeka nodded. "And now I'm playing catch up on my schoolwork."

Anak let out a sympathetic huff and then stared down at the wrapped statue. "Well, I gotta say, that's quite the gift. I would normally payout big time for such an item."

"No payment necessary," Taleeka said, grinning broadly, "let's just say you owe me one."

The Grand Turine ringing in the Zorian Harbor, marked the last run of the cycle before breaking for the Kan. The twenty-passenger hackney bus plodded past the Seven Sisters Slums, filled to capacity with citizens getting off work, eager to return home.

The cloaked figure sitting by the vehicle's door shifted nervously when they passed the second side street heading into the blighted neighborhoods of the High Holy City. When the third boulevard came into view just ahead, the figure suddenly stood, produced a pistol crossbow from under his cloak and pointed it at the driver's head.

"Make a right up here!" he demanded gruffly.

The terrified driver stared wide-eyed at the weapon trained on him, swallowed hard and nodded. Passengers now cried out in panic and he spun to face them.

"Everybody shut up and stay calm!"

The bus slowly turned the corner and floated another twenty feet into the squalor of the Seven Sisters.

"Stop here and open the door," he growled to the driver, who anxiously complied.

"All right folks, this is where we play my version of pass the hat," he said, taking out a canvas sack folded over his belt and handing it to the driver. "I'm going to send my new assistant here around to collect your money, jewelry and anything else you might have of value."

He then motioned for the driver to begin in the back. "If we make this quick, I can be out of your lives and you can be on your way in no time. Now, HURRY UP!"

The driver moved down the aisle, between the five double rows of seats, clutching the bag with trembling hands. Nineteen petrified faces watched his trek, paralyzed in fear.

"GET YOUR SHIT OUT NOW! the thief screamed.

He pointed the pistol at the nearest passenger. With the imminent threat, all scrambled for their valuables.

"If you're not ready when that bag gets to you, you're gonna die on this bus!"

When the driver passed the bus's third row, it obscured the thief's vision of the fourth row. At that moment, the only person in the vehicle not intimidated by the robber, pulled back her hood. Tantei quickly retrieved her Mark Six pistol and stood with weapon aimed.

Drop it Rogo!" she ordered, her face grim and lips taut.

The distracting cover worked, the Zorian Guard almost magically appeared from behind the driver, taking Rogo completely by surprise. A panicked look swept over his face and he started to train the weapon on Tantei when a male voice came from the bus's open door.

"Ah ah *ahhh*."

"A quick side glance revealed Talib standing in the street with his pistol trained on him. Rogo's face fell, his shoulders slumped and he lowered the pistol in defeat. An immediate roar of cheers and applause erupted from the relieved passengers and Tantei cautiously moved toward the bandit, not relinquishing her aim.

"Toss the pistol out here, then put your hands on your head, then back out of the bus *slowly*." Talib's business like tone left little room for argument, and Rogo did as commanded.

"Sorry for the inconvenience folks, you can go about your business." Tantei announced, just before exiting behind her prisoner.

By the time she stepped out onto the street, Talib already had Rogo on his knees, legs crossed and his hands still on his now uncovered head. Tantei guessed his age as late twenties, sporting a round, scarred up face, unkempt short black hair and scraggly beard.

The bus silently lumbered off, leaving the two Zorian Guards and their detainee. Tantei reached down and picked up the thief's firearm and holstered hers.

"Damn Rogo," she said, examining the weapon. "This is a Mark Four. How did a low-level scumbag like you, get their hands on such heavy hardware?"

Rogo stared defiantly forward, saying nothing. Lashing out violently, Talib shoved the back of Rogo's head.

"The lady asked you a question!"

"Fuck you," Rogo angrily snapped. "Both of you!"

Tantei's demeanor remained calm, bordering on amused. "Ah, come on Rogo, why ya gotta be like that. We nabbed you fair and square with your pants down."

"Bad fucking luck," Rogo muttered.

"Oh, this was more than just a bad case of 'the wrong place at the wrong time.' The deck was stacked against you from the beginning. We've been tailing you for a while now, waiting for you to fuck up and what do you know, you handed it to us. See, normally if you tried this dumb-ass kind of stunt, I'd just as soon splash you as to look at you, but we need to talk."

"I got nothing to say."

Tantei gave a weary sigh. "Look asshole, we can work this one of two ways. You can tell me what I want to know, in which case we kick you loose—we'll keep the pistol though—or we march your sorry ass over to Judgement Square and put you in front of an Imperial Judge. So, let's see, we've got hijacking of a Zorian hackney and twenty counts of armed robbery, committed right in front of two Zorian Guards. Fuck cutting off your right hand, I'll bet they'll take the whole arm. Then, you're gonna have to train your left hand to beat your meat."

Rogo broke his defiant stare forward and peered at Tantei, his resolve crumbling. "What do you want to know?"

Tantei gave a satisfied smile. "There's a good fellow. So, four cycles ago, your good friend Wado was killed when he and three of his buddies tried another dumb-assed maneuver of ambushing the Konrad's. I think you probably know something about that."

Rogo gave a lengthy pause, his eyes shifting wildly.

"I'm listening," Tantei cajoled.

"The guy wanted to hire me too, but I had something going on that Kan," Rogo admitted in a vanquished inflection.

"Well, you lucked out there," she said. "What guy are we talking about?"

"He didn't give a name. Average height, dressed nicely, with short dark hair and a receding hairline. His moustache and goatee didn't connect on the side of his mouth."

Stovle, which means Banavor, Tantei thought with an accepting nod. "All right beat it!"

The thief didn't need to be told twice. He bounded to his feet and dashed down the street into the anonymity of the slums and rising Kan fog.

"We know Banavor's behind it." Talib said, watching Rogo's hurried exit. "Why can't we go arrest him right now?"

"Because an Imperial Judge is going to need something more than the word of a second-rate street thug to sign an arrest warrant on one of the most powerful men in the Goyan Islands."

Talib sighed in frustration and Tantei put a reassuring hand on his shoulder. "You should be proud new guy. You did good today."

"Why doesn't it feel like it?"

Tantei smiled and shook her head. "Patience, sooner or later both our bus hijacker and Banavor are going to fuck up. When they do, I'm going to be there to shove it up their ass.'"

"If the stories are true," Talib scoffed, "Banavor would like that."

"Not the way I'm going to do it."

With the rising of the Kan fog, the Zorian residence of 2300 Kasada Drive, better known as Konrad House, came to life. Peshk prepared a delicious dinner and Taleeka delighted in entertaining her friends, but something seemed amiss in the hostess that all her guests couldn't help but notice. She had been unusually sullen and quiet before and during the meal. Barr-Ani, the Bailian sensitive, became the one most affected by Taleeka's frame of mind and brought it up first once Peshk had cleared the table.

"Tally, I'm sensing some sadness in you. What's wrong?"

"Yeah, why so glum, chum?" Nibira chimed in.

Taleeka paused for a long, reflective moment and then filled her empty wine glass.

"My folks left yesterday," she began wistfully, watching the swirling red liquid in her glass, "and, I don't know, it feels weird."

"I understand," the Bailian replied. "You were close and now they're gone. It's natural for you humans."

"Yeah," Nibira concurred. "It only makes sense. You all were practically joined at the hip for a long time now."

"But that's just it," Taleeka said, shaking her head. "How close were we *really*? I mean we worked well together. We all knew our work roles like the back of our hands, but I don't ever recall a time when they were just mom and dad."

"They are not your birth parents, is not that, correct?" Noorim asked.

Taleeka silently shook her head, deep in thought.

"What happened to them?" Noorim pressed.

"They were killed in a mining accident when I was six. I survived on the streets until Mal and Alto rescued me and took me in."

"And how old were you at that time?"

"Nine."

"I would agree with the others," the Amarenian assessed coldly. "Your feelings are natural. They will pass after you become accustomed to your new life."

"And you're starting it off right my friend," Nibira said enthusiastically. "I mean look at this place, and you've got the run of it!"

Taleeka's smile at her friend depicted both sweetness and a little sadness. She felt happy that her relationship with Karta brought this shy librarian out of her shell.

"You can still contact them, can't you?" Barr-Ani asked gently.

"Sure," Taleeka said, with a shrug, "but I'm not sure I'd know what to say. Looking back on it, almost all our conversations dealt with work. Now that we don't work together, we really don't have anything to talk about. Calling them up just to say, 'hello, how's your day' just seems so trivial."

"Don't knock the trivial and mundane," Nibira cautioned. "That's what most of family life is all about."

"I guess," Taleeka admitted.

"This is the perfect opportunity to connect with them as your parents," Nibira said optimistically."

"Did they go far? Can you visit?" Barr-Ani asked, sensing her friend's dilemma.

"Sure, I can visit, but I have to be careful. I can't let anyone know where they are."

"Why so?" the Balian asked with a perplexed look.

"Because of the nature of their work," Noorim answered for Taleeka. "They would have no peace."

"That's right," Taleeka agreed. "They made me promise not to tell anyone where they went."

The Bailian gave a sympathetic nod. "I'm truly sorry my friend. Unresolved family issues are difficult."

Taleeka gave a wry chuckle. "Yeah, and now that they're gone, I can't help but feel, I don't know, kind of abandoned."

Noorim's eyes narrowed at her friend's statement. "Did they not provide for all your needs?"

"Sure."

"Did they not leave you with access to their vast network of clients and contacts?"

"Well, yeah."

Noorim scoffed. "Taleeka, I feel you are looking at this in a most unproductive manner. Your parents must have great faith in your abilities and trust in your judgment to leave you with such a great responsibility to the family name. You were not *abandoned*. You were given the keys to the kingdom!"

Eamil de Uutu tossed the last fifty-pound bag of grain onto the back of the wagon's bed and paused to wipe his brow. The burley Zorian warehouse worker silently rejoiced at the cycle's completion. The last few had been especially exhausting, because a sizeable load arrived four cycles ago from the agricultural islands, needing distribution across the Goyan continent. The shipping company, now on a tight schedule, had to get the wagons loaded and on their way. With a deadline looming, they pushed their laborers hard.

Eamil thought about the new guy, Karmi, who had just started yesterday and immediately his heart went out to him. *A brutal introduction to the job*, he thought while watching the wagon speed off.

Once out of sight, he decided to check on the kid he had unexpectedly taken under his wing. The scrawny seventeen grand old seemed hardly suited for the job and the first day almost killed him. By the time lunch break of the current cycle rolled around, the poor kid looked exhausted. Feeling sorry for the youth, he shared with him a new potion on the market making its way through the city's labor force called Dawa. The stuff was a real pick-me-up and rapidly gaining in popularity.

Strolling through the busy warehouse, Eamil reveled in the cool autumn breeze which swept through the massive open doors at both ends. He loved the fall and winter months. The cold air invigorated him, and the warm taverns seemed to make the ale taste better.

Stepping out onto loading dock three, he couldn't help but notice Karmi. The skinny young man with long dark hair and the first indications of facial hair worked feverishly, tossing bags of grain around as if they were pillows. The broad smile on his face told Eamil that the Dawa still coursed through his system. The seemingly magic elixir really made the mundane, backbreaking work enjoyable.

The Grand Turine in the Zorian harbor rang five bells when he approached the industrious young man. The Kan would be starting soon, it was time to break for the cycle.

"Quitting time!" Eamil announced. "Hey kid, what do you say we get an ale over at the Stormwatch. They got a new serving wench I really think you're gonna like. We're talking tits out to here, and she loves to get them right up in your face."

Karmi briefly paused, smiling at the thought.

"Gimme a few," he said, sounding extremely chipper. "I just wanna finish getting this wagon loaded."

Eamil put his large, calloused hand on Karmi's shoulder and gave him a fatherly look.

"Kid, ya never work past quitting time. The bosses won't appreciate it or pay you for it and it sets a bad example. They'll expect you to work for free all the time and that's what slaves are for. You ain't a slave, are you?"

"No," Karmi answered with a sheepish smile. "I'm a freeman. But the wagon?"

"The wagon will be here tomorrow. Don't you worry. Now it's time for ale and tits. Come on."

"Ok Eamil," Karmi said reluctantly. "Hey, ya got any more of that stuff you gave me?"

"You mean the Dawa?"

"Yeah, that's it. That's some really good shit."

The assessment made the older Eamil laugh and he slapped him on the back as they exited the warehouse.

"Yeah kid, I think I can scare up another vial for you, but you know you can buy it at any apothecary shop?"

Farmi's eyes twinkled in delight. "Really?!"

"Sure enough, and each vial is only a single copper."

"Wow, that's cheap!"

"Sure is kid, but I'd stock up. The stuff sells out fast."

Maluria Konrad sighed contently and took a sip of warm tea. This newest phase of her life in which she found herself could be described as nothing less than domestic bliss. For the first time in her existence, she wasn't running or fighting someone or thing and she had to admit it felt good.

It had been a full three clusters since she and Alto departed Zor for the final time and set up house on land bequeathed them by the very queen herself. Now, with the renovations completed on the once abandoned farmhouse, she could truly relax and enjoy the benefits of a prosperous career fraught with danger and excitement.

The moon had risen a short while ago over the fields of Taia-Dor in western Amarenia. Its reflective light, coupled with the sun permanently fixed low in the western sky, gently illuminated the modest grounds of Konrad House East. Mal basked in its warmth standing at the kitchen window with teacup in hand.

Each time she lifted the vessel to her lips, the morning light refracted off the violet striations in the blue Lolite ring Zau gave her as a parting gift. The bauble, so big it only fit on her thumb, became one of her most prized possessions. The Singa adamantly instructed her to always have the Etheria Crystal near, especially when sleeping. The enchanted gem's psychic shielding properties blocked anyone attempting to locate her by magical methods.

Part of Mal missed the crew of the *Haraka* because they were indeed more than that, they were friends that shared the bond of conflict through comradery. The comradery she would miss, the conflict, not so much. They all, however, had moved on in their own lives. Taleeka decided to stay in Zor. Kumo opted to live amongst the Cevot spider people of the Twilight Lands, where she was all but worshiped as a goddess. Zau moved to the Twilight Lands, setting up residence outside Immor-On.

As for her and Alto, she sighed contentedly, glad they decided on the peaceful remoteness of Amarenia. With her bequeathed land and title of Valorous Sister, it became an obvious choice.

The retired adventurer found herself smiling, watching Alto running through his sword forms on their patio in the side lawn. The swordmaster never omitted his morning ritual. With such a placid existence, his main concern had always been deteriorating technique. Defari also enjoyed the daily activity, giving off joyous barks every time the Etheria blade dramatically arced through the morning air.

The children from the nearby farms and hamlets, all young girls, seemed to enjoy the morning show. They gathered under a large tree and sat cross-legged enraptured by the spectacle. Many had only experienced men as slaves, forbidden to carry weapons. Now, this free man lived in their midst and performed a deadly dance at the beginning of every luna. Afterwards he would plunge Defari into the ground and allow the children to swarm around the sword, eager to get close to the magical blade and pet the canine spirit residing within.

Today happened to be no different, Alto finished with a grand flourish and a bark from Defari. The moment the sword's tip pierced the ground the children rushed over to Alto's admonishment of the blade's sharpness. This time, an adult stood in the audience, and she followed the crowd of children over to the swordmaster.

Mal noted her height, as tall as her, and she wore the traditional Amarenian court dress. The long and flowing, bright blue garment cinched at the waist with breasts exposed. With winter coming on, she wore a half cape, tied in the front, covering the woman's small twin orbs. Her exceedingly pale skin indicated her breeding as a High Amarenian and a head full of short red hair sat atop an angular face.

Mal recognized her as the matriarch of the neighboring Napp Plantation. Her estate's proximity to the capital Mostas and the queen identified her as a powerful figure in Amarenian politics.

Alto gave a friendly smile as she approached, moving through the crowd of children gawking over Defari. The dog's essence seemed to love the attention and it contently panted as they ran their tiny hands over the flat of the blade.

"Good morning," the swordmaster greeted. "This is the first time I've seen you at my practices."

The woman returned the smile and then glanced around at the children enraptured by the sword.

"My granddaughter told me about you and I had to see for myself. I must say, she did not exaggerate your abilities."

"Thank you for your kind words," Alto said with a modest grin. "Alto Konrad, at your service."

The woman gracefully extended her hand. "I am Kennari Napp. My estate is just to the east. I must apologize for not greeting you sooner, but you all appeared very busy getting this place back in shape."

"No apology is necessary," Alto replied. "For the most part we have been warmly received. Even me, though I have experienced a bit of distrust."

The Amarenian matriarch gave a knowing smile. "Yes, my people's ways are changing, albeit slowly. Still, it's not every day that an obvious sword master and Valorous Sister become your neighbors, so I offer my somewhat tardy welcome."

Off to their right, Defari had grown weary of the children's relentless attention and levitated several feet in the air to their gasps of surprise. Without breaking from his conversation, Alto extended his hand and the Etheria blade flew over to him slipping into his grasp.

"That's quite the trick," Kennari noted, staring at the sword.

"It is a long story," Alto said, lovingly glancing at his blade.

"And one I would love to hear, but I wanted to ask you about your footwork," Kennari said, watching Alto sheath Defari. "It was most intriguing, especially the transitioning between stances. Tell me, what discipline do you practice?"

"It is called Rohina Taki, a style native to the eastern Goyan Islands."

"Do all practitioner's carry possessed blades?"

Alto gave a forlorn smile and placed his hand on the sword's hilt. "No, Defari and I are special, forever friends."

Kennari returned the grin and peered down at the sheathed weapon resting in his waist sash. "Now I *really* want to hear that story!"

"You speak very knowledgably," Alto said curiously. "Do you train?"

Kennari peered wistfully downward. "I used to teach our national martial art called Kovos."

"Used to?" Alto noted. "That is a story *I* would one day like to hear."

Kennari then looked up and put a hand on the swordmaster's shoulder. "Alto Konrad, I think there's much we can learn from each other. In fact, you are the first person in a long time, that I feel is capable of training with me."

"You honor me," Alto said humbly. "It would be a great pleasure training with you. And you would not be the first. I took great pride in training with and calling friend a Valorous Sister from this very Dor, named Wostera."

A look of pleasant surprise lit up Kennari's face. "You knew Wostera?!"

Alto sorrowfully nodded. "We battled the insect plague together. She recently died beside me in combat."

"It's I who am now honored," Kennari said, all trace of melancholy now gone. "It's settled then. Tomorrow, at my estate. We begin at moonrise!"

A naked Banavor looked on in sadistic glee at two members of the Piety Watch holding the terrorized homeless woman firmly to the floor of his basement temple. He felt the first twinge of arousal when she whimpered and cried while peering about fearfully.

"You should be happy," the young cleric said placidly. "My Lord is about to give your miserable existence some meaning."

He then turned to the black and fawn colored mongrel Mawl beside him and nodded. When the cat-woman shredded their captive's grimy, tattered dress and gruffly parted her legs he felt his cock begin to rise. When the woman screamed in agony as the Mawl's single claw began to cut around her anus, Banavor's member jutted out obscenely in front of him.

Sheaths of blood streamed out onto the floor around the kneeling Mawl and the smell of excrement scented the air. Banavor started breathing heavily when the humanoid cat began slowly pulling out the woman's intestines in a long fleshy cord. His throbbing erection grew almost painful, and he looked questioningly when the Mawl paused with only ten feet of entrails extracted.

"Care must be given here," she explained. "The auger must be removed intact."

Banavor nodded through labored breath at the explanation and the Mawl gently resumed pulling on the living tendril. When the woman finally gurgled and shuttered before dying, Banavor doubled over in ecstasy, ejaculating hands free, onto the cold stone floor.

He righted himself and felt his breathing return to normal, before he stared at the woman lying lifelessly on the floor. A sea of blood pooled between her spread legs after the Mawl fully extracted the still attached large and small intestines. They stretched out sixteen feet and the pink flesh contrasted against the crimson bed it lay on.

With exacting precision, the humanoid cat began arranging the guts into a swirling pattern on the blood-soaked floor. Once arranged, she intently studied the gruesome form of divination. After several long moments she pointed towards the center of the swirl.

"The one you seek, the one called Maluria, is no longer in the city." She then pointed to a spot midway out from the center. "She will not be returning."

"Where did she go?" Banavor asked excitedly. "Where is she?"

The Mawl pointed to the end of the intestinal pattern and shook her head. "Her location is being blocked, my lord. I cannot see."

Banavor gave a frustrated sigh. "Keep looking, I don't care how many of those leeches on society you have to go through. I'm going to try a more hands on approach at finding the elusive Mz. Konrad."

Talib arose early before the Kan fog receded, dressed and headed out for Clerria House. He had a little time before reporting to headquarters and he hadn't visited his father in over a cluster. Twinges of guilt stabbed about in his mind and he couldn't help beating himself up while hailing the hackney. Work, especially the Banavor case, kept him and his partner busier than he ever thought possible.

Quickly navigating through the main infirmary, he made his way to the long-term care unit and his father's cubicle. To his astonishment, he found the bed empty.

"I'm sorry," came a kindly female voice from behind. "Your father passed away four cycles ago."

Talib froze and the world seemed to move in slow motion. A rumbling in the pit of his stomach warned that he might be on the edge of throwing up and all he could do was stare at the empty bed.

"How?" he asked, finally facing the purple robed Clerria.

"He just drifted off. It was peaceful and he was in no pain."

"The body?" Talib heard himself asking over the rushing in his ears.

"Standard procedure," she said with a sad, sympathetic look. "The body was taken over to the university's medical school for examination, and then sent to the Vurr pyres."

"Why wasn't I informed?" Talib asked mournfully.

"We don't have the resources to do that," she explained patiently. "You were always free to visit at any time."

"Thank you," Talib said weakly, before turning and leaving.

He vaguely remembered wandering back to Judgement Square in a tearful fog, bumping into people while ambling through the busy Zorian streets. When he finally made it back to his office, Tantei sat at her desk, concentrating on a stack of papers in front of her.

"Hey new guy," she said, not looking up. "I think I got something."

When she got no response, she looked up at her partner's tear-stained face. "What happened?"

"My pops died," He replied dolefully.

Tantei sat back and grimaced. "Oh man, I'm really sorry."

"That's not the worse part."

"It gets worse?"

Talib sorrowfully nodded. "He died four cycles ago. I couldn't be there to say goodbye or take care of his body or anything. I was too wrapped up in this damn job!"

"I feel your pain partner," she said, standing. "My mom died a few grands ago when I was on a stake-out and I didn't find out for a whole cluster."

"I don't know what I feel more of, guilt or grief," Talib said, staring at the floor.

"New guy, you just put your finger on it," she said, stepping over to him. "It's the damn job. And I hate to sound like a cold, unfeeling bitch, but things like... you know... not being there for important events, comes with the job. It sucks and there's no way around it. It's also really hard on relationships. Ask me how I know."

"I guess," he said with a mournful nod.

The senior detective reached over and patted his shoulder.

"Right now, let's get you a drink, preferably something strong."

"I really don't drink."

"No time like the present to start. Come on, I know where the boss stashes his spare bottle."

With moonrise over the Amarenian province of Taia-Dor mere moments away, male field slaves already busied themselves preparing for the luna ahead. Zaharrena Napp, eldest daughter of matriarch, Kennari, exited the main house and watched the plantation coming to life.

As with all plantations dotting the landscape, the Napp's estate mimicked the culture's circular architectural designs. Unlike the modest Konrad home, the Napp plantation consisted of six small buildings arranged in a circle around a large two-story central house. The barn and servant's quarters lie a hundred yards away from the main house.

In-between the main and orbiting structures, Zaharrena's sister, Tengah Napp, berated her younger brother and head field slave, Dasht, in front of several of his charges. Seeing this, Zaharrena sighed forlornly and shook her head.

She wished her ill-tempered sibling wouldn't, but she really could do nothing to stop it. It seemed bad enough that he suffered because of the randomness of birth. Being born male, he had been deemed unworthy to carry the Banja's name of Napp, forcing him into slavery and it weighed on her. Her sister despised him, as well as his older brother Gunat, and it showed.

Approaching her siblings, she could see her sister screaming, but she couldn't make out the words. The alabaster skinned middle daughter waved her hands wildly and pointed out into the western fields. The public dressing down ended with Tengah giving Dasht a vicious backhanded slap to the face, snapping the twenty grand old's head violently to the side. The young man's smooth clean-shaven features now sported a glaring red mark and he slunk off; head humiliatingly bowed.

"You shouldn't reprimand him like that in front of the Dags," Zaharrena said, watching the field slaves moving out of view.

Tengah scoffed loudly. "He's nothing more than a Dag. I'll discipline him as I see fit!"

"He's your brother!" Zaharrena countered incredulously.

"You needn't remind me," Tengah said, sneering. "It's his and his brother's fault our Banja dropped in status! Our Banja is now last, *dead last*, because of *them*!"

Zaharrena sighed in frustration. This argument between them went on constantly. Over the grands it became more than just feeling superior to her brothers. Because of her alabaster skin, indicating High Amarenian blood, Tengah looked down on everyone in the Banja, except their mother.

"Mommy, can I go watch our neighbor sword dance?" came a tiny female voice from behind.

Both looked over to see Zaharrena's five grand old daughter Sisu, gleefully bounding over to them. The rambunctious child, dressed in traditional Amarenian children's attire, halted and looked expectantly at her mother. Zaharrena lovingly gazed down at her daughter and brushed some dirt off her light green, floor length dress.

"You're not bothering the man, are you?"

"No, Mommy, but last luna Grandmama came along and she talked to him."

"Alright but come straight back afterwards."

"I will Mommy," Sisu said, before bolting off in the direction of the Konrad's home.

"I don't much care for that either," Tengah said, not bothering to contain her disapproval. "It's bad enough we trade with the Goyan Dags. Now we have one living amongst us!"

"Times are changing sister. We can either change with them or be left behind."

Tengah's scowl remained, rancorously contorting her face. "The old ways were the best. Everyone had their place and we knew our enemies."

Zaharrena, now actually enjoying her sister's uneasiness, gave her a resolute stare. "Look at how our society has improved since opening up to the west. Our queen is guiding us into the future. For some of us, it means being drug kicking and screaming."

"Mommy, mommy, look who I found!" Sisu excitedly interrupted Tengah's rebuttal.

Both gazed over to see the exuberant young girl leading Alto by the hand.

"He was coming to see Grandmama!" Sisu cheerfully reported, guiding the swordmaster over to the bickering sisters.

Both Amarenian women stared openmouthed in surprise at Alto's arrival. Their reactions following, however, could not have been more different.

Zaharrena smiled at their approach, charmed at her young daughter making a new friend. Tengah's eyes narrowed suspiciously and her already pervasive scowl deepened.

"Hello," Zaharrena greeted cheerfully. "It's good to finally meet our new neighbor. I am Zaharrena, this is my sister, Tengah, and you've already met my daughter, Sisu."

"Alto Konrad, at your service," he said with his customary bow.

"So, you're here to see mother," Tengah all but spat. "Are you expected?"

"Not merely expected," Alto said charmingly, "but invited."

The rattling of the beaded front door to the main house drew everyone's attention to Kennari, standing in front of the still rattling beads with her hands on her hips looking slightly irritated.

Dressed in the traditional Kovos uniform, the Vardee, the Kovos mistress stood bare foot and bare chested, wearing baggy, black floor length divided pants, flared at the bottom, resembling a skirt. A wide waistband, set high on her abdomen, underscored her two small, but perfectly formed breasts. The blackness of the solitary garment starkly contrasted with the matriarch's pale white skin.

"You're late!" she admonished, glancing past them at the moonrise on the horizon.

◯ ◯ ◯

The ominous sizzling sound immediately preceded the smell of burning flesh and a piercing scream.

"Perhaps if I rephrase the question," Banavor calmly wondered aloud. "Where is Maluria Konrad?"

They had tied the naked man, with sweat drenched long black hair, securely to the chair with thin wires, which dug into the flesh of his arms and legs.

"I told you before," he cried out, while violently shaking his head. "I don't know where she is! I haven't seen her in over six cycles! She just disappeared!"

The dark cleric sighed heavily. "Yet another answer I don't like."

The man's terrified gaze followed Banavor as he reached over for the handle of the poker whose tip lay buried in red hot coals. Pulling it out, Banavor examined the glowing sharpened end and small barbed hook.

"As I understand it, you were one of her most trusted street contacts. Do you really expect me to believe you?"

"I swear," he cried out when the young man approached with the glowing tip of the poker leading the way.

Remaining transfixed on the poker, he thrashed back and forth rocking the chair until two henchmen grabbed him by the shoulders and held him firmly in place.

The man's response took on a shriller, pleading edge. "The last time I saw her she told me she was gonna retire and she was gonna take off, but she didn't say where and I didn't ask. She said her daughter was taking over and that I'd be working with her."

Banavor stopped. his brow slightly furrowed and his face took on a pensive look.

"Yes, a daughter," Banavor said contemplatively. "Now that you mention it, I have been hearing a bit of a buzz about that."

He then stared at the amber colored tip. "Go on."

"The daughter's name is Taleeka," the prisoner said. "They... they call her Tally. She still lives in the Konrad's house. She goes to the university."

"Interesting," Banavor said softly. "Very interesting. I'd be willing to bet any one of your lives she knows where her mother is."

Banavor returned the poker to the fire and began to gently rotate the implement in the base of the flames.

"We can't take any chances though," he addressed the henchmen. "The kid may not know anything either. Get word out to all our people throughout the Goyan Islands. If she surfaces, I want to know!"

"Yes, Lord Banavor," they chanted.

"And let's put out a bounty," he added. "One hundred secors to the sentient that brings me her alive."

"Don't you mean dead or alive lord?" one of the henchmen asked.

"No!" Banavor snapped. "I want to kill her myself, slowly, like her friend here."

The man's eyes widened at the statement. He watched Banavor pull out the freshly heated rod and give a lecherously evil smile when he stepped before the captive.

"I just hope I can last till the end," he said, indicating the erection plainly visible through his skintight bodysuit.

The man now sobbed and quaked uncontrollably. "No, no, please, I've told you everything!"

"I know," Banavor said, moving the super-heated barb between his legs, "and I believe you."

He then leaned forward and kissed the man on the mouth, biting down hard on his lower lip until blood flowed. "This is just for fun!"

Eamil became concerned about his young friend Karmi. The kid didn't look good. He had always been thin, but now it looked like he hadn't eaten in quite a few cycles. His eyes were sunken and he appeared jittery. The gangly teen still managed to work like a whirlwind though, with boundless energy thanks to the Dawa.

When the Grand Turine in the Zorian harbor rang twenty bells, indicating time for the first break of the cycle, Eamil decided to check up on him. He found him sitting away from everyone, staring at the unloaded pile of grain bags and twitching, unable to sit still.

"Hey kid how ya holding up?" Eamil said, sitting down next to him.

Karmi peered at his friend with an almost panicked look.

"Fine, fine, I'm fine," he blurted out quickly. "But we're just sitting here, when, when, there's work to be done!"

"Yeah, mid-morning break," Eamil replied suspiciously. "Just like always."

"Well, it just, it just seems like we're wasting time!"

"You okay, kid? You seem jumpier than normal."

"I'm good, good!" he replied quickly shaking his head. "I just had to take an extra dose this morning. Now, I just want to get *going*. I mean those wagons, they're, I mean… *they're not going to load themselves!*"

"Kid those sacks aren't going anywhere, and I'm not sure taking a second dose was a good idea."

The young man actually vibrated where he was sitting. "I'm fine. Don't worry about me! FOR THE LOVE OF THE GODS, CAN WE GET BACK TO WORK?!"

Eamil glanced around to see their coworkers staring at the overzealous young man.

"Kid, you need to calm down."

Karmi rose to his feet wildly flailing his arms and screaming. "CALM DOWN! HOW CAN I CALM DOWN WHEN THERE'S ALL THIS WORK TO DO AND WE'RE JUST SITTING AROUND?!

"Okay kid, now you're worrying me. Maybe we should get you checked out."

"NO, I DON'T NEED TO BE CHECKED OUT I NEED TO GET BUSY! I see what you're doing! Don't think I don't see what you're doing! You're *trying* to get me fired! Then I won't be able to work. AND I'LL DIE! YOU'RE TRYING TO KILL ME! *KILLER!* I WON'T LET YOU!"

Before any could react, Karmi snatched a crowbar off a nearby crate and lunged at the startled Eamil. With a bellow of rage, the much smaller Karmi brought the iron bar down on Eamil's bald head, splitting it open. Blood erupted from the open wound and a startled Eamil dropped to the floor with a blood splattered Karmi falling on top of him, continuing repeated forceful blows.

"I WON'T LET YOU KILL ME! I'LL KILL YOU FIRST! *DIE, DIE, DIE!*"

By the time the workmates rushed over to the altercation, Karmi's iron bar had reduced Eamil's head to something unrecognizable, beaten to a bloody pulp. It took two men on each arm to subdue the raging teen, who struggled and wrenched violently against their grip, all the while maintaining a fevered paranoid rant.

Suddenly Karmi froze up, stopped struggling, gurgled once, and went limp in their arms. The crowd that had gathered from the other loading docks looked around anxiously as they slowly lowered his body to the floor.

One of the men restraining him reached down and felt his pulse. When he peered back up at his fellow workers, he shook his head.

"I think his heart gave out,"

Alto had lost count of how many times he had hit the floor in Kennari's private training hall. For two solid decis, the Napp matriarch had tossed the swordmaster about like a rag doll, with movements resembling nothing more than the waking moments of a child.

Giving a frustrated sigh, Alto slowly climbed to his feet and gazed over at the smiling older woman with pale white skin. He had always considered himself proficient in empty-handed combat, until recently.

"Your timing, speed and form are impeccable, Mora," she said, noting his fatigue and disappointment. "It is your distancing, your reliance on your sword's length that handicaps you now."

Alto shook his head and rubbed his sore arm.

"Geta," he began, making sure to use her proper title while training. "I thought I was used to moving in circular patterns and off angles, but nothing like this."

"Mora, it is merely distancing and learning to work in close. Worry not, it will come."

Alto nodded his acknowledgement and Kennari gave a satisfied grin.

"I think we're done for the luna," she said, and both bowed to each other. "It's lunch time, let's go see what the kitchen staff have prepared."

The two exited one of the orbiting structures and headed for the main house. Tengah watched from a second story window, seething with indignation. Not only were the dark-skinned Goyan Dags living amongst them, now her very mother taught him that which the law deemed forbidden for outsiders to know.

Something had to be done to right this great wrong, but she felt powerless. The matriarch held supreme authority within the Banja. While it was true, in this instance she could do nothing, there existed one she knew of who could.

Taleeka felt mentally exhausted leaving the university library, but at least she now felt caught up. It surprised her how much she had missed from Zekoff's class those few cycles in Awa. Nibira had been a great help and she looked forward to life getting back to some semblance of normal.

She noted a lighter than usual Kan fog this cycle, which would make the short flight home a bit easier. Heading for the stairs leading to the roof on the side of the building, she fished around in her pocket and pulled out her airship fob.

When she rounded the corner, she halted suddenly. Standing in front of the staircase to the roof, Boraton Jefferies barred her way. His handsomely aloof features were now twisted into a scowl.

"You're in my way," she said tersely, resuming her trek.

"There's someone who wants to see you," the older student said belligerently.

"Have them make an appointment with my secretary."

Taleeka heard footsteps approaching from behind and pivoted to see both Boraton on her right and two younger students, she recognized as part of his crew, on her left.

"Look, I'm tired and I just want to get home. Why don't you boys go play somewhere else before this gets ugly."

One of the two recent arrivals silently produced a pistol crossbow from under his jacket and pointed it at her.

"And, it just got ugly," Taleeka wearily said, raising her hands.

"Like I said before," Boraton stated confidently. "Someone wants to see you."

"And I said I'm tired," Taleeka replied, surreptitiously swiping her thumb down on the fob and subtly pointing her already raised hand over the gunman's head.

She didn't need to look at them, Boraton's face said it all. In a flash, his demeanor went from commanding to startled.

"Guys, above you!" he cried out in alarm. The warning came much too late. *The Mala*, Taleeka's four-seater airship, plunged to the ground crashing down on top of the two student thugs with a loud wet crunch. The assaulting craft then settled to the ground, inches from the bodies bleeding in the street.

Taleeka took full advantage of the confusion. Deftly reaching back into her pack's holster, she retrieved her cudgel and launched it at the shocked leader. The baton struck him squarely in the groin, doubling him over and propelling him back onto the stairs, crumpled in agony.

Taleeka snapped on the lanyard and the club flew back into her hands.

"Like *I* said," the teen softly growled, bending over so their faces were close. "Make an appointment with my secretary."

"I lost two friends to that bitch!" Boraton fumed, barely able to control his rage.

"Your friends are dead because you underestimated your adversary," Banavor said sternly, sitting back in his chair. "The events of last Kan should serve as a lesson. You have also failed me and more importantly, the Lord."

"I'm sorry Lord Banavor," Boraton said remorsefully, head bowed. "Please give me another chance to redeem myself."

"Perhaps we've been going about this too directly," Banavor mused coming to his feet. "Does Mz. Konrad have any less formidable friends?"

"Yes, Lord Banavor. She has several but she's closest to this fat librarian."

"I see," the dark cleric said, coming out from behind his desk. "Perhaps that is the answer."

The unnerved college student swallowed apprehensively when Banavor began peeling off his bodysuit.

"And yes," the dark cleric said, stepping out of his skintight garb. "I do believe you deserve another chance to serve the Lord, and myself, but first, you must pay a price for your failure."

Boraton fearfully watched Banavor's smooth hairless body stepping closer, causing a chill to overtake him.

"Take off your pants and bend over the desk," Banavor ordered salaciously, his cock stiffening.

The command sent a wave of panic through the young man. He reeled in confusion, simultaneously repulsed and yet, somewhat mysteriously aroused.

"Let's not be all day about this," Banavor said flippantly to the stunned youth. "As you can see, I'm ready to administer your punishment."

When his pants finally dropped, Banavor grinned in surprise at Boraton's growing organ. "Or, perhaps you don't view it as punishment at all. Well, we're going to have to raise the stakes."

Boraton amorously shuttered when Banavor touched his back, forcefully shoving his chest down on the desktop. When Banavor cupped the light brown globes of his buttocks and spread them, Boraton, whose preference had always been women, couldn't help but notice his now throbbing erection and the opposing sensations of fear and arousal.

"Nice ass," Banavor assessed. "I may just keep you on as my permanent bitch. Would you like that?"

"No, sir, please, you don't need to do this. I'll do better next time."

"Oh, I know you will," Banavor cooed mercilessly. "I find it highly amusing that you beg me to spare you, while maintaining such a regal boner. Now, spread your legs."

He begrudgingly complied, gritting his teeth in expectation of the impending pain, when Banavor walked over and opened the door to the outer offices of the Zorian Monetary Council.

"Jeanne," he called out to his secretary. "Gather the clerks and have them come into my office. There's something I want you all to see."

Returning to his compromised henchman, he ran his stiff member through the cleft in his ass cheeks while stunned, murmuring assistants filed into the room.

"Now," Banavor snarled in his ear. "I'm going to fuck you bloody in front of all these people. And you're going to loudly say, 'Sorry, sir, thank you, sir,' with every thrust, until I'm through with you."

"I told you it was just a matter of time," Vanir said, watching the milky white Etheria screen on his office wall. "Sooner or later greed was going to get the better of them."

The display revealed a lone man seated at a small table in a very stark interrogation room. The suspect appeared to be in his mid-fifties, balding on top with wispy white hair and beard. His eyes darted nervously around his surroundings and he fidgeted in his seat.

"His name's Borc Veren," Tantei said, glancing over at Vanir and Talib.

"The textile guy?" Vanir clarified.

"Yep," Tantei confirmed. "We caught him red-handed trying to use his influence on the Monetary Council to corner the market on importing Merebi Silk."

"You really think we can get this guy to roll over on Banavor?" Talib asked skeptically.

"Look at this guy," Tantei said, nodding towards the Etheria screen. "This guy's as nervous as a teenager on his first visit to a whore house."

Vanir smiled at the analogy. "Only one way to find out. Okay, he's simmered long enough. It's up to you two."

Tantei brightened at the assignment. "You got it, boss. Come on, new guy, let's go stoke the flames under this character and see what his boiling point is."

The interrogation room for the Zorian Guards consisted of a freestanding, windowless two room building just off Judgment Square. From headquarters, the short, chilly walk caused both investigators to pull their wraps tighter. A shiver went through Talib when he took off his coat and hung it on the rack just inside the front door.

The mostly empty room only contained several chairs set before a long horizontal window. Next to the window, a single door led into the interrogation room proper. Peeking through the window, Talib could see Borc seated at the table.

"Follow my lead," Tantei said, before opening the door.

The textile merchant's face, riddled with anxiety, watched the detectives enter. Tantei wasted no time once she met his nervous gaze.

"Si. Veren, I'm Inspector Tantei and this is inspector Talib, we've got a few questions for you."

I... I don't believe I have anything to say to you," Borc said defiantly.

Tantei leaned over the table and brought her fist down hard in front of him. The sudden loud crash caused both Borc and Talib to jump.

"Are you trying to piss me off!?" she growled intensely. "Because you're doing a good job of it right out of the gate!"

Borc sat stunned at the abrupt, violent outburst, his eyes blinking furiously.

Tantei remained relentless. "Look, we got you dead to rights. You cooperate and tell us who else was in on your little silk deal and we'll put in a good word with the judge."

"I don't believe I've broken any laws. I'm an honest textiles merchant," Borc said meekly.

"Yeah, I'm gonna call bullshit on that one!" Tantei said, leaning on the table, uncomfortably close. "For getting caught with your hand in your pants is good for at least two clusters worth of naked time in the stocks out in Judgement Square. Winter's coming, my friend. You don't want to spend any naked time outdoors."

"Si Veren," Talib said calmly and friendly, taking a seat directly across from him. "We're all reasonable people here."

"Some more than others," Borc snipped.

"Don't push me asshole!" Tantei exploded, pointing a finger in his face.

Talib raised a hand for calm. Tantei backed off with an angry huff and Talib continued. "We might be able to work something out."

"Like what?" Borc asked in a mixture of suspicion and promise.

"We're greatly interested in what you can tell us about the head of the council, Lord Banavor."

At the mention of the dark cleric's name, the man's face went pale.

"Lord Banavor is a financial genius!" Borc blurted out in a panicked rote. "It is an honor and a privilege to work under him!"

"Banavor's a greedy little pervert," Tantei interrupted loudly. "We're gonna nail his ass to the wall and I'm gonna rub one out in celebration, right in front of him!"

Talib once again held his hand up for calm. "We know Banavor is responsible for a number of deaths in and around the council. We also know you know something. Your testimony in front of an Imperial Judge will be all we need to bring Banavor to justice."

A look of panic swept across the merchant's face and his eyes darted back and forth between the detectives. "Lord Banavor is …"

"Yeah, yeah, I know, a real fucking financial genius!" Tantei leaned in again on the table deliberately invading Borc's personal space. "Here's another scenario asshole. We put you in the stocks for just a single cycle, and then kick you loose. Banavor thinks you cut a deal. He takes care of you in his own special way and we're there to catch him. I just hope we get to you in time before he works his magic. We both know how creative he can be."

Borc nervously licked his lips and looked about wildly. "Lord Banavor is a financial genius! It is an honor and a privilege to work under him!"

Talib leaned forward on the table keeping his demeanor calm. "You're going to be in front of an Imperial Judge before the cycle is over. What you tell that judge is going to affect your future for better or worse. Why don't you help us help you?"

Borc, trembling badly, appeared to be on the verge of tears. "Lord Banavor is a financial genius! It is an honor and a privilege to work under him!"

"Okay, dipshit, have it your way," Tantei said, grabbing him by the arm and yanking him to his feet. "We've got a date with an Imperial Judge. You're gonna get fucked without even a kiss."

They marched him out into the viewing room and Borc offered no resistance, keeping his head lowered. When

Talib started binding his hands, Borc looked up with a doleful, resigned expression.

Suddenly, jerking his hands away from Talib, he leapt over to the coat rack. Before either of the two investigators could act, he grabbed both sides of the rack and smashed the front of his face into the only peg that didn't have a garment hanging from it.

The four-inch-long post penetrated his eye with a plop and a cracking sound. It drove straight through the eye cavity directly into the brain, killing him immediately.

The body went limp and dangled for a moment before the weight became too much for the peg and it broke off sending Borc's corpse toppling to the floor.

Both Talib and Tantei stood frozen in shock.

"Damn!" Tantei cried out, rubbing a hand across her bald head. "Fuck! What kind of mojo has he got over these people?!"

Nibira placed the last book on the shelf from the returns sorting cart and gave a satisfied sigh. As a second grand library intern, they reduced the dreaded chore of shelving to one cycle per cluster. She longed for the next grand when she would be exempt, and the task would fall to the first and second grand students.

Rolling the now empty cart up to the front checkout desk, she smiled at her friend, Dosata, who just finished checking books out to the last few students of the cycle and passed the last few centis of the library being open straightening up.

"That's it for me today," Nibira announced, placing the cart by the counter.

"Any big plans for the Kan?" Dosata asked, pausing her cleaning for a moment.

"Yeah," Nibira said, barely able to contain her excitement. "There's a new eatery that just opened up on Meridian Street. Karta is working late, so Tally and I are going to go and check it out."

"They seem to be popping up everywhere nowadays," Dosata said, returning to her duties. "You'll have to let me know how it is."

"I'll give you the full review tomorrow," Nibira said, heading for the front doors.

Nibira reflected on the other librarian's interest with appreciation. She had always loved well-prepared food and absolutely adored the burgeoning trends in the urban culinary world. Gone were the days when the only place to get a solitary meal served at the owner's whim, happened to be inns and taverns. Now, eateries as they were affectionately called, stayed constantly open and served a variety of fares off a menu.

With the unprecedented growth and prosperity raging across the Goyan Islands, cooks from all across Lumina flocked to Zor, the most cosmopolitan city in the Annigan, to ply their trade and hopefully attain fame and fortune. She valued a friend like Tally who, like her, very much appreciated a fine meal.

Moving down the wide stairs to the street, she pulled her jacket tighter and crossed her arms against the damp autumn chill of the Kan. Peering all about for her friend's airship, she hoped the wait wasn't going to be too long.

Nibira considered contacting Tally on her talking stone when she suddenly became aware of a presence behind her. She attempted to scream when two sets of hands grabbed her arms and held her mouth closed. Muscled into a nearby side street, she saw the figure of Boraton Jeffries appear out of the fog.

"So, I guess you're the secretary I'm supposed to make an appointment with," sneered the arrogant youth.

Nibira had no idea what he meant and continued to try in vain to cry out. He gave out a whistle and a lizard drawn wagon sped to a stop beside them.

"We're gonna go on a little ride and, you know," he said, "I might just let my guys here have a little fun with you before we turn you over."

Boraton's next statement halted before even starting, with him freezing in place, eyes wide in surprise.

"Bory, what is it?" one of the thugs holding Nibira asked quizzically.

"What you're feeling," came Taleeka's calm and deadly serious voice from the shadows behind the leader. "Is the tip of a very sharp blade at the base of your spine. The slightest pressure from me and you never walk again. Nod if you understand."

Boraton slowly nodded.

"Good, now tell your boys to let her go, then back off."

"Let her go, let her go!" he said shrilly.

"Now, pay attention, because I'm only going to say this once. I don't know who you were supposed to deliver her to, and quite frankly, I don't care. But as my mom would say, 'this fucking bullshit ends here and now.' You and your crew are going to leave me and my friends alone or I'm going to get cranky. Got it?"

"Boraton gave another frightened nod.

"Excellent, now that we understand each other, you and your playmates are free to go. Get outta here!"

All three of the college reprobates piled into the wagon and it quickly sped off into the fog.

"Are you okay?" Taleeka asked slipping her knife back into its holster on the side of her backpack.

Nibira nervously nodded. "Just a little rattled."

Taleeka shook her head in disbelief. "Would you believe he tried to snatch me last Kan from darn near this same spot?"

"Well, you're here so he must have failed."

"Yeah, and two of his toadies didn't make it. I'm just a little surprised he tried something so stupid, so soon."

Sighing, Nibira's breathing finally returned to normal. "Why is he doing this?"

"Beats me," Taleeka said with a shrug, "but if there is a next time, it'll be his last."

"I'm just glad you came along when you did," Nibira said, her trembling finally subsiding.

"I've actually been waiting," Taleeka replied, reaching for her airship fob. "I got here a little early and saw them waiting to ambush you from the air."

Raising the Etheria shard, she swiped her thumb vertically down its surface and the *Mala* descended from its airborne parking area.

"So, if we don't know where, when, or even if, he's going to try something again, what do we do in the meantime?"

"Dinner," Taleeka said, climbing into the craft hovering inches above the street. "I'm starving!"

They set the long, polished dining table for two and Banavor, its sole occupant, sat at the head. He delicately cut off a bite of succulent fowl from the plate before him and gracefully brought it up to his mouth. Stovle and a female dining attendant devotedly stood on either side, directly behind the lone diner.

The young priest of Pa-Waga didn't look up when two members of the Piety Watch escorted Boraton Jeffries and his comrades into the dining hall. Several tense moments inched agonizingly by while Banavor continued eating, completely ignoring the new arrivals. Unsure what to say or if they even dare speak first, they traded anxious looks.

He finally paused and sighed, looking down at his interrupted meal. When he finally peered up into the three frightened faces, he demurely dabbed his mouth with the napkin in his lap and then set it on the table next to his plate.

"Si. Jeffries," he said, perplexed. "You seem to be missing someone. Where is the fat librarian I was promised? We've set a place for her and a meal has been prepared."

"We're sorry, Lord Banavor, we ran into a problem."

"A problem?" Banavor's icy expression cut through the nervous youth.

"Yes, sir, it was the Konrad girl."

Banavor glanced thoughtfully at the ceiling for a brief moment before serenely gazing back at the now apprehensive young men. "You're telling me that a teenage girl bested three strapping young men such as yourselves?"

"It's not that simple sir," Boraton nervously sputtered. "She snuck up on us."

"I see," Banavor said, calmly getting to his feet.

"She held a knife to my back. She said I'd never walk again."

"Really?" the dark cleric said in a mockingly quizzical inflection. "Show me where."

"Sir?"

"Show me where she held the knife on you," Banavor ordered, stepping over to the now terrified young man.

"Uh, right here sir," he said, pointing to the base of his spine.

"I can understand your trepidation," Banavor said, examining the area being pointed to.

"Tell me, Si. Jeffries, by allowing a teenage girl to defeat you, do you feel worthy to walk amongst *real* men?"

Boraton waivered anxiously, stunned by the insulting question. "Well, uh, yes, sir. Like I said, she snuck up on us."

"Well Si. Jefferies," Banavor said, reaching over and removing a dagger from the belt of the nearby Piety Watch member. "I accept your apology."

"You do?" Boraton said, immediately relieved. "Thank you, Lord Banavor!"

"However," Banavor softly continued. "I completely disagree with your assessment."

Before Boraton could respond, Banavor plunged the dagger into the spot he had been shown, severing the lower spine. The wounded young man cried out in agony and dropped to the floor.

"You don't deserve to walk among anyone." Banavor said as a pungently disturbing odor filled the air when Boraton's bowls and bladder gave way. "And, you have completely ruined my dinner with this mess you've made,"

Banavor stared down dispassionately at the injured Boraton. "Still, there may be some use for you."

"Get him down to the temple and put him in holy restraint," he ordered the two members of the Piety Watch, before fixing his gaze on Boraton's friends, "and then strip these two down and get them ready for initiation."

The Piety Watch member nodded and picked up the now paraplegic Boraton, Banavor smiled at his two comrades staring at their mutilated friend in horror. "The Lord is about to give your pathetic, privileged lives some meaning. You should be happy."

He stepped away from the table and headed for the arched doorway.

"Clean this mess up," he ordered before leaving. "I've got an initiation to prepare for."

Mid-cycle bells rang out from the Grand Turine in the Zorian harbor. They echoed across the city and Narian Bay as two hackneys arrived in front of a large nondescript warehouse on the outskirts of the southern docks.

The plethora of city guards and red boundary cords surrounding the immediate area denoted tragedy within. They had slid the warehouse's massive front bay door all the way open, hinting at the building's spacious interior.

Shurta and Vanir hopped simultaneously out of their respective cabs and grimly nodded upon meeting.

"Thanks for the heads up on this one," Shurta said, watching the cold stiff breeze blow about the captain's red hair and jacket.

"I figured the Society needed to be in on this," replied the lead investigator.

The pair passed through the small crowd of murmuring onlookers, crossed the red cords and approached an older Zorian Guard with haggard features.

"What have we got, Sergeant?" Vanir asked, eyeing the open door.

"We've got a real mess in there sir," the sergeant replied. "I've never seen anything like it in my twenty grands of service."

Vanir gave a stoic sigh and cast a distraught glance at Shurta. "Alright, let's have a look."

The sergeant led them to the entrance, but before they could step through, both caught the cloying metallic smell of blood. The two investigators surveyed the complete shambles constituting the interior. Scattered amongst the broken crates and their contents' littered debris, lay twenty warehouse workers dead and bleeding. All showed bludgeoning or stab wounds, and giant pools of blood painted the floor around each altercation site.

"It looks like one massive deadly brawl," the sergeant noted.

"What about that one?" Vanir asked.

He pointed to a man lying on his back next to a badly mutilated corpse. He stared at the ceiling, his face frozen in rage, with four crossbow bolts buried in his chest.

"He was the last one standing," the sergeant explained. "When we arrived, we found him tearing up the body next to him. He started to charge us when we fired."

The sergeant then pointed to a naked woman off to the side with the top of her skull completely crushed in. "That's the warehouse manager over there. We think she was the first to die."

"Rape?" Shurta asked, noting her nudity.

"We don't think so. This looks like pure rage," offered the sergeant. "What in the name of the Gods caused this?"

"Until the Clerria can examine the bodies, we can't be sure, but I'm willing to bet my next cluster's wages that there's Dawa running through all their systems."

It is said the very definition of a fanatic is someone who can't change their mind and won't change the subject. Sorgina Napp, the youngest of the three sisters in the Napp Banja, didn't care if she fit that description perfectly. As a new acolyte to the Derek Witches, she left home several grands ago to join this ancient coven of midwives, healers and shamans.

This powerful, roaming cabal of women were also the keepers of Amarenian traditions and the old ways. Sorgina had returned home, beckoned by her older sister, Tengah, with news that trouble had come to the Napp plantation.

Sorgina caught sight of the circular rooftop of her family home a little after moonrise. She had walked all moonless to get here and thankfully, when she got the message, she had been only a few miles away.

In true Derek tradition, she arrived dressed only in simple robes with a walking stick as her sole possession. Also, in Derek customs, and Sorgina's basic nature, no warm homecoming greeted her when she encountered Tengah directing a party of field slaves to their next task.

"Where is mother?" Sorgina asked, typically austere.

"Training," came Tengah's solitary reply.

The young Derek merely nodded and walked over to the satellite building across from the main house, which served as the matriarch's private training hall. Knowing better than to interrupt a session, she sat down beside the door with legs crossed and staff resting in her lap.

Just before mid-luna she heard the latch on the door turn and she stood. In mere moments, Kennari and Alto exited deeply embroiled in a discussion about proper technique. The swordmaster appeared sweaty and fatigued. In contrast, the Amarenian Kovos mistress looked fresh and tireless.

"Mother," Sorgina greeted gruffly, before turning her repulsed gaze towards Alto. "You were training with *that*?!"

Alto reeled, taken aback by the open hostility. Kennari's face, at first happy at seeing her youngest, fell in anticipation of the inevitable forthcoming conversation.

"Well, I'm pleased to see you too, Sorgina, welcome home. Alto, this is Sorgina my youngest daughter."

256

"Alto Konrad, at your service," the swordmaster said, with his typical shallow bow.

Sorgina remained silent, glowering intently at the man in their midst.

"A word, mother," she said, not breaking her hostile gaze on Alto. "*Alone!*"

"Perhaps I should go and see what they have prepared for lunch," Alto said, before quickly walking away from the tense exchange.

Once Alto moved out of earshot, Sorgina pounced. "Mother, what are you doing teaching a Dag? You know it is forbidden!"

"I am not teaching him. I am training with another master. I will thank you not to call him that, he is our new neighbor and a renowned swordmaster."

"But he's a *man!*"

Kennari smirked at her daughter's vehemence. "So, I noticed."

"Mother, this is serious! I cannot allow this!"

It was now Kennari's turn to be indignant. "Cannot allow?! Young lady, I am a Kovos Master Geta as well as advisor to Lidari and queen! I will train with whomever I wish!"

The daughter's face flushed in rage. "It is wrong to share our secrets with an outsider, much less a Dag!"

"I told you not to call him that!" Kennari said angrily, her eyes boring into her daughter.

"I will call him that, because that is what he is!"

"Times are changing Sorgina," Kennari said, regaining composure. "There is nothing that can be done to prevent it."

"Perhaps not, Mother, but I will not stand idly by while you flaunt the very law that has been in place for thousands of grands!"

"You have nothing to say about which laws I choose to follow or ignore."

"We shall see about that," Sorgina said, before starting to leave. "You have not heard the end of this."

The Mawl shaman didn't care if the humans hadn't bothered to learn her name. They couldn't pronounce it anyways. They got what they wanted in the form of information and she got what she wanted. For every act of divination performed, every reading of the entrails, her power and ability increased.

The human's leader, called Banavor, kept her with a steady supply of humans for her incantations, mostly homeless and street people but he occasionally thew in an enemy. She performed one Zhanbu per cycle, keeping tabs on Banavor's enemies and searching for the one who would suffer the cleric of Pa-Waga's vengeance when found.

A wave of disappointment swept over her when she stared down at the nude carcass of the woman. She lay face down with her entrails pulled out of her anus and arranged in a circular pattern between her spread legs just like the others. Still, she saw nothing. Whatever Banavor's enemy was using to block her search had to be powerful.

She looked up from her examination of the long flesh rope when she heard the door to the basement temple open. Banavor, along with two members of the Piety Watch, escorted a barely conscious naked man down the stairs.

She had long since gotten over her revulsion at their hairless bodies, they were merely a vessel to increase her power. She also thought the Piety Watch, now used as Banavor's private army, looked ridiculous in their red shirts and high collard black capes which resembled cat ears over their heads. She always purred with happiness when she saw them, however, because they always brought fresh people to work on, but she found it curious they provided her with a second offering so soon. This seemed odd, because the body before her was barely cold and she had yet to give Banavor her report.

"Lord Banavor," she said, when the humans reached the bottom of the stairs. "I apologize. The one you seek is still being hidden from my view."

"Keep up the search," Banavor said, directing the Piety Watch to lay out the man beside the dead woman. "Right now, I need to know about the daughter of the one you seek. Tell me about Taleeka Konrad."

With the morning session almost over, Alto felt more than a little frustrated. Being a swordsman, he struggled getting used to working this close to an opponent. To force himself to think close quarters, he began leaving his long and short sword at home and, just like the old days, carried just a knife in his boot.

The single technique Kennari attempted to explain she called, Makamashi Kwarara and it continued to be the main reason for his failed attacks.

"It is not enough to just move out of the way into a position beneficial to you," Kennari said patiently. "That is strategy and you mastered that long ago. You must feel the direction of your attacker's energy. Only then, will you be able to redirect it."

Alto gave a weary nod and Kennari smiled confidently. "Strike me. Any way you wish."

Without winding up, Alto lashed out with a lunging punch at full speed. Kennari spun in a tight outward circle, caught Alto's wrist and pulled him in the direction his fist traveled. Instead of throwing him across the room like she had been doing, she slowed the technique down.

"See what I did?" she asked, peering at the swordmaster's awkward extended position. "I felt the energy release and helped it along its path, pulling you off balance. I can now redirect the energy any way I choose."

Kennari then tugged slightly downward. "I can throw you forward."

She then jerked his arm back, bending the elbow she grabbed with her free hand, and pulled him slightly backwards. "Or I can send you onto your back."

Straightening his arm out again, she slipped her arm under the elbow and pushed upward on the elbow joint. Alto rose painfully to his toes.

"I can also bar the arm and lead you anywhere I want you to go."

To illustrate her point, she marched the helpless swordmaster around the room before releasing him.

"Amazing!" Alto said, rubbing his sore appendage.

"Come," she said, beckoning him over. "Show me some of your in close techniques. That way I can help you feel the energy flow."

They stood facing each other, a little over a foot apart.

"As before, attack any way you wish."

When the swordmaster lashed out and she deflected it with a simple circular block. Alto kept his forearm against hers, following the path her limb had taken. The two masters began snaking their hands and arms gracefully together.

"Very good," Kennari praised. "You are now feeling..."

The door flew open, cutting short her next direction. Both spun in surprise to see three stern-faced Mahilia guards standing in the doorway, with sisters Sorgina and Tengah behind them.

The stocky and almost six-foot-tall Mostas city guards wore red cropped pants, cut off at mid-ankle. A decorated sash, with two weighted balls on either end, draped diagonally across their bare chests. The balls met on their hips and the marking on the material nestled between their breasts indicated their rank.

"See, didn't I tell you?!" Sorgina said loudly, pointing at her mother. "She teaches the Kovos art to a Dag!"

"Is this true?" the lead Mahilia, a ruddy skinned redhead, asked gruffly.

"I am a Kovos Geta and well within my rights to train with a fellow master!"

The Mahilia paused in uncertainty, the title of Geta, equivalent to that of Valorous Sister, commanded respect in their society.

"I accuse!" Sorgina shouted defiantly, pointing directly at Kennari.

With the formal statement of accusation now made, the city guards had no choice. All three stepped into the room.

"Kennari Napp, Alto Konrad," she said officially. "I am placing both of you under arrest."

Vanir took a big swig of whisky and then put the flask away when the hackney slowed and came to a stop. All around him, the squalor of Zor's Seven Sister's Slums rose as a testament of human resilience. Ramshackle wooden structures, some nothing more than mere boxes stacked precariously upon each other, constituted what most inhabitants of this swath of urban blight called home.

Vanir always marveled that, despite the rundown appearance of the living conditions, the streets by comparison remained remarkably clean. This proved true across the entire city, but nowhere more obvious than in 'The Sisters.' The Clerics of the Fire God Verr were the reason the boulevards and alleys of practically every city in the Goyan Islands remained clear of refuse and corpses. Their pyres burned constantly, fed by their roaming carts. They were also the reason that brought him out on this crisp autumn morning.

He got out of the cab and could see three patrol guards keeping back a crowd of onlookers from an open top lizard cart being drawn through the narrow street.

"Two for the price of one this morning, Captain," a patrolman said, passing. "Last time I saw anything like this was when we cleaned out Tiger Town awhile back. Boy, talk about a mess. Those Tiikeri sure trashed that section of the city before they got kicked out."

Vanir ignored the chatty guard and didn't reply to the cynical comment. He pushed through the crowd and stepped into the narrow alley.

He stopped and exhaled loudly when he saw the bodies, immediately understanding the guard's assessment. The naked man and woman, obviously street people, lay face down on the ground. They had stripped the man's thighs completely of flesh down to the bone. On both bodies, someone had pulled out the intestines, careful to leave them still attached, through their severed anuses. The long fleshy tendrils lay haphazardly behind the carcasses, resembling gruesome tails.

The head investigator stood staring for a long moment until the voice of a patrol guard pulled him out of it.

"Sir, here's the cleric that found them."

The bald young man stood naked, except for a long-hooded cloak and pair of sandals. His filthy body had streaks of an unidentifiable substance marring it and he smelled like a smokey pile of trash. He pulled his cowl back out of respect and peered meekly downward.

"You found them?" Vanir confirmed.

"Yes, yes, right after the Kan," he said quietly, continually bowing. "Not the first. Not the first."

"What do you mean, not the first."

"Every cycle, every cycle."

Vanir gave a suspicious tilt of his head. "For how long now?"

"Six cycles, yes, six cycles."

"Six cycles?! A body every cycle? Why wasn't this reported?"

"Only one, only one, today two, very strange."

Vanir nodded in acknowledgement and went back to examining the bodies. The patrolman couldn't have been more correct. This had all the earmarks of a Mawl feeding. By the bite radius it appeared too small to be a Tiikeri or Singa. A mongrel more than likely did this. The removed intestines continued to still be a mystery.

One thing he was willing to bet on, Mawl or not, this act of macabre depravity had Banavor's name all over it.

The Amarenian Citadel of Justice is located near the heart of the capital city of Mostas. It is the primary and highest court on the entire continent. Lesser and more regional crimes were handled in their respective Dors and officiated by travelling judges. Capital and only the most serious offences made their way to the Citadel.

Alto and Kennari sat anxiously peering around the giant circular amphitheater style main courtroom. To their left, two stout Mahailas guarded the large double beaded doors leading outside. To their right, the judge's desk, now empty, sat on an elevated stage. The prosecutor's station loomed directly across the room.

A young High Amarenian, with thick, wavy white hair, pale skin and freckles, stared disdainfully at the two captives. They all knew her as Vakila Coben and her white legal robes, combined with her general appearance, gave her an almost angelic look, but her scowl gave away her reputation as a fierce litigator. Directly to her left, the accuser, Sorgina Napp, sat stony faced.

Across the room, Vakila's twin sister, Affekot Coben, sat next to the accused. She earned her reputation as defense council who was just as ferocious as her sister was a prosecutor. The identical twin's rivalry in the Amarenian courts constituted that of legend.

The seats, gently cascading up three of the walls, filled almost immediately with fans of the 'Battling Cobens.' They murmured excitedly, anxious for the show. Mal decided to sit in the gallery directly behind Alto, where she could hear anything said between counselor and clients.

Just off center on the floor, rose a small circular platform with a railing where the ones being questioned stood.

"Alright this is just a plea hearing," Affekot said softly. "I'll do most of the talking. All you have to do is answer the judge's single question."

Both nodded they understood and the beaded door behind the judge's desk parted.

"Okay, here we go," Affekot said, smiling confidently.

"All rise for Astute Sister Sudiya Blount," the Mahalia ordered.

The room complied and a High Amarenian in her mid-thirties gracefully stepped into the room. She wore floor-length white robes, the same as the lawyers, but her garment also had an added cowl, revealing only a portion of her pale white face.

The judge carried in her hand a palm sized. metal ball, which she held ceremoniously out in front of her. She stepped up behind her desk, scanned the crowd and then rapped the ball once on the desktop.

"This citadel of truth is now in session," she formally announced, before pulling back her cowl and sitting.

Alto noted, once he and the rest of the room had been seated, how the judge's long, straight, black hair contrasted quite strikingly against her alabaster skin.

"Are the councilors ready to proceed?"

Both of the Coben sisters briefly stood to answer affirmatively.

"Is the accuser present?"

"Yes, Astute Sister," Sorgina said, standing.

"Your accusation has been recorded. Does it still stand?"

"Yes, Astute Sister."

"Very well," Sudiya said turning her attention to the captives. "Kennari Napp and Alto Konrad."

With the mentioning of their names both rose.

"Kennari Napp, you stand accused of teaching the hidden art of Kovos to an outsider. How do you plead?"

"Innocent, Astute Sister."

"Alto Konrad," the judge announced, "you stand accused of taking part in willfully learning the hidden art of Kovos.

"How do you plead?"

"Innocent." Alto's solitary statement resonated across the courtroom.

"Very well, your pleas have been recorded. I will set trial for three lunas from now."

"Astute Sister, if it please the citadel," Vakila said, standing. "Three lunas is not enough time to prepare a case…"

"I object!" Affekot said, rising to her feet. "Astute, the Tenable Sister was all too quick to accept these accusations as fact. If she wasn't sure she had a case, why would she be so quick to waste the citadel's time?!"

"Astute, this is outrageous!" Vakila said, glancing over at her sister and then back up at the judge. "I must be allowed time to interview witnesses and gather evidence! This is an obvious ploy by the defense to sabotage my case!"

Affekot all but sneered at her twin. "Yes, and while you take your sweet time, my patrons languish in jail!"

"Sisters," Sudiya cried out with a rap of her metal ball, quieting both down immediately. "This is just a plea hearing. Put away your claws and save them for the trial.

"Tenable Vakila, I am sustaining the defense's objection. Three lunas should be more than enough time. And, if you will recall, I was the one who set the date, not the defense. I can assure you I am not trying to sabotage anything.

"The trial will be in three lunas, beginning at moonrise. This hearing is adjourned."

With a rap of the ball the courtroom became abuzz with the crowd's excited chatter. The sisters never failed to deliver.

"Thank you, Astute," both lawyers said meekly, before stepping down from their stations.

Mal sat tensely fuming in her chair.

She leaned over Alto's shoulder and put her lips next to his ear. "I don't like the way this is fucking shaping up. I'm going to see if I can get some more help."

Alto gave a surprised look but before he could say anything, Mal quickly kissed him on the cheek.

"I'll visit when I know something," she whispered.

With that statement, she quickly got to her feet and took off, heading out of the courtroom. Once outside, she found a quiet spot and retrieved her Larimar talking stone. She placed her thumb on the milky white Etheria shard and thought of her daughter.

"Tally, are you somewhere you can speak?"

"Sure, Mom," Taleeka's voice resonated inside her head. "What's up?"

"Okay, here's the deal, your dad's been arrested."

"*My dad*?!" Taleeka blurted out in shock. "You're talking about Alto, right?"

"Yeah, he was working out with our neighbor and apparently, the powers that be didn't fucking like it!"

"You've got to be fucking kidding!" Taleeka said, before remembering her conversation with Noorim. "Mom, I've heard about this. They take that stuff seriously."

"Yeah, well they're putting him and his workout partner on trial in three cycles."

"Who was his workout partner?"

"Our new neighbor, an older woman by the name of Kennari Napp."

"Mom, what can I do to help?"

"We've got a couple of fucking jerkwad twins for defender and prosecutor. These quims are too wrapped up in their sibling rivalry and can't seem to get out of their own fucking way! They're so determined to outdo each other that your dad could end up getting fucked like a dog in the street! If you've made any Barrister contacts, I sure could use them right about now."

"As a matter of fact," Taleeka said confidently, "I think I can help."

"Whatever you're going to do, make it quick. We're fucking running out of time here."

"Understood, I'm on it!"

As the connection broke, Taleeka sighed and shot a worried look over at Peshk who had just prepared the evening meal.

"Is there something wrong with your mom?" the Picean asked worriedly.

"Yeah, Dad's in a bit of trouble."

"Oh my, is there anything I can do?"

Taleeka smile sadly. "You're doing it right now. The girls will be by shortly for dinner; we'll put our heads together. Tomorrow, I've got some favors to call in."

The table had been set for a feast and her friends, assembled. The mood however, because of Taleeka's news, hardly felt festive.

"You three are now the only ones, besides myself, that know where my folks are, and we need to keep it that way," Taleeka said solemnly. "The only reason I've told you, is because I've got to help them and I'm probably going to need your assistance as well."

"Of course," Barr-Ani said sympathetically.

"An outsider being taught Kovos is a serious offence," Noorim said grimly. "For the teacher, if convicted, it most certainly spells death. Did your mother mention who your father's training partner was?"

Taleeka picked at her meal while searching her memory. "Mom said it was Ken, Ken something."

The Amarenian's pale white features froze in recognition and she slowly gave a startled nod. "Kennari Napp?"

"That's it!" Taleeka said, pointing at her friend. "You've heard of her?"

"There is none who practice the art who have not," Noorim replied. "She is considered the greatest living Kovos master in all Amarenia. I cannot imagine her breaking such a sacred vow."

"And my mom's not happy with the legal talent over there. I'm going to go see Karta tomorrow at the lifting of the Kan. He owes me one and I've got to get him to Mostas."

Taleeka's declaration set off a wave of protest from around the table.

"Tally, you can't do that," Nibira said pleadingly. "You know good and well that Banavor is watching you. You'll lead him right to your mom!"

"What can I do?" Taleeka asked. "My folks need legal help and Karta is one of the best legal minds in the entire Goyan Islands."

"Yes, but he is ignorant of Amarenian law," Noorim countered.

"He's a quick study," Taleeka said optimistically. "Seeing the world in legal terms is a process, despite the individual laws, and Karta's one of the best."

"Please don't go," Nibira asked meekly.

Taleeka dropped her fork on her plate and waved her hands in frustration. "Look, I've got to do something! My mom asked for legal help and I'm going to deliver."

"*I'll* go with Karta," Nibira said, giving her friend an anxious yet resolved look.

A stunned silence descended on the dinner table.

Taleeka shook her head in disbelief. "What?"

"I said, I'll go," Nibira pleaded. "Tally, it only makes sense. You shouldn't go. With my memory and language skills I'm the *perfect* choice. I know it's your dad, but I really think I am better than you for this situation."

"They may need protection," Noorim spoke up suddenly. "I will accompany them."

Taleeka sat silently for a moment, touched by her friends unwavering willingness to help. Her eyes darted back and forth while a strategy percolated in her mind.

"You're both sure?" she asked hesitantly.

"Tally, it's the only thing that makes sense," Nibira said calmly, sensing her argument making headway.

"I agree with Nibira," Noorim said firmly. "She and Karta would be the most effective. Your presence will cause undo peril to the ones you seek to aid."

'Okay, I'm convinced," Taleeka said, a strategy finally composed. "Barr-Ani, it's going to be business as usual for you and me. Tomorrow we're going to attend Zekoff's class just like normal.

"Nibira, when you get home, get Karta on board and have him ready to go at the lifting of the Kan."

"I'll stop off at the university library on the way home," Nibira said, organizing her thoughts. "I'll grab any books I can find on Amarenian law to get a head start."

"Good idea," Taleeka concurred, before getting up and removing a one hundred secor Air Note from her desk. She returned to the dining table and handed it to the Amarenian.

"Noorim, bright and early, you need to be over at the air station. Locate a pilot that goes by the name Dusty. He runs an air taxi business and should be easy to find. Use my name and give him that. Tell him to deliberately file a flight plan for his next destination—he usually doesn't. You three will be a discreet detour. If he balks, remind him he owes me."

By the time Vanir stepped out of Marassa Sajarah's office, half of the cycle had passed and he felt exhausted. The wild-eyed head of the Samine School of History and Lore could be enthusiastic, to say the least. He had a million stories and eagerly regaled them to anyone, whether they cared to listen or not. Despite the fact that he had just endured several decis of historical trivia and arcane

270

traditions, it turned out the Marassa only suggested for him to try the recently formed School of Nocturn Studies.

He pulled the flask from his jacket, took a long swig and then set off across campus. The calm fall air felt crisp, making his lengthy walk invigorating. He had forgotten about the newest school at the University of Marassa, as it only formed three grands ago to process the volumes of information gleaned from the ruins of the Tiikeri cities and breeding centers at the end of the Etheria War.

By the time he made it all the way across campus to the newly built structure, lunch time was upon him, and the halls and walkways filled with hungry students converging on the cafeteria. After making a few inquiries, he learned that Marassa Tarr-La always took her lunch in her office. When the head investigator arrived, he discovered why.

After a few brief raps on the door, he heard from inside a muffled, "Come in."

Vanir stepped in and encountered a young human/Yagur female with long black hair which took him completely by surprise. Marassa Tarr-La sat at her desk in the middle of eating her lunch. He found her primarily human appearance, accented by Yagur markings on her face and hands, intriguing. He assumed they covered her entire body, but the red Marassa's robes left that musing to his imagination.

The muffled greeting had been due to her mouth being full. Before her lay a plate of partially eaten raw chicken. He watched the Marassa finish consuming the whole leg, bones and all. She swallowed and smiled up at Vanir while holding the bony end of the leg up.

"This is the reason I eat in my office. Can I help you?"

"I'm sorry to disturb your lunch," Vanir said, still a little stunned at the scene before him. "I'm Captain Vanir of the Zorian Guards."

"No need to apologize," she said, popping the bony, grizzled end into her mouth and crunching away. "Have a seat."

"I need to pick your brain, if I could?" Vanir asked, sitting in one of the chairs facing her desk.

"That's what Marassas live for," she said, eyeing the half-eaten carcass in front of her. "I would offer you some but..."

"Quite alright," the detective said, retrieving his flask. "I'm having a liquid lunch."

"So, how can I help the Zorian Guards?" she asked, rending the breast and rib cage from the bird. "I hope you don't mind if I continue eating. I've got a class to teach in about a half a deci and I'm starving."

"Go right ahead," Vanir said, taking a sip of whisky.

"So, pick away." She bit down on the breast and a large chunk disappeared into her mouth, punctuated by the crunching of chewed ribs.

"Is there any kind of ritual over in Nocturn that involves removing the entrails?"

Tarr-La's brows raised and she swallowed the mouthful.

"As a matter of fact, there is," she said, now extremely intrigued. "It's a Mawl divination ritual called 'Zhanbu.' Why do you ask?"

"It's for a case I'm working on."

"In Nocturn?" she asked, clearly puzzled.

"No, here in Zor."

The Marassa stopped eating and stared inquisitively at Vanir. "Someone's practicing Zhanbu here?"

"So, it would appear," Vanir said fatalistically. "And they're using homeless street people."

Tarr-La blinked in astonishment. "Zhanbu is almost never practiced on anything larger than a goat. The entrails are completely removed. Placed on a field of the creature's own blood and then arranged by the shaman for reading."

"These are still attached to the body and arranged in a swirling circle," Vanir said, noting the slight difference.

Tarr-La's eyes shifted back and forth while she tried to make sense of what he had just told her. "How long has this been happening?"

"Every cycle for the past seven."

The Marassa exhaled loudly and sat back. "Every cycle, *really?*"

Vanir nodded solemnly.

"Well, you're probably dealing with a Mawl mongrel, and a powerful one, given the size of the victim and the frequency, maybe even a team of them."

"What's the purpose?"

"Like I said, it's a form of divination," Tarr-La repeated, resuming her meal. "Someone asks a question and the shaman goes to work."

"So, with this practice they could be keeping an eye on the activities in the city?"

"Not just the city," Tarr-La said, before tearing the chicken in half and feasting on the dark red meat underneath. "With human sized sacrifices, they're more than likely able to see across the entire Annigan."

"What's the significance of keeping the guts attached?"

"Well, given they're fresh kills, I would say the shaman is using any residual PSI in the victim's body to boost the power of the spell. I gotta say, though, the circular patterns are new to me."

Vanir brought his hand up to his mouth and stared out reflectively. *So, that's how Banavor is staying one step ahead of us.*

"Captain," Tarr-La said, breaking him out of thought. "I'd like to be of more help. Not to mention this new Zhanbu variant is fascinating and needs to be studied. If you could call on me, if and when the next body is found, and I would be happy to lend any type of expertise I can."

"Thank you, Marassa Tarr-La," Vanir said, standing and putting away his flask. "I'm gonna do just that."

Dusty's Air Taxi Service cut a prominent fixture on the Zorian flight deck of the *Putkin*. Noorim had been pleased to find the pilot, Dustoff (Dusty) de Lomen, personable, amenable to anything Taleeka requested and didn't ask questions. Seated beside him in one of the command chairs, Noorim glanced back down the aisle consisting of four rows of double seats per side.

Both her friends in the rear of the craft studiously perused the stack of manuscripts which littered the seats around them, talking softly. Nibira and Karta began pouring over the books pertaining to Amarenian law the moment the *Putkin* left Zor's Air Station Three.

Dusty turned out to be the perfect cabby, with an aptitude for small talk and an absolutely encyclopedic knowledge of the geography of the Goyan Islands. The thirty-five grand old with boyish good looks, stood average height and had very light brown skin. His short brown hair was neatly groomed which diametrically opposed his moustache and very short beard bordering on slovenliness.

"So how is it you know Taleeka?" Noorim asked in an attempt to get the pilot to talk about something other than his tour guide's monologue.

"About three grands ago, Tally saved my ass," he said, staring out the windshield. "I was actually an afterthought. Her mom, Mal and her crew, were pulling a job in Penith over on Moreen Island in the Otoman Group. I had just delivered a group of, what I didn't know at the time were, mobsters from the Silent Partner, attending some kind of meeting with the local mob. Turned out to be an ambush. It got pretty hairy there for a few centis until Tally and that spider woman pilot of the *Haraka* pulled me out of it."

"I knew Taleeka was competent, but I was unaware of most of her past," Noorim said, now extremely interested in the pilot's tales.

"Yeah, she doesn't talk much about it," Dusty said wistfully. "You know, the entire time she was dealing with those mobsters she never lost her cool or raised her voice. I guess that comes from travelling all over the Annigan *looking* for trouble."

"I can only imagine."

"Her family has a bespoke name for a reason. They don't just hand those things out. You gotta earn them."

"I am only now becoming familiar with the customs of the Goyan Islands."

"Yep, 'Heroes of the Realm' is what they call them. You're from Amarenia aren't you?"

"Yes, even there, Taleeka's mother, Maluria, has similar status. Her title is Valorous Sister."

"No kidding!" the pilot said, bobbing his head enthusiastically. "That's *bad ass!*"

In the last row of seats, Nibira paused her reading and peered up at Karta beside her.

"I've found a lengthy passage on the law concerning Kovos," she said, excitedly leaning in close. "It does go back thousands of grands, but there seems to be some inconsistencies here."

"Really?" Karta replied, staring down at the text she read.

"Yeah, right there and there," she said.

She handed him the book. The barrister's brow furrowed and eyes narrowed reading the passage.

"Interesting," Karta noted. "When we get to Mostas, I need to visit their ancient archives."

For someone who had acquired all of her mom's organizational, strategic skills and more, Taleeka always found herself running late.

Today had been no exception. With backpack slung casually over one shoulder, she hopped out of the *Mala*, palmed her Etheria fob and sent the four-seater airship upward to the designated parking altitude.

The morning classes already in session explained the sparse foot traffic. That, combined with the cold wind blowing the fallen leaves about, gave the university plaza an eerie, deserted feeling.

Barr-Ani stood waiting for her at the base of the stairs out in front of the lecture hall, fidgeting nervously. Taleeka could plainly make out her large blue eyes darting from side to side searching for her.

"Yeah, yeah, I know, we're late," Taleeka said, rushing up to, and then past her friend.

"Yes, 'we' are," the Bailian replied nervously. "It's not that."

Taleeka spun back to face her friend. "What?"

"We're being watched. I can feel their presence."

Taleeka surveyed the area and grinned when her focus centered on two men in their mid-thirties lounging on the library steps next door. Both dressed shabbily and one had an open book in front of him he constantly peered over.

"You mean like those two?" Taleeka asked, nodding at the out of place duo.

A quick peek by Barr-Ani and she nodded, her beautiful pale blue face awash in anxiety.

"Good," Taleeka replied happily.

"Good?!" Barr-Ani's timbre transformed from frightened to unsure.

"Yeah, good," Taleeka said reassuringly. "It means they're following us instead of our friends. You know, just like we planned?"

"Oh yeah," Barr-Ani said, suddenly calmer.

"Gimme a centi," Taleeka said, starting off in their direction. "I'm gonna mess with them."

"What?! Tally no! I can feel waves of radiating hostility."

"Ah, what's life if you can't have a little fun?"

The short walk over to them caused the men to grow more uneasy with every step the confident teenager took. When she stopped in front of them, she stood at eye level, due to their seated perch on the third step.

"Hey guys," she greeted cheerfully at two angry, confused faces. "I just came over to tell you your book's upside down."

Shock quickly followed and both examined the tome in a panic. Comically fumbling, they righted the book and both now carried a much humbler bearing.

"Look guys," Taleeka continued in her friendly countenance. "We're going to that building right over there. We're kinda late for class so we're going to be walking faster than normal. Don't worry, it's not you, we're just in a hurry. I can appreciate your position though. So, if we get too far ahead just give a little wave and we'll slow it down a bit, but only a little bit."

Without waiting Taleeka spun and walked off, leaving two stunned henchmen staring at each other.

"What was that?!" Barr-Ani asked excitedly when they walked off together.

"It's like my dad taught me, always keep your enemy off balance in combat."

◯ ◯ ◯

Stovle watched the *Putkin* take off from the flight deck with Taleeka's three friends on board. Huffing in frustration, he turned to the small wiry man with an unshaven scowl next to him. "We have to find out where they're going."

The accomplice nodded and an idea swept over Banavor's assistant.

"Wait here," he ordered, and then rushed off for the ticketing and flight scheduling counter. He arrived in front of the multi-station windows seemingly out of breath and exasperated.

"Excuse me," Stovle said to a bright looking young lady in the traditional green Valdurian jumpsuit, standing behind the window.

"Yes, sir," she beamed. "Would you care to purchase a ticket?"

"No," he replied uneasily. "I'm hoping you can help me please. That ship that just left, The *Putkin*, I left my bag on that ship."

"Oh, I'm so sorry sir," she said empathetically. "Nothing has been brought up here. Would you like us to contact the pilot?"

"No, no, that's not necessary. Where are they going? I may just wait for them to get back."

The young lady gave a sympathetic pout and reached for a stack of papers on the counter in front of her. "

"Let me see," she said, leafing through the stack. "He may have filed a flight plan."

"May have?!" Stovle stammered apprehensively.

"Yes, sir," she replied, not looking up from her search. "It's not like commercial or military aircraft, you know the official ones. Independent pilots don't have to file one if it's a quick pick up and there's no time to."

"I see."

"I imagine that's going to change as the skies get more crowded... Ah, here we are," she said, victoriously lifting the sheet to read. "It looks like a plan *was plotted* to Aris, up in the Outer Zerians. He'll probably be back next cycle."

Stovle feigned disappointed resignation. "Very well, thank you. I'll come back tomorrow. There wasn't anything in there except for dirty laundry."

They said their goodbyes and Stovle returned to his companion. "Get word to our people in Aris to be watching for that ship," he ordered gruffly.

Affekot Coben did not have anything against men personally, she just couldn't help disregarding them as a species. The high strung Amarenian lawyer grew up during an era when they captured, enslaved and brutalized human males as a way of life. It had only been in the last ten grands that things had changed after thousands of grands under the old system.

The reason for the deep-seated hatred of men lay buried long in the past, with a group of enslaved women rising up against their captors and escaping to the shores of the land she now called home. After establishing a colony, they turned the tables on the slavers of the Goyan Islands, raiding, pillaging, as well as taking male slaves. The logical side of Affekot's brain told her a vengeance-based lifestyle is inhumane and unsustainable, but entrenched prejudices die hard.

Now, as she looked down the table at the young male barrister introduced as Karta, she found herself struggling to keep those errant prejudicial thoughts at bay. Not helping her opinion was the fact that he seemed a bit brash and full of himself.

Then again, what lawyer wasn't?

What held her tongue could have been that he had a brilliant legal mind. She kept returning to the amazing fact that he and his younger mate Nibira managed to learn the basics of Amarenian law, *and* specifics about the statute being argued, on the trip here.

Differences in opinion had arisen since their arrival in Mostas last luna, but that had to be expected. The stakes couldn't have been higher and the defendants happened to be famous. This case would have serious ramifications on Amarenian law.

Looking across the table at Mal sitting next to Alto, she had to admit the thing that really bothered her was that Valorous Sister Maluria thought it necessary to bring in legal assistance. It said, in effect, that her skills did not measure up to the task.

"Are you really proposing we challenge what a witness saw with her own eyes?" Affekot said, leaning on the table and staring at Karta.

"Did she?" Karta countered. "I would like the chance to hear exactly what she saw."

"I think you're splitting hairs pursuing that line of questioning," Affekot said with a shake of her head.

Karta's eyes twinkled in amusement. "Isn't that what the law is all about. It sure is where I come from."

Affekot bristled slightly at the comment. "Yes, and I feel the need to remind you we are here, not there."

"We still have a single judge to convince," Karta replied, "just like over there. Speaking of judges, what do we know about the one we've got?"

"We're fortunate," Affekot said, calmed by the change of topic. "Astute Sister Sudiya Blount is known to be fair and just. Still, I think it would be wise if I presented the case."

"Agreed," Karta responded immediately. "I don't think the visuals of me vigorously cross-examining a woman would play very well."

Affekot nodded, thankful of one less potentially contentious point to iron out.

"I don't see why we aren't challenging this insane law!" Kennari said, frustratingly waving her hands.

Affekot peered over at the Kovos master with a conciliatory look. "Geta, unfortunately the law is not on trial here, you are."

"Not so fast," Karta said, the twinkle returning to his eyes. "Nibira and I spent the better part of last luna in your royal archives. We might just have something."

◯ ◯ ◯

Shurta stood casually in the doorway to Joc' Valdur's office, collaborating about lunch choices, when she caught sight of Vanir turning off the Zorian Forum's busy main corridor, heading their way.

"I take it you're not here to join us for lunch," Shurta said, catching the look on the investigator's face.

"Afraid not," Vanir said, nodding a greeting to Joc'. "I just got word from the Sister Superior over at Clerria House. They've got the alchemy reports on those bodies from the warehouse. You're following the Dawa trail, so I figured you'd want to tag along."

"You figured right," Shurta replied. "Sorry boss, looks like you're on your own for lunch."

Joc' grinned. "I think I can figure something out."

The redheaded captain thoughtfully stroked his beard.

"She also said she's got something new on those gutted bodies that continue to turn up."

"I heard Gasata has doubled the patrols in The Sisters," Joc' said, his gaze fixing on the head detective.

281

"Yeah, so far nothing," Vanir said, shaking his head. "The population there is getting pretty jumpy."

"I can imagine."

"Come on," Vanir said to Shurta. "We'll walk and catch a bite along the way."

Joc' watched the pair walk off together, pondering how many calamities the city could bear before they could catch a break. With a resigned sigh, the Valdurian Ambassador decided to ponder the subject over a quick bite to eat.

Halfway on the short walk over to the Kampo Plat and Clerria House, Shurta glanced over at Vanir who had set a brisk pace, matching the chill of the air.

"Uh, Vanir."

"Yeah?"

"I thought we were going to stop for lunch?"

"Yeah."

"So, like, we've already passed at least half a dozen food vendors. You got a specific one in mind?"

The question snapped Vanir out of his brooding.

"Oh, yeah, sorry," he said with an embarrassed grin. "Pick the next one that looks good to you."

They stopped at the next open front food shack and while Shurta ordered a deluxe meat stick, Vanir pulled out his flask and opened it.

"Aren't you going to order anything?"

Vanir shook his head lifting the container.

"Damn, don't you eat?!" she asked, watching him down a gulp. "By the Goddess if I drank as much as you, someone would have to carry me around."

"Clears my head," the detective confessed, returning to his ponderings. "So, you gotta ask yourself, if this Dawa stuff is in this report we're about to see—and I'm betting it will be—why hasn't it been deemed a public threat and declared illegal?"

"I think it has everything to do with the person in charge of production and distribution," Shurta replied, accepting her lunch from the vendor.

"Banavor," Vanir replied, his voice trailing off.

"Yep," Shurta said, taking a bite and then starting off again. "That little shit has wormed his way to the top of the heap in the financial world. Some of the most influential people in Zor think he walks on water. No one wants to oppose him. Let's face it, he's making them an obscene amount of money."

"Yeah, I guess," Vanir said, putting the flask away.

By the time they made it to Clerria House, Shurta finished her meal.

"Damn," she said, opening the door. "Lunch is sitting like a lump in my stomach."

"Good thing we're at an infirmary in case you get sick," Vanir said with a chortle.

After announcing their arrival, a Clerria led them back to an autopsy room where Sister Superior Sararwaan oversaw an unidentified human male being systematically taken apart. The bald, stern faced sister in purple robes closely observed another Clerria in gloves lifting the liver out of the body cavity, weighing it, and then reporting the findings to a much younger Clerria who recorded it.

When she saw Vanir and Shurta enter, she broke away from her supervision.

"I'm glad you could get here so fast," Sararwaan said seriously. "This way."

She led them down a long corridor which connected Clerria House to the morgue of the university's Isarod School of Medicine.

"Captain," she began, not slowing her pace. "I want to stress my concern in the strongest terms. We are getting bodies in so fast we can't keep up with the staff I have."

"Dawa?" Vanir asked.

"Yes, but there's something else I want you to see."

"What about the ones from the warehouse?" Shurta asked.

"The report is on my desk," Sararwaan said." I'll spare you the medical mumbo jumbo, but they all had highly elevated levels in their bodies. All except the warehouse foreman. She was clean."

They could feel the temperature dropping the closer they got to the heavy door at the end of the hall. The Sister Superior opened it and the policing duo shivered when a cold blast of air escaped. Inside, the walls were lined floor to ceiling with narrow six-foot-long shelves. All of them filled with human corpses.

"Wow," Vanir said appreciatively. "It looks like you're at full capacity."

"That's what I'm trying to tell you," Sararwaan said, her frosty breath streaming out with each word. "Most of these are Dawa deaths, some are the murders with their bowels removed. We're taking in so many casualties, it's becoming more difficult to keep up with the number of bodies we normally get on a daily basis.

"Captain, this is ridiculous, you have to get a handle on this situation."

"We're working on it," Vanir tried to assure her unconvincingly. "We'll pass your concerns along to the security council. Now, you said you had something else to show us?"

"Yes, right back here," she said, leading them to the rear of the room. "This one arrived shortly after the Kan lifted."

The body of a young woman with clean attractive features lay lifelessly on the stone tablet. They coiled her intestines and stored them on her stomach like the rest of the victims, but this unfortunate fatality definitely did not fit the description of a street person.

"The Vurr clerics found her in the Shimol Platt," the Sister Superior said grimly.

Vanir exhaled loudly, watching the steam escape his mouth. He absentmindedly retrieved his flask and took a quick shot while deep in thought.

"Well, the Shimol Plat is quite a distance from The Sisters. I'd say our killer or killers expanded their reach."

At only twenty-three, Jacon de Honis took pride in being the newest and youngest trader on the floor of the Commodities Exchange in Zor. He had moved his small family to the High Holy City less than a grand ago to seek his fortune as a commodities trader. The clean-shaven young man with wavy brown hair had always been good at math and trader seemed like the perfect vocation.

Jacon could have applied at any one of the several exchanges around the Goyan Islands but chose Zor because he would be in close proximity to his idol, the financial genius, Lord Banavor. It had been a fanciful daydream of his that Banavor would one day take him under his wing and teach him the secret ways of wealth.

Right now, standing in the head of the Zorian Monetary Council's office, he felt as far from that dream as he possibly could. He had suffered the humiliation of being dragged off the busy trading floor by two large members of the Piety Watch and gruffly escorted into his 'idol's' presence.

Now, with a dry throat, sweating palms and pounding heart, Jacon fearfully stared at Lord Banavor. The beautiful dark cleric sat behind his desk composing a piece of correspondence, completely ignoring him. The two Piety Watch thugs stood menacingly behind the frightened trader.

"So, Jacon," Banavor finally said serenely, not looking up. "How are you getting along in your new position on the floor?"

Jacon nervously paused, taken by surprise at Banavor's friendly deportment at this obvious disciplinary meeting.

"Uh, fine sir."

"Good, good," Banavor said, finally looking up. "You do know why you're here?"

"It's about last cycle," he meekly replied, lowering his head.

"That's right. See, you really are smart. Now you need to be taught a lesson in obedience."

"But sir..."

"But nothing," Banavor interrupted, his eerily calm demeanor further unnerving Jacon. "You were advised to short sell that block of rubber commodities, but you didn't."

"But, sir, my client did well."

Banavor gave a frustrated sigh and rubbed the bridge of his nose. "Jacon, did it ever occur to you that I might have wanted that client's sell order to fail?"

"Sir?"

"This exchange and monetary council serve the Lord, and I am the Lord's representative here in the Annigan. This is *my* trading floor, and you *will* obey every order and advisory issued by this office. Is that clear?"

"Yes, sir, I'm sorry, sir, it won't happen again, sir!"

"Oh, I'm certain of it," Banavor said, an evil smirk crossing his face. "We need a punishment that will make an indelible impression on you."

At the mention of punishment, a wave of panic swept over the young trader. Banavor had an infamous reputation for his creative forms of discipline.

"Yes," Banavor thoughtfully said, stroking his smooth honey brown chin. "Nothing too extreme, perhaps I should fuck your wife? I hear she's very beautiful."

"Sir?!" Jacon said on the verge of pissing himself.

"What, you don't think I'm good enough to fuck your wife?" Banavor asked with a touch of indignance.

Jacon's mind whirled, unsure of what to say that wouldn't make the situation worse.

"No sir, of course not, sir. It would be an honor for you to fuck my wife."

A lecherous smile returned to Banavor's face. "Splendid, this evening then. You and your daughters will be in attendance to watch. Still...

The Vicar of Pa-Waga looked Jacon up and down, his gaze finally settling on his crotch. "I have also heard that you have been greatly gifted between your legs. Is that true?"

"Sir?"

Banavor rolled his eyes. "Your cock, Jacon, show me your cock!"

"Sir?" Jacon pleaded.

Sighing, Banavor nodded at the two Piety Watch members who reached over and shredded his expensive silk pants. Jacon's massive organ tumbled into view reaching halfway down his thigh with a girth of almost two inches.

"Impressive," Banavor praised, not taking his eyes off the mortified man's flaccid member. "I imagine that keeps her quite happy. Tell me, can she take it from behind?"

Jacon could now barely make out what his boss was saying over the rushing sound in his ears.

"Sir?"

"In the ass Jacon, do you fuck your wife in the ass with that monster of yours?!"

"No, sir," Jacon said on the verge of tears.

"Pity, and I'm afraid with the size of my cock, I doubt if she would even know I was there."

Banavor sat back stroking his chin while contemplating his salacious dilemma. An idea struck when he glanced down at his hand. Holding a raised fist up, Banavor glanced at his forearm and then over at Jacon's similarly proportioned member.

"Yes, I believe this will do the trick."

Jacon, paralyzed with dread, could feel himself vibrating on the verge of a panic attack.

"Who knows," Banavor pruriently continued with a wink. "I might just get that ass of hers opened up for you, too. You can thank me later. Right now, you can go home and tell your little girls that mommy is going to be putting on a special show this Kan."

"Sir, I…"

"Have her cleaned and ready by seven bells," Banavor said dismissively, returning his attention to the papers on his desk. "Now get out!"

The two Piety Watch thugs seized the half-naked man and led him out the door. Passing them on his way in, Stovle gave a chuckle at the trader's precarious position.

Banavor saw the look on his assistant's face and set his pen down once more.

"And pray tell what news you have that could potentially ruin this cycle for me?"

"Sorry Lord Banavor, but I just heard from our people in Aris. That air taxi, the *Putkin*, it just arrived, a cycle late and without the passengers."

Banavor paused, silently assessing the news. Slowly, the young man's face went from contemplative to stern.

"What happened?" he asked.

"Unknown, sir. The pilot supposedly picked up a quick fare and was gone before our people could talk to him."

Under his calm calculating exterior, the dark cleric seethed. The Konrad's had bested him again.

"Find that pilot, Stovle," Banavor said, radiating cold malevolence. "Bring him to my temple. I want to have a little talk with him."

With a rap of her round metal gavel, Astute Sister Blount brought the Citadel to order and everyone took their seats.

"Are both parties prepared to bring this matter before The Citadel.

Briefly standing, both Coben sisters indicated they were.

"Very well, I'll entertain brief opening statements. Tenable Vakila the floor is yours."

"Thank you Astute," she said, positioning herself in front of the judge's desk. "Astute, quite simply, the prosecution will show that with great malice and forethought, the accused, Kennari Napp violated one of our most sacred traditions and laws by teaching the hidden art of Kovos to an outsider and a man. Not only did she commit this heinous act, but she flaunted it in front of several witnesses that will give testimony before the Citadel of Truth.

"We will also show the accused, Alto Konrad, was a willing student of our secret national treasure, defiling its sacred nature.

"We will be asking this hallowed court to impose the maximum sentence on both. Thank you Astute."

The judge nodded and looked over at the defense table.

"Tenable Affekot, you may proceed."

"Thank you Astute," she said, taking her place before the judge. "Unlike the prosecution's rather dramatic opening we plan to show that the accusation is completely baseless and immaterial. Thank you, Astute."

Blount smiled and nodded. "I asked for brief and you both complied. Thank you. You both also displayed a civil demeanor. I would like to see that continue."

She peered over at Vakila. "Bring forth your accuser."

The youngest Napp sibling got up from behind the prosecution's table and stepped into the witness circle.

"Please state your name for the record," Vakila said, standing between judge and accuser.

"Sorgina Napp."

"And the accused, Kennari Napp, is your mother?"

"Yes."

"Formally state your accusation for the Citadel."

She stood stiffly with her hands resting on the rails and stared insolently forward. "I accuse Kennari Napp of teaching the hidden art of Kovos to an outsider!"

An excited murmur rippled through the crowd with the formal accusation and the judge rapped on the desk.

"Order!" she demanded and then faced the prosecution. "You may examine your accuser."

"Thank you, Astute," Vakila said, strolling over in front of the witness circle.

"Sorgina Napp, are you a Venerable member of the Derrek Sisterhood?"

"I am."

"Are not the Derrek Sisters dedicated to serving their Amarenian sisters faithfully in all matters of maternity..."

"Objection!" Affekot said coming to her feet. "This is immaterial to the case at hand."

"Astute, I am merely establishing the accuser's credibility for the Citadel."

The judge scowled, realizing the Coben sisters were just getting started. "Overruled, I'm going to allow the question."

"Thank you Astute, so Venerable Napp, the Derrek Sisterhood is known for its forthright nature and service to the community?"

"Yes," Sorgina replied, proudly puffing out her chest.

"And you personally witnessed this offence?"

"With my own eyes," she said, throwing her mother a disdainful look.

"How is it you witnessed this? I was under the impression Derrek's wandered the countryside, going where needed."

"I was called home by my older sister, Tengah, who was concerned, because mother was meeting every other luna with her new male neighbor to train."

"Objection! Hearsay!"

"It's not hearsay if it's true!" Vakila said, her bearing betraying a touch of annoyance.

"It makes all the difference if your actions are based on something you haven't witnessed yourself!"

Blount rapping on the desk silenced the bickering.

"Overruled, Tenable Vakila is within her rights to establish how the accuser came to witness the crime."

"Thank you, Astute," Vakila said, smiling triumphantly. "Venerable Sorgina, can you identify this person?"

"Yes," Sorgina said, pointing at Alto. "The one called Alto Konrad."

Vakila allowed for a dramatic pause. "Thank you, Venerable. No further questions."

"Your witness, Tenable Affekot."

"Thank you, Astute. Venerable Sorgina, it is my understanding that these alleged lessons took place in your mother's private training hall?"

"That is correct."

"Were you inside the room?"

"No, mother does not allow any observers."

"Is there a window in the building?"

"No."

A perplexed look crossed Affekot's face. "Hmm, tell me do you possess the ability to see through walls?"

"Objection!" Vakila said sternly. "Badgering the witness!"

"How am I badgering?! It was a single, simple question to determine her ability to witness this so-called lesson!"

"You know very well she cannot see through walls!"

"I know no such thing!" Affekot said with a shocked expression. "She *is* a Derrek Witch and may very well possess such powers."

"Overruled, answer the question, Venerable."

Sorgina's lips tightened. "No, I can't see through walls."

Affekot scratched her head and scrunched her face. "Then how is it you 'saw with *your own eyes*,' what was transpiring inside?"

"When they came out, she was dressed in her traditional Kovos garb and he was sweating."

"So, you didn't actually *see* your mother instructing him?"

Sorgina's face tightened and she bristled at being challenged. "If it acts like a duck, I can only assume it to be one."

"But you didn't actually *see* it. They could have been doing anything in there. I mean he could have been doing calisthenics, for all you know."

"Objection" Vakila said, shaking her head. "This calls for the witness to speculate."

Affekot spun to face the judge. "Astute, I propose that the entire accusation is based on speculation. We have no credible witness to this so-called crime!"

"You would slander the reputation and word of a Derrek Witch?!" Vakila asked indignantly.

"I'm slandering no one!" Affekot countered. "In this case, she didn't actually *see* a crime being committed. I'm just trying to establish the possibility they could have been doing any strenuous activity!"

The judge nodded. "I'm going to allow the question."

Affekot returned her attention to Sorgina with a questioning gaze.

"I know what they were doing!" Sorgina spat obstinately.

"How could you? You admitted you couldn't see them."

"I just know!"

Affekot paused and stared at the young Amarenian with a condescending smirk.

"I'm afraid that's just not good enough for the law, especially when someone's life is at stake." She then brusquely snapped her attention back to the judge. "No further questions, Astute."

"Hey, new guy, pass me one of those meat sticks, will ya?" Tantei asked, not taking her eyes off her vigil at the window.

Talib sighed and pulled a skewer from inside the bag on a nearby table. He did a reverent swirl of his hand and mumbled a quick prayer of thanks, before handing it to her.

"You know I have a name," he said, peering across the street at the large pawn shop she intently watched.

The operation, run by a member of the Zorian Monetary Council named Katan Kotuttavar, appeared busy. The two investigators had identified him as the next weakest link in the chain leading to Banavor.

"Yeah," she said, accepting the food, "but if I start using your name, you might actually think I like you."

"Well, we can't have that," Talib said with a smirk.

"I know, right?" she quipped, her mouth full of roasted meat.

She swallowed and waved the skewer in his direction.

"So, I noticed you do a lot of short prayers and that swirly thing with your finger, what gives?"

"I, as well as my pops, are followers of the Sun God Santi," he said. "I was just offering thanks for the food."

"You do it a lot."

"I have a lot to be thankful for."

"I guess," she said, returning her attention back out the window.

"Anything going on over there?" he asked, sitting at the small table, retrieving his own meat stick and offering the same devotion.

"Are you kidding?" Tantei shook her head. "That place is busier than a whore house on payday."

"It only makes sense," Talib said, taking a bite. "If you're too small to deal with the Imperial Bank, Majestic Pawn is your next best option."

"Not to mention all the stuff he sells from the pawned shit people never reclaim," Tantei noted. "Most of the foot traffic I've seen have been buyers. Only a handful of people have been bringing shit to pawn."

"We've been at this for the past four cycles. Are you sure this isn't a colossal waste of time?"

"Right now, it's all we got. Sooner or later this guy's gonna do something dirty and we're gonna be there waiting. The hard part will be getting him to roll over on Banavor."

Talib started to complain about their cramped quarters when Tantei bolted to her feet.

"Woah! Okay, didn't see that coming," she blurted with a stunned expression.

The junior investigator made it to the window just in time to see a medium sized airship descend to the street.

From the side hatch the tall, bearded figure of Mukavar led four studious looking accountant types and two uniformed city guards onto the sidewalk.

"Hey, I've seen that guy around," Talib said curiously.

"Me too," Tantei said, watching the group enter the pawn shop and leaving a guard out front. "Mukavar de Oris, he's the new Calden mechanic."

Tossing her now empty skewer onto the table she headed for the door. "Come on, let's find out what's going on."

"Aren't you worried about blowing our surveillance?" Talib asked, navigating quickly across the busy street.

"I'd say that ship has sailed," she said, walking up to the patrol guard outside the door.

"They're closed," he said curtly.

"Tantei and Talib, Investigation Division," Tantei announced, indicating her partner. "We were staking this place out. What's going on?"

Once identified, the sentry's demeanor swiftly changed to a friendlier bearing. "The Calden Commodities Exchange thinks this guy's been playing it fast and loose with some of his numbers, so they arranged a surprise audit."

Tantei's mind raced, arranging pieces of the puzzle. The Commodities Exchange's involvement explained Mukavar's presence. One thing she felt certain of. The walls were definitely closing in on Lord Banavor.

Sorgina glowered disdainfully at Affekot walking back to her seat. She stared straight ahead, making no remarks nor acknowledging the prosecutor seated next to her.

Blount consulted a sheet of paper on the desk before her, and then gazed over at the prisoners.

"The accused will now be allowed to answer the charges leveled against them. The Citadel calls Geta Kennari Napp, step into the witness circle."

Upon hearing her name, the Amarenian Kovos master stood and gracefully glided to the center of the courtroom leaving Karta, Affekot and Nibira at the table whispering legal strategy back and forth.

Vakila slowly approached the Witness Circle with a sly smile. She paused for a thoughtful moment.

"Geta Napp," she said, keeping her intonation calm, but accusatory, "how long have you been training in Kovos?"

"I have been a practitioner of the art for forty-six grand lunas," Kennari replied, her attitude serene.

"You are considered a Grand Mistress, are you not?"

"I am."

"How many students do you think you've had over the grands?"

"I don't know, hundreds I suppose. Many of them are now instructors in their own right."

"And being a Grand Mistress, you are no doubt familiar with the regulations which govern your art?"

"I am."

"Geta, I must ask, knowing the laws which govern you, why did you choose to flout them by teaching an outsider and a man?"

"Objection!" Affekot said sternly. "Tenable Vakila has not proven that she broke any law!"

"I'll withdraw the question."

"No, it's quite alright," Kennari said, totally unphased. "I will be happy to answer the question."

From the defense table, Affekot gave her an uneasy look as she sat back down.

"I was not teaching Mora Alto," she said pleasantly. "And the way I know I *wasn't teaching* was *because* of those hundreds of students I have trained over the grands. This was a totally different situation."

"Different in what way? Enlighten us."

"Alto Konrad holds the title of Mora, which is equivalent to our title of Geta. This was two senior instructors training together."

"I see," Vakila said, icily and unconvinced.

Kennari remained unflappable. "Tenable, I don't believe you do. Otherwise, this trial would be over."

"You have not yet proven your innocence," Vakila said, her upper lip curling.

"Objection!" Affekot called out. "The burden of proof rests with the accusers."

"Sustained," the judge said authoritatively. "Tenable Vakila, you would do well to remember that this is all on you."

"Yes, Astute," she sheepishly said, before returning her attention to Kennari. "Geta, if you were not instructing, exactly what went on in these *training sessions*?"

"I was mostly critiquing his form."

"What critiquing was needed, I thought he held the equivalent title as you?"

"Mora Alto is a sword master. One of the greatest. My comments concerned his empty-handed techniques. More especially his distancing. He was used to a ranged weapon."

"And that required no instruction on your part?"

"I merely pointed out any weakness in his own technique, nothing more."

Vakila stared at Kennari, still unconvinced, yet out of questions. "Your witness."

Affekot deliberately positioned herself between Kennari and the prosecution table. "Geta Napp, what was the reasoning behind the prohibition of teaching to outsiders, especially men?"

"We are very selective in accepting students. Kovos is a deadly art. Students must have the right temperament and natural abilities. The reason men were not taught was because, until recently, the only men in our land were slaves. It would be unwise to teach slaves something that would allow them to kill their masters."

"No further questions, Astute."

Blount gazed expectantly at Alto while Kennari returned to her seat. "The Citadel now calls Mora Alto Konrad to the Witness Circle."

By the time Alto made it to the floor, Vakila was waiting.

"Mora Alto, how would you describe your relationship with Geta Napp?"

"Humbling."

The answer set off a round of laughter, silenced by a stiff rap on the desk from Blount. "Order!"

"Go on, Mora."

"I would attempt to attack her and for the most part I was unsuccessful. She would then point out the flaws in my methodology."

"And she didn't instruct you in any way?"

"Instruction was unnecessary."

A brief look of frustration flashed across Vakila's face before turning away. "Your witness."

Karta, remaining behind the table, whispered something to Affekot just before she rose to her feet .

"Mora Alto, can you perform any Kovos technique for us here now, even the most basic?"

"No."

"No further questions, Astute."

"You are excused, Mora," Blount said, before addressing the attorneys. "The principles have been heard. You may now call any corroborating witnesses, Tenable Vakila."

The prosecution, in turn, called up the rest of the Napp family. All told basically the same story, which withered under cross-examination. Eventually, the facts became clear; no one actually saw Alto being taught.

Once the prosecution had run through their list of witnesses it was the defense's turn. Karta leaned over to Affekot.

"Alright," he said in a defiant whisper. "It's time to drive a stake through this and kill it."

"Astute," Affekot said, standing. "The defense has only one witness. We call to the Witness Circle, Royal Head Scribe Gragir Nalaa."

A gentle murmur went through the crowd and the announcement clearly surprised Vakila. All watched a small stout woman with short grey hair step into the circle carrying three large books under her arm.

"Learned Nalaa, a member of my legal team came to visit you did they not?" Affekot asked, in a friendly yet business-like tone.

The scribe's sour expression broke into a matronly grin.

"Oh yes, the western barrister and his associate spent several lunas with me in the royal archives."

"What were they looking for?"

"They were researching the very law being debated today."

"Did they discover anything of substance?"

The question caused the scribe to practically tremble with excitement. "Indeed, they did!"

She picked up the top book and opened it to a place she had marked.

"This is from the ancient archives," she explained enthusiastically. "Written over a thousand grands ago. This book of ancient law has the passages specifically dealing with today's mix-up."

"Wait, you said 'mix-up?'"

"Oh, my yes, and it's a big one."

"Explain."

"Right here," she said, pointing to a specific line. "The word in ancient Amarenian is Parampara. Which means tradition."

She then picked up the second book and opened it. "This is from the modern archives. The word has clearly been mis-translated to Kayado, which means law. A clear and very distinct difference."

"Learned," Vakila interrupted. "With over a thousand grands the word could easily have been changed to reflect the severity of the law."

"Oh, I thought of that," Gragir said, putting the second book down and picking up the third. "This is part of the legal registry with a record of any official changes to the original entry. It was not ordered changed. It was simply... *mis-translated*."

Vakila remained relentless. "Objection! Astute, I see no reason for this trifling difference to have any bearing on these hearings."

"The difference is hardly trifling," came a commanding female voice from the back of the audience.

All peered up at the last row to observe a hooded figure pull back her cowl. A gasp of shock rippled through the crowd. Queen Omaris Atona stood regally, flanked by two Hill Sister guards in similar disguises. Her beautiful, porcelain white face turned somber and her eyes bore into the prosecutor's.

"The difference, Tenable," the queen said, "is that *laws* carry a penalty imposed by the state. *Traditions*, while they might carry a penalty if violated, are only valid on members of the group authorizing the tradition."

Vakila's face fell.

The Amarenian queen continued, "I've heard enough. This case is closed and the defendants are hereby exonerated. Furthermore, I am abolishing this tradition as of this very luna, so that this will never be brought up again. I find this court steeped in intelligent people, but there is a quality of wisdom severely lacking here.

"Have you forgotten that Alto Konrad and his mate Maluria saved our lands from ruin? For that I bestowed on her the title of Valorous Sister, while he received *nothing*."

Another low rumble passed through the audience.

"That changes now!" Queen Atona commanded. "From this luna forward, men shall be able to hold the same rank and title as any sister. The Annigan is changing, sisters. We've had a good relationship with the Goyan houses for ten grands now. We can either change with the times or be left behind.

"You can expect more laws concerning the inclusion of men in our society very soon, but for now, Alto Konrad, I, Queen Omaris Atona, bestow upon you full citizenship in the land of Amarenia and the title of Valorous Brother, with all the rights and privileges that comes with it!

"This court is dismissed!"

The bed creaked and groaned one last time when a naked Alto rolled onto his back trying to catch his breath. Lying beside him, Mal's labored panting matched his cadence and the two stared at the ceiling.

"I must admit, that was quite the homecoming," he said, finally looking over at her.

"Yeah, I've got a thing for guys that have recently been in jail," she said with a satisfied smile.

"Hmm, perhaps I should consider a life of crime."

"Yeah, I think I prefer you getting out of jail over going in," Mal said, still staring upward.

"There's always conjugal visits," Alto offered.

Moving only her arm, she playfully swatted him on the chest with the back of her hand. "Asshole."

Both snickered, enjoying the moment, when they heard a whimper from the next room.

"Defari?" Alto asked, concern replacing happiness.

Mal rolled onto her side and propped her head on a bent elbow. "Yeah, I've been meaning to talk to you about that."

The swordmaster sat up and glanced in the direction of the whimpering and then back to Mal. "What is it, my love?"

"Alto, she's lonely. She's been like that for the past ten lunas, ever since you started training with the Napp woman."

Alto sorrowfully shook his head. "How could I have been so thoughtless. I will resume my sword forms immediately."

"Alto, it's not just that." Mal reached over and gently touched his leg. "The sword forms are barely enough. She craves the excitement of our old life. We were *ready* to retire... she wasn't."

"What do you suggest?"

Mal sat up and peered into his eyes. "She needs to be with someone who still wants to get out there and kick some ass."

"I don't know if she'll take to anyone else. Remember she bonded with me, alone, when she left the On'Dara herd."

"I can only think of one person," Mal said optimistically.

Alto quizzically tilted his head.

"Our daughter, silly."

"Taleeka?"

"Do we have another daughter I don't know about?"

"An intriguing idea," Alto said, stroking his goatee.

Mal now became animated. "Think about it. When we travelled, she always slept with your blade. And she's got the perfect vessel for her, that Ukko Wood cudgel Zekoff gave her for her twelfth birthday."

"Yes, but getting her all the way to Zor," Alto pondered.

"I'm working on it," Mal said, her eyes shifting back and forth forming a plan.

"Until that time," Alto said, getting up and reaching for his robes. "I should spend some time with her and get her used to the idea of leaving us. Perhaps I will run her through a form or two."

"Hey, where did you suddenly get all that energy?"

"I did not say the pace would be vigorous," he said, stepping through the doorway. "You did an excellent job of draining the stamina from me."

Mal got dressed, made a cup of tea and then settled on a garden bench to watch Alto. The swordmaster elegantly glided from stance-to-stance, wielding Defari through the cool fall air. In between each form, he would hold the Etheria long sword up in front of him and pensively rest his forehead on the pummel. She watched him mouth some words and knew he had begun the process of saying goodbye.

Mal felt a touch of nostalgia with the passing of an era when the squawking of a gull overhead broke the solemnity of the moment.

The bird circled, dove, swooped the swordmaster and landed several feet in front of him. It then walked in a series of tight circles, edging towards Alto, all the while continuing its shrill cries.

He sheathed Defari, reached down and picked the bird up. The animal didn't resist, and Alto plucked the note attached to its leg, before sending it on its way.

Mal sipped the warm tea and watched Alto read the message. She always prided herself on being able to gauge Alto's mood, but in this case when he finished studying it, his face remained inscrutable.

"What's up?" she asked apprehensively when he stepped over to her.

"The note is from my Aunt Motra," he said, handing it to her. "My mother died two cycles ago from a jungle fever. Her funeral is in seven cycles. Motra has requested my presence to pay my respects."

"Yeah, and she seems pretty fucking adamant about it." Mal said, finishing reading and handing it back to Alto.

"Yes, Aunt Motra is the eldest of the four sisters. I remember her as quite overbearing."

"Wow, your mom, aunts, I mean you never really talked about them. Also, and I gotta say it's a little disturbing, blade slinger, that you don't seem overly moved by the news."

"I haven't seen or heard from my mother in over thirty grands. The last time I saw Beleza de Kaiea was when she put me on that Whitmar slave ship. I was nine."

"So, what are you going to do?" Mal asked, watching Alto wrestle with the notion.

"My presence has been requested by a family elder for an onerous event. I must go, but first I think I shall make a quick stop in Zor. It is time to reunite our daughter with Defari."

ACT THREE

Ward of the Craft

Haserre de Goya stormed across the Southern Zorian docks with his fists clenched and mouth drawn tight. It wasn't fair. His co-workers had been holding out on him.

Like all the dock workers, he got his free daily dose of Dawa from the Forman when he showed up that morning, but being a big guy, no one took his size into consideration. As usual, the single dose only lasted until right after lunch. Traditionally this wasn't a problem. Several of the guys didn't want to take the drug and there always seemed to be someone willing to sell or even give him their dose.

Not today. Everyone had either chosen to take theirs or had already gotten rid of their allotment. Desperate, he even tried nearby warehouse six, where the laborers that still had theirs flatly and rudely refused him.

He made it twenty feet from the warehouse's wide double doors when he felt his anger reach a boiling point. He halted and peered back at the warehouse where he had been treated with such disrespect. His eyes narrowed into slits and his already taut mouth curled into a cruel sneer.

When he saw the food vendor's cart by a single office door, an alarm went off in his head and his sanity snapped with a loud ringing in his ears. Strolling up to the cook, busy roasting meat over an open flame, he drew his heavy bladed utility knife.

"Be right with you," the older man in a greasy apron said, turning a rack of ribs, not looking up.

Haserre came up behind him and drove the blade upward into his back so hard he lifted him off the ground. The unfortunate merchant silently fell into a heap beside the cart from which he made his living, his face frozen in shock.

Several long metal fire tending tools hung on the side of the cart and a diabolical idea came to Haserre. Removing them, he slid one across the latch to the office door. He then pushed the cart to the double receiving doors.

The wide entries remained closed because of the cold weather and he pulled one open the width of the cart. An immediate protest came up from the people inside when they felt the first chilly blast of air.

With one door now partly open, he saw his target, a wagon with several barrels of oil and a short distance from it, several wagons of baled grain. The nearest worker, at least forty feet away, had no time to sound the alarm when Haserre pushed the food cart over to the grain wagon and turned it over. Grease fueled flames exploded under the wagon, rapidly engulfing it in an out-of-control blaze.

The enraged dock worker exited the opening to a chorus of warning shouts. Quickly sliding the door closed, he barred it with the remaining two fire tools and stood back, his anger unsated. He grimaced listening to the anguished screams from inside and the pounding on the locked entrance. Smoke now billowed out the cracks and the beating on the door became even more frantic. Many of the shrieks quickly rose and ceased when he heard the barrels of oil exploding.

He still felt unsatisfied watching the warehouse and its occupants burn, unbridled fury raged inside. He tightly gripped the handle of the knife and ground his teeth.

People started to gather and stare at the flames. He knew it wouldn't be long before the Fire Division of the Zorian Guards and the Air Workers Guild arrived to rescue any survivors and put out the blaze.

That suited him just fine. He would be ready for them.

Barr-Ani loved dinner nights at Konrad House West. Great food, comradery and conversation always marked the once-a-cluster event. Being a foreigner in such a large city so far from home, she felt truly fortunate to have found such good friends so soon after arriving.

Looking around the table, the Bailian sensitive marveled at how very different they all were. Noorim Sheed, the Amarenian, appeared serious and formal, but she could feel her compassion deep within, even if she tried to conceal it. Nibira, the shy librarian constantly teased about her weight, proved herself time and time again as the smartest of all of them. Barr-Ani could feel her timidness receding with every cycle in the company of such a supportive group of women.

Then she focused her attention on Taleeka, sitting at the head of the table munching on a roasted drumstick. Everyone at the table recognized the thin sixteen-grand-old with short black hair as the glue that bound them. She had demonstrated herself as a smart, strategic thinker who radiated absolute calm in the face of danger. Barr-Ani could only imagine the things she must have experienced in her young life to earn her the title, "Hero of the Realm," as well as her bespoke name.

Reaching for a serving spoon on the platter in the center of the table, the sensitive prepared to respond to a statement Noorim just made when they heard latch on the front door loudly click.

All eyes anxiously focused on the sound's origin. Peshk, just coming out of the kitchen, reached into Taleeka's backpack hanging on the wall. She quickly retrieved her pistol and tossed it underhand. Taleeka caught and cocked the weapon in a single fluid motion, aiming it at the opening door. All heaved an immediate sigh of relief when Alto stepped into the foyer.

The swordmaster closed the door behind him and then surveyed the table and its occupants. An amused smirk crossed his face when he saw the pistol trained on him.

"Please accept my sincere apology for interrupting your dinner. I had no idea it carried such a dire penalty."

"Dad!" Taleeka squealed in delight.

Bounding from her seat, she raced across the room and threw her arms around the man whom she had now grown to his same height. Barr-Ani felt the waves of love and relief emanating from the two, but she sensed another presence she couldn't see or define. One radiating both sadness and excitement.

The Bailian sensed Alto's urgency and knew he wasn't going to stay long. Father and daughter had a brief, quiet conversation none could hear, but she could feel the wide range of emotions emanating from them.

Finally, Taleeka nodded and stepped over to her backpack. Putting the pistol away, she removed her cudgel from the side holster. When Alto drew his long sword, Barr-Ani could strongly feel the other entity's presence. The sensations of apprehension and enthusiasm, as well as the feelings of love and loyalty, almost overwhelmed her.

Alto kissed the bronze Etheria pummel of the weapon and mouthed a few words, and then raised the blade into the air, pointed at his daughter. Taleeka did the same thing with her club. When the two weapons touched, a large blue spark erupted, and a course of the same-colored lightning surged from the blade into the cudgel.

The wave of power that filled the room swept over the Bailian and she felt on the verge of passing out. When her head cleared, she smiled knowing exactly what kind of spirit had just passed between them. It felt canine in nature and it could sense Barr-Ani's presence.

Father and daughter spoke briefly before hugging and he gave her a kiss on the cheek. The swordmaster then turned and formally addressed the diners.

"Ladies, once again, I apologize for interrupting your meal. Now, I must take my leave. Have a pleasant Kan."

With that, the swordmaster slipped out the door and Taleeka sat back down with a sad smile. All but the Bailian stared at her in astonishment.

"What in the name of the Goddess was that?!" Nibira managed to stammer out.

Taleeka set her cudgel beside her plate and all could hear it softly panting. She gently rested her hand on the weapon and stared around the table at her stunned friends.

"I'd like to introduce everyone to the newest member of our little group. Her name is Defari and she's been with my family for quite a while now."

Banavor peered up at the naked figure of Dusty de Lomen hanging from a beam in the ceiling and heaved a frustrated sigh. He had to admit, the man proved to be a lot tougher than he looked. Although they had reduced both his legs to burnt, smoldering stumps, it became obvious the man would not talk.

"I must commend you on your integrity," Banavor said with a congratulatory nod of the head. "Loyalty to your clients is a trait some would say is vanishing."

Dusty gurgled something unintelligible while staring off in a pain-induced fog. He had hung there by his wrists for the past three deci, ever since they snatched him from the flight deck of Air Station Three. When they started burning him, he figured himself as good as dead, which stiffened his resolve not to give them what they wanted.

"Still, there is a way you can be of use to me, besides being this evening's entertainment." Banavor said.

The dark cleric nodded to the Piety Watch member standing guard by the door at the top of the stairs. He opened the door, motioned, and stepped aside. The Mawl shaman stepped onto the landing and padded slowly down the stairs.

"I'd like you to meet an associate of mine," Banavor said, brightening. "All the way from the Land of Mists."

Banavor smiled broadly up at Dusty when the Mawl joined him at his side. The humanoid cat eyed the tortured airship pilot dispassionately.

"I would introduce you, but quite frankly, I can't pronounce her name," Banavor shook his head in mock confusion and then seemingly snapped out of it, raising his forefinger. "No matter. She possesses a very special ability and, seeing you won't willingly help me, she is going to see that you unwittingly assist me in my endeavor."

If Dusty saw the Mawl's single claw flick out from its finger, it didn't register. He grunted in pain when she sliced his abdomen open and by the time his blood and intestines spilled out on the floor before him, he had long since perished.

The mongrel intently eyed the mound of bloody tubing before severing them completely from the corpse. Dropping to her knees in the field of blood, she arranged the strands while the various groupings of X's and I's began strobing all across the walls of Banavor's basement temple.

The priest of Pa-Waga watched in raptured fascination while the Mawl meticulously moved the long strand of flesh into a large swirl, stopping occasionally and pondering along the way, sometimes adjusting the placement. When finished, she stared intently at the display, and then back up at Banavor with an excited look.

"My lord," she said enthusiastically, while pointing to the center of the swirl. "I have something!"

"Is it Maluria?!"

"No, my lord, it is her mate. He has appeared."

"Banavor stroked his chin and stared intently. "Go on."

She pointed outward on the macabre wheel. "He was in the city a short time ago, but now he heads north."

"Does it say where?"

"The Spice Islands," she replied consulting the outermost strand. "I can't be more specific until he gets closer."

"Well, well, well, we may have finally caught a break on this," Banavor said, his mind racing.

He snapped his attention upward to the Piety Watch member by the door. "Put a team together, secure an airship and, for the sake of all that is holy, get her another street person!"

"So, exactly what is a Defari?" Nibira asked, staring at the cudgel on the table.

Taleeka smiled at the question. "Defari was my dad's dog who was mortally wounded in a battle over in the Barrens about ten grands ago. She was hurting real bad and dad ended her suffering, but because he had an Etheria sword, her essence traveled into the blade and that's where she lived. They were always together."

"And now her spirit resides with you," Barr-Ani said knowingly.

Taleeka nodded at her friend. "Yes, my dad hardly uses his swords nowadays since their retirement. Dad said she was bored and lonely."

"Something tells me she'll be neither, hanging out with the likes of you all," Peshk said cheerfully, clearing the table.

"That was a most impressive light show," Noorim said, handing her dirty plate to the Picean.

"Yeah, it kinda surprised even me," Taleeka said, giving the club a pat. "It's Ukko wood, so it was able to contain her. And watch this."

Holding the club in the air, she gave it a toss and it levitated, causing the friends to gasp.

"She can obey simple commands, too. I saw Dad do it in Otomoria."

"I can feel her love and devotion to you," Barr-Ani said, staring at the floating baton.

"Dad says holding the handle gives you the ability to smell and hear like a dog. She can probably do other stuff too. I'll have to get used to her. Tomorrow I'm going to have Ukko slats inserted in the walls. That way, when she's not with me, she can have the run of the place."

Noorim nodded in approval. "This should come in most handily when dealing with that Banavor person who insists on vexing your family."

"Yeah, dealing with that power crazy punk and his band of religious whack jobs has to end," Taleeka said.

She held up her hand and whistled. Defari sped into it. When she set the club back on the table, it continued softly panting.

"I need some leverage on him," she added.

"How are you going to do that?" Nibira asked with a touch of concern.

Taleeka gave a sly grin. "I've got eyes on him now. As soon as he leaves town, I need to drop by his place and poke around."

"That sounds dangerous," Barr-Ani said nervously.

"It probably is," Taleeka said with a shrug.

Taleeka abruptly sat up straight and pulled the Larimar talking stone on the chain around her neck out of her shirt. Gripping it, a male voice filled her head.

"Talk to me," she said aloud.

The short conversation proved decidedly one sided, with Taleeka throwing in a few, "uh huhs" and general sounds of approval.

"Thanks, Mannee, I owe you one," Taleeka said, ending the conversation.

Looking around the table, Taleeka waggled her eyebrows mischievously. "That was my guy over at Air Station Three. Banavor's assistant just hired a large luxury airship for tomorrow. Looks like this is going to happen sooner rather than later. It's on!"

Alto, intent on not calling any unwanted attention to his arrival, grinned in satisfaction. His ruse seemed to be working. From the Amarenian capital of Mostas, he took an air taxi to Zor, where he dropped off Defari with Taleeka. From there he secured a vedette boat for the trip north, up the Zerian Reef Chain. The fast-moving Ukko wood craft hugged the west side of the reef with its Ukko propulsion rudder submerged deep in the water.

The swordmaster felt a twinge of sorrow when they sailed past Makatooa and he could see the rebuilt wharf. His mind flashed back to that fateful Kan seven grands ago, the riot, the fire, his school going up in flames. He was glad when the city slipped out of sight and Padan, the northernmost island in the chain, came into view.

When the swordmaster saw the fishing village of Kaiea Point on the island's far western tip, he readied his backpack and checked the weapons in his sash. Once he leapt out onto the dock, the boat sped away down the coast to the capital of Honia, where it stood a better chance of picking up another fare.

After making a few inquiries, he had been directed to the small fish market just off the docks. The open-air, covered area contained several long tables lined with fish of various sizes with people milling about inspecting them. A fishing boat had just come in and dockworkers studiously unloaded the catch.

He found the woman he looked for on the dock proper, waving her arms all about in a heated debate with the boat's captain. All around the tables and wharf, several men and women carrying a strong family resemblance, tended to the duties of carrying and selling fish.

Alto casually approached and winced slightly at the pungent aroma, while smiling and nodding at the people who halted their labors to stare.

By the time he made it over to the woman, she had finished berating the captain and now regaled her confrontation with another woman, who he assessed to be her sister. Both measured just over five feet tall with thick features and medium brown skin. Their shoulder length greying brown hair framed scowling faces.

When Alto stepped up to them, they halted their conversation and glared guardedly at him.

"Aunt Motra?" he asked respectfully. "I'm your nephew, Alto."

With the introduction, both women's faces immediately dropped their antagonistic scowls and broke into broad grins.

"Alto!" Motra cried out. "You came!"

"As requested," he said, watching the two women rush around the table.

314

Motra threw her arms open and gave the swordmaster a surprisingly tight hug, and then held him out at arm's length. "Look at you, all grown up and with the fancy swords too.

"This is your Aunt Arreba," she said, indicating the slightly younger woman smiling demurely next to her. "And wandering around here somewhere, are her husband and children who are pretending to work."

She then turned to the curious group of onlookers, who now openly stared at the reunion. "Everyone, come say hello to your cousin, Alto!"

All dropped what they were doing and gathered around the swordmaster and family matriarchs.

"This is Arreba's husband, uncle Osaba," she said, indicating a thin man with short cropped white hair and a permanent dumfounded expression.

She then pointed to the three adult children, two men and a woman. "And these are their children, your cousins, Zarmik, Rodak and Kajina."

Alto smiled pleasantly and gave a traditional, shallow bow. "Alto Konrad, at your service."

When he stood back up and peered around, everyone stared with stunned, awestruck expressions and scrutinized every aspect of him, especially his swords.

"You really *are* him!" Kajina said wondrously, her youthful face blushing.

"Him who?" Alto asked innocently.

"The one the travelling bards sing about," she replied, surprised by his humble demeanor.

"Bards," Alto said with a bewildered expression. "I had no idea."

"It is him!" Kajina squealed and everyone crowded around, bombarding him with questions.

"Have you really been in all those battles?"

"Do you really work for kings and queens?"

"Do you really have your own airship?"

"Have you really been to Nocturn?"

"Are those swords really magical?"

"Alright everyone, settle down!" Motra yelled, her voice cutting through the clamor. "We'll have a family dinner at my place tonight to catch up. Meanwhile, back to work, the lot of you!"

The throng of enamored relatives excitedly, but reluctantly, dispersed with pats and handshakes for their famous cousin.

"Where are you staying?" Motra asked once the others returned to their various jobs.

"I literally just arrived," Alto said, gesturing towards his backpack. "I have yet to secure lodging."

"Eh, you stay with me," she insisted. "I have plenty of room. We'll have a big feast tonight and you can tell us all about your adventures. Your Aunt Bona should be back from Honia by then. She's been making funeral arrangements with House Nur."

Oh, there will be no immersion ceremony here?"

"No, Kaiea Point is too small for a Nur temple. Come, I'll get you settled. Tomorrow morning at the lifting of the Kan, we start the funeral procession to Honia where we say good-bye to your mother."

"It is most kind for you to open your home to me," Alto said when they started off.

"It's nothing, *you're family*. One thing though?"

"Yes?"

"Do you always talk that way?"

Vanir sat back and scowled. He and Tantei, sitting next to him, watched Talib replace one name on the chalk board with another. All six names had lines connecting them with each other and then to Banavor.

"How many original members are left?" he asked, not taking his eyes off the board.

"Two," Tantei replied. "Three dead and one removed after that audit four cycles ago. He's systematically replacing the Monetary Council with his people."

"Does it really matter?" Talib asked, taking a seat across from his partner at the small conference table. "He kept the old guard in line with fear, so he still got his way."

Vanir took a swallow from his flask, shook his head and pointed at the posted list. "You can bet all the new members carry his mark. The old representatives may have gone along out of fear, but these new folks will obey out of devotion to him, and that infernal god of his."

"We're running out of people to lean on," Tantei said, optimism draining from her overall attitude. "His new toadies won't roll over on him. Religious fanatics would rather die than betray their cause."

All three investigators sat silently staring at the board, desperately attempting to craft their next move, when a knock on the door pulled them from their plotting.

A smiling Shurta poked her head in. "Everybody ready for some good news?"

The Zorian Guards stared warily at the grinning redhead's pale freckled face.

"We could use some right about now," Vanir said sitting up. "Come on in."

"I testified this morning to the Security Council," she said, stepping into the room and closing the door. "Then stuck around for the vote."

"And?" Vanir asked, his gaze becoming inquisitive.

"Dawa has just been designated a public health threat and a danger to society. It's now formally illegal."

The mood in the room immediately became buoyant and all broke out into broad grins.

"Finally, a break!" Tantei said hopefully.

"It gets better," Shurta continued.

"Hey, I'm liking this," Talib said, unable to contain his enthusiasm.

"I just ran into Muuky on the way over here. The pawn guy, the one that was audited, Koṭuttavar, wants to talk."

"Hot damn!" Vanir said, quickly hitting his flask once more. "That *is* good news!"

Tantei chuckled lecherously. "Yeah, it's amazing what a few cycles naked in the stocks can do. With winter almost upon us, he probably spent the entire time shivering with his nut sack shriveled up into his body."

A now energized Vanir bounded to his feet. "This is just what we've been waiting for."

He then addressed his two detectives. "Put together a uniformed strike team for each of the apothecaries in town. Seize all the Dawa. If they resist, arrest them."

He then glanced back at Shurta. "You and I will lead the team to take down his alchemist. We hit them first thing next cycle. The Kan will start soon. Get Koṭuttavar out of those stocks and in protective custody."

"Muuky's already got you covered," Shurta replied. "Si. Pawn Dealer is already in a holding cell with a guard outside the door."

"Excellent!" Vanir said exuberantly. "The smug little bastard's officially in violation of his agreement with the city. The pieces are almost in place. Now we can start dismantling Banavor's empire."

This particular Kan fog proved to be cold and thick. Taleeka bolted from one position of cover to another and could feel the damp, dew covered grass under her feet. The well-manicured grounds of the Banavor estate were mostly quiet with the lord of the manner out of town.

Ducking behind a low wall bordering the garden, she scanned the rear entrance to the mansion less than twenty yards away. Her orange, Trinilic coated spectacles revealed the heat source of a lone Piety Watch sentry, standing rigidly by the back door. The house appeared dark and still. In the distance, she could hear the Grand Turine in the Zorian harbor chiming the lateness of the hour.

Quietly she removed Defari from the sheath on the side of her pack, held it up to her mouth and whispered, "Quiet girl, strike," before kissing it.

Bounding up from behind the wall, she launched the club at the sentry. The canine possessed projectile streaked across the lawn striking the startled guard in the forehead, dropping him to the ground.

Taleeka leapt over the wall and rapidly made for the door. Halfway across the grounds, she reached out and grabbed a returning Defari in mid-air. She dragged the unconscious guard into some nearby bushes and retrieved her utility knife from the pocket of her ghost suit.

When she examined the lock she smiled, recognizing it as a relatively easy one, and she didn't see any traps or alarms. It required only a moment's effort after selecting the proper pick before she heard the tell-tale click and felt the tumblers fall into place.

Opening the door just wide enough to slip through, she silently entered the Banavor manor house. She found herself in a narrow pantry with a long hall directly in front of her leading to the front foyer and door. Off to her left, through a wide-open archway, she saw a kitchen. To her right, was an expansive dining area.

She softly padded down the hall and passed a door that, by the smell, led to the privy. Then, a short distance away she encountered a large receiving area on her left. Directly across to her right, the study, the room she sought, came into view. She had burglarized enough rich people's homes to know that most valuables were kept there.

Garish tapestries covered the the walls next to a huge picture window looking outside the expensively appointed, thirty-foot-square room. A sizable solitary desk, with a throne-like chair behind it, appeared to be the only furniture in the room.

She quickly checked behind the wall hangings and, finding nothing, turned her attention to the desk. All six drawers were unlocked and contained the usual writing sundries. The bottom right drawer, however, turned out to be locked and covered.

"That's more like it," she whispered to herself, taking out her knife once more.

This lock happened to be one of the newer models and Taleeka felt a rush of excitement. You didn't use this kind of a lock to safeguard trivial possessions. She sat down in the lone chair, carefully chose a tool from the assortment and went to work. The lock proved decidedly more difficult than the previous, but on her third try, it finally gave way.

Cautiously lifting the lid, she peered into the deep drawer and saw an inch tall stack of one hundred secor commodity notes within its recesses. Smiling with satisfaction, she slipped them into her backpack.

A small black leather bag sinched at the top caught her attention. Opening it, she found it full of diamonds. With a gratified nod of her head, it joined the notes in her pack.

The final item, a large book, looked intriguing. She placed it on the desk and opened it. The numbers and notations in columns indicated it might be some sort of ledger. She wasn't sure what the inscriptions meant, but she didn't want to take any chances, so, into the pack it went.

Just as she prepared to close the drawer, she heard shouts coming from the rear of the house. They must have found the guard or he regained consciousness. Either way the manor came to life and she felt trapped, desperately looking around for an avenue of escape.

Taleeka heard the sound of rapidly approaching footsteps coming from the only doorway and the hallway beyond, eliminating that option. Seeing no other alternative, she pulled Defari from her holster and hurled it at the window.

The large pane of glass shattered with a loud resounding crash. She jumped through the broken window followed by several crossbow bolts. Landing in the wet grass, she took off running. With a whistle, Defari returned to her hand and she stopped sprinting after only fifty feet.

She watched Stovle, still in his bedclothes, come out of the window, leading six Piety Watch thugs armed with light crossbows. She grabbed the club by the end of its lanyard and spun it propeller style in front of her. With her other hand, she pulled out her airship fob out of her pocket, held it aloft and called the *Mala* from its parked position overhead. Now, she only had to hold off this armed, fanatical group until relief arrived.

The first round of bolts, caught up in the spinning Ukko shield, flew harmlessly away. This, however, gave her little solace because she saw the men advancing on her.

Defari managed to catch all of the next round of projectiles except one. The bolt struck her in her exposed upper arm and knocked the fob to the ground. Taleeka winced in pain with the impact that almost knocked her over. The Ukko fibers running through the Valdurian ghost suit proved enough to stop the light crossbow bolts from penetrating but did nothing to stop the force of the strike.

That will undoubtedly leave a mark, she thought.

Now, forced to stop spinning her club in order to pick up the fob, she felt another bolt smash into the outside of her thigh. She cried out in pain and frustration.

While her attackers busied themselves reloading, she snatched the fob from the lawn and hobbled quickly over to her ship settling to the ground a few feet away. She just had time to open the top hatch when another volley of missiles sailed her way. Each bounced off the Ukko wood hull of the craft but one, which found its mark in the square of her back. It bounced off her pack with a dull thud and propelled her forward onto the flight deck.

She kept her head down, climbed into the cockpit, jerked back on the flaps and hit the accelerator. With the hatch still open, the *Mala* rocketed upward to the sound of projectiles bouncing off the lower hull.

Once safely away, she closed the clear canopy and heaved a sigh of relief. She wasn't certain if anyone recognized her, but one thing had become clear; her personal war with Lord Banavor was on.

As promised, Motra had everyone up early and by the time the Kan fog had receded, Alto's entire extended family followed behind the solitary slow-moving, horse-drawn cart carrying his mother's lifeless body. As per local tradition, the sixty-mile trip to the Capital of Honia had to be completed on foot and without stopping. The swordmaster and Motra walked side by side at the head of the line directly behind the cart. For the longest time no one spoke. All that could be heard was the lone clacking of the wagon wheels on the hard packed road winding through rows of neatly planted fruit trees. Alto, who had so many burning questions, broke the silence first.

"Aunt Motra, I had not seen my mother in over thirty grands. Why did you feel the need to reach out to me?"

"That is the reason," she said, keeping her eyes straight ahead. "After thirty grands, I thought you should see your mother one last time before we feed her to the fish. I'm curious though, why you didn't return to her after your term of indenture was over?"

Alto sighed and thought for a moment. "My life was saved by a sword master. I watched him kill six men who robbed us in the most beautiful and graceful dance I had ever witnessed. Instead of returning home I sought that man out."

Motra gave a sad smile and continued to stare ahead. "You have told me *what* you did nephew, not *why*."

"For the longest time, I told myself that I was proud knowing my indentured service helped feed my mother and village. Upon reflection, I realize I really felt abandoned."

"And now?"

"And now I realize how hard the decision must have been. My father and uncle were dead. That left her with no means of supporting herself. We both would have suffered greatly and perhaps even perished if she did not take the course of action she did."

Motra nodded her acceptance of the answer. "After you didn't come back, she returned to us a broken woman. Always sad, never smiling, the joy of life completely sucked out of her. She always regretted sending you away, selling her baby boy. It haunted her. There was not a day that went by she didn't miss you. Sometimes, when the Kan was still, you could hear her crying in her room."

Upon hearing this, a sorrowful wave of guilt swept over the swordmaster. "I should have at least written."

"Yes, you should have nephew, yes you should," Motra said, finally looking over at him, her disposition reflective and nonjudgmental.

"I wonder what my life would have been like if I did return to her?"

Motra gently touched his shoulder. "The road not taken will always be a mystery. You weren't alone in your feeling of abandonment, however. Our entire family felt abandoned by her when she ran off with your father. We hardly welcomed her back with open arms, especially your Aunt Bona. After a while though, we realized she did what she did out of love. The longings of the heart can't be denied."

"Still," Alto said hauntingly.

Motra shook her head and her demeanor became matronly. "Do not wallow in regret, nephew. From the stories you told last Kan, you have led an exciting and successful life. You have a beautiful wife and daughter that share your bespoke name. These are things to be proud of. Not to mention saving the entire Annigan on a few occasions. Just think, if you had returned and not chosen the path you did, none of us might be here."

"I had not considered that," Alto said, feeling a bit better about himself.

Still, he couldn't stop reflecting on choices of the road not taken, the life not lived and a desperate mother's love.

A hackney the size of a small bus pulled suddenly to a stop in front of the lab of Hemicar the alchemist. When the back door flew open, Shurta, Vanir and four Zorian Guards with medium crossbows poured out onto the streets of the Kampo Plat. All around them, students on their way to the nearby university stopped and stared at the martial spectacle.

"Alright," Vanir said, frost trailing from his mouth into the nippy air. "He occupies the entire third floor. Secure it."

The guards nodded and rushed the front of the building, causing the onlookers to scurry out of the way.

"This is gonna cause that little bastard to bust a gut," Vanir said with vindictive glee.

Shurta shook her head and grinned. "You are enjoying this way too much."

"You have no idea. Lord Banavor has been a monumental pain in my ass for the last six grands." Vanir said, following his strike team into the building.

When the pair reached the second story landing, they heard their men crashing through the door a flight up. They passed workers from the second story jeweler peering out the door, curious about the commotion.

When they finally made it to the top floor, Vanir's heart sank and his stomach knotted with anger when they found the room completely empty. Shaking his head in dismay, he paced around staring at the blank walls.

"They must have cleared out during the Kan," a patrol sergeant said, disappointment punctuating every word.

"Yeah," Vanir begrudgingly agreed, reaching for his flask.

Taking a drink, he peered over at Shurta. "I've got a bad feeling about this."

The head investigator then reached into his pocket and grabbed his Larimar talking stone. "Tantei? Talib? What have you got?"

Talib's youthful voice came through first. "The Dawa's gone chief. The apothecary said the short haired woman running point on Banavor's Dawa operation showed up last cycle and confiscated all of it. When he complained about being compensated, she threatened him."

"Pretty much the same story here too boss," Tantei chimed in.

Vanir exhaled loudly. "Okay let's meet back at headquarters and see where we stand."

"Roger that."

"How is he keeping one step ahead of us?" Shurta asked, rubbing the back of her neck.

"He's using Mawl divination magic," Vanir replied.

"Until we find that Mawl we're going to be playing catch-up," Shurta said through tensely pursed lips.

Vanir took another swig. "Dammit, just dammit! This is a giant step backwards."

"A setback perhaps," Shurta said confidently, "but I might just be able to get us to skip ahead, so to speak."

"I'm all ears."

"Earlier this morning I heard from one of my contacts on Lurd Island. They're getting ready to ship out another three crates of Jabule Beans. I'm gonna hitch a ride on a Quartermaster's Interceptor and see where they're bound."

Vanir immediately brightened at the news. "That's fantastic! I could kiss you!"

The half Amarenian's pale, freckled face reddened and she shyly looked away. Yeah, well… we're not done yet. My problem is going to be keeping the Ironmark they send in check. They tend to want to get heavy handed when it comes to smugglers."

Taleeka awoke to the feeling she wasn't alone. Not prone to paranoia, she could definitely feel a warm presence down by her legs. Whatever it could be, Taleeka could feel the slight rhythmic breathing, but otherwise the form didn't move. Feeling her heart beating faster, she swallowed hard and cautiously reached her hand down to touch whatever it might be.

To her utter amazement she found nothing there. Yet she could still feel the presence.

She bolted up in bed and threw back the covers, frantically running her hands over the area. She only felt warm sheets, but her movements caused a canine whimper to resonate in her head and the presence disappeared.

Surprisingly, Taleeka felt no apprehension at the phenomena. It gave off no feelings of animosity, quite the opposite. In a strange way, it comforted her. With a curious smile, she swung her feet over the side of the bed and stared excitedly around the room.

"Defari?"

A solitary bark, seemingly coming from everywhere, reverberated off the walls.

Taleeka's mouth dropped open and her eyes grew wide in astonishment. They only completed the installation of the Ukko wood slats inside the walls one cycle ago.

When she returned home that Kan, she remembered how happy the canine spirit felt when she touched her cudgel to the inside door jamb, allowing the dog's essence to flow between the Ukko objects. She actually felt the animal's spirit joyously racing around the walls of the house at full speed, overwhelmed by its sudden freedom.

The ability to project its presence into the room was an unexpected and pleasant surprise. One that she could see would come in very handy someday.

The next big act of wonderment came when she stood up. A short distance away, on a clothes peg on the wall, her robe began to shake. Curiously tilting her head, she found herself grinning broadly at the oddity. After a few undulations the robe then flew off the rack at her, covering her head.

She slowly pulled the robe partially off her head and peered around in wide eyed wonder.

"Uh, thanks girl," she said uncertainly, peeking over the garment.

The reply came in the form of another lone bark.

Taleeka's mind raced, she thought she knew all of Defari's abilities, obviously she had been mistaken. Her best guess was that with more territory to cover, she could exercise more of her powers. The confined space of a sword or club limited the canine spirit in its abilities.

Taleeka considered this nothing short of amazing. She couldn't wait to tell Mom and Dad.

Taleeka also couldn't help but wonder what else Defari could do?

Alto silently reflected on the wide range of emotions he had gone through concerning his mother, watching the EEtah priestess from House Nur preparing her body for immersion. What started out as a repressed, deep-seeded resentment, gave way to ambivalence, and finally, just recently, a loving acceptance.

A lingering feeling of guilt gnawed at him for not reaching out to her. He realized that simple act might have saved her from the suffering she experienced in her life. The swordmaster also considered that the only way he knew his mother came through the eyes of other people.

The funeral procession from Kaia Point to Honia had taken two full cycles, giving him ample opportunity to learn about her from his aunts and cousins. The opinions, as well as the remembrances, of her were varied. Aunts Motra and Arreba thought of her as a sweet, but tragic figure to be pitied. Meanspirited Aunt Bona considered her a troublemaker who made poor choices in life and had to pay for them. His cousins recalled her as a kind but aloof relative bathed in melancholy.

Suddenly, alarmed cries and murmurings from the end of the docks interrupted the EEtah priestess' staccato benedictions and Alto's contemplative musings. He snapped out of his fog in time to see a dozen men with crossbows trained, swarming onto the docks.

The swordmaster instinctively reached for the hilt of his blade when a commanding, youthful voice rose above the confusion, "Let's stay calm everyone, shall we."

Banavor, dressed in a black, Kell skin body suit and carrying a pistol crossbow, confidently stepped in front of his henchmen.

"I'm truly sorry to disturb the solemnity of this moment, but Si. Konrad and I have urgent business to discuss."

The EEtah priestess scowled, baring rows of serrated teeth and pointed at the brash young man. "You dare interrupt this sacred ceremony!"

The dark cleric ignored the humanoid shark's indignation and continued his monologue, "So, if Si. Konrad will kindly hand his swords to the person next to him and come along with us, we can leave you in peace to say your good-byes."

The mourners all remained frozen in place, surprised by the interruption and uncertain what to do.

Banavor gave a resigned sigh. "I hate to be overly dramatic, but you can comply with my request, or we will start shooting people. The choice is yours."

Alto and the EEtah stared warily at Banavor while everyone remained still, anxiously peering around.

"Very well," Banavor said, sighing once again.

He calmly raised his pistol crossbow and fired. The bolt struck Alto's Uncle Osaba in the middle of his chest, propelling him backwards onto the dock. Immediately, the wharf descended into chaos, with people screaming and running while crossbow bolts flew.

Alto bounded to the nearest attacker, while simultaneously drawing his blade in an upward strike.

The EEtah bellowed loudly and raised both fists into the air. The mystical cue caused the water around the docks to begin churning violently. Long tentacles of water erupted from out of the froth. The thin cyclonic tendrils lashed out from the sea, impaling some of the attackers. The water tips turned a grisly shade of red exiting their torsos. The aquatic tentacles grabbed some of the others and drug them screaming beneath the turbulent water.

Alto's attention focused on Banavor and he moved in his direction. The dark cleric, however, seeing the effects of the EEtah's water-based magic on his forces, quickly slipped away in the confusion.

A henchman thwarted Alto's pursuit, managing to reload and raise the crossbow at him. Before he could train the weapon, the swordmaster slashed horizontally across his torso. The diamond Etheria blade severed the body cleanly in two and the bleeding halves toppled to the deck, leaking their hematic contents.

By the time Alto's attention returned to the waning fray, Banavor had escaped the scene. With the brief violent encounter over, the water appendages returned to their source and a relative silence replaced the sound of the chaos.

The realization of what had just happened descended on the family like a dark cloak. Arreba screamed and rushed over to her husband, his eyes stared vacantly upward, with the projectile lodged in his chest. Her sister, Bona, lay next to her husband who had met a similar fate, with a bolt completely impaling her neck. An arrow protruded from the upper arm of her son, Rodak, and he moaned in agony. Everyone else appeared shaken up but unharmed.

"He seemed to know you," the EEtah said in a growl watching Alto sheath his sword. "Who was that?"

"His name is Banavor and he was attempting to get to my wife through me."

The priestess looked around at the carnage and sneered. "He has made a great enemy of House Nur and the EEtah people!"

Vanir's mood kept fluctuating from fist clenching frustration to pure rage, watching the city go by from the back of the hackney. He had almost emptied the open flask in his lap and took the last giant swallow when the cab came to a halt on the outskirts of judgment square.

He got out, saw the crowd around the entrance to the city's jail and he knew this was going to be a long cycle.

Tantei greeted him first, when he stepped from the small crowd of Zorian Guards. "They found him when they changed shifts a little while ago boss."

"What about the guard on duty during the Kan?" Vanir asked, entering the open jail door.

Nowhere to be found," Tantei replied, following him in.

The Zorian jail changed little since its inception. A large facility simply wasn't necessary. Judgement square with its barristers, Imperial Judges and readily available implements of punishment proved an efficient method of administering justice. Confinements inside were always temporary.

The small entryway led to a short single hall with six staggered cells on either side. Standing outside the last cell, Talib and Mukavar quietly talked while gesturing at the cell's interior. They broke off their conversation when they saw the lead investigator approach.

"I don't get it sir," Talib said, his youthful face haggard and confused. "I mean, there were two guards on duty. One at the front door and one right here. How?"

Vanir stared into the cell. Koṭuttavar, their witness, knelt facing inward right beside the door. The thin wires tightly binding his ankles, wrist and neck to the bars cut into his flesh. They sewed his lips shut with the same type of wire, caking his gray beard with blood all around his mouth. More disturbing still, his severed tongue lay on the floor just in front of him.

Vanir exhaled loudly, closed his eyes and shook his head in exasperation. "The guards must have been the weak link. If we don't find their bodies, it means they've joined him."

Shurta stood on the foredeck of the Quartermaster's Interceptor *Jieju*. The sea spray tingled her skin and her auburn hair flowed wildly out behind her. Standing beside her, the Ironmark known as Mizore kept his intense gaze straight ahead. Like all of the Quartermaster's enforcers, he was an imposing figure, with thick features, short white hair and a permanent, penetrating stare.

The sleek blue-gray Ukko craft rapidly gained on an old two masted smuggling ship they had been following since it left Lurd Island with a shipment of Jabule Beans. The onetime Air Marshall turned Valdurian Mechanic was willing to give the captain the benefit of the doubt. It could very well be possible he remains unaware of the new law establishing the beans as contraband outside of the Spice Islands. If the ship containing the beans headed west towards Zor, they followed a preset route and likely didn't know the beans were recently deemed illegal. If the ship set any other course, however, they would be guilty of knowing the bean's current status. At that point, a safe bet would be they were delivering them to Banavor's new, secret location.

When the schooner turned eastward along the northern Goyan coast, Shurta knew the answer.

"Take them," she commanded and a sadistic grin broke out on Mizore's face.

Once the smugglers spotted them, they tried to make a run for it but were no match for the sleek, open top ship regarded as the fastest on the water. When the *Jieju* got within a hundred yards of the fleeing craft, Mizore gave the order to run up the colors. A deckhand quickly raised their flag, while the two EEtahs stood amidship, in front of the driver, and readied their Yudon harpoons.

"Don't kill them unless you have to," Shurta called out to the boarders. "The dead can't answer my questions."

The much faster interceptor quickly closed the distance with the fleeing ship. Shurta could see the panicked crew scrambling around the deck with several aiming bows and arrows at them.

The smugglers had just enough time to release a volley of ten arrows, which either bounced off the Ukko wood hull or plunged into the waters of the Shallow Sea with a swish.

Coming along side, the EEtahs launched themselves onto the sailing ship's deck to another volley of arrows which lodged harmlessly into their tough skin. The enraged man-sharks bellowed and speared the two nearest smugglers. One of the EEtahs lifted the impaled sailor over his head and shook him, showering the deck with blood.

The sheer ferocity of the attack caused the remaining crew to quake in fear, drop their weapons and raise their hands.

"I'm glad that ended quickly before either of those EEtahs went into a blood frenzy," Shurta said, casually following Mizore and the EEtahs on board.

"Everybody on deck," the Ironmark barked. "On your knees, legs crossed!"

Once the EEtahs verified the full crew of twenty were present, Mizore coldly surveyed the sea of frightened faces.

"Which one of you is the captain?"

"I am," replied an older, clean-shaven man with long, gray hair pulled back into a ponytail.

Shurta and Mizore stepped over in front of him.

"I'm placing you all under arrest for smuggling," he said to the captain loud enough for all to hear. "Smuggling contraband carries a sentence of punishment slavery. The length of the sentence will depend on your cooperation with my associate here."

"We weren't smuggling," the captain protested. "We were just…"

Mizore delivered a savage backhanded strike to the side of his face, cutting short his explanation.

"And a lie is a poor way to cooperate," he admonished with a sneer.

"Where were the beans going?" Shurta asked calmly but firmly.

"I… I don't know," the captain said, groveling.

When Mizore raised his hand once more, the captain cowered. "No, no I swear! We were supposed to drop them off on a remote beach not far from here. That's all, I swear!"

"Who paid you?" Shurta pressed.

"Someone from the Kenzie Plantation paid us. The one who brought us the beans paid us and gave us the location where they were to be dropped off."

Shurta pondered the information for a moment before an idea formed.

"Captain, you're going to keep that rendezvous," she said before gazing over at the Ironmark. "I'm going to need to borrow your EEtahs. After you drop us and the beans off, the prisoners are all yours."

"This place gives me the creeps," Talib said, getting out of the hackney in front of the Banavor mansion.

"Given the way his religion has some sort of hard-on for yours, I understand," Tantei said.

She instructed the driver to wait and then joined Talib on the wide portico. The racket made by a team of six laborers repairing the large, shattered window off to their left, made communicating difficult.

"Hmm, looks like there was an unreported incident last Kan," Tantei said, before using the large ring knocker to rap on the door. "Let's see what Lord Banavor has to say."

Moments later, one of the house slaves, a young woman with a slender body and dark brown skin, and nude except for a slave collar, opened the door.

"Inspectors Tantei and Talib to see Lord Banavor," Tantei officially announced.

The woman smiled and nodded. "Just a moment please."

She turned away and, with her back facing them, both detectives could plainly see the engraved X and I on either side of the base of her spine before she closed the door behind her.

"Looks like we don't get an invitation to step inside," Tantei noted with a smirk.

"Just as well," Talib said, when the door opened and Stovle stepped outside.

"What can we do for the Zorian..." the seneschal of Pa-Waga halted his greeting upon recognizing Talib. "Inspector Talib, how good to see you again. How's your father?"

"He died," Talib said bitterly.

Stovle shook his head and pursed his lips. "It's a pity you couldn't get the prompt medical attention he needed."

Talib's face flushed and his fists clenched. He started to lunge for Stovle but Tantei's arm streaked out in front of him and blocked his path, preventing it.

"We're not here to chat with the help," Tantei said demeaningly. "Go get your boss."

Stovle remained unphased and gave a smug, superior smile. "Lord Banavor is abroad on business. He is expected to return tomorrow."

Tantei looked at him suspiciously while Talib silently glowered with his fists still clenched.

"If Banavor's out of town what happened to the Dawa?" Tantei demanded.

"The moment the council declared it illegal, I ordered the operation shut down and any product left at the apothecary shops removed and destroyed."

"*You* ordered it?" Tantei asked, clearly unconvinced.

"Yes, as Lord Banavor's assistant, I have been entrusted with the day to day running of things when the master is away. We, of course, want to be in compliance with the law."

"But of course," Tantei replied, sarcasm dripping from her words.

An uneasy silence descended on the conversation and both sides stood staring at each other for a moment.

"Please inform Lord Banavor of our visit and to expect more visits," Tantei said, finally breaking the tension.

"Indeed, I will inspector," Stovle said with a mockingly pleasant emphasis.

The two sleuths had walked halfway back to the cab when Stovle called out cheerfully above the noisy repairs. "So good to see you again, Inspector Talib. Sorry to hear about your father."

Talib abruptly halted and started to turn, when Tantei grabbed him by the arm. "Come on new guy, get back in the hackney."

Talib stared silently out the window, scowling as they left the grounds.

"He was baiting you," Tantei said, glancing over at her fuming partner. "You can't let them get to you like that. It clouds your judgement."

"You didn't believe him, did you?" Talib said, continuing his brooding stare.

Tantei scoffed loudly. "A follower of Pa-Waga voluntarily getting rid of a highly profitable commodity? Do I look like I just fell off the turnip wagon?"

Through her spyglass, Shurta watched the lone wagon carrying six men approach the two wooden crates of Jabule Beans sitting on the white sand beach. She lay on the crest of a small dune amongst a large patch of waving sea oats and had an unobstructed view of the deserted coastline stretching off in both directions. The two EEtah's waited submerged just offshore, keeping an eye on the crates.

When the wagon stopped, the six passengers jumped out and muscled the crates into the back of the open top bed. Once loaded, they hopped back in and the wagon lumbered off down the beach.

She followed the wagon on the opposite side of the line of dunes and she knew the EEtahs ran the beach from under the water just in case another boat was involved. The lizard drawn wagon plodded through the soft sand for another two hundred yards to where the beach became narrow and rocky. When the shoreline became comprised of large rocks and boulders, an inlet opened up on their right.

A small hamlet of five single-story, wooden buildings surrounded a covered well in the deepest part of the inlet, all but invisible to any passing watercraft. Just beyond the hamlet, encircling the inlet, the tree line of a wooded terrain isolated the buildings from the land.

Shurta noted the considerable amount of activity for such a tiny, remote outpost. Retrieving her field glass once more and kneeling behind some bushes, she poked the extended end through the foliage. Shurta counted twenty men moving boxes from two small open-air boats out to several other parked wagons. The wagon she had been following rumbled noisily over the rocky ground where it pulled up beside the other parked carts.

She smiled in satisfaction when the bald, bearded figure of Hemicar exited one of the buildings next to the petite Tumuh. The two appeared engaged in a conversation walking over to inspect the latest shipment.

"Got ya," she whispered to herself.

Putting her eyeglass away, she traded it for her Mark 7 pistol and cocked it. She quietly moved through the wooded area and came up behind the building closest to the trees.

Shurta felt ready and the EEtah's knew to wait for her attack before charging up from the water. She gave them standing orders to kill any of the henchmen workers who resisted but spare the leaders for questioning. She knew Tumuh, a full acolyte of Banavor probably would not talk. The alchemist, however, was another story.

Pulling a small orange Trinilic grenade from the side pouch of her ghost suit, she unlocked the cap and pushed down on the plunger underneath. When the Trinilic core met the body of the grenade's interior, the two volatile Etheria crystals began to get hot and spark. The Valdurian mechanic quickly threw the magical bomb at the back of the structure twenty feet away. The orange orb silently exploded on contact, setting the rear of the wooden structure ablaze.

Soon after, a column of smoke billowed skyward. She heard screams and shouts from the front of the compound.

Then, the roar of the man-sharks charging ashore rose above the commotion in the complex.

When the first two thugs came into view, Shurta leaped from the bushes and fired. The Mark 7 pistol misfired and the bolt didn't launch. She looked down and saw a twig stuck in the triggering mechanism. The thugs, now seeing her in their path, raised their swords and charged her. Her thick fingers struggled to get a grip on the small branch. She looked up and could see the whites of their eyes and the yellow of their smiling teeth, as they closed within striking distance.

Shurta finally yanked the branch free and pulled the trigger. She felt the reassuring kick of it releasing the Na-Kab Carbon bolt. The slug hit the one in the lead just below the ribcage and vaporized his entire lower half. The thug behind him had no time to be grossed out at being sprayed with the contents of his comrade's bowels. The bolt, continuing at its incredible velocity, blew a massive hole through his chest and then blasted several tree trunks into splinters behind him.

Two in one shot, she congratulated herself, *that'll be good for bragging rights over a tankard of ale.*

Down by the water she could hear the pandemonium of combat, punctuated by the EEtah's bellows.

She bolted through the compound and saw another goon fleeing the combat, heading her way with sword in hand. Not bothering to aim or slow down, she raised the pistol and fired. The projectile struck square in the chest, obliterating the upper half of his body before blowing out part of the wall behind him. His lower torso continued running for a couple steps, like a mobile fountain of blood and shit, before tumbling forward and spilling its entrails across the ground.

Through the ruins of the wall, she saw a dozen dead bodies on the rocky ground down by the water. One of the EEtahs finished running a man through, while the other held Tumuh, Hemicar and the remaining four blood-soaked survivors at harpoon point. Seeing the situation well in hand, she slowed to a determined walk and lowered her weapon.

"You are all under arrest!" she proclaimed loudly.

Shurta stepped over to the alchemist and Banavor's point person. "Especially, *you two*."

Tumuh's attractive features contorted into a maniacal scowl. "You have no power over me! I serve a mighty god!"

"Glad to hear it," Shurta said with a bored expression. "Why don't you go shake hands with him."

Shurta quickly raised the pistol and pulled the trigger. Tumuh's petite frame completely exploded, spraying the area crimson, leaving only her two feet still standing. Hemicar's eyes went wide in horror and his blood-spattered body trembled violently.

"Have I made myself clear?" she asked over the chuckling EEtahs and the crackling of the burning building.

All stood paralyzed in silent shock.

"Good," she said holstering her weapon, and then addressed the man-sharks. "Get them bound and in the boats. I'm going to finish off the rest of this operation."

"Yes ma'am," one said, watching her heading towards the nearest building and pull another Trinilic grenade from her side pouch.

When the skyline of Aris came into view, Taleeka saw Nibira heave a sigh of relief from the corner of her eye.

"We're almost there," Taleeka said calmingly.

"I'm sorry, it's no reflection on your piloting. I'm just not comfortable when I can't see land."

"You've flown before," Taleeka reasoned.

"Yes," Nibira admitted, "and you'll remember I always had something to occupy me. This time, not so much."

Taleeka gave a sympathetic smile and banked the *Mala* gently to the west over the massive docks of the Aramos ancestral capital and up the mouth of the Vakai River. The city hummed with life on either side of the wide waterway. There was a steady flow of transport barges below bringing harvested agriculture from the interior as well as transporting goods and people.

When they reached Guardian Bridge, leading from the bustling central Baka Sector to the restricted, sparsely populated Aramos Sector, she turned the craft north. The landscape below transformed. Dotted with large estates and sprawling, well-manicured lawns, the area screamed wealth. Up ahead, the Aramos Palace and grounds loomed on the outskirts of the elite neighborhood and city itself,

"Do you think he'll see us?" Nibira asked, peering out at the palace as the airship settled to the ground.

"Oh, he'll see us," Taleeka said confidently, watching two Forsvara Guards heading their way. "My name all but guarantees that and I'm pretty sure once he's informed of what you discovered, he'll hear us out. Whether it will do any good or not, well, that remains to be seen."

Taleeka popped the craft's canopy, grabbed her backpack and jumped out onto the ground just as the soldiers came up on them. Both brandished medium crossbows.

"This is a restricted area. State your business!" One said gruffly.

Taleeka remained unruffled. "Taleeka Konrad to see Cedar Aramos."

The sentry paused upon hearing the bespoke name. "Do you have an appointment?"

"No," Taleeka said assertively. "But we have a matter of the utmost importance for him."

"Lord Cedar is a private person and sees no one without an appointment!"

"Look, humor me," Taleeka reasoned. "Just tell him I'm here and that I've got information on the council and Banavor. Believe me, he's going to want to hear this."

The guard wavered, and then reluctantly nodded for them to follow. He led them up to the wide portico with the other guard trailing behind them.

"Wait here," he ordered, before disappearing through the ornate double doors.

He returned a few moments later and led them through the opulent interior to another set of double doors. He knocked respectfully and then opened one and the two teens stepped into a spacious library, lined floor to ceiling with books. A massive window on the far wall looked out onto the grounds, with a desk and reading station in front of it.

Nibira looked around in reverential awe at the private library and Taleeka focused on the room's lone occupant, a thin, well-dressed man with short grey hair and beard who ignored the pair. Instead, he inspected a book he pulled off one of the shelves.

"They said you had information of the *utmost importance* for me," he said distantly, not looking up.

"Uh, yes, Imperia," Taleeka said, realizing her sudden slight nervousness.

"I am not an Imperia anymore," he said, returning the book to the shelf. "I am now merely a private citizen."

"Yeah, about that," Taleeka said, taking off her pack and feeling her confidence return. "How would you like your old job back?"

This caused the ousted head of the Zorian Monetary Council to finally look over at them.

"They can keep it!" his reply dripped with scorn. "As far as I'm concerned, every one of those spineless council members, as well as an Imperial Judge or two, can be fed to the EEtah's. And don't get me started on that disgusting little freak that now heads it."

"You don't have to worry about the council members," Taleeka replied assertively. "Most of them are dead, killed by the disgusting little freak you refer to."

"Speaking of which," she said, pulling out the ledger. "Banavor's personal ledger has come into my possession, and it has some entries you're going to want to see."

Cedar's eyes widened in surprise and then narrowed suspiciously. "How did you get ahold of that?"

Taleeka shrugged. "What can I say. I've got a knack for getting into places."

"Very well, young lady, you have my attention."

Taleeka gave a sly smile and handed the tome to Nibira. "My friend Nibira has been studying it since I got it. She's the one that found the fun parts."

Nibira walked over and laid the book down on the desk while Cedar and Taleeka gathered around.

"Okay." Nibira began opening the book to a page she had marked. "I'm not going to pretend to know anything about accounting or finance, but the notation on the individual entries caught my attention."

She then pointed to several entries at various positions on the page. "Those are the names of Imperial Judges and that's a lot of money being paid out to them."

"He's got half a dozen Imperial Judges in his pocket!" Cedar gasped. "No wonder he gets away with whatever he wants."

"Yep, they're paid regularly, every quinte," she said with an accomplished grin, "and it gets better."

Nibira excitedly opened to a marked page in the middle of the book. "Banavor had you brought up on charges seven grands ago."

"A day I will not soon forget," Cedar said resentfully.

"Well, here's the page for that quinte. Look, here's his normal payment but here, two cycles before your trial, is an additional payment." Nibira peered up at a very concerned Cedar. "You were sandbagged, sir. This proves it. I'm sure there's a lot more things in here which, frankly, are beyond my expertise."

"But not mine," Cedar said with an air of self-assuredness. "Leave this with me. I'll study it. Come back tomorrow and I'll let you know what I find."

"You bet," Taleeka said, nodding.

"The guards will see you out," he said, returning his attention to the ledger.

"And by the way," he added when they opened the door. "Mz. Konrad, Nibira, thank you."

"*You bet!*" Taleeka enthusiastically repeated.

Walking over to her airship, Taleeka glanced over at her friend. "Well, it looks like we're spending the Kan in Aris."

"Sounds like a golden opportunity to experience this city's culinary scene," Nibira said enthusiastically.

"My friend, you are reading my mind," Taleeka said, climbing into the cockpit.

When Taleeka and Nibira returned to the Aramos palace the reception was decidedly warmer than their first visit. Cedar Aramos seemed excited to see them and, by the stacks of handwritten notes beside the open ledger, he had been busy all of the Kan.

"This is fascinating!" Cedar said enthusiastically. "It gives a complete picture of his entire operation. There are so many tentacles into so many pies that without this we would have been hard pressed to untangle them."

"So, you're saying things don't add up or they're out of balance?" Taleeka innocently asked.

"Oh, my no," Cedar reverentially replied. "This is perfectly in balance and all the numbers add up beautifully.

"In fact, this is one of the most meticulous set of books I've ever audited. It details the scope of his operation and the ingenious ways he's generating income. He's found a way to get a cut off of practically everything that comes through the Zorian docks. That's not necessarily illegal, of course, but I'm no barrister.

"What *is* illegal, besides the judges he has in his pocket, is his cut of the smuggled goods traded around the western Goyan Islands. He's also started reaching out to the eastern agricultural islands."

"Yeah," Taleeka interjected. "My mom and dad shut down his plans to steal some sizable mineral rights on Wou-Late' Island."

"Yes, I know," Cedar confirmed. "I saw the entries for that little incident. You'll be pleased to know the thwarting of those plans cost him dearly."

Taleeka chuckled. "Couldn't happen to a nicer guy,"

"He's also getting a tithing cut every quinte from all businesses owned by a follower of Pa-Waga," Cedar continued, "and those numbers are growing. Then, there's the Piety Watch. He's increased its funding and it looks like he's building a private army of zealots under his sole command. It all sounds like organized crime to me and from what I understand, that's always been frowned upon over in Zor. He must be stopped before his people outnumber the city guards. We need to get this, and me, in front of an Imperial Judge."

"But he's paying them off!" Nibira said in exasperation.

"Not all of them," Cedar corrected, "and we've got a list of the ones he controls. My suggestion is that we go straight to the top, Grand Justice Epaile. His name is not on the list and I'm sure he's going to be very interested in the way some of his justices are supplementing their income."

"I'd say we better get moving on that," Taleeka said sternly. "The instant he finds out that ledger is missing he's going to panic and turn this town inside out to get it back, and he's not going to be gentle about it."

Through the Kan fog, Banavor watched the wagon containing five Piety Watch thugs pull to a stop in front of 2300 Kasada Drive on the upper Tuath Plat in Zor. All five quickly got out and the dark cleric stepped up to greet them.

"There's no one home," he said ominously. "The person who lives here stole from me and we are here to retrieve my belongings. I want us in and out quickly. You are looking for a ledger book and a small bag of diamonds."

On the outside Banavor exuded his usual calm deportment. Inside, however, he seethed with anger and more than a little concern. The ledger more than the diamonds needed to be found. His Mawl shaman identified the Konrad woman's daughter as the culprit.

Without further instruction he reached into his pocket and pulled out an oblong green Etheria shard with red striations. Examining the smooth featureless wooden door, he placed the crystal in the vicinity of where a latch would normally be and nothing happened. Furrowing his brow, he moved the Agress crystal around the immediate area with no results.

"Shall I kick the door in Lord Banavor?" the largest of the five, a tall burley acolyte, offered.

Banavor peered over at him with a mockingly amused expression and stepped aside gesturing toward the secured barrier. The man swept back his cape, puffed his chest and lashed out with a savage kick. The instant his heavy boot contacted the wooden surface, he found himself repelled backwards by an unseen force onto his back in the street, groaning in pain.

"It's Ukko wood," Banavor admonished, leaning over the prone figure. "Now, if you're finished with this line of buffoonery, I will proceed."

Placing the Etheria crystal back against the door, he addressed the rest of his men while the fallen one got to his feet. "We're not dealing with street people here. She doesn't carry a bespoke name for no reason. So, stay sharp."

Running the stone around the entire edge of the door, he heard the tell-tale click when he passed it along the top and the door cracked open.

"Fan out, search everywhere," he ordered.

The Piety Watch quickly entered and disbursed with Banavor bringing up the rear. The moment the priest of Pa-Waga entered the home, he heard the growling that seemed to emanate from everywhere and he sensed something most certainly amiss.

"Quick, but thorough," he called out just before he heard one of his men cry out from the kitchen.

He rushed over to the archway leading into the food prep area but froze in shock when the knife drawer on the opposite side of the room suddenly opened and the sharpened utensils flew out, seemingly on their own. They targeted a thickly muscled man with a bald head, already wounded with a large chef's knife protruding from his arm.

The canine growling and snarling grew more pronounced and seemed to come from everywhere, as Defari's essence raced through the newly fitted Ukko wood slats in the walls.

Banavor heard a loud crash and a howl of pain, He spun to see an interior door rapidly opening and closing, battering another of his henchmen.

"The house is alive!" one called out from the living area.

A small metal statue flew off the mantle of the fireplace and struck him on the side of his head. He dropped to the floor in a silent heap.

Banavor's attention, pulled in several directions, began to crack. He could do nothing but watch, as everyday items lashed out all over the residence, punishing the trespassers. When a letter opener sped past his head, narrowly missing him, he had to admit defeat.

"Grab the fallen and let's get out of here while we can!" he called out before heading for the exit.

It was now clear to the dark cleric that other, perhaps more drastic measures would be necessary.

Joier de Zor happened to be one of the High Holy City's prominent jewelers. The thin, clean-shaven man with a head full of short blond hair was known for his meticulous eye and attention to detail. His shop on the outskirts of the upscale Bogat Plat served the city's elite, as well as some more nefarious citizens, in his constant pursuit of quality product.

When a half dozen diamonds came into his possession with the same color, cut and clarity matching a group he had procured for Lord Banavor several clusters ago, he naturally became suspicious and reported it.

"You say these came in late last cycle," Banavor asked holding one of the gems aloft and examining it.

"Yes, Lord Banavor. He said his name was Betoro and that he needed money to buy passage out of town. I know all of the high-end jewel thieves and didn't recognize him."

"And this was all he had?"

"Yes, lord, but he indicated he had more."

"I see," Banavor said.

He scooped up the remaining jewels and put them in his pocket. Joier's eyes nervously followed the gems into the dark cleric's pouch but he said nothing.

"I made him an unusually low offer and was quite surprised when he immediately took it. He seemed very nervous."

"What did he look like?"

"Older guy, my height and build, bald, clean shaven."

Banavor nodded. "Very well. You were right in contacting me. The Lord will bless your loyalty. I trust you will alert me immediately if he returns."

"Of course, lord, but he did say he was leaving town."

Banavor gave a knowing grin. "Yes, many people say many things. Let me know if he returns."

"Yes, my lord."

Banavor nodded his good-bye and headed for the front door with Stovle by his side.

"Uh, lord," Joier said meekly, when Stovle opened the door for his boss.

Banavor paused and peered back at the intimidated jeweler. "Yes, Joier?"

"Uh, sir, about my compensation for purchasing the diamonds. As I said, it wasn't much but..."

"Joier," Banavor said disappointedly. "Your reward comes in the form of prosperity from the Lord. Rejoice, you serve a mighty god."

"Yes, lord," he said, sounding quite defeated.

The pair stepped out onto the street where they joined the two Piety Watch bodyguards just outside.

"Get to our people on both the north and south docks, as well as the air station," Banavor ordered Stovle. "I'm going to get these diamonds over to our Mawl soothsayer and see if she can locate the rest of them. Hopefully, if we find them, we find my ledger."

"I'm really worried about Tally and Nibira," Barr-Ani said, shifting her textbooks from under one arm to the other. "I feel this dark cloud trying to surround them."

Noorim sympathetically glanced over at her Bailian friend's concerned expression.

"I understand your dismay," Noorim replied brushing aside her single braid of jet-black hair, "but our compatriots are more than capable of taking care of themselves. Taleeka won't allow anything bad to happen."

"Yes, but this is different, it's growing in size and becoming more aggravated."

The Amarenian stared thoughtfully down at the rising Kan fog, now up to their knees. With luck, they would make their way across campus to the dorm building before the entire university became completely socked in.

"I could not help but notice you were distracted in class. Is your trepidation the reason?"

"Partially," Barr-Ani replied. "It's also because Marassa Smuka is really boring. She's got that low, sing-song voice that can put you to sleep in no time. I remember my first class with her I thought…"

Noorim stopped listening and concentrated on the shadows cast through the fog on the wall just within her range of vision. They appeared to be several humanoid figures with cat ears protruding from the top of their heads.

She recognized them as Piety Watch and silently stepped ahead of Barr-Ani to shield her.

"Excuse us ladies," one said, sounding very youthful. "Do you have a centi to talk with us about our Lord and prosperitor, Pa-Waga?"

"We have no time to talk about your god," Noorim said, watching six caped figures spread out in front of them.

"But believing in him ensures your success in life," the same youth rationalized.

"I said we have no time. Kindly stand aside!" The Amarenian's pitch became aggressive.

The young man stepped in close and reached out for her shoulder. "You don't have to be rude about it..."

Noorim captured the arm before it got to her and barred it straight. Stepping back, she pulled him out of balance and then brought her other forearm forcefully upward on the exposed elbow. The joint cracked loudly as it broke and the youth howled. Then, spinning to her right, she tossed him into two of his companions.

From the corner of her eye Noorim saw the vehicle come to a stop behind them and more Piety Watch members piled out. She engaged two attackers when she heard Barr-Ani's books drop and her shrieks of terror before sudden silence.

Noorim added another broken Piety Watch thug to the ones already littering the ground, writhing in pain, when their reinforcements joined the fray. Now completely surrounded, Noorim awaited the next attack.

Just before feeling a blow on the back of her head and everything going black, she saw the panicked, pleading Barr-Ani being drug into the back of the vehicle by three of the fanatics. One of which had his hand securely over her mouth.

Noorim awoke with a start and sprung up in bed with a disturbed look on her pale white features. The back of her head throbbed and she had a terrible headache. The curtained partitions around her revealed her location as the Clerria House infirmary and she breathed a sigh of relief seeing Taleeka standing beside the bed. A wave of guilt flooded over the Amarenian warrior.

"They took her," she lamented, falling back in bed. "I failed to protect her!"

"Okay," Taleeka said calmly. "First things first. I'm really glad you're not badly hurt. Secondly, who took who? What happened?"

Noorim sighed deeply, taking a moment to compose herself. "Barr-Ani; the Piety Watch ambushed us on the way back from class and took her."

Taleeka's lips went taut at the news and she felt her fists tightening.

"If the Piety Watch was involved, that means Banavor was behind it," she said, scowling. "The fact that they didn't kill you outright, means he wants something, and I'm pretty sure I know what it is."

The sound of approaching footsteps and the curtain being pulled aside broke the brief contemplative quiet. A purple robed Clerria poked her head in and nodded when she saw Taleeka. She stepped aside and a young man of the Piety Watch stepped through with her.

Taleeka immediately noted his short stature, close cropped brown hair and a smooth baby face that bore a superior, disdainful expression. The traditional red shirt looked smartly tailored and the high collar of the half-cape poked above his head resembling cat ears.

"Leave us," he gruffly ordered the Clerria, and then fixed his scurrilous gaze on the two young ladies.

"Heretics, you've stolen something from my master and he wants it back," he said, righteous indignation dripping off each word. "He's prepared to trade you for the blue skinned foreigner."

"Actually, I'm not a heretic," Taleeka said, unphased by the attempted intimidation. "I think *all* religion is stupid."

"Very well," he sneered. "That makes you a heathen."

. "Good enough." Taleeka gave an uncaring shrug "Hey, you piety guys do know that those capes make you look like real idiots, right?"

The young man said nothing, but by the way his eyes bore into her she could tell he seethed on the inside.

"Bring it to Lord Banavor's estate at nine bells."

"And if I refuse?"

The young man's contemptuous look vanished, replaced by an evil smirk. "She will be sacrificed in the name of the Lord, slowly."

Taleeka's expression went from bored to deadly serious. The Piety Watch thug flinched under her penetrating gaze.

"Well, in that case let's raise the personal stakes, shall we," she said menacingly. "If she's harmed, I mean *at all*. I'm coming for *you*, personally, whether you had anything to do with it or not."

'Nine bells, heathen," he said before turning to leave.

"Hey, I'm curious, "Taleeka mockingly said, just before he stepped through the curtain. "How many of you nut jobs did she manage to bust up before you ganged up on her?"

The young man sneered scornfully over his shoulder and then disappeared when the curtain closed behind him.

"Okay, I've had just about enough of that smug little bastard." she said, unslinging her backpack.

She pulled out a small pouch, removed a tiny brown ball and handed it to Noorim. The Amarenian peered quizzically at it in the palm of her hand.

"Dreeat confection," she said, noting the look. "Eat it. It will make you feel better. Then, we're going to get our friend."

Noorim looked skeptical. "Just the two of us?"

"Nah, I've got a delivery to make," Taleeka said, pulling the Larimar talking stone necklace from under her shirt. "Then, I'm going to round up some muscle."

Placing her hand over the stone she looked off into space.

"Vanir," she said aloud, when his face appeared in her mind. "I'm headed your way with a gift. Get us an audience with Grand Justice Epaile."

Tucking the necklace back under her shirt, Taleeka smiled at her friend.

"I gotta go. Take that," Taleeka said, indicating the piece of candy in Noorim's hand. "It'll fix you right up, then meet me over at Judgement Square. As my mom would say 'I'm about to *fuck* this guy up!'"

◯   ◯   ◯

Captain Vanir stood outside the row of judge's chambers, took a swig of whisky from his hip flask and stared around the plaza known as Judgment Square. The city's miscreants, some captured by his very own investigators, filled a half-dozen of the stocks, as well as several gallows.

The cycle, so far, had been clear and cold. Thankfully, the chilly winds subsided last cycle and the citizens of the High Holy City could be seen on the streets beyond, rushing about, enjoying the bright sunshine.

Vanir hoped he wasn't going to have to wait much longer; Justice Epaile was a very busy man and didn't like to be kept waiting. He had beaten a hasty path across the plaza and convinced the Grand Imperial Judge to clear his morning schedule after Taleeka's cryptic call earlier this morning.

He heaved a sigh of relief when he saw the *Mala* descend onto the street just outside the plaza. Taleeka jumped out, strapping on her backpack, followed by a thin, elderly man with short grey hair.

Her passenger climbed out of the craft much slower than the pilot. Vanir studied him as they approached and felt sure he had seen him before.

"Hey Vanir!" Taleeka said excitedly. "This is Cedar Aramos."

The two nodded at each other. Taleeka peered at the judge's chambers.

"Is the justice ready?" she asked.

"He's waiting on you," Vanir replied. "What's this all about?"

"I'm pretty sure we've uncovered something that's gonna help you nail Banavor to the wall!"

Vanir's face brightened. "Well, you did say it was a gift. This I gotta see."

The chambers of Imperial Grand Justice Epaile, much like those of the other justices, actually mimicked a mini courtroom, with barrister stations before a large, elevated desk at the far end of the room.

The Grand Justice looked up from a desk full of paperwork when Vanir knocked once and then entered. His purple robes disguised any bodily attributes but his greying hair and beard conveyed wisdom.

"Your honor, thank you for seeing us on such short notice," Vanir said respectfully. "May we approach the bench?"

Wordlessly, he raised a hand and beckoned them over.

"All right, Captain," he began, when they stood in front of him. "What's so all fired important that warrants me clearing my schedule?"

"Yes, once again thank you for…"

"Yes, yes, get on with it!"

"Well, your honor I'm not sure of the details. I'll be hearing it at the same time as you. Your Honor, this is Taleeka Konrad and Cedar Aramos.

"The Honorable Aramos and I know each other," The judge sympathetically replied. "Finally venturing out, Cedar?"

"Hello Dunkan," Cedar replied with a sad smile. "Mz. Konrad here is the one responsible for breaking me out of my self-imposed exile. She's come across some damning evidence about this city's most flamboyant citizen."

"You're referring to Lord Banavor?"

"I am."

Epaile glanced down at the young woman standing confidently between the two much taller men. "Well, young lady, what have you got to show us?"

Slipping the pack off her back she reached inside and pulled out the ledger.

"Your Honor," Taleeka said, placing the tome on his desk. "This is Banavor's personal ledger. It's quite telling."

The judge glanced quickly down at the book and then leered suspiciously back up at Taleeka. "How did this come into your possession?"

Taleeka gave a quick grimace and shrug. "I would rather not say. What's important is why we came directly to you. Those entries show that six of the nine justices under you are on his payroll."

Epaile's expression turned from curious to stern. "Those are serious accusations."

"Accusations I don't make lightly," she assured, "and the entries in that book will back me up. Especially interesting are the payments made to the justice that presided over Cedar's trial."

A look of surprise crossed the judge's face. "You mean?"

"Banavor wanted me out of the way so he could take over the Monetary Council," Cedar explained patiently. "He cooked up fake charges accusing me of, well, you know what they were. He then paid off the judge."

"This is incredible!" Epaile said with a sputter. "If true you will be reinstated immediately!"

"It's true sir," Taleeka said positively. "I've seen it and that's only a small part of his dirty dealings. Cedar, here, will guide you through it all. It looks like I can be of no further help here, besides, I've got some errands to run."

"Going through this is going to take some time," Epaile said, fanning the pages.

"I think you'll find it interesting reading, Your Honor. I would keep that in a safe place and be careful who knows about this. As it turns out, Banavor has people everywhere. The good news is their names are in that ledger."

"Those will be the first ones we round up," Vanir said resolutely.

"Well, Your Honor and gentlemen, I'll leave you to it," Taleeka said, starting for the door.

"Taleeka," Vanir called out, causing her to pause. "Thank you for this."

"Yes, many thanks, young lady," Epaile concurred.

"I guess the Konrad's title of Heroes of the Realm is well deserved," Vanir said, with a grateful look.

"Aww thanks," Taleeka said, blushing slightly. "You owe me one."

With a wink, she left. Once outside, she found Noorim standing beside her airship.

"Feeling better?" Taleeka asked, popping open the cockpit canopy.

"I am," Noorim replied, obviously amazed. "What was that candy?"

"The Dreeat Empire in Otomoria makes them. They have incredible healing powers. We helped them out right before the Etheria War and this is how they showed their gratitude."

"I am most impressed," Noorim said, climbing aboard.

Taleeka started the Etheria engine. "Yep, it doesn't hurt having a race of humanoid crocodiles in your debt."

"What about the judge?"

"They've got the ledger. It's officially out of my hands. I can now concentrate on getting our friend back."

"Did you tell the judge about Barr-Ani's abduction?"

"Nope."

"Why not?"

"Because they'd have sent city guards and they would just get in my way," Taleeka replied lifting off. "Let's go get some muscle. You're gonna love this."

Just as it had done since its construction three thousand grands ago, the rebuilt Grand Turine in the Zorian Harbor rang out six bells, announcing the risen Kan fog's arrival.

Talib and Tantei followed three Piety Watch members escorting a mysterious cloaked figure from the Banavor estate and trekking eastward across the city on foot. The two investigators maintained a discreet distance but always kept the quartet in sight.

It struck Tantei as odd they chose not to hail a hackney. When they turned north on Canal Street, heading into the Seven Sisters Slums, she became downright suspicious.

"Hey, new guy, what's wrong with this picture?"

The junior detective's face soured. "You mean besides the fact that we're walking around in the cold and damp and I'm hungry?"

Tantei shot an irritated side glance. "Yeah, besides that."

"Well, wherever they're going," Talib replied, "they're taking the long way,"

"That's part of it," Tantei said quizzically. "Why didn't they hail a hackney? And why in the name of my boyfriend's balls are they heading into the Sisters? There's nothing but poor people in there, and they *fucking hate* poor people."

"I didn't know you had a boyfriend," Talib said innocently.

"I don't... and that's not the point. They have absolutely no reason to go..." Tantei stopped, and her mouth went wide in recognition. "I've got a bad feeling about this."

She reached into her pocket for her communications shard. The Zorian Guards modified the Larimar Etheria crystal allowing for more than just communication and translation. Now, four small Etheria crystals set into the top and bottom of the stone glistened, performing complimentary activities including locator tracking and visual capabilities.

Holding the Larimar in front of her mouth, she pressed her thumb on it and spoke. "Patrol Dispatch, this is Investigator Twelve."

"Go ahead twelve," came a female reply.

"I'm going to need all available patrols in the area routed to where Canal Street enters the sisters. We're going to need immediate back-up. We've got a possible homicide. We're going in and I'm turning on my tracker."

"Copy that, Crash Team being rerouted to your signal."

Tantei pressed on the amber tracking crystal at the top of the Magitech device and pocketed it. "Okay, let's go."

She drew her pistol and started off after her quarry. Talib nervously drew his weapon and followed.

The Sedam Sestasra, or Seven Sisters Slums were as old as the High Holy City itself and had always been an embarrassment for the officials who kept the metropolis running. Many attempts were made over the grands to clean up the community's most dangerous neighborhood, all of them failed.

Talib's nose twitched in revulsion at the dank smell of the canal's stagnant water next to the street. The boulevard went from cobblestones to hard packed shells and cut completely through the area of urban blight, avoiding the naked panhandlers and sexual acts of all sorts in the alleyways.

Keeping their weapons down, so as not to attract attention, the two investigators caught up to the suspicious foursome. They watched as a nude woman with long, greasy, matted hair approached them with her hands out pleading for relief. In true Piety Watch fashion, one of the caped men backhanded her and she cried out, reeling in pain.

For the detectives this no longer constituted an alarming sight. The Piety Watch routinely beat beggars, most often with thin ratan canes. In the beginning, they were arrested, but because of Pa-Waga's influence on the city, never punished. After a while, the guards ceased the useless apprehensions. Tantei gasped they grabbed the woman and then abruptly turned left, out of sight into an alley.

"Oh shit!" the senior partner said, before taking off at a dead run with Talib in tow.

When the duo reached the alley entrance, the pursued were nowhere in sight. A brief, solitary scream from a small plaza midway down the side street gave away their location.

Sprinting between the ramshackle wooden huts stacked precariously on top of one another gave Tantei a slightly claustrophobic feeling. Talib, who had traversed these streets on his days in Patrol Division remained unphased by the tight quarters.

When they arrived at the plaza's entrance, neither could have been prepared for what they found. In the brief moments it took to run there, the scene they came upon had turned gruesome.

The naked woman lay spread eagle in a large puddle of her blood. The mysterious hooded figure knelt over her dead body. It pulled its cowl back, revealing the mongrel Mawl. It had already opened up the vagrant's abdomen and began the prosses of disembowelment. The Mawl's hands and the front of its garment were stained red and steam escaped from the open wound into the cold Kan air., The three Piety Watch thugs stood merely five feet away observing the disturbing spectacle with bored expressions.

"FREEZE!" Tantei screamed, when she and Talib jumped out, weapons trained.

All four perpetrators quickly scanned the plaza for an escape route but found none. One of the caped men sneered and began walking towards them, arms extended, speaking a language the investigators did not understand. When blue sparkles began emanating from his outstretched palms, both investigators fired in unison.

The man's body vaporized when both Na-Kab Carbon bolts struck in unison, spraying the entire courtyard in a fine red mist. The others stood paralyzed in shock.

"That wasn't freezing," Tantei said coldly to the sound of alarm whistles drawing closer.

"All right, here we go," Taleeka said, navigating the *Mala* low over the wrought-iron fence of the Banavor estate. "Everybody stay frosty and let's get this done."

"Are you certain this will work?" Noorim asked from the co-pilot's seat.

"Well, it's the only plan we've got, so I say we *make* it work," Taleeka replied, searching for a spot to land the airship.

"Sure hope I get to bust some heads," Larzz said gruffly from the back seat.

"And as much as I would like to watch that, I hope you don't," Taleeka said, settling the craft to the ground just inside the driveway's gate. "If you get involved, that means things have gone sideways."

The half EEtah chuckled revealing his mouth full of razor-sharp teeth. "For what you're paying me, I'll sit around and knit all day if you want."

Noorim turned and peered back at the human/EEtah hybrid stuffed into the inadequately sized accommodations.

"You knit?" she quizzically asked.

Larzz shrugged and gave a shy grin. "It calms me."

"And, right on cue, here's our welcoming committee," Taleeka said, watching Stovle lead five Piety Watch members onto the front portico.

"I don't see Banavor," Noorim noted, when Taleeka popped the canopy.

"Yeah, he's smart to keep this whole situation at arm's length. Looks like we'll be dealing with number two. That's fine," Taleeka said, standing and grabbing her backpack. "You two stay back and be ready just in case you're needed."

Taleeka left the engine running and the three jumped to the ground. On the porch, all five caped men fanned out behind Stovle.

"Do you have it?" Stovle called out.

Holding the pack by the straps she opened it, retrieved a ledger book and held it aloft.

"Where's the Bailian?" Taleeka demanded.

"Put the ledger down on the ground and back away," Stovle said forcefully. "Then we'll send her over."

"Do I look like I was born last cycle?" Taleeka said dismissively. "This is going to be a mutual exchange or it's not going to happen."

"We could just kill her," Stovle replied mockingly.

"How do I know you haven't already?" Taleeka remained steadfastly resolute. "Look, we both have something each other wants. What say you quit screwing around and we complete this transaction!"

Stovle and Taleeka glared defiantly at each other for a tense moment until he looked back at the front door and nodded. One of the double doors creaked open and another Piety Watch thug muscled a terrified Barr-Ani into view.

"Tally!" she cried out upon seeing her friend.

"Everything's going to be fine," Taleeka said calmingly, stepping forward, holding the book for all to see.

When she reached twenty feet from the airship she halted. "All right, I'll put the book down here, Start her walking."

"I hope you don't mind if we escort her and retrieve our property," Stovle said with an evil smile.

He raised his hand and all of his henchmen pulled pistol crossbows. "And if you try anything stupid, she dies."

"Suit yourself," Taleeka said, placing the book on the ground and stepping back.

The Piety Watch member, a large jowly man with a crew cut, led Barr-Ani gruffly by the arm over to where Taleeka stood by the book. They locked eyes for a taut moment while the frightened Bailian struggled in his grasp.

"Are you gonna let her go?" Taleeka asked, breaking the stalemate.

With an insolent sneer, he released her and reached down to pick up the book.

"Get to the ship, quickly!" Taleeka ordered in a whisper when a trembling Barr-Ani hugged her.

The Bailian locked eyes with her friend.

"Quickly," Taleeka urgently repeated.

Barr-Ani nodded and then broke and ran for the *Mala* while Taleeka cautiously backed away not taking her eyes off the weapons trained on her.

While Noorim helped her friend into the ship, Taleeka watched the henchmen deliver the ledger to Stovle.

Banavor's seneschal immediately opened the book for an inspection. Upon seeing blank pages, he peered up in a rage.

"KILL THEM!"

Taleeka had wisely kept her pack close at hand. Quickly pulling out her baton, Defari howled and the teen began spinning it propeller style by the lanyard just as a volley of crossbow bolts streaked her way.

The spinning Ukko wood cudgel deflected two of the projectiles and three of them embedded in the thick skin of Larzz's chest. The half EEtah bellowed in rage at the annoyance and reached over to the wrought iron fence. The two balusters groaned noisily when he wrenched them free.

Taleeka, continued backing up, while the Piety Watch thugs advanced off the porch, firing as they went. Defari snarled and barked with each projectile deflected and several more peppered the enraged Larzz.

Reaching back, the half EEtah wound up and launched one of the pointed iron rods at his attackers. The fence part hummed when it streaked through the air, and then plunged completely through Stovle's chest with the crack of his bones being crushed.

The Piety Watch members looked on in stunned surprise at the shocked look frozen on their leader's face and the six-foot-long piece of iron impaled completely through his torso. Stovle retained the shocked expression as his legs gave way and he toppled to the ground.

Taleeka took advantage of the brief lull in the fighting to hop into the flight deck. Larzz gripped the remaining metal baluster like a spear and charged towards his assailants. The Piety Watch thugs got off another ineffective volley which lodged harmlessly in the charging sentient's chest. By the time they decided to run, Larzz caught up to them.

He drove the spear through the nearest one, lifted the fresh kill above his head and bellowed in rage. The man bounced about on the end of the shaft before being cast aside.

The remaining Piety Watch member, seeing their leader dead and their weapons useless, broke and ran.

"The half EEtah considered giving chase until Taleeka's shouts snapped him out of his murderous rage. In a final act of aggression, he hurled the baluster at the fleeing thugs.

"Come on, get in," Taleeka said, pulling the *Mala* up beside him.

Larzz climbed aboard breathing heavily and scrunched himself in the back seat next to Barr-Ani.

"Thank you all for rescuing me," the Bailian said, still trembling.

"You killed Banavor's right hand man," Noorim said appreciatively. "He won't be happy about that."

Larzz cackled through ragged breath, while pulling out the embedded crossbow bolts. "Yeah, lucky shot."

"There's gonna be a bunch of upcoming events that's going to make Lord Banavor unhappy," Taleeka said, guiding the airship over the Zorian rooftops. "We're done playing defense. It's time to bring the fight to him."

Hemicar shivered uncontrollably watching the morning fog recede. This last Kan had been the coldest one yet and he knew winter was well on its way. It had been five cycles since his capture. Mercifully, the boat ride was short. They bound him to the other prisoners and the EEtah's escorting them in the water ensured no escape attempts.

Upon reaching Zor, they took him immediately before an Imperial Judge where they rendered his sentence. He spent the last four cycles on the cold cobblestones of Judgment Square, naked in the stocks. They hung a placard around his neck announcing his crime for all to see, *"Smuggler."*

The mild-mannered chemist's back and legs ached from standing bent over. His buttocks stung from the random whippings from sadistic passersby. His beard served as a constant reminder. It smelled like rotted fruit from the assorted foodstuffs thrown at his head by taunting children.

The misery laden echoes of the other condemned around him endlessly assaulted his ears. Being forced to face away from them, all he could do was listen, which somehow made it worse. By cycle number two, his own sobs added to the chorus of despair.

The most awful sounds, however, turned out to be the hangings, which also took place behind him, and started every cycle, just after the lifting of the Kan. The quick ones proved bad enough. The sounds of the trap door opening and the body dropping caused him to wince each time, but at least they died quickly. For truly heinous crimes, they slowly winched up and strangled the hanged. He tried to block out the sounds of their gurgling and thrashing about in mid-air but found it impossible. They left the bodies to dangle for a full cycle, which amused and served as a warning to the citizenry. Then, just before the Kan they took them down, only to be replaced by the next group of unfortunates.

When he heard the first hinges creak this cycle, followed by the crash of wood giving way, and the dull thud of a body suddenly jerked taut at the end of a rope, he had had enough.

What in the name of the gods am I doing here? coursed through his head. He was just a simple alchemist who now wished he had never met Lord Banavor.

"GUARD! GUARD!" he heard himself scream above the din of woe crying out across the plaza.

He called out many more times before he caught the attention of a middle-aged man with cruel, hard features wearing a sergeant's rank on his tunic.

"What do you want, *meat*?!"

Hemicar peered up into a blank expressionless face with tears streaming down his cheeks.

"Tell Captain Vanir *I'm ready to talk!*"

The closer Taleeka and Barr-Ani got to the commodities exchange the more anxious the Bailian sensitive felt. Taleeka kept catching side glances of her friend staring wide eyed up at the pillars lining the extensive porch. All around them a crowd of humans and Piceans swarmed in and out of the large double doors furiously jabbering away.

"I don't like the feel of this place," Barr-Ani said apprehensively. "Why am I here?"

"Hey I'm sorry. I know you just went through a lot, but this is Banavor's back yard," Taleeka replied starting up the steps. "I said we were going to bring the fight to him. I just want to snoop around and see if you can get a reading on anything."

"Aren't you worried about Banavor spotting us?"

Taleeka shook her head. "We've never met. His number two was the one who snatched you. Just keep a low profile. It's pretty crowded and he may not even be in there."

Barr-Ani gave a resigned sigh. "Exactly what are we looking for?"

"Anything that may give us an edge."

"There is something very unsettling about this place," Barr-Ani said, crossing the porch towards the doors. "The feeling gets stronger with each step."

"Probably because this is such a cutthroat place, monetarily speaking that is. Heck, even I feel…"

Taleeka realized her friend no longer walked beside her. She peered back and saw the Bailian staring at the doors wide eyed and with lips quivering in terror. Protesting traders stacked up behind her. Taleeka, fearful of calling attention to themselves, took her friend by the arm and guided her out of the flow of foot traffic.

"Wow, this place really does get to you, doesn't it?" Taleeka said sympathetically. "Look, you don't have to go."

"It's that self-serving mercenary attitude that's been building in Zor since the end of the Etheria War," Barr-Ani explained ominously. "It feels like it originates from this very structure."

"Okay, if it's too much, you can stay out here if you want. We can meet for lunch later."

Barr-Ani took a deep breath and composed herself. "No, I'll be alright. Besides, I want to do my part in bringing this sentient down. He did have me kidnapped after all."

"That-a-girl," Taleeka said, patting her arm.

The two stepped back into the flow of those entering and found themselves transported to a scene of apparent turmoil. The trading floor contained mostly humans, screaming and waving their arms around, while runners frantically moved about with slips of paper in their hands.

Along three of the walls were balconies with private alcoves for elite traders. The other wall contained several giant Larimar screens with multiple lines of ever-changing numbers and symbols streaming across them.

On a tall pedestal in the center of the trading floor, the black statue of Oldmar Calden, the founder of the exchange, stood for all to see. The simple, mostly featureless effigy looked down on the controlled chaos he created so long ago.

"What in the name of the Goddess!" Taleeka said, staring around at the pandemonium with her hands on her hips.

When Barr-Ani remained silent, Taleeka glanced over at her friend. The Bailian stared up at the statue with a horrified expression. Her mouth went agape, and tears welled up in her wide, unblinking eyes.

"Barr-Ani, what is it?!"

"Pa… Pa-Waga!" she breathlessly stammered before her eyes rolled up in her head and she tumbled unconscious into Taleeka's arms.

Somber described the mood in the small meeting room at the University of Marassa. Three friends sat around the rectangular table while the library, just outside the closed door, hummed with the usual daily activity.

Taleeka looked into Noorim and Nibira's worried faces and gave a helpless shake of her head.

"And she just passed out?" Noorim asked.

Taleeka nodded with a concerned look. "She was apprehensive all the way there and actually froze up before going in. I feel guilty asking her to go with me."

'Is she at Clerria House?" Noorim asked.

"Yes, and they don't know if and when she'll regain consciousness."

Nibira reached out and reassuringly touched Taleeka's arm. "What caused it?"

"We were just standing on the trading floor amongst all the craziness, when she looked up at the statue of the founder, called out 'Pa-Waga,' and out she went."

Nibira gasped. "What exactly did she say?!"

"Pa-Waga," Taleeka repeated bleakly.

"Is not that the god those violent fanatics the Piety Watch worship?" Noorim asked.

Nibira's face, already somber, went grim. "As well as Lord Banavor. Pa-Waga is a Mawl demi-god from Nocturn. He is the god of greed, selfishness and desire."

Taleeka nodded. "My mom and dad spent a good deal of time before I came along tangling with Stryder Aramos, his acolyte on this plane."

"Yes," Nibira concurred. "The story goes he slowly lost his humanity and was exorcised on this very campus. He was then summoned back by the Mawls when they lived here in Tiger Town. That was just before they were expelled, and the war that followed."

Taleeka gave a wry chuckle. "Yeah, I'm very familiar with that conflict."

"They've actually got a copy of his prayer book over in the Language Arts building," the librarian continued. "It's Professor Zekoff you should be talking to. He was right in the thick of it."

"Do you think Pa-Waga possessed that very statue?" Noorim asked, struggling to comprehend the past events.

"It would go a long way explaining the climate of greed which has been growing since the end of the war," Taleeka said, her mind racing.

"As well as the Piety Watch and Banavor's sudden and seemingly unstoppable rise to power," Nibira added. "I can tell you this, if Pa-Waga is on our plane of existence, it is unprecedented. Gods dwell in the Middle Realms and use their proxies here in the Corporal Reach to do their bidding. If he's crossed over into our plane, it would dwarf any other god's influence here."

"That seems an undue amount of power," Noorim said, finally catching on. "Surely the other gods cannot be happy about that?"

Taleeka suddenly bolted up in her chair. "That's it!"

"Tally, what's it?" Nibira asked, her curiosity piqued.

Taleeka's eyes twinkled in excitement. "The map on your boyfriend's back! The cave, the runes, I've got a feeling we were being played."

"You believe you are a game piece of the gods?" Noorim asked, confusion returning.

"It would seem so," Taleeka replied.

"So, what are we supposed to do?" Nibira asked uncertainly. "I mean, if we've been being guided all along, shouldn't there be something pointing the way?"

"Maybe we've got all we need," Taleeka said, "so let's think this through. Gods can't be killed, right?"

"Right, only banished. The only way gods die is if people stop believing in them."

"And if we do manage to banish it, some other power-hungry idiot in the future could just bring it back?"

"Yep."

A sly grin slowly inched its way across Taleeka's face.

"I've got an idea, but first, I'm going to need to talk with some people."

371

The four naked Piety Watch members knelt on the cold stone floor of Banavor's basement temple trembling in fear. They bound their hands and feet, placing them there on their master's orders upon his return. An equally naked Banavor calmly paced before them, his rigid erection bobbing in front of him, the head glistening with precum.

"So, let's recap the events of the last few cycles in my absence, shall we?" he asked malevolently. "You lost my ledger, my prisoner *and* my assistant, as well as one of your very brethren killed doing their duty. You four, however, chose to run. Am I missing anything?"

"Lord Banavor, there... there was this huge half EEtah," a young man in his early twenties stammered. "Our weapons didn't hurt him and you saw what he did to the front gate!"

The dark cleric paused in front of the man giving the explanation and scowled. Without warning, his right hand lashed out. Banavor's long sharp forefinger sliced open his throat and the man's face strained in shock. He opened his mouth to cry out but only gurgles could be heard.

Banavor then reached down and grabbed either side of his head by the ears. Yanking it close, he rammed his hard member into the open wound and began pounding the man's head on his turgid organ like a gruesome sex toy. After this brief moment of murderous degradation, he grunted out his release and pushed the body backwards to the floor.

The other three winced in disgust at the brutal act, fearful of his still hard penis coated with dripping blood and slime. The next in line gulped hard when the bloody rigid appendage wagged in front of his face.

"Now, let's hear *your* clever excuse. You do have one, don't you?"

With a panicked expression, he shook his head but remained silent.

"No?" Banavor asked, mockingly disappointed. "Well then, put that mouth to good use. Clean up my cock."

The man looked up at him with pleading, fearful eyes, mumbling something incoherent while shaking his head.

"The penalty for disobedience is death," Banavor stated calmly before slashing his throat.

He kicked him in the chest and sent the hemorrhaging body toppling backwards, spraying blood everywhere. Stepping before the last two, he stared down menacingly.

"Your compliance, just might earn you your master's forgiveness."

Two mouths and tongues immediately began running across his bloody organ and he watched them, casually assessing his situation.

They had dismantled his drug operation and his alchemist was talking. His judges and Mawl shaman had been arrested. His damning ledger was in enemy hands and his assistant was dead. These were all things that would rattle a lesser man, perhaps cause him to contemplate fleeing, but he was not a lesser man. He would see this through and prevail, for he served a mighty God.

Taleeka stood on the windswept flight deck of Air Station Three and watched the small, scout class airship bank towards her over the Zorian rooftops. The sun shone brilliantly in a cloudless autumn sky and she watched it glint off the cockpit's canopy when it quickly approached.

Following the craft on its trek to a nearby slip, she made her way past the milling mechanics and flight crews. She smiled when the craft's lone passenger disembarked. The Gila stood just over five feet tall. His scaly blue green skin perfectly matched his black floor length duster jacket and the eyes on the side of his head rotated independently of each other, taking in his surroundings.

He hasn't changed, she thought when he caught sight of her and headed her way.

"Tally," he greeted, offering her his hand.

"Da-Olman, it's been a while," she replied, warmly shaking it.

"The last time I saw you, you and your folks were fighting undead in the Dark Waste," he said with a nod of the head.

Taleeka gave a knowing chortle. "Yeah, undead that *you* summoned as I recall."

"Details, details," the Gila replied with a wave of his hand. "So, what brings me here?"

"Let's wait until we've got a little more privacy. My ship's right over there. I'm more than likely being watched, and I want this to appear like two old friends reuniting."

"Ooh, cloak and dagger, I like it!" he said, following the teenager over to the slip containing the *Mala.*

Once inside with the canopy closed, the Gila's curiosity got the better of him. "Okay, let me just say, I knew the Konrad name had some pull within House Valdur, but I didn't know how much, until now. How in the name of the empire did you get me pulled off an existing project for a private job just for you?"

Taleeka smiled and hit the accelerator on the air boss' signal. "Joc' Valdur and my family go way back."

"Well, alright," Da-Olman said, watching the craft sail out of the hangar and into the Zorian sky. "You've got me on loan for as long as you need me. What's up?"

"Don't worry, I won't take up much of yours and House Valdur's time. I need you to build me something special and I need it fairly quickly."

"Etheria in nature I would imagine?"

"Taleeka nodded. "Yep, and you're one of the best."

"Thanks for the vote of confidence. Truth be told, I needed a little time away from the Dwarf."

Taleeka snickered. "Yeah, I heard he can be a *wee* bit intense."

"You have no idea!" he said, laughing.

"I just use the toys you Landagar research folks make," she said, "but like laws and sausages, I don't want to see them being made."

"What's a sausage?"

"Never mind."

Da-Olman smiled and the *Mala* began its descent towards Konrad House West. "Well, once you brief me on what this thing is you want me to build, I'll put together a shopping list of what I'm going to need. Most of it could be pretty exotic, not to mention expensive. That's not going to be a problem, is it?"

"Nope, when you've made the list give it to my seneschal, Peshk, she'll make sure you get what you need."

"Impressive," the Gila said, watching the Konrad's hangar door open. "You're not sticking around?"

"Nah, I've got to make a quick trip over to Immor-Onn. I'll be back in a few cycles."

"I guess I'm staying with you?"

"Yep, I want anyone who might be watching to think this is a friendly visit."

"Again, with the cloak and dagger. I've got a feeling I'm going to like this project of yours."

"And don't think you're not going to be compensated," Taleeka said, steering the ship into the specially designed hangar above the main residence. "There's an Etheria Tablet below your seat.

A pleasantly surprised look crossed the Etheriat's face and he reached under the seat and retrieved the four-by-six-inch rectangular slab of Larimar Etheria Crystal.

Settling the craft down, she pulled a two-inch-long black Obsidian shard from her pocket and handed it to him.

Without need of instruction, Da-Olman snapped the Obsidian storage device into one of the series of grooves carved into the edge of the Larimar tablet.

They sat in the *Mala* while the Gila stared blankly at the multiple pages of strange runes which appeared on the milky white surface.

"What's all this?'

"We pulled them out of a cave in the mountains of Awa Island. According to the Marassa's over at the university, it's an ancient language that predates anything they have ever seen. Get this, its very nature is based on Etheria. Those first, solitary runes are the alphabet. The lines after are Etheria combinations."

Taleeka paused for effect. "Congratulations, like I said before, you're one of the best, but that document makes you the most powerful Etheriat in the Annigan."

The entire two wall chalkboard in the small conference room contained a massive flow chart displaying the numerous tendrils of Banavor's operation, many of which were now adorned with a large X. With a satisfied stroke of the marker, Vanir added one more over the entry denoting the corrupt Imperial Judges.

"The little bastard's gotta be feeling *that*," Vanir said triumphantly, returning to his seat across from Tantei.

"Alright, the judges are off the table," the bald investigator said. "What about the ledger?"

"Cedar Aramos and a team of accountants are pouring over it. They should be finished soon. I've spoken with him recently. There should be more than enough to have an Imperial Judge issue an arrest warrant."

"You mean from the three judges that are left," Tantei said disparagingly.

"You're a real glass is half empty kinda girl, aren't you?" Vanir playfully said, taking a sip of whisky from the tumbler in front of him. "I mean, we've shut down his drug operation. We've got his alchemist, his judges and his ledger. It's only a matter of time. As far as the judges go, the High Council will be filling those vacancies by the end of the quinte."

"I always play the pessimist, boss," Tantei said with a sarcastic grin. "That way, when things go right, I'm always pleasantly surprised."

"I guess that's one way to look at it," Vanir conceded before pointing at one of the few unmarked entries on the board. "The biggest thing left to tackle is the Piety Watch. We may have Banavor reeling, but we can't forget he's still got his own private army of fanatics."

Talib, who sat silently studying the board, finally sat forward. "You know, with the bad judges out of the picture, we can finally start arresting the Piety Watch when they assault the homeless. In fact, there's really no reason we can't start leaning on them *hard*. They've been acting with impunity for so long, they think they're untouchable. I say it's time we prove them wrong."

Vanir and Tantei froze and stared at each other with looks of shared recognition.

"I like it," Vanir said with an enthusiastic nod.

"I think that'll work!" Tantei agreed ardently.

The room suddenly became energized with the new idea.

Vanir took a quick swig, draining the glass. "Alright, you two get over to Gasata's office in Patrol Division. Have him get his men in on the party. Then I want you to lean on any they arrest and try to get them to talk. Maybe bring in Rafel to help persuade them."

'You bet boss," Tantei said enthusiastically, rising to her feet. "Come on, Talib, let's go see how many religious whack jobs' balls we can bust."

"Hey," Talib said, standing up with a broad grin, "you called me by my name!"

"Yeah, yeah, let's not make a big deal of it," she said nonchalantly, heading for the door. "You don't think like a new guy anymore."

The moon recently set over the western Twilight Lands, leaving the city of Immor-Onn basking in a brilliant canopy of stars exposed by the weakened rays of the sun on the distant horizon. The faded light, however, couldn't conceal the two Bailian teenagers making their way on the main road out of the city and into the Os'Tor Forest.

Both girls shared similar Bailian features, pale blue skin, large almond shaped eyes and whiteish yellow hair. One, however, carried herself with an air of confidence, while the other seemed decidedly timid.

"I can't believe you talked me into this," Derra-Has said uneasily, her eyes darting nervously.

Nera-Bea glanced over at her friend and gave a superior smile. "You want to see if the rumors are true, don't you? This is the only way."

"I guess," she replied anxiously.

"Mother says it's a sentient lioness all the way from the Land of Mists," Nera-Bea said excitedly. "She's supposed to be a sorceress."

"I hope she doesn't put a spell or a curse on us."

"Will you quit worrying. It'll be fine. All we need is a quick peek."

The surroundings grew measurably darker when the cobblestone road turned into hard packed dirt at the entrance to the ancient forest. They had only traveled a short distance through the gloom when they saw light from a cabin just beyond the trees. The teens slowed and quieted their pace when they stepped off the trail.

"Alright, we'll go up to the window and see," Nera-Bea said quietly.

"Maybe I should just stay here," Derra-Has suggested nervously.

"What are you talking about?!" Nera-Bea's whispered harshly. "You've already come all this way! We're *here*. Now quit being a frightened rabbit and follow me."

They skulked as stealthily as two urban girls' abilities allowed through the underbrush and up to the lit window. Nera-Bea cautiously peered inside first, she then beckoned to her overly cautious friend to join her.

They saw the spartan interior of the single room shack, just a table, two chairs and a straw bed. A hinged metal arm suspended a cooking pot over a hearth on the far wall.

A female Singa with an eye patch sat at the table carefully arranging several sheets of paper into an overlayed pattern.

"What's she doing?" Derra-Has whispered.

"Shhh," Nera-Bea shushed, raising a finger to her lips.

"You know," Taleeka's stern voice reverberated out of the woods behind them. "It's not nice to spy on people."

The Bailian teens spun in a panic, screamed and took off running. A moment later, the door opened, filling the area with light and casting shadows amongst the trees.

"Tally!" Zau greeted her warmly. "I've been expecting you. Please, come in."

"Zau, long time no see," Taleeka said, stepping inside.

Taleeka was about to ask how she knew of her unannounced arrival when she saw the astrological Tanem Charts displayed on the table.

"You've grown quite a bit since I saw you last," the lioness said, closing the door.

"Yeah, six grands will do that," Taleeka replied. "So, what's with the impoverished hermit routine? You made plenty of money working with my mom."

"Yeah, I lost a lot of money too," Zau said pensively. "You know I could have kept going with your folks, but I really got tired of that fast-paced dangerous lifestyle. I prefer solitude and the simple life."

"They just finally retired," Taleeka said sullenly.

"I know, I saw." Zau said, indicating the charts on the table. "I just can't see where. I guess she's using the ring I gave her."

"Yeah, she's blocking *anyone* from finding her. Which is part of the reason I'm here."

"Ah," Zau said, stepping over to the table and pointing at one of the charts. "I also saw that you came here to ask for my help."

Taleeka gave a pensive shrug. "More like offer you a job, and it pays pretty good."

Zau cleared the papers off the table and sat in the chair facing the door.

"Have a seat," she offered. "If you're anything like your mom, I can't wait to hear this."

Anak Bramoul peered through the oversized magnifying glass and sighed in frustration. His attention focused on a miniscule section of his latest acquisition, a ten-foot-long portion of carved whale bones, standing on prominent display in his private museum. He hadn't been mistaken, *there it was*, a small fault in the ivory, barely visible to the naked eye.

The eight-foot-tall rack of ribs served as a canvas for intricately carved reliefs of various pastoral scenes from the lives of its creators, the Rhune Whalers of the southern coast of the Ice Lands. A race renowned for their unusual hunting and preserving practices.

Now, this rare artifact, usually lost to the sea, belonged to him, *but how could this have happened?* Or could it be he had missed it upon initial inspection when delivered last cycle? The defect, while small and all but invisible amongst the elaborate engravings, still bothered him.

His assistant spoke and gently broke him from his diligent scrutiny, "Uh, sir?"

"Yes Redati?" he said, peering up at his aide's approach.

"Taleeka Konrad is here to see you, sir, and she has some rather... *unusual* sentients accompanying her."

"Really?!" he said inquisitively, lowering the glass. "Did she say what it was about?"

"No, sir, just that it was important and potentially of great interest to you."

"Well, leave it to the Konrad girl to get my attention," the Antiquary stood up and adjusted his suit. "Show them in."

"Yes, sir."

Redati disappeared and returned a few moments later with Taleeka accompanied by Zau and Da-Olman. Anak smiled with an admiring nod at her companions.

"Mz. Konrad, you never fail to surprise me," he said, smiling at Taleeka before turning his attention to Zau.

"If I'm not mistaken, you are a Singa, are you not?"

The lioness gave a sly smile. "You get the prize, bubby!"

Anak returned the grin and looked the Gila over. "You *however*, I have never seen the likes of you!"

381

Da-Olman smirked and trained both his independent eyes on the man in front of him. "Unless you've visited the Dark Waste, I understand."

Anak returned his attention to Taleeka. "So, Mz. Konrad, I see you're as intriguing as usual. To what do I owe the pleasure of this visit from you and your friends?"

Taleeka smiled slyly. "I've got a proposal that I think you'll find very interesting and quite satisfying."

"I'm intrigued, but I must ask, why me?"

"Quite frankly," Taleeka admitted, "you're the only one who comes to mind with the resources to help pull this off,"

"Go on."

She formally introduced her associates, "This is Zau and Da-Olman. I've got an idea that will benefit the both of us, and they're here to make it happen."

It was mid-morning, and the trading floor of the Zorian Commodities Exchange hummed, immersed in its everyday controlled chaos. Banavor, arms folded in front of his chest, confidently watched the seeming mayhem below from his private balcony and gave a condescending smirk. The thought of how much money the frantically scrambling traders would make for him today greedily played at the corners of his mind.

While true that he had suffered some setbacks of late, the brash young man remained confident. His God, so close at hand, would never abandon him. After all he had been a loyal servant and faithful to His cause.

Pa-Waga's prosperous influence could now be felt, to some degree, all across Lumina because of his deity's current residence on this plane of existence. Spreading at its

current rate, it soon would be the predominant faith of the Annigan. He remained a dutiful vassal and had no doubt his God would deliver him from these trifling annoyances, lifting him up to even greater glory.

He felt it first, a tingling around the base of his neck. It then trickled down his spine and soon his whole body prickled with the odd sensation. Fearing something definitely amiss, he quickly surveyed his surroundings, but observed nothing out of order.

The dark cleric cried out when he saw the blue sparkles appear around the base of the statue of Oldmar Calden, but no one heard him over the roar of uncertainty on the trading floor. When a blue cyclonic vortex formed swirling at the statue's feet, a gale force wind swept across the crowded area, blowing about papers and almost anything not secured. Traders panicked, trampling over one another to get away from the intense disturbance.

When the whirling blue tempest swallowed the statue, the very embodiment of his deity, Banavor heard himself screaming, *"NOOO!"*

Once Pa-Waga disappeared from sight, the Flavian portal began shrinking, and the fierce winds diminished until it all evaporated in a shower of blue sparks, the way it arrived. Silence fell over the Zorian Commodities Exchange, slowly broken by stunned traders cautiously milling about the disheveled room wondering what had just happened.

Banavor leaned paralyzed on the balcony's railing, staring at where Pa-Waga once stood, his mind racing with a flood of unnerved questions. *Did his god abandon him? Did his god not feel him worthy? Did he do something to displease him? Why would he leave? Or perhaps something else?* Whatever facilitated the departure, Pa-Waga was gone and Banavor could no longer feel his influence.

The sensation of abandonment and concern caused him to feel sick to his stomach and he fought back a wave of

nausea. In an instant everything had changed, and he suddenly felt extremely vulnerable. Plans must be altered, quickly.

In the Antiquary's museum Taleeka shot Anak a worried look. Neither dared speak for fear of breaking Zau's concentration, but both thought the same thing.

I hope this works!

Beside them, Da-Olman stood looking at the device he created with the same hope going through his mind. The Gila Etheriat carefully crafted the ten-by-ten Etheria cage to ensure it could magically hold any creature, ward off any attack and block any psychic activity in or out of its confines.

Zau stood beside the cage, eyes closed, chanting softly while rubbing one of the runes on her seashell belt. In her other hand she held a green Vivante Etheria shard which doubled her PSI output. She lifted it just above her head towards a purple Etheria disk mounted several feet above the cages open top.

When Taleeka felt the hair on the back of her neck begin to stand on end, she knew something was about to happen. Watching blue sparks begin to dance across the disk's surface all but guaranteed it. They all looked up when the sparks swirled in a tornadic fashion moving ever faster.

Da-Olman stared at the opening portal with his long tongue snaking nervously out of his mouth, licking his eyeball, while his hand fidgeted on a long lever. When the portal fully opened, the air became electric, and wind gusted around the room, blowing hair and garments wildly about.

This should have worked by now, Anak anxiously thought holding his jacket closed. *Somethings wrong!*

The Antiquary knew failure could easily spell all their deaths. He didn't know specifically what an angry god would, or could do, he only knew he didn't want to find out.

When Stryder finally dropped out of the rotating turbulence feet first, he no longer resembled the founder of the commodities exchange. He had reverted back to the featureless cat statue standing erect. All across his smooth black body, fields of X's and I's strobed furiously blue and the creature's enraged bellow resonated through their minds.

There was a ten-foot drop between the purple Azurite disk in the ceiling, now open to the Middle Realms, and the open cage top. During that short plunge, all in the room were subject to Stryder's desperate psychic attack. Wave after wave of destructive energy emanated from the falling demi-god and all but Zau reeled.

Taleeka placed both hands on either side of her head and fell to her knees wincing in pain. Da-Olman staggered back from the lever and struggled to maintain his balance while a ribbon of blood escaped the side of his mouth.

When Stryder dropped into the cage the attack lessened but he quickly recognized he could still escape through the cage's open top.

"DA-OLMAN!" Taleeka screamed when she saw the Gila not at his post.

The humanoid lizard shook his head to clear it, and then saw the black figure begin to levitate upward to freedom. The Gila lunged for the lever just as the black statue reached the top of the cage. It slammed shut with a crash and the psychic onslaught immediately ceased.

Zau's hands fell to her side, shoulders slumped and her head lowered in exhaustion. Taleeka slowly got to her feet, wiping away some blood running out of her nose.

"Is everyone okay?" she managed to pant out.

Through labored breaths everyone indicated they were. They all then stared at their captive, whose clenched his fists by his sides and raised his face to the ceiling in a silent scream. The runes continued to blink feverishly all across his body with no apparent results.

"Don't worry," Da-Olman said reassuringly. "The cage is shielded. He can't get in our heads. If he wants to communicate, he'll have to do it the old-fashioned way."

"Alright, good job everyone," Taleeka said, her breathing finally returning to normal, "and Anak, it looks like you've got another addition to your collection."

"My greatest addition," the Antiquary said, stepping over to the cage and reverently eyeing Stryder, who in turn malevolently surveyed all in the room.

"Yeah, it's not every day you get to add a god to your menagerie," Zau said, joining her comrades around the cage.

"I don't know how to thank you," Anak said to Taleeka, unable to take his eyes off his prized addition.

Taleeka gave an indifferent shrug. "Eh, you owe me one."

She then looked directly at the possessed Stryder knowing she peered into the eyes of Tiikeri god Pa-Waga.

"I hope you like your new home," she said contemptuously. "You're going to be here for a long, long time. Now, we're going to unravel that web of corruption and greed you fostered. Personally, I'm starting with your main bitch boy, Banavor."

After an eventful day that Anak Bramoul would never forget, when the Kan fog began to rise, he and Redati went out for a celebratory dinner. Upon his return, the Antiquary couldn't help visiting his newest prize possession.

Standing in front of the cage, he marveled at the standing cat statue. He had just finished a detailed inspection of the binary glyphs covering its body when he noticed it staring ominously right at him.

"You cannot hold me forever human," it finally spoke in a deep bass tonality filling the room.

Anak, initially startled, recovered quickly. "Perhaps, but for now you belong to me."

"I am *Pa-Waga!* I belong to no one!" he thundered.

Anak remained calm. "Your situation seems to indicate otherwise."

"Release me!"

Anak gave Stryder an incredulous look. "Release you?! I just acquired you. Why would I want to do that?"

"Release me and I will make you rich and powerful beyond your wildest dreams."

An amused grin crossed the Antiquary's face. "I already *am* rich and powerful. And now, I have something beyond *anyone's* wildest dreams. I have a god in my collection."

When Taleeka saw the two Piety Watch members enter the pub and scan the room for threats, she knew Banavor had accepted her invitation. She chose a table at the far end of the room, away from the bar, with a few patrons and a roaring hearth. When they spotted her, they exited. One of them escorted Banavor back in and stood guard at the door.

The dark cleric dressed in his typical cold weather outfit, a skintight Kell bodysuit accompanied by a fur lined blue silk cape. He swaggered over to her table, but Taleeka could see the strain on his youthful features.

"Mz. Konrad, I presume?" he queried formally.

"Lord Banavor, have a seat," Taleeka said, indicating the chair across from her.

"So, we finally meet," Banavor said coyly, sitting down.

"I figured it was about time." Taleeka raised her hand to attract a serving wench. "Join me in a drink, won't you?"

"Why not."

They ordered two ales and Taleeka sat back confidently in her chair. Banavor eyed her warily.

"So, to what do I owe the pleasure of this invitation?"

"Well," she answered, "we've been sniping back and forth at each other for a while now and I thought we might finally meet and have a farewell drink before you leave. Kind of a last meeting of two adversaries."

A confused look crossed Banavor's face. "Leaving, who said anything about leaving?"

Taleeka cocked her head in surprise. "You're not?!"

"Why would I?" The dark cleric's bearing became suspicious.

The conversation paused when the drinks arrived and Taleeka immediately took a sip from her tankard.

"Well, let's see," Taleeka said, setting her ale down, "your god and judges are gone, so you're completely without protection. Your operations are in shambles and, as we speak, one of the Imperial Judges that wasn't on your payroll is drafting an arrest warrant for you. If it were me, I'd be looking for the next ship leaving town."

"I still have my Piety Watch," he said defiantly, warily eyeing his tankard.

"I have it on pretty good authority that they're about to be labeled an organized criminal gang and disbanded."

Taleeka took another sip and watched the young man continue to skeptically stare at his ale.

"Oh, for the love of the Goddess!" Taleeka said frustratingly, before reaching over, picking up his mug and taking a sip. "There, satisfied?!"

She set it back down in front of him. Banavor cautiously stared at her while taking a drink and Taleeka joined him.

"So, you're really not leaving, huh?"

"No, I'm head of the Zorian Monetary Council. The Goyan Islands owe me a debt of gratitude!"

"Not for long you're not, "Taleeka said assuredly, raising her tankard once again. "They've drawn up a list of charges against you the length of my arm. When the judge signs the warrant, you're gone. It wouldn't surprise me if they hung you in Judgement Square for all your mischief."

Banavor became defiant. "I... I..." he stammered and then stiffened and his facial expression became confused before freezing in place.

"Yeah, there was something in your drink," she said before downing the remainder of her ale. "The antidote was in mine." Sitting back again, she smiled triumphantly. "Don't worry, it's not poison. Just a little something to temporarily keep you from going anywhere.

"You know, Banavor, for all our back and forth, you were always a pain in my rear end, but at least you were mildly amusing. Of late, you've just been a pain, and you tried to kill my mom and dad. Can't let that slide. I actually thought about killing you and being done with it but someone convinced me of another course of action."

A sudden gust of wind violently threw the door open, causing the few patrons at the bar to stop and stare. A male Avion stood in the doorway, retracting his long, white wings. On the ground behind him, Taleeka could see the prone body of the Piety Watch member who had remained guard outside.

When he stepped into the pub, the other fanatical guard charged him. Not taking his eyes off Banavor, the Avion lashed out with blinding speed, grabbed the attacker by the throat with one hand and easily lifted him off the floor. Taleeka heard the loud crunch of the neck shattering before the winged man casually tossed the body through the door and onto the street next to his comrade.

Banavor could do nothing but get a good look at the Avion eyeing him with cold disdain. He stood tall and thin, with bone white skin and long jet-black hair, wearing a pair of loose cotton pants and crossed bandoleers over his chiseled chest. With a quick flick of partially extended wings, he hopped across the room and landed directly before Banavor, ignoring everyone else.

"Banavor de Moras," he softly announced, yet still reverberated throughout the room. "I am Julius, Harbinger of Balance. Your crimes and misdeeds are many, but it is your spreading influence which now threatens the balance of this world. This dangerous shifting causes the Black Mural to teeter. If it falls, all life on the Annigan ends. And with no more followers, the gods themselves perish. I take you now to be judged by those gods and *they* will decide on your suitable punishment."

Julius reached across the table and grabbed the front of Banavor's body suit, easily lifting him out of the chair, before he faced Taleeka.

"Taleeka Konrad," he said with a thankful smile. "You have served the gods well and will not be forgotten."

Taleeka grinned broadly and sat back in her chair.

"Well, let's just say they owe me one."

EPILOG

Taleeka and Noorim exited the Mengjes Inn, a popular and upscale bed and breakfast spot in the Shimol Plat of Zor. Taleeka had invited all three of her friends to a celebratory breakfast, however Barr-Ani and Nibira had class and were unfortunately unable to attend.

"I'm pretty sure that's the last we're gonna see of Lord Banavor," Taleeka said, before going after a lodged piece of food with a toothpick and taking in the morning traffic of the city's main mercantile district.

Noorim shook her head at the fantastical story. "And you say this Avion just flew off with him?"

"Yep, picked him up like he was a doll."

"So, 'the judgement of the gods?'"

"That's what he said," Taleeka replied. "He called himself a Harbinger of Balance. I met another Harbinger in that cave on Awa. I don't know how many of them there are, but I guess they're always watching."

"A truly amazing tale," Noorim noted before pausing with a puzzled look. "What are they doing to your ship?"

"What?!" Taleeka cried out, spinning to face the small vacant area beside the inn where she had parked the *Mala*.

Two young men about the age of twelve stood suspiciously around her airship, while a third was inside her cockpit busily tinkering with the controls.

"Hey, you little bastards, get away from my ship!" she yelled, before she and Noorim took off towards her craft.

She kicked herself for being so careless. When the youths saw her, they cried out and jumped in her ship. The one that had been tampering with her dashboard started up the engines and lifted off to a few feet from the ground before taking off.

It travelled erratically down the side street bouncing off buildings and colliding with boxes on the side of the road. Occasionally, it would gain five feet of altitude, only to return to being used as a ground craft.

"Damn it, just damn it!" Taleeka cried out in frustration, frantically looking for anything that could come to her aid.

She saw a hackney parked fifty feet away awaiting a fare beside a corner. This one appeared slightly different than the others' common box shape. The sleek nose of the taxi and aerodynamic shape contained a mysterious ring on the front. It held six passengers including the driver, as well as a small cargo area in the rear.

The cabbie leaned nonchalantly against the hood of the vehicle feeding a four-foot-long lizard from a bag of treats. The harnessed reptiles commonly pulled various wagons and coaches in the Goyan Islands, but this one appeared to be a pet. It bounced happily about the drivers crossed legs snapping up the morsels from midair, and then nuzzling affectionately on her boots before jumping back up, ready to receive another.

The female cabbie stood as tall as Taleeka, with dark black skin and a buzz cut with geometric patterns shaved into the very short hair. She stopped the feeding when Taleeka and Noorim sprinted up to her. Both the driver and lizard looked over at the two out of breath teens.

"I need to hire you, *now*!" Taleeka said, waving a fifty secor commodities note.

The woman took one look at the amount being offered and recoiled in shock at the large sum.

"Damn, heck of a way to start the day!" she said.

She closed the bag and took the note from Taleeka. She motioned for them to get in and opened the driver's door.

"Come on Brzo, were going for a ride!"

The animal danced around excitedly, and then hopped over the driver seat and into the passenger seat, where it began happily panting. Taleeka and Noorim climbed in the back of the carriage.

"Where to?" she called out after everyone had piled in.

"That way," Taleeka cried out, pointing in the direction she last saw her ship speeding away. "They stole my ship!"

"You got it!" The driver said, pulling away from the curb.

The customized hackney moved a bit faster than most but would prove no match keeping up with the fleeing airship.

"Can't this thing go any faster?" Taleeka asked frustratingly.

A mischievous smile crept across the driver's face. "Are you sure?"

"Yes, I'm sure!" Taleeka pleaded. "We'll never catch them this way!"

"Suit yourself," she said, reaching up and throwing open the sunroof.

She briefly looked over at her lizard who excitedly vibrated in its seat and stared expectantly at her.

"Bang bang, Brzo, bang bang!" she said enthusiastically.

In a motion so quick it was hard to detect, the reptile launched itself out the opening in the roof. It vaulted onto the hood and slipped its head through the harness on the front of the cab. The driver pulled a lever on the dashboard and the whole harness structure separated from the front of the vehicle, allowing the lizard's legs to reach the ground.

The hackney lurched forward at an alarming speed which pushed Taleeka and Noorim back in their seats and caused the driver to erupt in laughter. It barreled along the side streets, whipping around what little traffic could be found until it met the main road. Without stopping, or even slowing down, it made a sharp right turn into oncoming traffic, forcing drivers to veer to avoid it with shouts and curses.

"My Brzo, he loves to run!" she yelled, guiding the racing lizard with the steering wheel which now controlled the reptile's harness. "There was this one time, a couple of grands ago, when this rich guy needed to get to the air station fast. So, me and Brzo get him to his flight on time and the guy was going to stiff us and woah…"

The cabbie swerved to avoid a pedestrian. Taleeka peered over at Noorim out of the corner of her eye and found the normally stoic Amarenian anxiously watching the buildings and traffic flying by on either side as the hackney deftly maneuvered through the streets of the crowded metropolis.

Noorim cried out when the lizard scrambled ten feet up the side of a row of tall buildings. To the passenger's delight, the vehicle's carriage leveled out, righting itself along the wall, while the lizard continued his vertical scramble.

"Nice!" Taleeka noted ardently.

"Thanks," the driver replied with a broad grin. "I had a disk of Gyronite mounted underneath, right after the first time Brzo ran a wall."

Taleeka grinned at the visual and then pointed downward towards the road ahead. She could tell they chose the right direction and gained on them by the spectacle of crashed vehicles, overturned carts and general mayhem left in the stolen craft's wake.

"Here we are," Taleeka said, finally catching sight of the *Mala* just ahead.

As predicted, the airship blundered through the crowded streets causing panic and destruction in its wake.

"Why do they treat it like a ground vehicle? Noorim asked, watching a large swath of pedestrians scatter and duck to get out of its way.

"They're kids," Taleeka replied. "They may know how to steal one, but they sure don't know how to fly it."

"They are causing much mayhem," Noorim noted shaking her head disapprovingly.

"Yeah, well, I'm about to toss a wet blanket on their little joy ride," Taleeka said.

"Hey, what's your name?" she asked the pilot, while removing the *Mala's* control fob from her pocket.

"I'm Gidaria," she answered staring intently forward, precisely maneuvering the steering wheel.

"Gidaria, how close can you get me?"

The driver replied by pushing the steering wheel forward, releasing tension on the lizard's collar, allowing him to accelerate. Within a brief moment, they ran parallel to the stolen airship down in the street.

"Hey, that's pretty good, I'm finally in range with all theses buildings around," Taleeka praised, aiming the fob at the fleeing vehicle. "You interested in a job?"

Pushing the power button on the remote control effectively killed the Etheria engines in the *Mala* and it began to slow.

"I don't know," Gidaria said, braking her reptilian pet, skimming back down the wall and onto the street.

"What do I have to do and what's it pay?" Gidaria asked, spinning the hackney around and retrieving a very happy Brzo back into his seat.

Taleeka smiled at the scene of Gidaria attempting to drive the craft, while the overjoyed lizard happily licked the side of her face. "Same thing you're doing now, only I'd be your sole customer. If you liked what I paid you before, I think you'll be happy with your compensation."

Just ahead they could see the panicked looks on the young thieves' faces when they scrambled out of the flight deck to the sound of multiple guard's whistles rapidly closing in on them.

"Will it be dangerous?" Gidaria asked, slowing the hackney beside Taleeka's abandoned ship.

"Sometimes," Taleeka replied honestly.

"Good!" the driver said, bringing the cab to a stop. "To tell the truth, driving people around the city is kinda boring."

She baby talked the lizard next to her, "Isn't that right, Brzo, yes, boring people."

Her adoration was met with another excited lick across her face. Noorim opened the door and stepped out, while Taleeka pulled another fifty secor note from her pocket.

"Splendid!" she said, handing Gidaria the money. "Here's an advance. You start immediately."

"At your service," Gidaria said, pocketing the Ukko wafer.

"Okay," Taleeka said, following Noorim. "Head back to twenty-three hundred Kasada drive and wait for me. I'll be along soon."

"Sure thing," Gidaria said. "But one minor item…"

"Yeah, what?"

"If I'm going to be working for you, shouldn't I know who my employer is?"

Taleeka snickered at her social ineptness. "Yeah, sorry about that, things got a little intense back there and that just flat slipped by me. My Name's Taleeka Konrad, that's my friend, Noorim."

"Hey, I've heard of you!"

"And still want to work for me?" Taleeka asked glibly.

Gidaria gave a sly smile and patted the money in her pocket. "Sure, like I said, driving fares around is boring."

"Good, I'll meet you back at my place," Taleeka said, closing the door.

She joined Noorim inspecting the ship when several city guards came into view with the three captured thieves.

"There appears to be little harm done to your ship," Noorim assessed, nodding in appreciation.

"Ya gotta love Ukko wood. I could have settled for Ukko slats along the outside. I'm *so* glad I splurged for the whole hull. It looks like they caught our little hoodlums."

When Taleeka watched the city guards walk up, she finally got a good look at the thieves. The two who stood watch appeared around ten grands old, younger than she originally assessed. The older one, who actually bypassed the engine controls, appeared to be around twelve. He stood taller than the others at just under five feet, with short black hair and a baby face streaked with grime.

"Hey Kwincee," she greeted, recognizing the patrol sergeant. "I see you managed to track down the hooligans that pilfered my ship."

"Hey Tally," Sergeant Kwincee replied. "I take it you can ID these three as the guilty parties?"

"Yeah, that's them."

"So how in the name of the gods did they get ahold of such a serious piece of hardware?"

Taleeka shrugged and sighed. "Me being stupid. We were running late for a breakfast reservation at the Mengjes, you know how strict they are about their reservations, and I left it parked in the vacant lot on the side of the building."

The sergeant scoffed and ran his hand across the greying stubble of his goatee. "Actually, the Mengjes is a little pricey for me, but I get it."

"Hey Kwincee, let me talk with the older one, will ya?"

"Sure, have fun," the sergeant replied with a wicked leer, fully expecting to witness a well-deserved beatdown before he carted them off to Judgement Square.

"Hey kid, come here," she ordered.

Sergeant Kwincee ordered the guard detaining the boy to let him go and the youth defiantly sauntered towards her.

"Yeah?" he scowled.

"So kid, what's your name?" she asked when he separated.

"Fuck you!"

Taleeka remained unphased by the hostility. "Wow that's a pretty weird name. Listen, you little hustler, you and your friends are looking at going through the rest of life minus a hand, for stealing. You're the leader. You're responsible for the debris trail you left through the Shimol Plat. They'll probably take *your* whole arm, or maybe more, depending on the judge. I'm here to throw you a lifeline. Now, what's your damn name?"

The youngster thought for a moment and Taleeka saw his blustery resolve crack.

"Jixie," he answered, defeatedly.

"Alright, Jixie," Taleeka said matter-of-factly. "You were pretty handy back there figuring out how to bypass the controls on my ship. You have promise. Your friends, however, don't strike me as the industrious type. I'm here to make you, and you alone, an offer. You can take it and make more money than you ever dreamed possible, or you can take a trip with the good sergeant over there with your friends to Judgement Square. The choice is yours."

"What about the Zorian Guards?" Jixie asked skeptically.

Taleeka gave a lone sarcastic chuckle. "You let me worry about the law. Now, I'm waiting on an answer."

Three cycles after Banavor's removal, the Zorian High Council, under advisement from the Zorian Security Council, voted unanimously, in an unprecedented action, to ban the worship of Pa-Waga, and banish any followers who refused to recant.

Mudir de Nir, harbormaster of Zor's southern docks, watched from his perch in the control tower two stories over the wharf, as the large cargo ship pulled up beside docks three, four and five. The vessel lifted its massive three oar Ukko rudder system out of the water, to the sound of groaning wood and protesting metal, berthing the two-hundred-foot transport ship into the pier.

A small army of armed Zorian Guards kept close watch over a sea of Pa-Waga followers crammed onto the three central docks. As soon as the three gangplanks lowered, the prisoners began an orderly procession aboard the ship.

"I'll be glad when they're all on that ship and off my docks, Rocus," Mudir said to his assistant harbormaster, standing next to him watching the exodus.

"Yeah, the tension's got to be pretty high down there," Rocus noted, watching the parade of angry, disgruntled faces. "People generally don't like being forced from their homes and relocated."

Mudir ran a hand through his head of short-cropped greying hair and sighed nervously. "I say good riddance to them. This city's been turned upside down since they came to power. I'm just glad there wasn't more violence than the smattering it took to round them up."

"I don't know," Rocus challenged. "It seems like we were all doing pretty good under their influence."

Mudir scoffed loudly. "Some at the top did very well, but the rest of us were forced to live under oppressive religious fanaticism. Come on, you couldn't even enjoy a sunny day in the park without being beaten by the Piety Watch."

"Yeah, I guess."

"Guess nothing," Mudir said disdainfully. "My neighbor was beaten within an inch of his life for giving a copper piece to a beggar, who, by the way, didn't survive."

"So where are we sending them, Chief?"

"The only place that'll have them, The Free City of Tannimore. It's already a haven for their kind. I say good riddance!"

Banavor awoke attempting to scream in pain but the long fleshy tube inserted into his mouth gagged him. He was suspended spread eagle in space, a few inches off the ground, next to the birthing pit in the Na-Kab hive located beneath Mount Goya. Every cycle, a nutrient dense liquid tasting like rotten cabbage and ammonia pumped into his mouth to keep him alive. Similar tubes penetrated his anus and through the urethra of his penis to remove waste.

Oppressive heat and humidity kept him constantly bathed in sweat and his joints ached under his restraints. The large boils covering his entire naked body, however, caused the real pain. Each of the gelatinous filled sacks contained a growing Na-Kab larvae, which fed off his life energy while they swelled.

The insemination process felt painful enough. The fire mantis' stinger tail resembles a barbed penis and the mantis creatures notoriously could impregnate any creature, no matter where they stung them on their body.

Now he could feel the six-inch boil on his chest painfully undulating with the creature inside ready to be born. He felt the already stretched taut skin ripping with a popping sound. Escaping disgusting smelling fluid from the ruptured sack flowed down his sweat drenched torso and he could feel the eight tiny legs pulling the larva from his flesh. Each birth sent waves of agony racking through his entire body until he passed out.

He would regain consciousness a brief moment later to find the slimy larva running its partially formed thorax over the gaping wound sealing and healing it. The baby Na-Kab then dropped to the stone floor and inched its way over to the pit. From there, it slithered over the side to join the other growing mantises in their steaming, foul smelling birth pit.

Banavor was heaving with relief at the passing of the pain, but knew his respite was short lived. He already felt another boil undulating, soon, another would be born and more Na-Kab would arrive and seed the now vacant areas on his body.

It was almost the end of autumn and Taleeka strolled through the streets of the Tuath Plat in Zor. The brilliant sunshine warmed her exposed extremities on that calm and cold day. Gidaria, dressed in a new, dark red jumpsuit, struggled to maintain control, walking beside her with an exuberant Brzo, straining at his leash while bounding around the pair.

"So, are you excited?" Taleeka asked when they crossed over into the more artisan Bogat Plat and paused in front of a large lone standing building with a wide bay door.

"You bet!" she happily replied. "I want to see what he's done to my ride!"

Both looked up at the sign above the door of the new business and smiled.

"Jixie's Garage

If it flies, floats, or rolls we can fix it."

"You sure called it with the kid," Gidaria said, nodding up at the placard. "He's turned out to be a real whiz."

"Yeah, I had a feeling about him," Taleeka replied. "Anyone who could boost an airship so quickly, had to have something going on. Sometimes, all you have to do is give a lost soul some direction and watch them thrive."

"Are you referring to yourself or Jixie?"

Taleeka gave an introspective smile. "Both."

"Well, I just want you to know I appreciate the opportunity you afforded me," Gidaria said gratefully.

Taleeka shook off the compliment. "You're a whiz in your own rite. Good drivers are hard to find."

Gidaria smiled at the praise. "Tally, you do realize that if you're going to be hauling my hackney, as well as me and who knows how many of your people around with you, you're going to need a bigger airship?"

Taleeka sighed, realizing she was right. "Yeah, I know, one step at a time."

GLOSSARY

Spoiler warning: The following is a master glossary for all the books in this series. Reading beyond a specific word or phrase searches could result in spoilers.

Adad Sunal – EEtah war collage belonging to House Bran, specializing in conducting internal security for House Bran.

Agress – A green Etheria Crystal with red striations which opens and closes doors, windows and hatches, negating any locks but not traps or wards.

Aiken – Semi-sentient clouds sent out across the Annigan from Mount Ghas-Tor, recording everything they witness on the ground and in the air. They are indistinguishable from other clouds against the backdrop of a blue sky. Aiken constantly send visuals back to the mountain, but recent images remain in their limited memory. Those possessing psychic abilities can access their recent memories by flying through and communing with them.

Akina – Humanoid fox creatures native to the Barrens in the Twilight Lands. Often sly and excellent thieves.

Amarenian – Female human race formerly noted for their hatred and slavery of men and piracy.

Angona – Roasted eel on a stick. Sold from vendors' carts all over the City of Immor-Onn.

Annigan – The name of the world which is the setting for the various stories in the Tales of the Annigan Cycle. It includes the two hemispheres of Lumina and Nocturn separated by the Twilight Lands.

Anointed Sister – The title for the Amarenian Queen.

Aquamarine – Pale blue Etheria Crystal which reveals something's true nature.

Ara-Fel Party – Political party of Amarenian farmers.

Arapa Fish – A large fish native to the back waters and tributaries of the Otoman River. Their tough scaly skin is coveted among the Dreeat as armor. The scales by themselves are so abrasive they are also sold as nails.

Ash-Ta – Avion term (winged monster) for the widespread colonies of humanoid bats inhabiting the rocky crags stretching across of the Spine of the World. Avion scholars record six tribes: the Molossi, Acero, Chiro, Ptero, Diaemus and Desmodus. The Ash-Ta allied with the Tiikeri due to their shared enemy, the Do-Tarr.

Astute Sister – Amarenian title for high level politician.

Aur-Quaz – Iridescent Etheria Crystal stimulating energy.

Available Regions – Uninhabited areas of Immor-Onn waiting for the residents displaced by the recent Black Pearl Revolution to return and inhabit.

Avion –Proud sentient rulers of Lumina's sky. Incredibly beautiful and graceful to behold and unabashedly elitist, especially towards their distant cousins, the Humans. Avions refuse to wear any armor and yet have led the way in almost every major war fought. Their scholars contributed a great deal to the knowledge of Lumina. Their four Great Houses occupy the airspace and mountain tops of the Goyan Islands.

Avion Great Houses:

House Azar - Avion House inhabiting the City of Mitar, on the Island of Dal, in the Tellasian chain, ruled by Queen Averin. Their territories include the skies over the Tellasian Chain, Otomoria, Zer-Tal Twins, and the

Zerk Atoll. They are known for their healing Clerics of Neami and their beautiful music.

House Eacher - Avion House inhabiting the Island of Wou, City of Picon & surrounding airspace. Ruled by King Sindil.

House Solas – Smallest of all the Avion houses. They inhabit the city of Adean on the Island of Temil in the Outer Zerians and control the surrounding airspace.

House Pyre - Eldest, largest, and most powerful of all the Avion Houses. They inhabit the skies above the Island of Goya. Their city stronghold, Darmont Keep, sits on the north face of volcanic Mount Goya. Unlike the other Avion Houses who utilize Air Magic, they mastered Fire Magic drawing their power from the volcano.

Awal – First of the ten Quinte Grand Cycle, Spring.

Azurite – Purple Etheria Crystal which connects to the Middle realms.

Bailian – Predominate race of the western Twilight Lands. Descended from the Piceans, they are a beautiful humanoid race with pale blue skin and large eyes.

Banja – The seventy-seven Amarenian noble families, eleven for each of the various seven provinces called Dors.

Banok Atoll – Island ring in the Southeastern Ocean of Lumina housing one of the largest permanent Flavian portals. Its psionic ripples extend out hundreds of miles and affect the entire southeastern Deep Ocean of Lumina.

Banok Run – The final test for admittance to the elite Brightstar Sailors where they must navigate a tight circle around the turbulent seas surrounding the Banok Atoll without being pulled into its giant Flavian portal.

Bespoke Lords – Members of prominent families who have Bespoke Names and serve as advisors to the sovereign in a respective noble human house in the Goyan Islands.

Bespoke Names – Honorary family names only bestowed by a Goyan Island governor or higher as reward for exemplary service to the crown.

Black Mural – A magical record of the Annigan located deep in the Rod-Ema Trench in the Ocean Deep of Nocturn. It slowly grows in size as it records every act of imbalance on the planet. If it grows too large, it will penetrate into the planet's core, killing all life and allowing it to start anew.

Black Talon – Special forces of the Aramos Army, the Fosvara Guard.

Boustian Mage – Bards who perform magic by singing, playing music and storytelling, found predominantly in the larger cities of the Goyodian Chain of islands.

Brightstar – Elite sailors of House Calden qualified to sail the Deep Oceans and the storm-tossed seas of the Twilight Lands. Captains in the Calden Navy must be Brightstar qualified. Brightstar only allows acceptance to their ranks upon completion of the treacherous Innaca or Banok Runs.

Brom – Horse size dragonflies inhabiting the steep southern foothills of the Amaren Mountains.

Calcite – Clear Etheria Crystal which aids in navigation.

Caldani – Privateers hired by Human House Calden to patrol their waters.

Calden Intelligencer Service – House Calden's elite spy agency and secret police. They draw recruits mostly from the Calden Maritime Legion.

Calden Maritime Legion – Marines for House Calden

Calisma – Main library in the University of Marassa.

Cali – Branch libraries and scriptoriums in the five Human capital cities in the Goyodian Island Chain.

Carbana – Chewing tobacco rolled into a tight tube.

Cavernite – A pale green Etheria Crystal with pink striations that can increase the physical dimensions of the interior of any structure it is placed within. The size increase depends on the amount of Cavernite used and the level of PSI used to power it. Without a constant supply of PSI power, the dimensions revert back to their original size. Often used with an Obsidian PSI battery backup.

Centi Elipse – Called a Centi for short. Unit of time in the Goyan Islands equaling a minute.

Celot – Amarenian term for a priestess.

Cevot – Large sentient spider creatures known for their silk, inhabiting the Os-Oni Mountains of the Twilight Lands.

Ched – Seventh of the ten Quinte Grand Cycle, Autumn.

Chanakans – An ancient race of sentient octopoids dwelling in vast underwater cities in the Ocean Deep of Nocturn. They worship the ancient ones of the abyss and practice a powerful water magic.

Cluster – The name for ten cycles, the Annigan's version of a week. There are five clusters to a Quinte (month).

Cobalcite – Deep pink Etheria Crystal used for healing.

Code of Tisina – Mobster code of silence in the City of Zor. Because of Zor's zero tolerance for organized crime, the various independent criminals adopted a "no cooperation" rule with city officials. The slightest violation of this code is punishable by death.

Common – The Common Tongue, a spoken only language used mostly by humans and those in business with them.

Cocoonessa – Cocoon city of the Tinian Moth people on Mount Natal in the Land of Mists. Also called the Silk City.

Corporal Reach, The –The prime material plain of the middle realms where the Annigan resides.

Coxeter – Both the language and magic system of the Tinian race based on a complex form of three-dimensional geometry. The written language is made up of cryptic mathematical notations using lines and dots. Tinian minds perceive all math as the three-dimensional mapping, best displayed in their silk weavings of intricate geometric patterns. When combined with Etheria Crystals, these patterns can be used to perform spells.

Croquis – Magitech mapping devise projecting a scalable three-dimensional holographic image of a desired location, including the other planes of the multiverse.

Cub Prince – A rare black tiger heir to the throne of the Tiikeri Empire. Once every generation, the Tiikeri king must breed an heir. All prominent Tiikeri families offer their most eligible daughters for breeding, but only one will conceive of a black tiger. All other cubs produced from this royal union are killed at birth. They move the complete family of the female who gives birth to the Cub Prince into the palace and considered them nobility. They immediately begin grooming the Cub Prince for the throne, and, when he comes of age, he must kill his father to take it.

Cul-Ta – Humanoid rat creatures found in almost every City in Lumina.

Cycle – Time period equivalent to a day.

Dag – Amarenian term for a common slave. A derogatory slang word for a male.

Darek Witch – Amarenian earth shamans acting as midwives and performing other shamanistic duties.

Darian Silk – High quality silk spun by the Cevot Spiders traded to the On'Dara.

Darwan – A cross between the Balians and the Fudomi, this race is the most prolific humanoid native to the Barrens. They situate their villages around Ghorn temples and must pay tribute to the Onay hordes of the region. Villages close to the borders of the hordes remain under constant threat. Darwans raise a herd animal called the Ng'Ombe which provides the major staple food in the Barrens.

Dasam – Tenth of the ten Quinte Grand Cycle, Winter.

Deci – Time unit equivalent to one hour.

Derde – Third of the ten Quinte Grand Cycle, Spring.

Diamond – Clear Etheria Crystal which transfers power.

Doggin – Derogatory term used for slave dock workers in the city of Aris.

Dolin – Etheria gem hunters, mostly of the Gila race, traveling the Barrens in small caravans and harvesting raw Etheria Crystals to sell to the Zadim lapidaries of the Oasis in the Dark Waste Desert.

Dor – Title of the seven various provinces in Amarenia. Taia-Dor, Denat-Dor, Mivira-Dor, Amoso-Dor, Kinning-Dor, Rackam-Dor, Durik-Dor.

Do-Tarr – Sentient, hive-minded mantid creatures from the Land of Mists in Nocturn. They comprise two large hives in the north and south with precise subterranean tunnels connecting them. They are expert builders and remain neutral in all forms of politics.

Dreamer in the Lake – Demi-God of the Os'Tor Forest and a Harbinger of Balance. She rests at the bottom of a large lake encased in mud and manifests herself on the lake's surface as a multicolored lotus. Her accolades, sentients from every race, sleep around the lake's shore, sending their ethereal bodies out into people's dreams and guiding them.

Dreeat – Humanoid crocodilians inhabiting the end of the western fork of the Otoman River in Otomoria. They grow sugar cane and make magical healing candies from it. They harvest river fish as a major part of their diet. For thousands of grands, ever since the arrival Human race, the Human families have tried to eradicate them.

Dronning Mare – Female horse chosen to breed with the On'Dara chief.

EEtah – Large, powerful and aggressive sentient humanoid shark creatures trained in martial schools known as Sunals to become the professional warriors of Lumina. After their egg birth in the hatcheries and their first year in the nursery, they are sorted into one of the various Sunals of their House. Females enter House Nur and the males go through a highly competitive Sunal scouting and recruiting process with the nursery's called the Garess. Sunals hire out bodyguards, sentries, mercenaries and virtually anything martial. This, along with weapon manufacturing and sales, provides the main revenue stream for the great houses.

EEtah Great Houses:

House Nur – This Noble house is female only. Co-ruled by a secular Queen Mother and spiritual High Priestess.
> Temple of Drulain headquartered in the High Holy City of Zor.
> Specialty: Scribes, Clerics, Healers, Politics, Domestics.

House Crom – Three Sunals in the Tellasian Chain.
> Sedar Sunal on Roe Island. Specialty: Bodyguard.
> Boril Sunal on Uma Island. Specialty: Crom Internal Security.
> Zorod Sunal on Tel Island. Specialty: Castle and Town Defense.

House Bran – Four Sunals in the Goyodian Chain.
> Garf Sunal on Quell Island. Specialty: Long term inland duty.
> Tukk Sunal on Mobis Island. Specialty: Shipboard Security.
> Adad Sunal on Creos Island. Specialty: Bran Internal Security.
> Farak Sunal on Roust Island. Specialty: Bounty Hunter, Vengeance.

House Zed – Three Sunals in the Wouvian Islands.
> Dakor Sunal on Owling Island. Specialty: Shock Troops.
> Jut Sunal on Tor Island. Specialty: Zed Internal Security.
> Morrak Sunal on Billow Island. Specialty: Police, Executioners.

Elipse – A unit of time equaling a second.

Ellie – Slang and abbreviation for an Ellipse.

Esteemed Sister – Amarenian title for Ambassador.

Etheria Crystal – Crystals containing magical properties mostly found in crystal trees in the Barrens of the Twilight Lands. Residents of the Dark Waste Desert harvest and process the oases' crystals. These crystals provide the primary form of magic in Nocturn.

Flavian Portals – Portals through space making different points in the Annigan instantaneously accessible by passing through the inter-dimensional Middle Realms. Each portal is different. There are several large, fixed portals on both Lumina and Nocturn and hundreds of smaller dedicated Flavians. Certain animals, intoxicants and magical items can open smaller portals.

Frozen Sea – The vast expanse of ice flows covering the majority of Nocturn and the largest centrally occupied area in all of Annigan. The ice ranges from a slushy mixture with icebergs near the land masses to several hundred feet thick in the eastern areas.

Forsvara Guards – A rank-and-file foot soldier army of House Aramos.

Fudomi – Sentient humanoid ram creatures inhabiting the western Os-Oni Mountains of the Twilight Lands. They steal and sell the Cevot Spider broods' silk and eggs, which they consider a delicacy.

Galeb – Sea Gulls with a psychic connection to a handler. They are used to transport messages across Lumina.

Garf Sunal – EEtah War college belonging to House Bran. Their specialty is long term inland duty.

Gar-Kal – Fish head humanoids living on the ocean floor of Nocturn. They are of low intelligence and aggressive.

Geta – Amarenian title for a master at a skill or craft, especially if they teach it.

Ghas-Tor – This is the tallest peak on the Annigan. It reaches upward 32,000 feet in the Os'Ani Mountain range of the Twilight Lands. More than a mountain, it is a sentient being and the epicenter of Air Magic in the world.

Ghorn – Necromancers of the Barrens in Twilight Lands.

Ghost Suit – A gray, skintight jump suit used mostly by Valdurian forces to blend into the Kan fog.

Ghosts of the Kan – Mariner's term for Rayth raiders. Due to their ghost white chalk covering their bodies and acting as camouflage when they attack during the Kan fog.

Gila – The main sentient race populating the Dark Waste. Hybrids comprising Bailian pilgrims and a now long-gone sentient lizard native to the region. They are an advanced race occupying the three large oases of the desert.

Golden One, The – Otick term for the Golden Avatar.

Goy-Ardia – Goyan fire mages trained at the University of Marassa.

Goyan Calendar – Method of time keeping found only in the Goyan Islands. It consists of a Grand Cycle (year) which is comprised of ten Quinte (months) named; Awal, Teine, Derde, Kvara, Peto, Sesto, Ched, Merve, Tisa and Dasam. Each Quinte is divided into fifty Cycles (days) with each cycle being divided into fifty Deci (hours) twenty-five in sunlight and twenty-five in Kan. Ten cycles equal a Cluster (week) with five Clusters per Quinte.

Goyan Rise – A 300-mile-wide sea mount in central Lumina acting as the floor of the Shallow Sea. Its volcanic vents fuel the volcano of Mount Goya.

Grand – Short for Grand Cycle. Unit of time equivalent to a year.

Grass Eater – Singa insult

Gustare' – Amarenian bath house and tavern.

Hackney – Etheria driven floating carriages found throughout the major cities of Lumina.

Hand of the Wind – The Assassin's Guild of Annigan. All members worship Orad, goddess of death. The upper levels are clerics of Orad.

Hakim – A judge in the High Holy City of Zor.

Harbingers of Balance – Sentient creatures of all types called to a secret society monitoring the balance of the Annigan and warning when something upsets it.

Hasteen – City of the Dreeat crocodile people.

Hill Sister – Hermaphroditic warriors inhabiting the northern foothills of the Amaren Mountains in Amarenia. Though they possess both male and female sex organs, they cannot procreate. Popular with Amarenian nobility as seneschal/bodyguards partly because they can have sex with them and not violate their "no man" pledge.

Hoon – Word used in Zor to denote a pimp or the manager of a brothel.

Howlite – Gray Etheria Crystal used for glamour, disguise and polymorphing.

Humans – The Human race descended from the Avion race. In 5070 PA, the rebellious Avions which joined Xandar the Mad's doomed Great Kraken Incursion had their wings severed as punishment before being banished and scattered to the Goyodian Chain. 171 years later the Seventh Avatar sang the "Song of Rebirth" evolving them into a separate race. They formed their Great Houses, spreading out across the Goyan Island Chain and beyond the Shallow Sea.

Human Great Houses:

House Aramos –The largest and wealthiest of the great human families directly descended from the First Men. The capital city of Aris is located on the Island of Vakai in the Goyodian Chain of Islands in the Northern Shallow Sea. They control banking and finance in Lumina and constantly hatch Machiavellian plots to expand their power over the other houses.

House Calden – This great house controls the seas with the largest military and commercial fleets. Their Capital City of Nader is on the Island of Tarla in the Goyodian Chain, but they command the island chain of the Zerk Atoll where their sailors are trained.

House Eldor – This great house controls virtually all the agricultural islands of the eastern Goyan Islands. Their Capital City of Rophan is on the Island of Tolle in the Goyodian Chain of Islands in the Northern Shallow Sea.

House Valdur – This house is known for their incestuous practices to keep the family bloodline pure. Their capital city of Dryden is on the Island of Atar in The Goyodian Chain of Islands in the Northern Shallow Sea. All but destroyed in a surprise invasion by House Eldor called the Unification War, only the discovery of lighter than air travel and a fleet of war balloons saved their home island. They lost the rest of their agricultural lands to Eldor. Their entire culture revolves around their powerful air guild, the Valdurian Air Service.

House Whitmar – This family runs the organized and sanctioned slave trade on Lumina from the City of Nier on the northern Goya coast. Their Capital City of Brinstan is located on the Island of Umin in the Goyodian Chain in the Northern Shallow Sea.

Immor-Onn – Large city known as "the Shining Jewel of the East" located on the western coast of the Twilight Lands. Home of the Bailian Empire.

Idonian Philosophy – The Avion prejudice that Humans are a scourge which should be wiped out. The driving belief of the Idonian Cabal of Avion House Pyre and Solas.

Innaca Deep – Giant whirlpool in the Northwestern Ocean of Lumina housing one of the largest Flavian portals. Its psionic ripples extend out hundreds of miles.

Innaca Run – The final test for admittance to the elite Brightstar Sailors where they must navigate a tight circle around the turbulent seas surrounding the Innaca Atoll without being pulled into its giant Flavian portal.

Ironmark – Brutal enforcers of the Quartermasters in the Goyan Islands of Lumina. Each island chain has their own Ironmark specializing in their own unique form of torture.

Itori – Insect Shamans found throughout the agricultural western Goyan Islands. Although they control mostly locusts, they can command any insect and are immune to all insect venoms and stings.

Jangwa – Elite desert commandos defending the outer parameter of the two civilized oases in the Dark Waste Desert. Capable of traveling under the sand and rapidly over the surface of the desert, they make frequent scouting missions to the untamed Qua-Raman Oasis and the Buried City of Nof-Saloom.

Kaefom – Traditional Amarenian breeding ritual overseen by the Darek Witches.

Kan – Period of the day in the Goyan Islands when the thick sea fog rises blotting out the sun, used mostly for sleep. It is an effect caused by geothermal activities only found in the Goyan Islands and Shallow Sea.

Kel – Flying lizards bred and tended by Avions for food and as beasts of burden.

Kharry Institute – Tiikeri medical facility located outside the Tiikeri capital city of Hai-Darr and run by the brilliant and ruthless Dr. Met-Ge, specializing in crossbreeding Mawl races to produce Mongrels for specific duties. The Institute created Cheepas and the Ves-Lari.

Kinjuto Dominator – Sex mage using BDSM techniques.

Konaleeta – Called the Island of the Lost. The entire island is caught in a permanent Flavian Loop. It bounces around from location to location across any of the planes of the Middle Realms, never staying in anyone place for very long.

Kusars – Mawl bandits from the Dasos region in the Land of Mists.

Kvara – Fourth of the ten Quinte Grand Cycle, Summer.

Ky-Awat – Sentient rat creatures of the Dark Waste Desert. They have bred them up from the Cul-Ta and are larger and more aggressive, but no smarter. Various factions use them as cannon fodder. They breed quickly and are plentiful, especially around the three main oases.

Land of Mists – The largest land mass in Nocturn. So named because the mixture of cold temperatures in the air combined with the warmth of the ground results in a uniform constant low hanging fog over the entire continent. Three distinct landscapes cover the surface of the land, separated by the Kel-Raku Mountain range and dimly illuminated by bioluminescence, outcroppings of Etheria Crystals and the moon and stars. The thick rainforest of Arboro lies to the north, and the vast savannah of Rovina runs to the south. They're connected by the Bor-Kaa Pass. The dense jungles and swamps of Dasos lie to the east.

Landagar Group – Research and Development Division of the Valdurian Air Service located in the balloon city of Landagar high in the mountain peaks of the Valdurian home island of Atar.

Larimar – The "Talking Stone," a milky white Etheria Crystal with blue striations, used for psychic communication between parties within proximity of the gem.

Learned Sister – The title given to Amarenian teachers, scribes & academics.

Legates – Suicide messengers hired through House Whitmar. Candidates are usually elderly or terminally ill. Upon their death, House Whitmar agrees to care for their surviving family for their remaining lifetimes.

Lor-Danta Oasis – The eastern most major oasis in the Dark Waste Desert. The large Obsidian field stretching from its shore contains six Tanum Charts of the skies used by the Arron-Nin Astrologers dwelling there.

Lumina – The hemisphere of the world in constant sunlight.

Luna – Term for the lunar cycle used by every culture in the Annigan except the humans in the Goyan Islands, who cannot see the moon.

Luroh – Bolo/sash weapon used by the Mahilia. The sash contains the person's rank and record. The two metal balls at either end become an effective weapon when twirled.

Magitech – The fusion of magic and technology. Mostly referring to the use of Etheria Crystals and specific mechanical items. i.e., Airship engines.

Mahilia – City guards in Mostar, the capital of Amarenia.

Makari – Inter-dimensional race of sentient spiders from the Pasture Plain of the Middle Realms. They seeded the Cevot race in the Os'Tor Mountains in the Land of Mists. The males resemble hairy wolf spiders, the females resemble black widows. The females have been known to allure any male of any race. They compulsively kill after sex.

Malachite – Light green Etheria Crystal, absorbs energy.

Marassa – A professor at the University of Marassa.

Masha – Amarenian for master.

Maudo Grass – Tall grass with a bright blue flowering tuft growing in the Land of Mists. The flowers are a favorite intoxicant for Mawls and especially coveted by the Tiikeri.

Mawl – Overall name for the humanoid cat races of the Land of Mists. It is also the term used for the common language they share.

Medikua – Medical officer aboard Calden naval vessels.

Merve – Eighth of the ten Quinte Grand Cycle, Autumn.

Middle Realms – Constantly shifting inter-dimensional plane between worlds. Sometimes referred to as the Fairy or Dream Realms.

Mongrel – The product of cross breeding between the Mawl races found all over the Land of Mists. Pure breeds mostly shun them and the Tiikeri use them for slave labor.

Moonfall – Period of the cycle when Nocturn's main illuminating body, the moon, dips below the horizon issuing in the Moonless

Moonless – The "night" period of the cycle when Nocturn's main illuminating body, the moon, orbits around to the Lumina side of the Annigan.

Mora – Term used for teacher or master in the Whovian Sword Schools of Rohina Takki.

Morasian Puff Boy – Male prostitute from the Port City of Moras on Goya's west coast. Known for their distinctly feminine demeanor.

Mostas – Capital City of the Amarenian Empire on the western shore of Amarenia.

Najuka – Amarenian emasculation ritual performed on all males except those used for breeding purposes in the Kaefom Ritual.

Na-Kab – One of the three insectoid groups originating from below the Land of Mists. They occupied the easternmost hive closest to Mount Natal. Their exoskeleton is made up of fire magic. Their tail has a penis shaped stinger capable of impregnating any living thing they sting.

Namesake – Term used for spouse when they share a bespoke last name.

Narrows, The – Remnants of an old iron mine forming the slums of the Hidden City of Toriss in Otomoria.

Nocturn – The hemisphere of the world in constant night

Nolton Boat – Ships made of Ukko wood in a secret shipyard on the Island of Zer, mostly used by Brightstar sailors. Hovering less than an inch above the water, their Ukko rudder guides and propels. The specific construction of the hull makes the boat unsinkable.

Noma – Poison from the Noma Viper.

Nurian Edicts – EEtah rules of conduct set down by House Nur forming the basis for all Sunal laws. The various Sunals add their own individual laws to this baseline.

Nyanja – Large seahorses ridden as sea cavalry by the Calden Navy.

Obsidian – Black Etheria Crystal storing psychic energy.

Ocean Deep – Name referring to any of the deep oceans of Lumina or Nocturn.

Ol'daEE – Person able to cast spells while having sex under the influence of Oldust.

Oldust – Hallucinogenic powder derived from the spores of the rare Impia Mushroom, increasing magical abilities and is essential for individual travel to the Middle Realms.

Onay – Humanoid wolf men of the Barrens, banding their various packs together in three distinct hordes.

On'Dara – Sentient horse creatures living on the Plains of Taka-Vir in the southeastern Twilight Lands. They raise and train horses, trading them for silk with the Cevot Spiders and selling them to the rest of the Annigan.

ooD – Shell worn on the back of the male Otick warriors as armor. They mark the warrior's rank and house on the outside of the shell and inscribe a record of their deeds on the inside. They place the ooD over the entrance to their homes in the sand.

Oracle of the River – Demi-God who dwells in the cypress swamp at the end of the western fork of the Otoman River for thousands of grands. It appears as a partially submerged giant catfish with its many whiskers sunken into the water. These whiskers perceive anything happening in, on, or around the waterway.

Orad – Air goddess of death and predominate deity of the assassin's guild, the Hand of the Wind. Her creed: *She comes as the wind. And takes whom she wishes. Her name is Orad. And she is death.*

Orad Dex – Initiates to the Orad priesthood. Street/entry level assassins.

Orad Con – (Taker of the Divine Wind) These are full priests of Orad. Their special skills are the Kiss of Death, the Poison Breath and the Phantom Dagger.

Orad Sto – (Giver of the Divine Wind) High priests of Orad who can also restore life.

Otick – Humanoid crab people inhabiting the Shallow Sea. Among the first sentient creatures to rise from the ocean floor they evolved into a proud, deeply spiritual and noble race. Goya's volcanic warmed waters provide home to the Otick's prolific oyster beds littering the floor of the Shallow Sea. From these beds arose the five great Pearl Avatars, creation gods whose songs brought life and sentience to Lumina. Otick society is divided into a highly structured caste system: Worker Class, Warrior Class and Mother Class, and organized into two main categories: domestic and military. The Shelled Triad, the three Otick Great Houses, tend their own oyster beds and compete for the birthplace of the next Avatar.

Otick Great Houses:

House Awa – Home of the last two avatars. Located in the Tellasian Chain, in the capital city of Hidet on the Island of Zod. Mother Class specialization.

House Pewa – Located in the Goyodian Chain, in the capital city of Oniack, on the Island of Zak. Worker Class specialization.

House Sensu – Located in the Otoman Group, in the capital city of Sunico, on the Island of Lakia. Warrior Class specialization.

Otomoria – Large Island continent in the western Goyan Islands. The main grain producing agricultural island.

Outer Clan EEtah – Humanoid shark creatures smaller in stature than regular EEtahs and cast out from the three great EEtah Houses hatcheries. The survivors band together into loose clans, contracting themselves out as deck hands or recently volunteering in the Valdurian Marines.

Padi – Regional demi-god of water worshiped in and around the High Holy City of Zor, associated with the peace and calming effect of water and represented by a calm pond.

Palu EEtah – Rare hammerhead EEtahs. They are as big as the Outer Clan EEtah but extremely intelligent. They tend to be reclusive loners.

Pappia – Members of the child street gangs of the Hidden City of Toriss in the slum section of The Narrows.

Pa-Waga – Lawful evil god of greed worshiped mostly by the Tiikeri. Its clerics practice binary blood rune magic comprised of the letters "X" and "I."

Peace Babies – Children born of a union between any of the five major Human noble houses.

Peto – Fifth of the ten Quinte Grand Cycle, Summer.

Piceans – Humanoid fish people of Lumina. Capable of breathing above and below the water and impervious to the ocean's depths. They have gill flaps large enough to fold over their ears and when the vocal sound waves pass through the membrane, it translates it. This makes them valuable translators in the seaports of the Goyan Islands.

Piety Watch – Militant, religious police faction of the Pa-Waga church. They arrest anyone caught begging, idle, or not being productive. Minor offences are punished by a beating with thin cane rods. They wear red shirts under black capes with high pointed collars resembling cat ears.

Pisar – Bailian title for a scholar.

Pomaku – Humanoid leopard people (Mawl) native to the Arboro region in the Land of Mists, Nocturn.

Protocol 13 – EEtah House Nur code phrase requesting a meeting between an intelligence asset and their handler.

Qua-Raman Oasis – An oasis in the central Dark Waste Desert. Due to its location just south of the Tur-Qua Pass, it serves as a major trading post for gems harvested in The Barrens to the north.

Quartermaster – Collector of taxes and tariffs in the Goyan Islands who use the Ironmark to enforce their rule.

Queen's Envoy Service, The – The Amarenian Empire's spy service and member of the Society of Whispers.

Quinte – Time period equivalent to a month.

Ramu – A gambling dismemberment game banned everywhere in Lumina, except the Free City of Tannimore.

Rayth – Pirate faction of the Amarenian people in open revolt and attempting to form their own nation.

Rod-Ema Trench – Massive abysmal fissure running along the equator in the western ocean floor in Nocturn. At its head is the Agar Goyot and the Black Mural is found on its north wall dipping into the ocean depths.

Rohina Takii – Sword school originating on the Island of Wou. Known for its strike while drawing technique.

Sardor – Amarenian title for a female warlord.

Salar Winds – Turbulent winds surrounding the peak of Mount Goya which must be navigated to enter the Avion City of Darmont on the mountain's northwestern face. Avion term of exasperation, "By the mighty Winds of Salar!"

Secor – Street name for the Imperial Gold Ingot equivalent to ten struck gold coins.

Sesto – Sixth of the ten Quinte Grand Cycle, Autumn.

Shallow Sea – The body of water surrounding the greater Goyan Islands covering the Goyan Rise. The depth is no more than thirty feet deep at its lowest point.

Si – The term for "mister" in the Common Tongue spoken in the Goyan Islands.

Sikari – Female Singa hunter/killer squads, traveling in groups of two or more. They arm themselves with crossed bandoleros covering their chests and filled with sickle shaped throwing blades.

Silent Partner – Seven cabals of organized crime families in the Goyan Islands.

Simikort – Round engraved coin acting as an Amarenian noble's calling card.

Singa – Humanoid lion people (Mawl) inhabiting the southern Rovina area of the land of Mists.

Skirting the Upwinds – Dangerous maneuver practiced by few airship pilots. It involves taking the airship up to the edge of the atmosphere and then plummeting down to your destination. Allowing long-distance travel in a short period.

Society of Whispers – The general intelligence cooperative of the five Human noble houses, the Zorian

Spymaster, the Calden Intelligencer Service, Suusho, and the Queen's Envoy Service.

Spice Rat – Smugglers operating in the Spice Islands chains (Zerian Reef Chain and Outer Zerians) and occasionally in the entire western side of the Goyan Islands.

Spooks – Street term for spies and operatives in the Society of Whispers.

Strasta – Ancient prophet in the folklore of the Cevot spider people of the Os-Ani Mountains.

Sunal – EEtah war college specializing in martial skills.

Suusho – The Bailian Empire's spy service and member of the Society of Whispers.

Szoldos Mercenaries – One of several small private armies for hire on the Goyan continent.

Taking it Upstairs – Airship slang for skirting upwinds

Tanum Charts – Six maps of Nocturn's night sky. The Arron-Nin Astrologers use them for divination and sometimes the opening of Flavian portals.

Teine – Second of the ten Quinte Grand Cycle, Spring.

Ten/Fifty— Cliché phrase in the Goyan Islands referring to the ten cycles (days) in the cluster (week) and fifty decis (hours) of the cycle (day). The equivalent of 24/7.

Tenable Sister—Title given to Amarenian lawyers.

Tiikeri – Sentient humanoid Tiger creatures of the Dasos region in the eastern Land of Mists.

Tisa – Ninth of the ten Quinte Grand Cycle, Winter.

Trinilic – Orange Etheria Crystal, fire magic connection.

Turine – Tidal clocks used in the Goyan Islands.

Twilight Lands – Area between Lumina and Nocturn in constant state of Twilight. Due to converging hot and cold air masses its weather remains perpetually stormy.

Ukkonite – Bronze Etheria Crystal with natural repellant properties. It is the crystal equivalent to Ukko wood found only in Nocturn.

Ukko Wood – Magical wood from the World Tree, harvested only on the Island of Zer in the eastern Goyan Islands. Its natural repellant properties are used in shields, weapons, Brightstar Nolton Boats and used as currency.

Ulana – Chaotic evil sea goddess worshiped by a small sect of Amarenian Rayth in the province of Durik-Dor

Unification War – Conflict started by House Eldor in 2 P.A. against the eastern agricultural islands of House Valdur. It ended as quickly as it began when House Aramos forced them to the negotiating table by threatening to freeze both houses' accounts in the Imperial Bank.

Valorous Sister – Amarenian title for heroic acts which affected the realm.

Vedette – Small fast Nolton Boats crewed by a single ex-Brightstar sailor and used for fast, anonymous travel around the oceans of Lumina.

Velocomite – Pale blue Etheria Crystal with red bands, increases or decreases an object's speed travelling.

Veros Pearls – Highest quality pearl cultivated in the Otick oyster beds. They are capable of holding a magical charge.

Ves-Lari – Mawl mongrels bred by the Tiikeri for rowing and poling. They are a combination of Pomaku (leopard)

and Duma (Cheetah). Crews can pole or row for hundreds of miles at a time without stopping.

Vurr Carts – Carts used by the Vurr Clerics to collect the City of Zor's dead and garbage. There are two types: stationary carts situated on every major street where citizens can deposit their waste and roving carts mostly dealing with collecting the bodies of the dead.

Vurr Clerics – Accolades of the Free God Vurr serving as waste disposal in the City of Zor. Once maintaining constantly pyres burning everything from corpses to ordinary refuse. The city upgraded the pyres to full crematoriums. Vurr clerics smell of smoke and generally work nude, wearing only a simple cloak.

Wraith – Deep cover agents for House Aramos drawn from the elite Black Talons unit.

Yagur – Humanoid jaguars (Mawl) from the Arboro region of the Land of Mists. They are seers, healers and shamans, serving all the various Mawl races.

Yudon – Harpoon with a rifled the shaft for throwing accuracy. The standard weapon of every Sunal EEtah.

Yupik – a.k.a. the Ice Clans, one hundred and sixty-five clans divided into three major groups. The nomadic wanderers of the Western Flows compete for resources while the Ash-Ta constantly hunt them as prey. The largest group inhabits the vast Eastern Flows with semi-permanent settlements surrounding the Ice City of Mos-Agar'.

Zadim – Lapidaries operating in the Dark Waste Desert.

Zerian Rangers – Woodsmen fighters belonging to any of nine different clans occupying the forests of the Island continent of Zer in the Goyan Islands.

Zoldak Group – A private mercenary army comprised of former Black Talons of House Aramos.

Zorian Monetary Council – A ruling body founded in 3850 P.A. controlling all banking in the High Holy City of Zor. The council coordinates with the Calden Commodities exchange to regulate the exchange of money, goods and services, and uses the Quartermasters Guild for the collection of taxes and tariffs.

MAPS

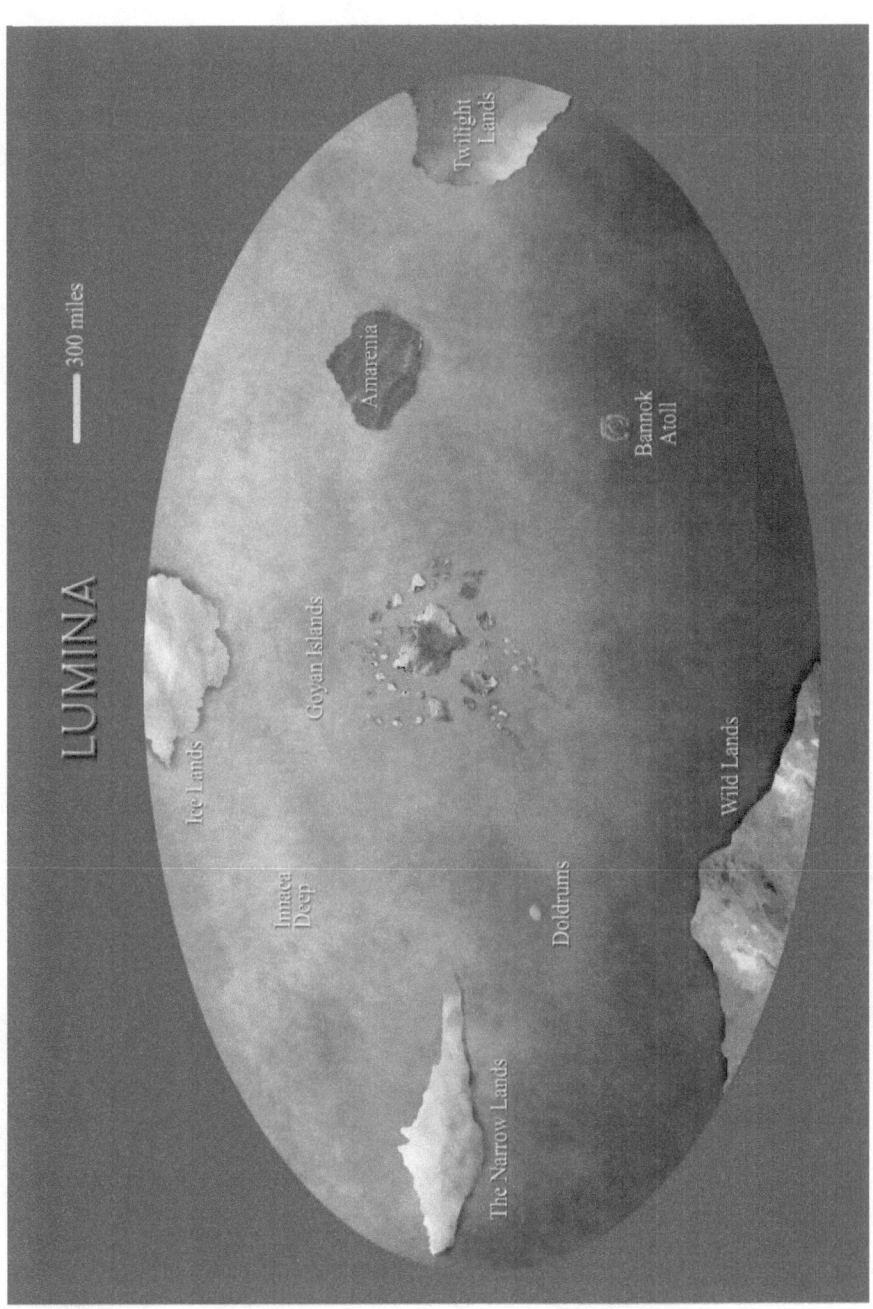

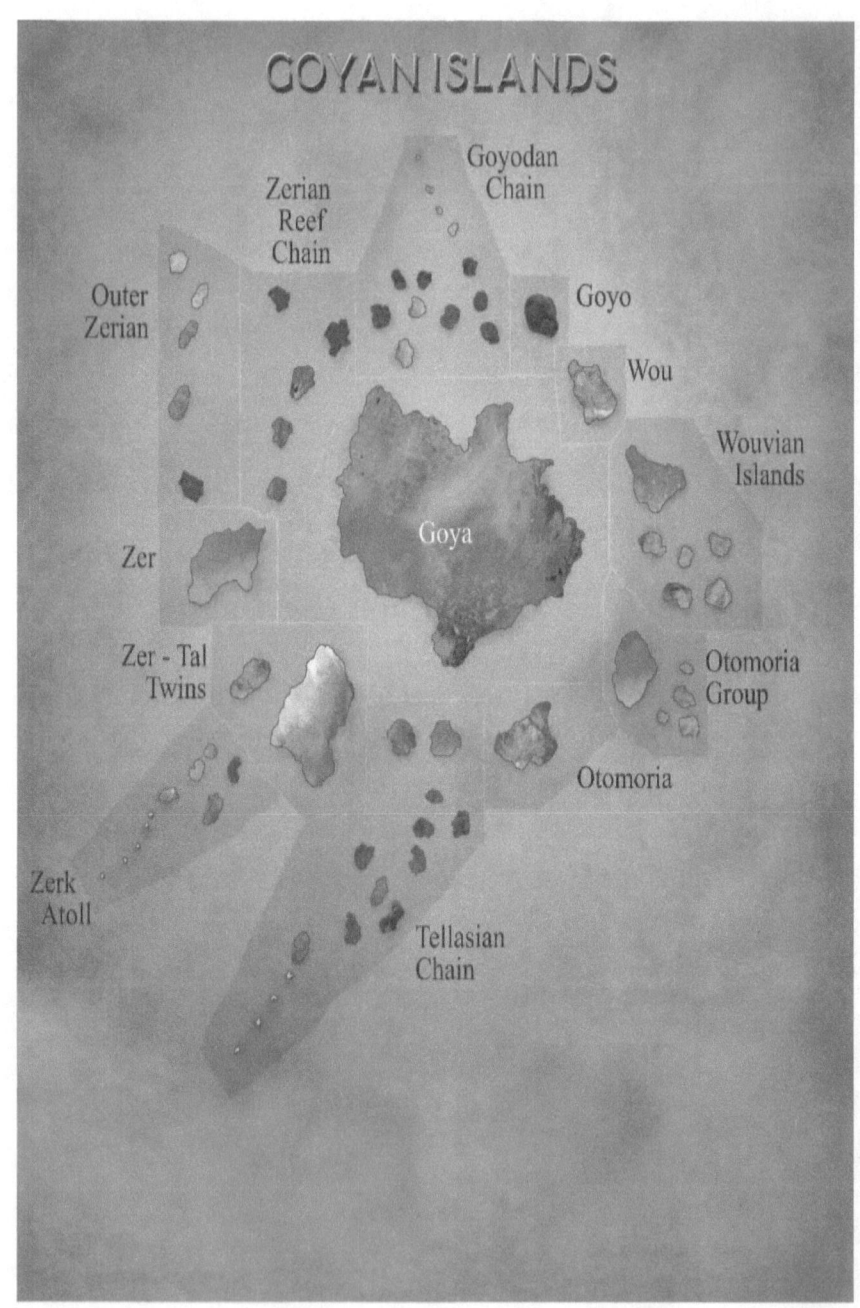

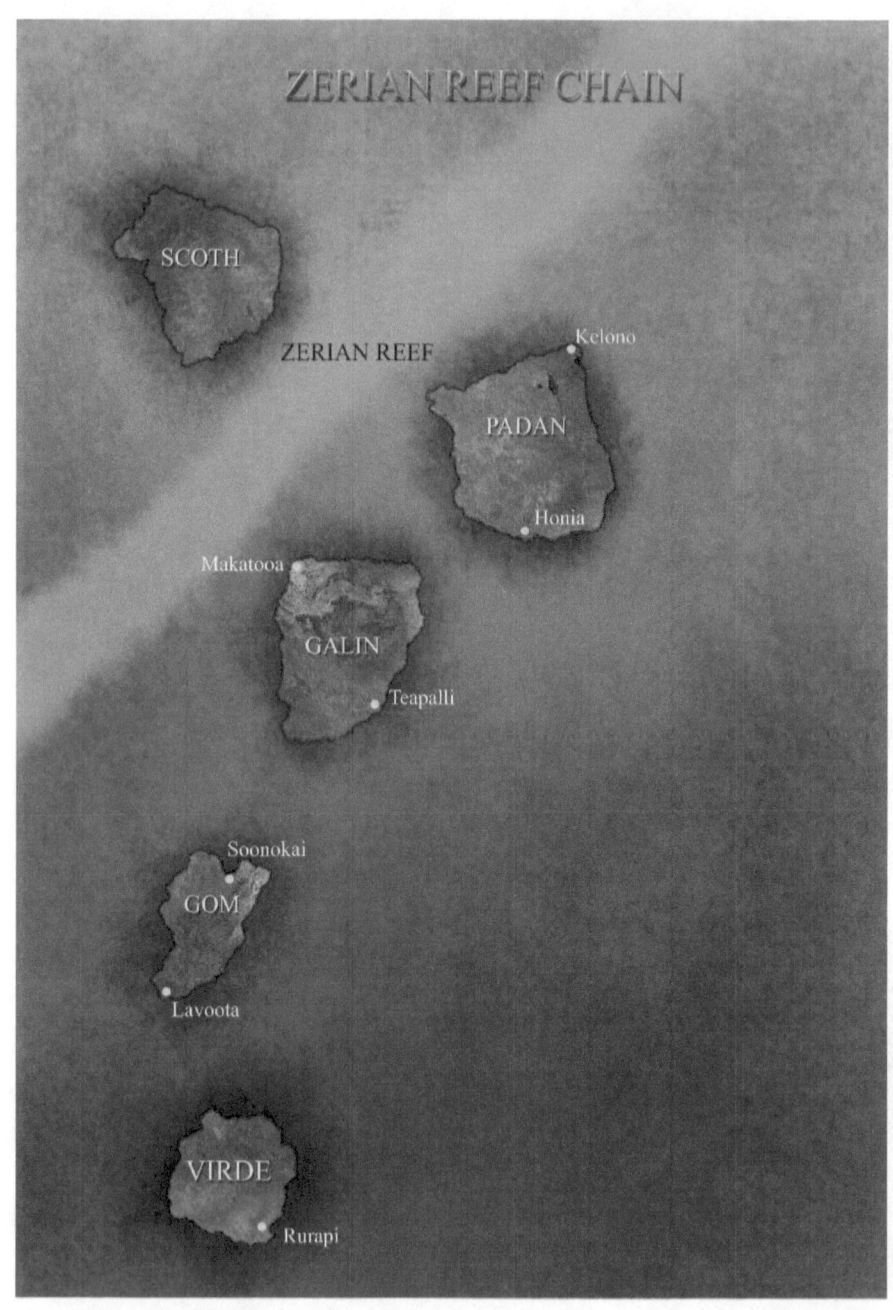

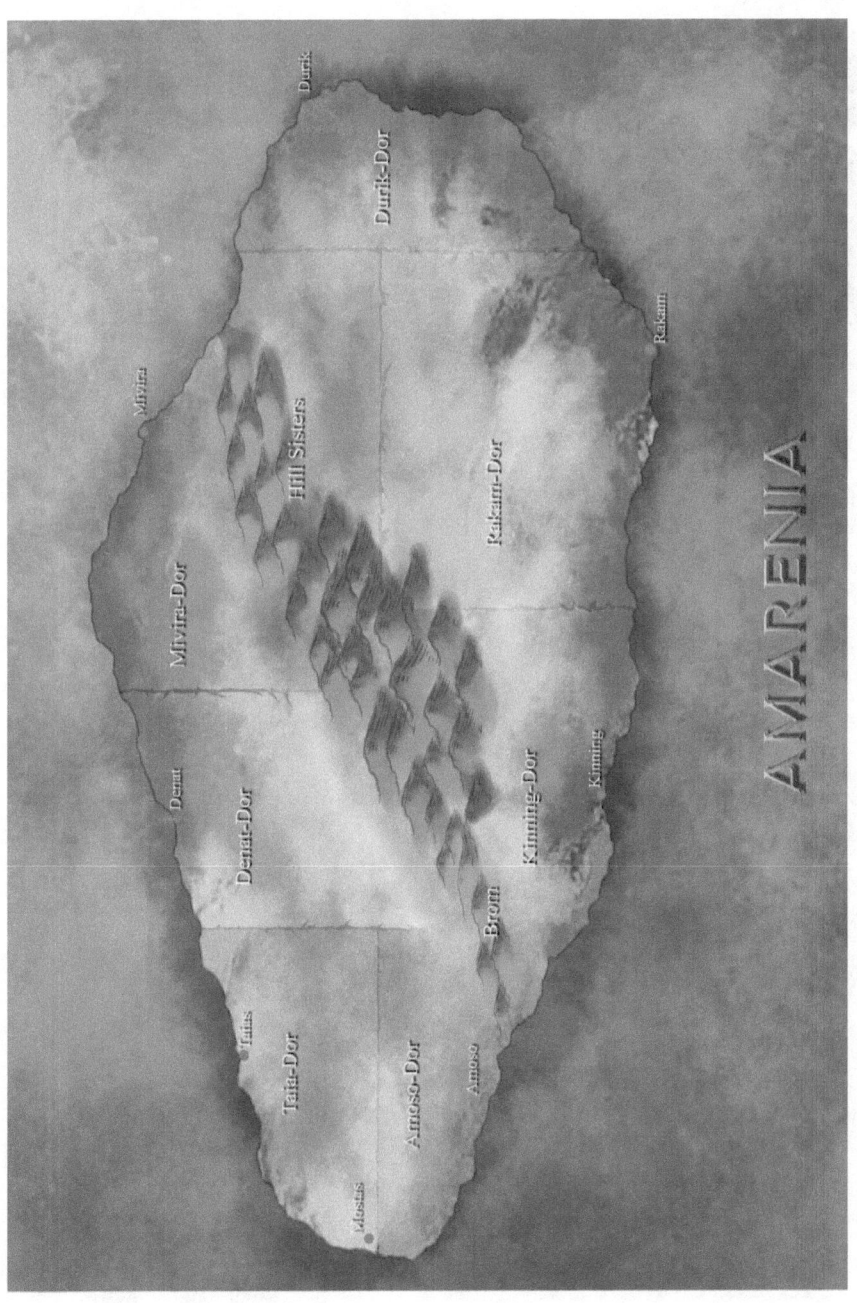

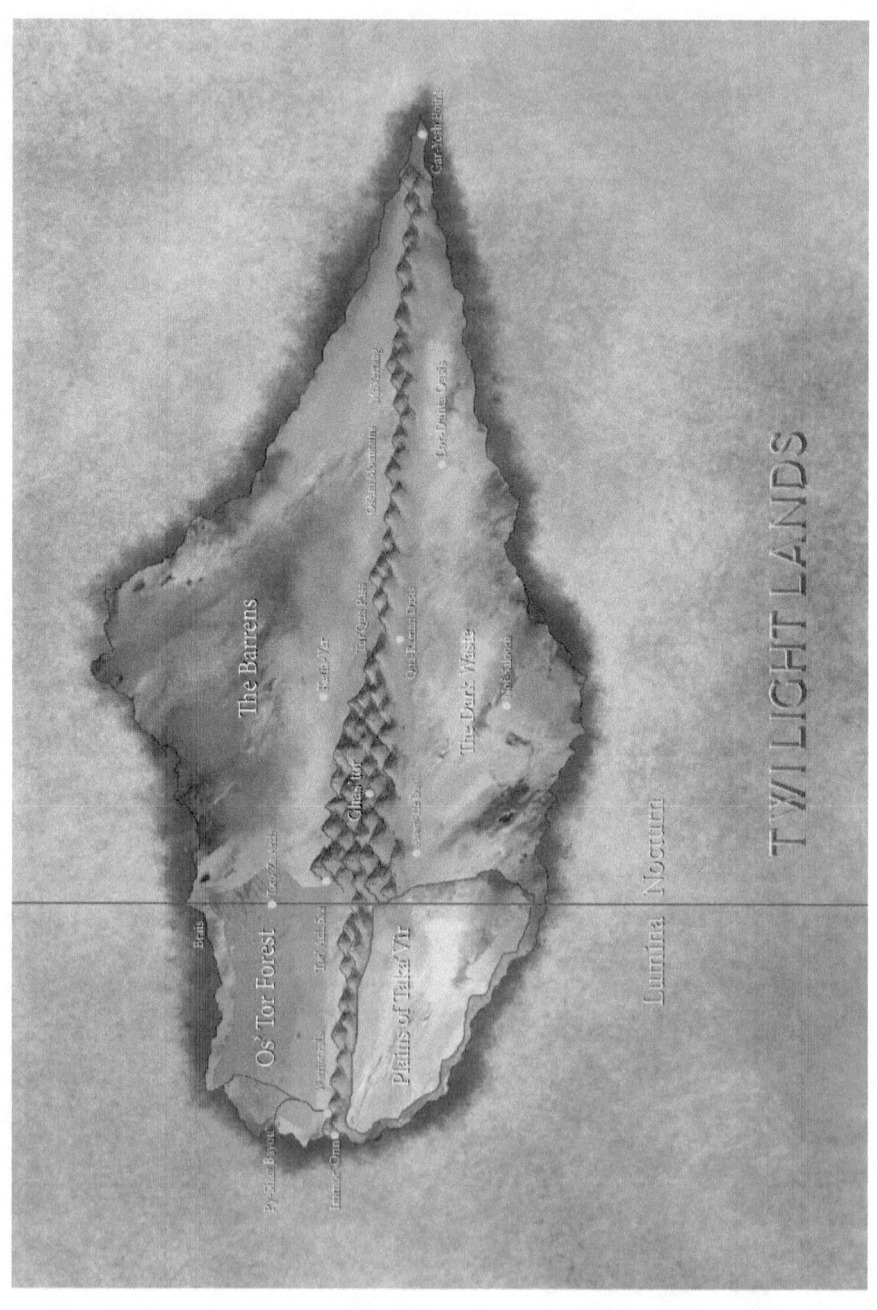

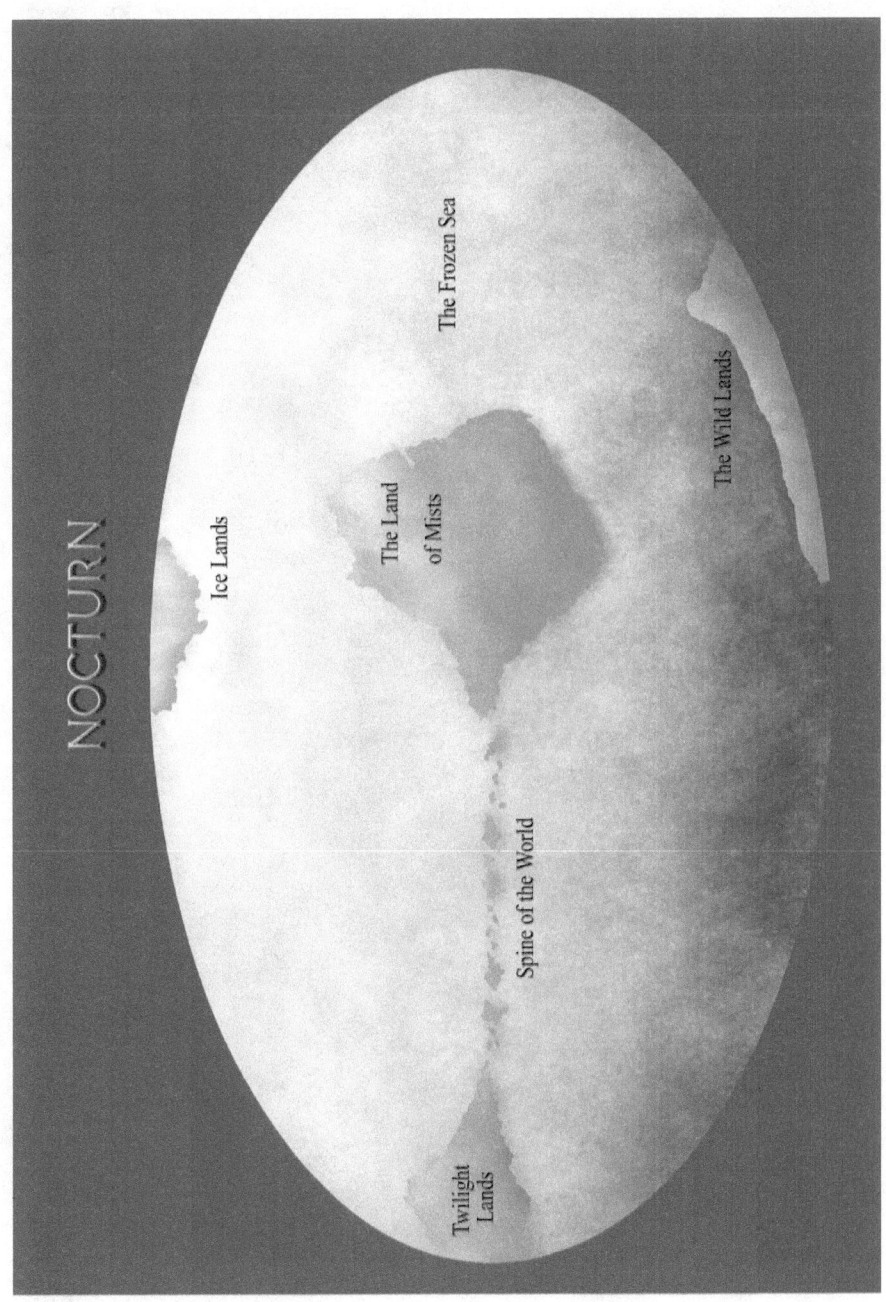

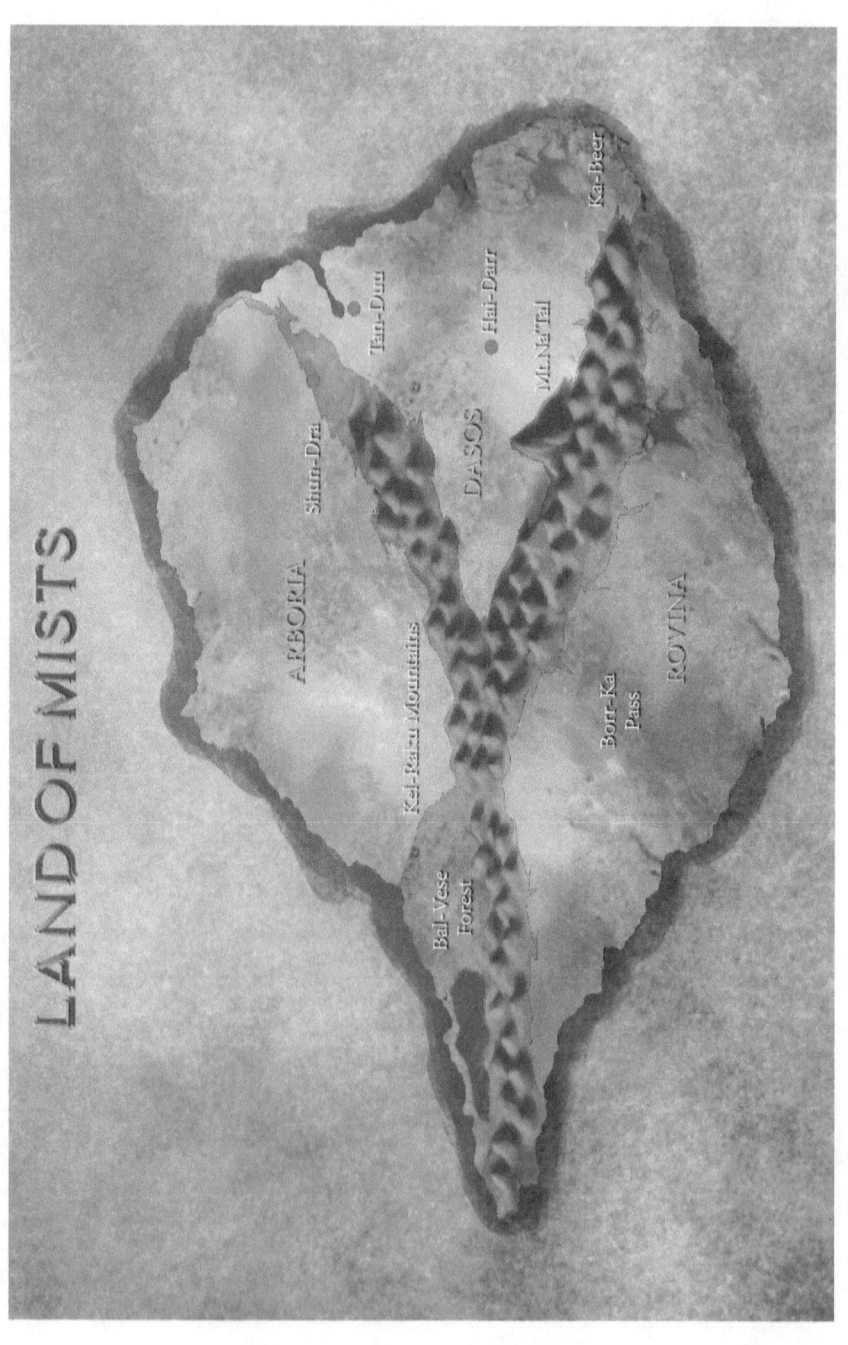

ABOUT THE AUTHOR

R.W. Marcus spent most of his life selling books. Along the way he managed to become a Falconer, 3rd Dan Black Belt in Yoshukai Karate, Freemason, Freelance Photographer, Ad Copywriter and WMNF Radio Disc Jockey. Marcus' radio commercials and freelance photography won numerous awards, including Best of Shows and Best of the Bay Addy Awards for work with Creative Keys and Laughing Bird Productions. R.W. Marcus was also Founder and Creative Director of United Game Masters, where he cowrote the UGM Universal Gaming System which he used to create and playtest a role-playing game based in the world of the Annigan Cycle. He formally held the title of Director of Incunabula at

Griffon's Medieval Manuscripts, where he penned his first nonfiction title, *The Ship of Fools to 1500*, which Amazon called "an authoritative guide to one of the most popular works of secular writing." Now retired, he created a new genre of fiction—Pulp Fantasy Noir—to exorcise the darker side of his good nature.

CONNECT
WEBSITE: https://AnniganCycle.com
FACEBOOK: https://www.facebook.com/noirrwmarcus/
TWITTER: @NoirRWMarcus
EMAIL: RWMarcus@yahoo.com

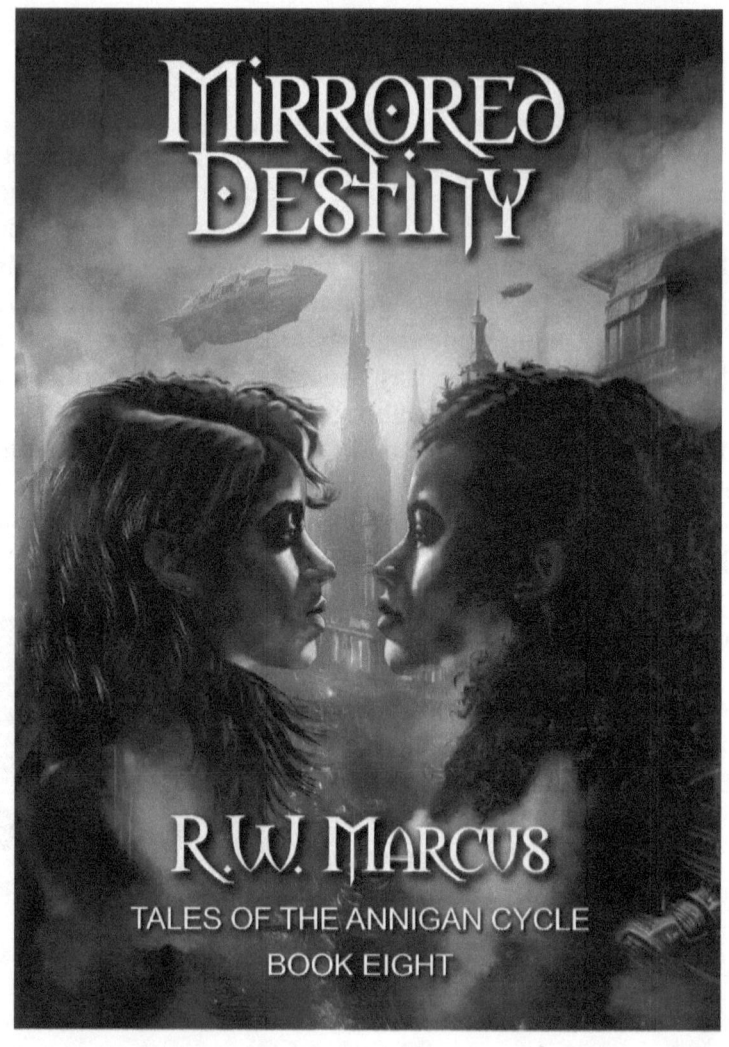

MIRRORED DESTINY
TALES OF THE ANNIGAN CYCLE
BOOK EIGHT
FROM LAUGHING BIRD PUBLISHING